LP
CHA

THE TIDE WATCHERS

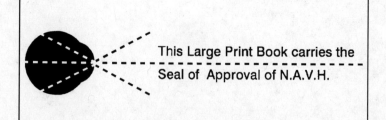

This Large Print Book carries the
Seal of Approval of N.A.V.H.

THE TIDE WATCHERS

LISA CHAPLIN

THORNDIKE PRESS
A part of Gale, Cengage Learning

GALE
CENGAGE Learning®

Farmington Hills, Mich • San Francisco • New York • Waterville, Maine
Meriden, Conn • Mason, Ohio • Chicago

GALE
CENGAGE Learning®

Thorndike Press® Large Print Historical Fiction.
The text of this Large Print edition is unabridged.
Other aspects of the book may vary from the original edition.
Set in 16 pt. Plantin.

LIBRARY OF CONGRESS CATALOGING-IN-PUBLICATION DATA

Chaplin, Lisa, 1962–
  The tide watchers / Lisa Chaplin. -- Large print edition.
    pages cm. -- (Thorndike Press large print historical fiction)
    ISBN 978-1-4104-8442-0 (hardback) -- ISBN 1-4104-8442-4 (hardcover)
    1. Fulton, Robert, 1765–1815--Fiction. 2. Napoleon I, Emperor of the French, 1769–1821--Fiction. 3. Napoleonic Wars, 1800–1815--Fiction. 4. Great Britain--History, Naval--19th century--Fiction. I. Title.
  PR9619.4.J38T53 2015
  823'.92--dc23
                          2015029693

Published in 2015 by arrangement with William Morrow, an imprint of HarperCollins Publishers

Printed in Mexico
1 2 3 4 5 6 7 19 18 17 16 15

*To Vicky, who asked me to write a book
that would last on the shelves;
and to Dad, who told me to be a writer
from the time I was sixteen*

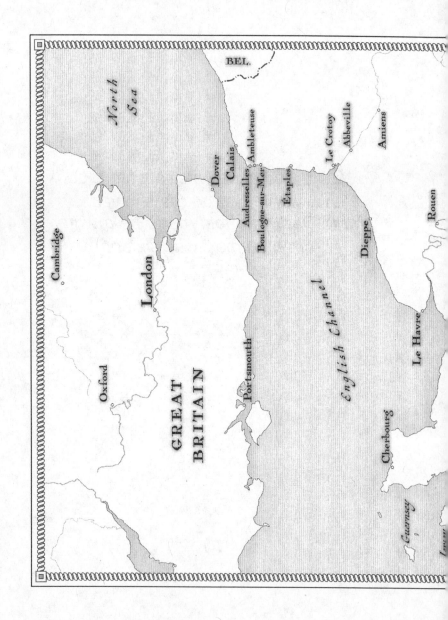

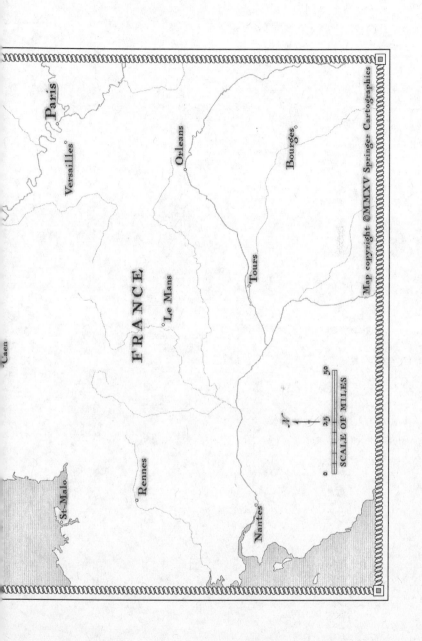

Paris

Versailles°

°Caen

Orleans°

FRANCE

Le Mans°

Bourges°

Tours°

Rennes°

°St-Malo

Nantes°

N

SCALE OF MILES

0   25   50

Map copyright ©MMXV Springer Cartographics

CAST OF CHARACTERS, FICTIONAL AND HISTORICAL

Fictional

DUNCAN AYLSHAM, King's Man and commander of spy ship (code name Tidewatcher)

SÍMON BEAUCHAMP, émigré and King's Man (code name Argenteuil)

JOHN BURTON, third lieutenant

JONAS CARLSBERG, ship's engineer

ALAIN DELACORTE, French spy, father of Lisbeth's child

EDMOND DELACORTE, Lisbeth's infant son

LISBETH DELACORTE, daughter of Sir Edward Sunderland

MARCELINE DELACORTE, Alain's mother

JAMES FLYNN, first lieutenant

CLARE FAÎCHOT, a French midwife-healer

ANTHONY HAZELTINE, second lieutenant

MARK HENSHAW, a cabin boy on Duncan's ship (French alias Marcus René Balfour)

MICHEL LEBRUN, colonel in the French army

JEAN LECLERC, a local in Abbeville

SERGE MARESCHAL, a former captain in the

9

French army

LUC MARRON, the son of the owner of Tavern Le Boeuf in Abbeville

MONSIEUR MARRON, owner of Tavern Le Boeuf in Abbeville

ALEC STEWART, Duncan's half brother (code name Apollyon: Greek, meaning "Destroyer")

CAL STEWART, Alec's twin (code name Abaddon: Hebrew, also meaning "Destroyer")

CAROLINE LADY SUNDERLAND, Lisbeth's mother

SIR EDWARD SUNDERLAND, King's Man and Lisbeth's father

LEO and ANDREW SUNDERLAND, King's Men, Lisbeth's brothers

PAUL TOLBERT, a local in Abbeville

BENJAMIN WEST, sailor

Historical

HENRY ADDINGTON, British prime minister 1801–1804

NAPOLEON BONAPARTE, French general 1793–1799, first consul of France 1799–1804, French emperor 1804–1815

ROSE "JOSEPHINE" BONAPARTE, Napoleon's wife, Fouché's spy

MARQUESS CHARLES CORNWALLIS, governor-general of India 1789–1792, lord constable of Ireland 1798–1800, British ambassador to France 1800–1802

ARTHUR RICHARD DILLON, former archbishop of Narbonne, French-Irish émigré

JOSEPH FOUCHÉ, Jacobin 1789–1794, minster of police 1798–1802, senator of Aix 1802–1804, minster of police and internal affairs 1804–1810, 1st Duc d'Otrante 1808

CHARLES JAMES FOX, secretary of state for foreign affairs, 1782–1783, 1806

ROBERT FULTON, American artist and inventor

LADY GEORGIANA GORDON, daughter of the Duke of Gordon

LADY ANNE GRENVILLE (née Pitt), sister to Thomas, 2nd Baron Camelford

LORD WILLIAM GRENVILLE, British foreign secretary 1791–1801, British prime minister 1806–1807

THE INCOMPARABLE, real code name for a top female British spy, name unknown (fictional name Sylvie Juneau, or Madame Recamier)

HORATIO NELSON, 1st Viscount Nelson, admiral of fleet and national hero, 1771–1805

DEVILLE O'KEEFE, French-Irish royalist and King's Man (real code name Tamerlan)

SIR EDWARD PELLEW, famed sea captain, later an admiral

THOMAS PITT, 2nd Baron Camelford, cousin to William Pitt ("The Mad Baron")

WILLIAM PITT ("Pitt the Younger"), British prime minister 1783–1801, 1804–1806

PRIGENT, first name unknown (code name

Le Brigand), Chouan/British spy/highwayman in Jersey

JOHN RUSSELL, 6th Duke of Bedford

SIR SIDNEY SMITH, Pitt's cousin, King's Man

LA HAYE ST. HILAIRE (code name Doisson), Chouan leader and British spy/highwayman in Jersey

LORD WHITWORTH, British ambassador to France, 1802–1803

WILLIAM WINDHAM, British minister of war (1794–1801, 1804–1807) head of the British Alien Office 1800–1804 (fictional code name Zephyr)

JOHN WESLEY WRIGHT, ship's captain, King's Man

CHAPTER 1

Étaples, France (by the English Channel)
August 16, 1802

"Commander, we got another semaphore message from the ship."

The muffled words were a shade too loud, proud, and English for their current position on the Étaples-Boulogne road. King's Man and unlisted ship's commander Duncan Aylsham parted the curtain of the hired coach and let the window right down. His skinny, freckle-faced cabin boy, Mark, met Duncan's quelling frown with a grin. Instead of knocking on the coach roof from his seat on the box as his commander had ordered, he'd leaped down and was hanging monkey-like on the running board of the moving coach. His eyes, blue as the summer sky behind, laughed too; even his shock of spiky red hair glistened as if in comical argument. The damn boy knew the protocol, the way to act and speak, but never did unless it was forced from him.

"*What* did you say? Who am I? And what country are we currently journeying in?" Aylsham demanded in French, in a tone calculated to dampen pretension.

"Lor' love yer, *monsieur,* I tol' yer, I *got* me cover." Mark switched to French while managing to keep his Cockney accent. Duncan longed to grab one of the ears sticking out from his head and pull it. "I ain't Mark Henshaw, I'm Marcus René Balfour, coach boy from the slums o' Paris. Ye're nobody's commander, an' you ain't got no ship. You're a gennelman of means — a *Frog* gennelman. But what's the point in wastin' time on the lies when there ain't a body about to appreciate it?"

Duncan spoke through gritted teeth. "You obviously do not *get* it, or you wouldn't half scream the word *semaphore.* And once you start using an identity, never leave it until it's dangerous or no longer needed. No self-respecting agent would dream of being so stupid."

The boy's face fell to ludicrous proportions.

"This is your first mission, and it will be your last with me." Duncan reinforced the lesson in icy tones. "I don't reward disobedience and insubordination."

The boy stammered, "But, monsieur, I didn't . . . you know I'm *good* —"

"What you'll be is thrashed before you're much older, boy, unless you respect your bet-

14

ters and obey," Second Lieutenant Burton growled from the box in flawless French.

Mark stiffened and muttered a sulky apology beneath his breath. If there was one person who *did* frighten him, it was the stiff-rumped Burton, who no doubt would thrash him . . . later.

Not even Burton would dare to beat Mark when their commander was near. Abusive sailors were sent back to England without pay or recommendation, a semaphore message sent ahead informing Duncan's superior officer so any complaints were cut off at the feet. Duncan might be irritated by Mark to the point of *thinking* about whipping him, but he'd never do it — even if the boy deserved it all too often. Naval discipline was harsh and inflexible; but they weren't in the Royal Navy, and Duncan's title of commander was a courtesy. Otherwise Mark's back would be flayed to shreds by now, his spirit cowed. What would an intimidated Mark look like? He'd never find out . . . no matter how tempting it was. Mark was a child.

Mark had been discovered picking pockets on a London street and was whisked to Whitehall before a local street gang could adopt him, and had been assigned to Duncan. The look in the boy's eyes when they'd met that day in London — the fear and the defiance — had sung a familiar song. Two peas from the same pod. Brothers from a dif-

15

ferent mother, the same kind of father: lessons learned at the end of a fist, or the point of a whip.

"You're not *good* yet. We're in a perilous situation, so for God's sake practice self-discipline. No one can become an effective team member — or leader — without it. Any. member of my crew is sent home without a recommendation for further work unless they display obedience and respect — and don't think you can get around that. You've worn out your chances. Do exactly as you're told, without argument, or you're gone."

"*Oui,* monsieur. I'm sorry, monsieur."

Duncan almost laughed at the boy's hanging head, the chastened tone — now in perfect, fluid French. The boy wanted to be a King's Man that much. "Now, unless Le Breton" — Duncan remembered Burton's cover name just in time — "decoded the flags, I won't hear it from you."

Mark nodded. "*Oui,* monsieur, I'm sorry, monsieur." Even his obedience managed to sound cheeky, a mystery Duncan, cut from another cloth, would never be able to unravel.

"What's the message, Le Breton?" he called, satisfied the boy understood he wasn't in charge of the mission.

In a long-suffering tone, Burton said, "He has it, monsieur, word for word." He hastened to add, "I didn't teach him."

Duncan almost chuckled at the thought of

it. Of all his crew, only First Lieutenant Flynn was more enamored of the rulebook or versed in respect for his betters than Burton. "It's as well I believe you." Speaking in harsh tones to inferiors kept order on a mission; but after almost a year on this one bloody mission, both order and patience were in short supply. Six months they'd trawled through Paris, which was barely any cleaner or more civilized now than during the hideous Reign of Terror. The past five months they'd combed the cities and towns of France, performing sundry missions for the highly secret British Alien Office as they went. But now, even he found it hard to find reasons to tell his loyal crew that Eddie's daughter was still alive. Both Burton and Flynn had told him the men were muttering about going home to their families. One or two men were bordering on mutiny.

Duncan had no family to go home to and owed Eddie too much to give up. A month ago he'd sent the worst two mutterers back to England on half pay, with no recommendation for further missions. The other mutterers were confined to the ship, with the austere Flynn in charge. Now Duncan had only the stoic Burton — and, reduced to desperation, Mark — on this final leg of the mission: the Channel Coast, the last stop before they returned to England. The boy had been begging and bragging of his abilities for months. How much of a disaster could it be?

Not quite a disaster, but no matter how hard he or Burton made it for the boy, the brat adored every moment of the experience. The boy reveled in showing off his fluent French — how he'd learned it was a mystery he wasn't sharing — and showing off other knowledge he'd gleaned by illegitimate means. Since joining the crew he'd been shooed away from beneath the ship's forecastle too many times to count. Fifty, sixty times he'd been caught memorizing the movement of the coder's arms and position of the flags that made up a letter, number, or a coded sentence. Burton and Flynn, his best coders, had thrashed the boy until a furious Duncan had forbidden it, but the little blighter only ever said, "Me da could show you lot a fing or free about a good whippin'," and laughed as he danced away.

If Mark had been born in France, no doubt he'd have led the rabble to the Bastille. Burton would have been one of the valiant guards that fell at the gates, fighting for his king — and the chalk and cheese of Duncan's current team made it bloody exhausting to be the commander.

Tiring of the wait, Mark jumped into the conversation, but kept low. Thank God for that. Even in Napoleon's France you never knew who was listening, or where. A wrong word and anyone could end up in prison to rot, or with their head lying beneath the guillotine. Memories of the Terror were slow to fade, especially from the minds of ambitious men, or spiteful women — and none were in greater danger than agents from the British Alien Office. "Mr. Zephyr sent the message, monsieur." His words were subdued, even a little respectful.

Duncan held in the laugh at the awed tone in which the boy gave their spymaster's code name, and the "Mr." in front. William Windham, code name Zephyr, didn't give a damn if he was respected or not. One simply obeyed, because one didn't dare to do otherwise.

During his few weeks of basic training, Mark had made the mistake of demanding while in Windham's hearing, "I want a code name like what the 'nob' agents got."

A haughty face, a single lifted brow, and the belligerence stuttered to silence.

"Code names are for those who have a position to uphold, a great deal to lose if they're discovered. *You* are bloody lucky to be here. If you don't like the way I conduct this office, go back to your East London stews." With that, Windham had turned his back on the boy.

Odd, how three sentences had done what months of thrashings and threats had not. Mark held a passionate admiration for, and morbid fear of angering, his spymaster.

Duncan had once been that boy with his first spymaster, William Wickham, now retired to Ireland. And with Eddie Sunderland. Always Eddie.

Leaning back against the badly sprung squabs of the coach, Duncan listened to Mark's bragging tone with half an ear, wishing the day wasn't so damned hot. He felt as if he was breathing in wet heat. If he could shrug off his jacket, as he would back on board ship — but his current cover was that of an up-and-coming businessman too conscious of his social position to ever let his inferiors see him *en déshabillé.*

"What?" he barked on catching a word. "Say that again!"

The boy refrained from rolling his eyes this time. "Mr. Zephyr said that bonkers Lord Camelford's on the lam again. Mr. Pitt, 'e's right upset about his cousin lobbin' off. Wants 'im found afore he kills some other poor blighty. Ought to 'ave been put in the Fleet years ago, or Bedlam, more like. Leastways, you're to look out for 'im. They fink 'e's headin' this way."

"Not that, the other," he snapped, but taking that piece of information into account. *Bloody Camelford, what's he up to this time? Mark's right, he ought to be locked up.*

After being tossed off a few ships in his early naval career, Thomas Pitt, known as the "Mad Baron," had stalked his former captain and caned him half to death on a London street in revenge for administering correct naval discipline. He'd been ousted from the navy for shooting a lieutenant for insubordination; but because of his rank, and being first cousin to Prime Minister Pitt — not to mention a great deal of hush money paid to Camelford's victims, or family — there had been no further punishment. Since then he'd been involved in two public duels, and probably several more Duncan hadn't heard about. Just four months ago he'd been deported from France for a spoken intention to kill First Consul Bonaparte. Boney's men had found him in Calais, confiscated his faux travel pass, saw him onto a packet for Dover, and made it clear to the British government that he was to never return to France.

Ten to one he was planning to kill Boney for the public humiliation to the great name of Pitt. In Camelford's mind, the Pitt family could only find their equal in the king and God himself (and being *German* Stuart descendants, mere Scots royalty, maybe even the king didn't rate).

So now, as well as trying to find the runaway girl and learn what her husband was up to, Duncan had an insane baron to add to the list. Wonderful. It seemed the aristocracy couldn't keep their family members under control.

Mark's loud expulsion of breath brought

21

him back to the words that had grabbed his wandering attention in the first place — and he noted with satisfaction that Mark had at last begun to use the mint paste he'd given the boy to clean his teeth and mouth. "Mr. Zephyr, he said" — pause, for dramatic effect — " 'Letter from Bertie Greatheed. He says you might find Eddie's girl in Abbeville, working in a tavern on the Amiens-Calais road.' "

Duncan's heart sank. "Turn the coach south, and spring 'em. I want to be in Abbeville by morning."

CHAPTER 2

Abbeville, France (Channel Coast)
August 17, 1802

The smells of wilted flowers, sweating cheese, salted pork, and overripe fruit hung in the air, a pall over the Tuesday farmers' markets. Stallholders swatted at flies, slow and indolent. The obligatory tricolor ribbons pinned to the front of each stall lifted a little now and then in a puff of air coming from the Somme: a tired nod to *vive la Revolution.*

Though perspiration beaded her back, Lisbeth Delacorte kept her cloak around the telltale checkered dress and cast-off boots. Taking the path behind the southern end of the Place du Marché-au-Blé, she kept her head down, her strides fast.

"Here comes the English whore, off to ply her wares again."

Every Tuesday and Friday when Lisbeth passed her stall, the woman said the same words, and she was tired of running past. Tossing back her hood, Lisbeth stared at her

23

tormentor. Iron-gray hair, ruddy cheeks in a square face, a sacking dress and mobcap tied beneath her chin. The tricolor ribbon pinned to her breast wasn't for show. The Revolution had been good to her. The former peasant now held the largest pork stall in Abbeville, and she never tired of crowing over less fortunate neighbors.

The woman's cheeks darkened at Lisbeth's unexpected challenge. "Lower your eyes, you haughty bitch." With the flat of her blade she swatted at a mouse nibbling on a pork slice. With a squeak, it toppled off the stall, landing at her feet. "Your father's not worth a *sou* here. *Citoyen* Delacorte should throw you out of France and wed a decent Frenchwoman to raise his boy."

Lisbeth only laughed. How she was no longer afraid she didn't know. "Do you mean yourself, madame? Would you take on the task of living with my husband for my son's sake, or would you perhaps send your daughter?"

At that the woman murmured something and made a little, stealthy sign of the cross. Though the people of Abbeville clung to the old respect for the Delacorte name, the gentleman her husband could have become had vanished when he was fifteen.

A hereditary knight of noble lineage, *Châtelain* Edmond Delacorte was one of a hundred thousand victims of Mademoiselle Death.

False information had been given to the Committee of Public Safety by a neighbor jealous of Delacorte's wealth, position, and pretty wife. Two days after his father's death, Alain came home to find his mother raped and beaten senseless by the same neighbor. Killing the man with his bare hands only fed Alain's fury and need for vengeance on enemies both visible and invisible.

How can one boy-man take retribution on a nation collapsing in on itself, a voracious people feeding on bloodlust and power, and remain sane? How had Lisbeth not once noticed during the weeks they'd met in secret? How had she not seen the violence and hatred in the romantic, poetic émigré until it was far too late?

Because I was seventeen and stupid, rebelling against Papa's arranged marriage for me. Because Alain had lived a life of romance, excitement, and danger, and I'd barely left Norfolk.

She couldn't let pity for his suffering change her determination. Getting her son away from Alain was all. It was everything. Alain was too damaged to raise a child; so he couldn't frighten her off or isolate her enough to make her go. Until he killed her she'd never stop trying to take Edmond back.

Seeing the mouse creeping away, the stall-holder kicked it. Lisbeth crossed in front of her, picked up the wriggling creature, and walked on, ignoring the jeering laughter.

When she reached the southern edge of the square, a lady approached from the western side of the stalls — a housekeeper for a good family judging by her cotton dress, poke bonnet, and the boy trotting beside her, carrying a laden basket. The moment she saw Lisbeth, the lady lifted her skirts and swept past as though she carried a contagion.

Only a year ago, that woman would have curtsied to her. A year ago Lisbeth would also have turned from a woman of ill repute. Now she knew tavern wench didn't always mean harlot, even in a notorious place like Le Boeuf. Sometimes it just meant hunger and desperation — and Alain was not the gentleman his father had been.

Despite her gentle caresses, the mouse quivered in her hand, its little eyes terrified. It cringed when her finger moved. A kindred soul in her hand: it also understood that a caress could be a prelude to pain.

She crossed the old stone footbridge across the Somme and laid the little creature in the nearest garden. "Be safe, and no more pork from that stall for you," she whispered as it vanished beneath crunching leaves fallen from the amber tree above.

She walked on, shaking her head and laughing. Reduced to talking to a mouse . . . laughing by herself. If Alain saw her, he'd have her put in an asylum.

Tavern Le Boeuf, Abbeville, France
It was her.

In an overwarm taproom filled with men yelling, singing, and groping the laughing waitresses, Duncan sat at an unpolished table in a corner far from the fire. Snuffing the candle or keeping his hood over his face would only draw attention, so he sat at the farthest corner from its muted light, sprawled across the crude bench seat as if sleeping.

He still felt naked. A man couldn't be alone here without people noticing. Almost all the girls had approached him about food or drink, or offering sex. Before long one man pointed at him with a nod, frowning, and then another.

When the next girl approached him, he paid for half an hour with her.

When they reached the room, he said softly, "Take a rest." The girl, tall and buxom, gave him a half-pouting smile of regret, and he felt his body respond. In other circumstances, he'd have relieved the tension; but after all he'd been through to find her, he wasn't letting his target out of sight. He climbed out the window, down the ivy, and watched her through a window.

It seemed appropriate.

When the half hour was done, he climbed back up the ivy, paid the sleeping girl,

27

returned downstairs, and asked for ale. Keeping on target. Watching her. Waiting.

The match to the kit-cat Eddie gave him was exact. The porcelain skin was touched by a dusting of freckles on her nose and cheeks, a giveaway to her tomboy childhood in the sun. The unique stripes of blond-and-honey hair were woven into a braid. Eddie said her unusual hair was the bane of her life, but it became a different hue in each light, glossy and changeable, more fascinating than one perfect shade. Skin flushed with hard work highlighted her cheekbones and brightened her slightly slanted green eyes, showing up laughter lines. Though she'd barely smiled beyond a polite stretching of lips, it was the tip-tilted, charming smile of her mother, giving an impression of crookedness that wasn't in her bone structure. She was by no means a classic beauty, yet he'd remember her face long after the current diamonds of London society became fat, overdressed breeders of the next generation of entitled brats.

He shrugged. What he thought of the girl wasn't important. He'd found her. He'd talk to her. Then his responsibility ended.

Watching her, he thanked God he wouldn't have to hide the truth of her occupation from Eddie. Le Boeuf promised willing girls, but she avoided groping hands, wouldn't sit on anyone's lap, and returned coins pushed at her by randy men. She wore an apron tied loosely over the tight, red-checkered uniform. A ruff of tucked-in lace hid her cleavage. She used a multitude of pins to push back rebel locks of hair falling in her face. Neat, modest, severe, she worked twice as hard as any girl in the room, never heading upstairs with a happy customer.

He might be relieved, but the men she served were less happy. "Bitch," one man nearby snarled when he groped her, and she tipped ale into his lap.

"*Pardon,* Monsieur LeClerc, the jug was overfull," she said in flawless French, her tone cool. "I will pour you another, on the house."

"On your wages, Elise," an older man shouted from the taps, as sulky as his thwarted patron. Duncan frowned. She was called Elise now? Had she become so French in a year?

The girl poured the glass, keeping the jug over the patron's lap the entire time. The sulky patron didn't move, didn't say a word. The girl had spirit, he'd give her that.

Near closing time he made his way out, keeping to the wall, listening as he went. Because of the singing, slapping, rattling of crockery, and general talk, he heard only snatches.

"My daughter's as ugly as my wife. *Le bon Dieu* only knows how . . ."

"If Fouchard's guillotined, his widow . . . the farm . . ."

"Fulton's new inventions . . . Fouché —"
The men stopped talking as Duncan passed;
but that they'd seen him at all was the
giveaway. Alerted, he slowed as he wove
among the tables, now knowing why a subtle
excitement had filled him on entering the
tavern. Too many of these seeming drunks
weren't drunk at all, and he'd have known it
from the start if finding the girl hadn't
distracted him. Ears honed, he kept moving,
weaving a little, a foolish smile on his face.
Touching, holding on to tables and chairs as
he went, as if for balance.

". . . October twenty-ninth, near Boulogne-
sur-Mer. The Gaillard brothers and O'Keefe
—" Again, the speakers stopped on seeing
him so close. Little wonder, for the names
were puppeteer's strings jerking him to a halt.
A glance gave him further information. He
forced out a belch, swayed, and grinned at
them all before forcing himself to keep walking toward the exit.

What were the odds of two different groups
of men being here tonight, discussing people
of interest to the British Alien Office, on the
exact night and place he'd found the girl? One
of the names mentioned was Deville O'Keefe:
French mother, Irish father, and a half-rogue
operative for the Alien Office. The Gaillard
brothers were also Alien Office operatives, but
again, their loyalties were always in question.
Loose cannons, all three of them.

On passing out into the darkness, Duncan frowned. Something had felt off, not quite right, for days now. Heavily armed soldiers had demanded his credentials to enter Boulogne-sur-Mer, a Channel port fifty miles distant. It seemed he needed written permission from General Soult, Admiral Latouche-Tréville, or First Consul Bonaparte himself. It happened again on every road he'd tried into the town. Semaphore messages from his ship reported the substantial French naval patrols on that part of the Channel, even by night. Soldiers had also challenged his entry on the main road into Abbeville today. They hadn't been as stringent as at Boulogne, allowing him in after seeing his papers. Yet something about the experience still rankled. Now this.

Something was happening on the Channel Coast. October 29 was only ten weeks off. The White and Red Rose teams in St-Malo and Calais were too well known. His team was new, unknown, so far unnamed (thank God for that; he hated all the classical or romantic code names Zephyr insisted on). His was the only team in the region . . . and the girl was right here at the hub, with every reason to return night after night.

Damp Breeches pushed past him in the night, his friend in his wake. "Haughty English bitch. I'll show her who's a man."

Duncan sighed.

■ ■ ■ ■

The moon was a harvester's sickle hanging low over the west as Lisbeth left the tavern via the servants' exit, her eyes hot and itchy, her hands rough and hard from scrubbing floors. The stiff night breeze softened the acrid perfume of spilled wine and wood smoke on her clothes, and cooled the sweat beading her face. Even after a pulsing-hot day, when the night Channel wind hit, it felt almost like winter. Drawing her cloak around her, she bid farewell to Elise . . . at least for the walk back to the place that would never be home. Elise lived in a cramped room in a *pension,* walked to work and back, took the insults and lower wages. Lisbeth was English to the fingertips, with carriages at her disposal, and home was a converted abbey snug in the rolling fields of Norfolk, with Mama in her sitting room reading or embroidering while her renegade daughter escaped on her spirited roan mare, and poor Ralph chased her on his hack. "Give over, Miss Lizzy! Go back to yer ma 'n' yer lessons. What'd yer da say if he was here?"

That was always the question nobody could answer.

As she reached the shadow of St. Vulfran's, a church again after years of storing either pigs or ammunition, she heard footsteps behind her. *Please, God, not again.*

"Elise, you can't walk home alone. You need protection."

She pursed her mouth. It seemed LeClerc hadn't forgiven her for the incident with the beer; the tone was aggressive beneath the persuasiveness. No doubt the second set of footfalls was his ever-present sidekick, Tolbert. Gritting her teeth, she strode on. She'd long ago learned that saying anything to them, even rejection, only encouraged these fools.

"Elise, end this foolishness." LeClerc's rough voice was impatient but held a note of would-be tenderness. "We've played your game long enough."

In grim determination she walked even faster.

Tolbert puffed as he trotted behind LeClerc. "You owe Delacorte no loyalty."

"He deserted you and stole your child — but you need not be alone. We want to be so kind to you."

Lisbeth closed her eyes for a moment, fighting the rebel ache, longing for a kind word, a gentle touch. *Perhaps they would be kind to me . . . at least until I'm not so young or the novelty of my birth and English blood palls.*

They hadn't been *kind* in mentioning Edmond. That type of ploy was far too clever for these two . . . but Alain knew how she loved her son.

In the precious minutes she'd held her baby she'd forgotten Edmond's conception, or how she'd prayed to miscarry at the start; she'd even hoped they could become a family. Then Alain took Edmond and disappeared, leaving her with medical debts and the rent.

What had she done to make Alain hate her so? She'd told him Papa didn't love her, yet Alain had been furious when Sir Edward Sunderland refused to allow either of them in the door after she'd eloped. By the time she'd discovered the reason Papa would never allow his new son-in-law into his home, it was far too late.

"That's it, *chérie,*" LeClerc said in an exulting tone, far too close. She must have slowed. Like a fox with hounds on her scent, she hitched up her skirts and bolted.

Booted feet pounded behind her. Jerked back by the hem of her cloak, she fell on the cobblestoned road. A jolt of pain shot up her spine. She couldn't breathe.

In the muted light of his lantern, LeClerc's thin, ordinary face came into view, his eyes red rimmed with drink and blazing with excitement. "Come, *chérie,* it's over now. Be sweet to us, and you'll see how good we'll be in return."

Oh, yes, Alain had taught her all about the *goodness* of men. She screamed as loud as she could. Not one light went up in response.

When LeClerc reached for her, she head-butted him.

"Salope!" LeClerc hauled her over his shoulder and carried her, kicking and screaming, to a mossy mound between the cemetery and the church wall. "Arrogant *chatte,* you'll pay for that, and the ale you threw on me. So you think you're above us? Here you're the same as any other girl in the tavern. *Liberté, egalité, fraternité. Vive le France!*"

The bitter irony tasted like gall. Yes, in post-revolutionary France there was equality and fraternity if you were rich, talented, or French. Liberty was yours if your neighbors didn't report you to the latest committee or paranoid leader, if you didn't work with whores by necessity, or —

LeClerc pushed her on her back, and the memory of her last birthday flashed into her brain. *Not again, never again!* She twisted and kicked, arms flailing. "Help me! Rape!"

No candle lit in all the row houses across the road. No sound from the presbytery she'd just passed. Echoes of the night at The White Goose were screaming from the abyss of memory.

She'd known all along these idiots worked for Alain, but this was cruel, even for him.

The knife! She pulled it from her cloak, but with a blow to her wrist, LeClerc sent it spinning. With an exasperated huff, he put a cupped hand over her mouth, the other hand pressing his fingers into her throat until she choked, fighting for air. "No more tricks, or I'll really hurt you."

She bunched her hand into a fist, gathering dirt and grass, and threw it in his face.

LeClerc's blow to her temple sent broken gravestones spinning behind her eyes. "Hold her." Tolbert grabbed her arms. LeClerc hitched up her skirts and loosened the tie at his breeches.

"Release the lady if you want to live."

CHAPTER 3

Abbeville, France
August 18, 1802

The growling voice came from the darkness close by. The unmistakable noise of pistols cocking followed. Tolbert and LeClerc gasped and released their grip on her.

Lisbeth's eyes snapped open. Was he a figment of her desperate imagining? But Tolbert's low-lit lantern and the uncertain moonlight illuminated a tall man swathed in a cloak, aiming two pistols at her attackers.

"I shoot with both hands equally well." With a subtle Spanish accent, he made her think of the *banditti,* professional killers. "But I don't have a shovel to bury you. So start running."

Tolbert bolted, tripping over crumbled gravestones, taking the low outer wall at a leap, arms windmilling in an attempt to go faster. LeClerc ran after him, holding his undone breeches with one hand while the other flapped, like a one-winged bird.

The stranger returned his pistols to his cloak pockets. "Did they hurt you, madame?"

The words barely penetrated the fog in her mind. She couldn't stop shaking. All she knew was that her bunched-up clothes exposed her to the waist like a harlot. If she still had her pantalets, as a lady of breeding . . .

Pull down your skirts! But her arms remained above her head, refusing to obey her will.

He stooped down. Energized by panic she scrambled back, but he only pulled her dress and her cloak over her. "May I see you home?"

She stared at him. *Beautiful manners. Pure Picardy-Norman French now, with no accent.*

Looming over her in the darkest hour of night, he was so *big*. With the hood pulled down, she couldn't see his face.

"Please tell me you're not hurt, madame."

Strange concern in his low murmur. *Faceless, anonymous, a stranger. I don't even know his voice, but he called me Madame. Does he know me?*

Stupid! Everyone knows you. You're the only British whore in Abbeville.

The random observations felt like a ship's log being filled, coming one after the other, adding to her confusion.

"Will you let me help you, madame?"

That he asked her permission felt like cement slapped over broken bricks: it smoothed the shards of her dignity, yet the cracks remained beneath. All she could manage was jagged breathing, and staring at that faceless space inside the hood.

"You're shivering." Gloved hands divided from his voluminous cloak, reaching to her.

She jerked up and pointed a shaking finger at him. "Don't touch me." She hardly expected obedience. Men never allowed women control: not fathers, brothers, husbands, or even chivalrous, hooded strangers.

Yet without a word he stood, pulled off his cloak, and laid it over her, shrouding her in its warmth. He laid his pistols by her and returned to sit at her feet.

He'd handed her his pistols? Why? She blinked and waited for him to speak, but he seemed content on the ground, waiting for her word to move. With the thin moon fallen behind the Channel, his face was a black silhouette in the dearth of light. Was he the phantom imagining of a desperate girl, an uncertain resemblance of what a gentleman ought to be?

The minutes ticked past while she shivered and he remained silent, waiting.

At last she whispered, "Help me."

He got to his feet. "I'm coming behind you. Now I'll put my hands under your arms, so. Are you ready?"

Overwhelmed, she could only nod. It hurt her throat, made it hard to breathe.

Touching only her underarms, he lifted her to her feet. When her legs trembled, he murmured, "May I carry you to the bench?"

After a long moment, tossing up whether speaking would hurt less, she nodded.

He set her on the bench in the belfry's shadow and wrapped his cloak around her once more. He retrieved his pistols and left them beside her. "Are you feeling warmer? If you take a chill, you won't be able to work tomorrow."

Lisbeth started. He'd been at the tavern? The man in the corner who'd turned from her whenever she approached him?

Why was he treating her as a lady when he'd seen her at work, and had just seen more of her than any stranger ought? How could he expect her trust when he wouldn't show her his face? Unwanted intimacy, respect, and concern coming from blackness. She wanted to pull her own hood over her face, run away. If she could make her legs obey her.

If only she could be sure LeClerc and Tolbert weren't waiting for the opportunity.

The stranger sat still, lost in the night. It seemed deliberate. He'd put her in the light while he remained in darkness and silence. She refused to speak first, or play the helpless damsel to this odd Galahad . . . but the silence grew and her curiosity hurt.

"Who are you? Do you know me?" she whispered at last.

She felt rather than saw his smile: a tiny hummingbird of satisfaction fluttering in the air. "You may call me Gaston."

Her mouth turned down as a cold sliver touched her bone. "No, I may not, monsieur. Not without ruining what reputation I have."

After a moment, a slow nod came. "Then you may call me Monsieur Borchonne."

She frowned at him, doubting. Somehow, despite his perfect accent, he didn't look French. Or maybe it was the lost Spanish accent? "It's not your real name, is it?"

He didn't answer. Knowing herself to be in the right, she didn't lower her gaze, but lifted her chin and waited.

Eventually he spoke. "You're still shivering. This may help." He held something out. Squinting, she caught the dull glint of a flask. "Brandy's good for shock."

"So is tea," she replied, feeling foolish.

Again she heard the smile in his voice. "I know tea is preferable to ladies, but I'm afraid this is all I have."

There was something in his voice, an expectation of obedience. Almost resenting it, she lifted the flask to her mouth. In seconds she spluttered and choked.

A low chuckle. "It always happens the first time. Sip slowly, and count to ten."

Saying that — understanding that she hadn't drunk brandy before when he knew she worked at a tavern — insensibly soothed her. By the time she reached nine, the pain in her throat eased a little. "*Merci,* monsieur." It was deliberate, leaving out the *Borchonne.*

She felt his disapproval in the long time it took to say, "I have a horse over there." His half-turned face indicated the street. "Do you think you could sit astride?"

The times she'd been in Mama's black books for wearing a pair of Leo's or Andrew's jodhpurs, and riding astride . . . she forced down a second bubble of laughter, lest he think she'd lost her mind. "Yes."

The stranger stood. "I'll fetch him."

She grabbed his jacket. "Don't leave me." *Thick broadcloth, warm and functional, a working man's jacket on a gentleman.* The understanding only added to the enigma.

The moment the silence grew painful, he spoke. "May I carry you to the horse?"

She couldn't walk, couldn't bear to be alone, and LeClerc and Tolbert could return with weapons — or God help her, with Alain, given her new suspicions — at any moment. "Yes."

He carried her through shadows in the darkest part of night. In the blackness there was only the faint silver of fading stars. When she squeezed her eyes shut, her other senses took over. Warmth and security and her pounding heart, too many impressions too fast, overwhelming.

She was tall, but he dwarfed her. His

clothes smelled clean, his skin fresh. No reek from beneath his arms. His breath smelled of peppermint water and hazelnut wood. She knew both scents from Mama's obsession with avoiding the dentist to have her teeth drawn. He'd probably rinsed his mouth and used a twig to clean his teeth.

The information clicked like a cog into a wheel. *Rough clothes, but newly washed. Clean teeth, sweet breath.*

Her arm around his neck, she felt the unevenness to his shoulders. It felt unnatural. An injury? Was he a soldier? Naval officer?

A horse nickered nearby. "The stirrup is by your left foot, madame."

All by feel, she slid her foot into the stirrup, found the pommel, twisted her body around, and swung up. When he untied his horse, she took the reins and covered her bare legs with her cloak.

She looked at him. He was looking down at her hands. His hair was thick and dark, tied naval style with a riband. "The trembling is much less. *Trés bien.* I see you like horses. You mounted astride perfectly."

"A misbegotten youth," she said with a chuckle. How could a stranger keep making her want to laugh, when he seemed so serious, and she'd barely even wanted to smile in the past year?

Without answering, the stranger steered the horse in the direction of her street. He stopped the horse on the uneven cobblestones in front of the *pension* on the rue Jeanne d'Arc.

He knows where I live. The scales of knowledge were too one-sided, too personal. Though her hands were still cold, her palms turned sweaty.

A room above them had a candle burning by the window, too soft to see him as he came around to the other side. He didn't lift his head, showing only his dark hair, the riband. He must have been in France for some time, to understand the danger of those who watched, listened. "Can you dismount unaided?"

She scrambled off the horse on the wrong side rather than let him touch her again and hit the ground with a shock in her feet. With a gasp she leaned on the wall of the *pension,* fingers digging into the mortar. The bulging cement with globs of plaster laid over to strengthen the painted wooden beams supporting the medieval house was cold to the touch, and she shivered.

"You need warm gloves, madame." Barely a whisper.

"I — forgot them today." Pot-valiant lie — but she couldn't rely on an eccentric Galahad who saw too much and gave too little. If he had gloves in his pocket, she didn't want them.

She handed him his cloak without looking

at his unshielded face. Discretion was the only gift she could give in return for all he'd done tonight. "Thank you for your rescue, your cloak, and your escort, monsieur."

"Those men won't give up." He pulled the cloak on, the hood down. "I can teach you to use that knife to greater effect."

So he was coming back. That meant he wanted something from her — then she sucked in a breath. "The knife isn't mine. Monsieur Marron will take it from my wages, and I can't —"

"Madame." When she looked up, he was holding the knife's hilt out to her.

A year ago, her greatest fear was Papa's arranged betrothal of her to a rich nobleman she'd never met. Now her life was reduced to avoiding unwanted attention, and worrying over the cost of a knife. Feeling small and stupid, Lisbeth mumbled, "You've been a godsend tonight."

"All this is unworthy of you," he said quietly. "You're a baronet's daughter. Don't you want everything you left behind? Don't you long to go home?"

Like fog rolling in from the river, sorrow enveloped her. Her rescuer had just inflicted more pain on her than any LeClerc or Tolbert could give. How could he speak so casually of returning to England, when she'd give her life's blood to go home?

"He burned my identity papers," she muttered, thoroughly trained in controlling every emotion around men during the past year. "A man legally owns his wife. With soldiers posted on every road, I can't even leave Abbeville without his permission."

A moment's silence. What had she said to grab his attention? Then another whisper: hooded temptation, anonymous desire. "You can. Just say the word. I can take you home."

Home . . . oh, the careless wound. Her sharp-drawn breath hurt her chest, like a thin dagger thrust. Yearning engulfed her, the hopes and dreams she'd buried since waking from a drugged sleep to find herself in France. To ride the fields of Barton Lynch once more . . . Mama scolding lovingly, always trying to make her hoyden daughter a lady . . .

He'd said *home* as if it was his home, too. So his name and both his accents had been a lie. After the past year, she refused to put her life in the hands of any man. And there was Edmond. "No." She pushed off the wall and headed on unsteady feet for the door of the *pension.*

"How long have those men been following you?"

Unwilling to answer, she owed him this honesty at least. She kept her back to him. "Since I began at Le Boeuf they've been propositioning me, touching me . . . following me."

46

"I can end that problem, if you'll trust me."

She almost laughed in his face. *Trust?* How *stupid.* No, he didn't know her.

Seventeen months ago she'd been an ingénue in pretty gowns and pearls, in London for the Season. With a smile and curtsy, she'd accepted dances with men she regarded as gentlemen because Mama said they were. Because they dressed the part, could speak the part, and made an elegant bow. The greatest judgment she'd made was on their looks, if they could dance, if their breath was sweet or rank, or if they'd flattered her enough. Boring fribbles that wanted her inheritance, the daughter of the wealthiest baronet in Norfolk, just as other men wanted her friend Georgy because she was a duke's daughter. The two of them had played tricks on those men, banded together against their matchmaking parents, and generally brewed mischief.

Now she was a fallen woman who'd made stupid choices she had to live with.

Turning to the door with its peeling green paint and ancient oak showing beneath, she tried to keep her voice even. "Thank you, but no. You've done more than enough."

"I'll be outside Le Boeuf tomorrow night."

No man could be as kind and disinterested without wanting something. She stared into the hood, fathomless darkness where a face should be. "I'd prefer it if you were not —

47

tomorrow or any night. I may be beholden to you, but I am not like the other women at Le Boeuf."

"You owe me nothing, and I ask nothing." Quiet, yet spoken with a hardness that made Lisbeth gasp and step back, and he softened. "I beg your pardon, madame."

With difficulty, she nodded. "Go on," she murmured.

"If I can't come to you, one of my men will do so. He'll use the word *Tidewatcher.*"

She blinked and tilted her head, frowning. "What — tidewatcher? What does that mean?"

"*Bonsoir,* madame." Before she could recoil he'd come around the horse, bowed over her hand, and, taking the horse's reins, slipped into the night.

She stared into the predawn emptiness, dark gray as his cloak. Had it been a dream? The thick curls of morning river mist added to the sense of unreality. If she'd stayed home, she'd be a future baroness, established in London's *haut ton,* surrounded by friends and family. Instead —

She could hear Alain's gloating voice. *Happy birthday, ma chère. Remember last year?*

No. Reliving the night at The White Goose only gave him power over her. There was no point in regretting the spoiled, headstrong child she'd been. She was a mother now.

Yet as she entered the *pension* and locked

the door behind her, her eyes fluttered shut. *I'm sorry I was a difficult daughter, Mama. I wish I'd stayed to meet the baron's heir for you, Papa.*

Thinking of her father brought her anonymous Galahad to mind. Despite his gallantry — or perhaps because of it — she saw him as a hawk on the hunt, circling above her. Her father had sent him, she felt certain of that; but there was some purpose beyond that, something he couldn't ask of her after she'd been attacked. But he'd be back tomorrow, and he'd ask then.

Given the woman she'd become, the only two options left her chilled to the bone.

CHAPTER 4

Abbeville, France
August 18, 1802

Duncan slipped into the saddle with a strong sense of *now is the summer of my discontent.* Even the small satisfaction of finding her had been snatched away, like a Captain Sharp cheating him at the card table. He'd found the girl. He should be able to go home, returning with a clean conscience, and report to Eddie that his runaway daughter was well and happy. Then he could go home. Put this waste of a year behind him. Get on with his life.

But when Bertie Greatheed wrote to Zephyr, it changed everything. The full message had come that morning. Greatheed, owner of the Royal Pump Rooms, traveler, dramatist, and font of all British gossip in France, had said, "French husband deserted her. Chit's put herself beneath contempt, working in a tavern where the girls whore themselves." Duncan could almost see the midlands squire speaking in his broad accent, shaking his round head. "If she joined the ranks or not don't matter. No family of good reputation would take her back."

As the coach rumbled south on bad coastal roads from Étaples to Abbeville yesterday, Duncan had hoped it wasn't the Sunderland girl. That she was somewhere else, or even dead.

Greatheed knew their world well, the world of British high society. A son was forgiven any and all peccadilloes and welcomed home, but a daughter must remain pure. If she married a rich nobleman, she might make it worth Society's overlooking her past, but the chances of that were minuscule if she wasn't a virgin. Though she *was* an heiress — Eddie's wealth was almost indecent — the scandal of eloping to Scotland with an émigré, and one who'd turned out to be a spy for the infamous French spymaster Joseph Fouché, meant the Sunderland girl had no chance of returning to Society. Especially because it seemed she'd be unwilling to desert the son she should never have had.

He'd set up his cover story, the Gaston Borchonne alias to hand. Armed with perfectly forged papers, the ever-efficient Burton had found the agent for the Borchonne house and obtained the keys. The entire Borchonne family was dead, apart from the long-missing Gaston and one missing cousin. Everything was in place, thanks to Zephyr's foresight —

How long had Zephyr known the girl was here — and how long had he been distracting Duncan with minor missions, allowing the girl to suffer? So typical of Zephyr, but if Eddie found out . . . then he chuckled. As if Zephyr would care.

Duncan had been to Abbeville months before, but he hadn't thought to come to Le Boeuf, the most notorious of taverns on the Amiens-Calais road. The tavern from which no redemption would come, if Eddie or anyone else found out the girl had even passed its portals.

With her unique face and hair, he'd recognized her at once. Even wearing a red-and-white-checkered dress spotted with sauce and ale stains, and ugly boots, the air shimmered around her. It was like she carried a pocket of hectic magic, resonating from another time or place, like a tale of the ancients. Not like the mythic Helen, or the glorious Lorelei on her rock. She didn't have the beauty that led to madness. It was something else . . . the girl had the same blind distance in her eyes as the mermaid figurehead on his ship. The Oracle — yes, the priestess hiding behind the wall who decided a man's future while she remained held apart from the concerns of ordinary men.

He clipped the side of his head. "Stick a cork in your stupid bloody myths and sailors' superstitions. Stick to the point."

He'd completed one mission only to stumble onto one more imperative. The girl worked in an obvious hub of French espionage. Without trying, she'd given him a way to ferret out the mysteries at Tavern Le Boeuf . . . and what it was they had scheduled for October 29.

He'd reached the Borchonne house. He opened the gate and headed to the small stable to get Blue settled.

A reluctant confession to make, but a small, mean part of him had hoped to find her life here less than blissful. He'd thought it a minor vengeance, considering all she'd put him through. But the way she'd been treated by the patrons at Le Boeuf, the owner, the men who'd attacked her — no one answered her screams for help. It felt . . . well, rehearsed. A Drury Lane drama.

His knowledge of Alain Delacorte gave the suspicions credence. A few months ago, Bonaparte had deposed Delacorte's mentor, Joseph Fouché, as the head of the secret police, even scrapping the entire portfolio. Though he'd been given over a million francs for his ousting, and was still France's unofficial spymaster, it was the power Boney denied him that Fouché craved most. One of his minions was Alain Delacorte — and, like his mentor, Delacorte enjoyed playing puppet-master. Arranging this dangerous, lonely life for the mother of his child was probably good sport to a man of his talents — a way to alleviate the boredom.

Why was Delacorte still in Abbeville? It couldn't be the girl; surely she was no threat. But given the sentries in the region, and the conversations at Le Boeuf —

The Treaty of Amiens had ended the war months ago, but in the Channel region, it didn't seem so. Something here smelled foul to the wind. Boney was up to something — and if Fouché knew, it explained Delacorte's continued presence.

Another semaphore had come from the ship this morning. A promising new recruit with the improbable name of Peebles had passed the guards stationed on the roads to Boulogne-sur-Mer. Armed with excellently forged papers and a French accent he'd inherited from his French mother, Peebles had bluffed his way in, along with the small set of portable semaphore flags and a shade cloth on poles to hide his actions from anyone else. All he needed was an empty roof.

Now Le Boeuf had become a link in the Channel Coast mystery chain — but despite his having saved her tonight, the girl had made it obvious she wasn't willing to play his game. Somehow she'd worked out that he'd waited to save her until the last moment, and it made her suspicious.

He must change her mind. Lucky for him,

he knew how to do it.

"Commander."

Without a sound Duncan wheeled around and cocked his head toward the house, covered Blue with a blanket, and left the stall.

When the door closed behind them, he snapped, "Three seconds to behave correctly. And you're supposed to be on ship."

"Pardon, *Monsieur Borchonne,*" Mark answered with abject humility, with the natural cheekiness still managing to shine through. When they returned to England, he'd hand the boy back to Zephyr. He wasn't built to guide a boy who seemed to thrive in a harder school than he was willing to teach. "A letter came from a passing ship. Hazeltine thought you oughta see it quick-smart." The wiry boy shoved a packet into his hand. By the looseness of the seal and the specks of dirt around it, Duncan suspected the flap had been pushed down hard after Mark read the missive.

He lifted his brows. "You found your way here in unfamiliar territory, at night?"

Mark rolled his eyes. "Ya fink I look fresh, monsieur? I got here afore sunset. I been waitin' for *hours.* I fell asleep in the shrubbery over there. Ruddy cold it were, too." The Cockney dialect mangled his French verbs, but was somehow apropos of a Paris slum-lad.

Duncan's mouth twitched as he opened the

55

packet. A bit of roughing it wouldn't hurt. Mark needed to learn obedience before he'd go anywhere in the Alien Office. Wily and cunning, bursting at the seams with raw talent, a loose cannon like him couldn't be let on his own, or he'd advertise their presence to all the wrong people.

Reading the packet's direction, he understood why Third Lieutenant Hazeltine had sent it. Only Zephyr and Eddie knew Duncan's new cover name — but the handwriting, slanted and hard without bothering to be copperplate, wasn't the spymaster's but his mentor's.

He read Eddie's letter first.

This information came to me. Leo and Andrew have verified it, but we cannot do more. I need you to meet with him in London — and for God's sake, display a little patience!

Intrigued, Duncan read the thicker letter. When he'd done, he looked up. "Return to ship and tell Flynn to prepare the crew. We must make the London docks by tomorrow's sunset."

Mark's brows lifted, but his eyes lit with excitement. "From 'ere to Lunnon in under a full day? It's what, nine hours in the packet boat from Calais to Dover, and that's less than a third the distance. We'd make a whole new record for that, Commander, um, monsieur!"

"Then a record we'll set," Duncan retorted.

Though she ached in every muscle, Lisbeth couldn't change into nightclothes; the craving battled exhaustion and even the fear, and won. In a few minutes she was in her oldest dress, her hair out of the tight chignon and in its habitual braid. She threw on a thick cloak and headed out on the street going south. When she neared the soldiers' checkpoint, she turned southwest, pushing into a small, tight forest by the river. She held up her cloak, allowing the brambles to tear her dress instead. Her hands were soon scraped raw and bleeding, but it was the only way. If there were a real walking path here, soldiers would man that, too.

At the northern end of the village of Eaucourt stood a white-and-blue cottage with sky-blue shutters, the last summer flowers flaunting their beauty in the windowsills. Winter herbs were thriving despite the heat. She inhaled the restful scent of rosemary, sage, and wintergreen.

Alain believed the child-wife he'd deserted in hostile territory wouldn't know how to slip past the soldiers guarding the roads out of Abbeville. He wouldn't begin to dream she'd be able to follow LeClerc and Tolbert as far as the Eaucourt road and time the minutes until their return.

Only one village was close enough to make a report and return in under an hour. Forging a path through the forest she'd searched Eaucourt by night until she'd found the house. Then she'd crept up the back stairs, found the nursery window — and she'd met her mother-in-law.

Using the edge of the outside stairs to minimize noise, she climbed to the second floor. Soft golden light told Lisbeth that Marceline was waiting.

Slat thin, with hollow eyes and frizzled gray hair bundled into a careless knot, Marceline rocked in the chair by the fire, holding Edmond in her lap, singing a ditty. Her damaged eyes stared dotingly into the sleeping face of her three-month-old grandson.

Edmond was flushed, so pretty in sleep. Lisbeth drank in the honey-tinted blond curls, the crooked dreaming smile — all the signs that this beautiful child had something of her.

She scratched on the glass. Though expecting her, Marceline started, her eyes pinched in the fear that never left her. Pity wrenching her, Lisbeth lifted the window and climbed in as quietly as possible. "It's me, Marceline. Where is Alain?" she whispered.

"He will be home at daylight," Marceline murmured, not looking at her.

"I understand." She took the baby into her arms with a spurt of joy that hurt her. "Thank you, Marceline, thank you."

The pale night rail and wrap Marceline wore made soft whooshing sounds as the older woman left the room on uncertain feet, still singing the ditty.

"My baby," Lisbeth whispered, staring at Edmond's face while she could. She had no way of knowing when Alain would discover her little trysts and move to where she couldn't reach them. She put her finger in the baby's palm. "I'm your mama. Can you understand, sweetheart? Can you remember me?"

His fist curled around her finger as if in answer.

Take him and go. Marceline can't possibly stop you. You could run, and —

And then what? With his resources, Alain would find her in hours. Though she hated to admit it, Edmond needed Marceline, this pretty cottage, the wet nurse, and all the time and attention *she* couldn't give him. Though violent to almost anyone else, Alain was an adoring son, and — so the women in town taunted her — a devoted family man. Perhaps he was, to anyone born and raised in France, or to anyone he didn't see as the destroyer of his greatest mission.

Lisbeth's throat filled with a lump she couldn't swallow. Though she shouldn't come — it brought nothing but pain — these minutes might be the only time she'd ever have with her son.

The first cockcrow came too soon. Edmond was in his cradle by the time Marceline appeared in the doorway, a tired ghost. "He's coming. Go."

With a panicked *merci* Lisbeth slipped out the window, tiptoed down the stairs lest a servant hear her, stumbled through the back garden, and bolted across the fields to the forest.

Pushing through the brambles, leaving skin, blood, and scraps of her dress behind; trudging back to Abbeville and the cramped room in the cheap boardinghouse she'd be ashamed to bring Edmond to, the hatred and need for revenge curled through her, a cat's claws pushing into her skin. No matter what it took, one day she'd have Edmond, and all Alain's beloved power games would avail him nothing.

An hour later, nestled in her bed trying to sleep, she caught her breath. The man without a name had offered to take her home. Would he do as much for her son?

CHAPTER 5

St. Pancras Church, London, England
August 19, 1802

The archbishop's gums were *purple.*

The dentures were the latest innovation for the wealthy, made in porcelain instead of ivory, fixed into his head with gold screws that flashed when he smiled. The ousted Archbishop of Narbonne looked like a Botticelli cherub, with chubby cheeks, a sweet smile, and a halo of white hair, but those teeth —

"You must be wondering why I asked you to meet me, Commander."

Click — the top denture dropped as the archbishop spoke, then *clack* — it moved back into place. A piece of half-chewed meat stuck above the denture showed every time the teeth dropped. And as for his breath — when Duncan was a child, he'd seen a two-headed goat at a fair. Now, he felt the same horrified wonder mingled with a churning belly.

"Commander, did you hear me?" Narbonne's voice was cold.

Caught out mid-run. He forced his gaze up to the old man's eyes and bowed — a swift, jerking movement, with none of the grace Eddie had taught him. "I beg your pardon, *Votre Éminence.*" If a man of the archbishop's exalted status requested a meeting in a tomb-cold church with underpriests stationed outside every entrance on the hottest day of the year, he must have vital news. Moreover, if he wore gentleman's attire rather than luxurious vestments of gold and purple, especially when inside the church he'd frequented since fleeing France, he must have information he didn't dare allow anyone else to overhear.

With a haughty nod, Narbonne forgave him. Duncan's jaw tightened, and his hands curled into fists. Oblivious, the old man waved his hand at the crypt and nave beyond. "This dates back a thousand years. So-called improvers with their gold leaf and plaster pots are fools." *Click-clack-click. Meat and spittle.* "These things tie us to the faith of ages past. In the Revolution, so much beauty was lost to the world."

Duncan suppressed a sigh. Elderly people liked to talk, and any informant of his standing expected and deserved a respectful hearing. But he wasn't saying anything that didn't happen during the Reformation, the Dissolution, the Wars of the Roses — name a war, or a country.

The silence stretched thin. It seemed Narbonne wanted an answer. "To lose your bishopric under the terms of the Concordat must have felt like betrayal."

An irritable look settled on the archbishop's face. "Don't patronize me, boy. You —"

Duncan's stomach jerked. *You are nothing. You will live up to the name you've been given, boy!* Even with his eyes open he saw Annersley's hand lifting, the whip descending . . .

Halfway to his face, Duncan forced his hand down. The scars had been there so long he mostly forgot they were there.

The old man sat ramrod straight on the pew: a highbred bird with ruffled feathers, every inch as imperious and easily offended as the old bastard at Mellingham Hall. He knew what Narbonne expected, but damned if he'd grovel. When he'd run from Annersley the last time, he'd sworn never to cringe or bow before any man again.

Eddie had asked him to display patience. "I will refrain from patronizing you if you do the same for me. If I was a boy, or not from your class, I doubt you'd have agreed to meet me."

Unexpectedly, Narbonne's lips twitched. "*Touché.* So which of your names do I use, the oh-so-English Commander Aylsham" — *click-clack* — "the equally French Monsieur

Borchonne, or perhaps I should call you Tide-watcher?"

Duncan stiffened with the quiet use of his code name, given by the British Alien Office when he was given his first Continental assignment, back in '93. "Commander Aylsham will do." He spoke with an edge of rigidity he couldn't control. "My ship leaves with the tide."

A slight nod indicated Narbonne's second gracious acceptance of an apology Duncan refused to offer. He pointed to a pew seat and crossed to it without bothering to see if Duncan followed. The silken whisper of the episcopal slippers the comte's son wore with the best tailoring London could provide ground at Duncan's patience, which was never his strong point. Wily old hypocrite played the man of God when it suited him, but the latest in his string of mistresses was rumored to be his own niece.

Duncan spoke through a tight jaw. "The tide turns in an hour, *Votre Éminence,* and my mission is imperative."

The archbishop lifted his brows, holding his haughtiness to the end. "With the signing of the Concordat, France and the Church abandoned me. Still, French, Irish, and Catholic dissidents here believe I share their causes and tell me their secrets as if in the confessional. They are sacred, and I will not reveal them without strong reason."

Click-clack. French. Irish. Duncan expected Narbonne, with Irish nobility for parents, but born, raised, and ordained in France, to have divided loyalties. "I know the rules of the confessional, *Votre Éminence.*" When would the old man finally get to the point?

"But one I must tell. There is a plot to kill the king."

Duncan stared at Narbonne. *Surely Eddie wouldn't recall me from France for this old chestnut?* Poor old Farmer George, why so many people wanted to kill a harmless, half-mad king who liked to potter in his garden was beyond him. *The Irish or the Catholics,* he thought wearily. *It's always the same.* "If you find it a serious threat, take it to a government representative."

Narbonne shifted on the pew, putting a cushion behind his back. "Sir Edward sent me to you. So don't waste my time, bo . . . Commander."

Frozen inside, Duncan bowed again. "Why did Sir Edward pass this to me?"

Narbonne's lips pursed. "His wife is . . . ill."

The ice inside Duncan broke into sharp pieces. If Eddie wouldn't leave Caroline even long enough to hold this single meeting, but had recalled *him* from France, she must be seriously ill. That meant he'd have to waste more time bringing the girl home — *if* he could make her leave without her child.

65

Damn it, it meant delaying the mission until he could find another woman. But where the hell would he find a lady of a similar age and the same perfect combination of ruin and innocence? "Can we please get to the point?"

Narbonne closed his eyes, as if asking God for patience. "As a French-born man of Irish nobility, and a displaced archbishop, I'm in a unique position to hear things. The plotters are not Jacobites or students preaching insurrection on the streets of London. Nor is it beer talk by the United Irishmen. These men lost titles and lands in Ireland and Scotland through ambitious men with social connections. The explosion is planned during the Opening of Parliament, which the king always attends, as do hundreds of those absentee lords raking in profits from their Irish and Scottish lands. A Colonel Despard is the ringleader — the former superintendent of Honduras, an Irishman with sufficient reason to want several men dead."

"I read about the case." The men in Honduras, who'd accused Despard of treason and had him imprisoned for their profit, had escaped perjury charges through connections to the king; but though he'd eventually been freed, Despard's life and reputation had been destroyed. "I don't see how they'd get close enough. Armed guards surround Whitehall —"

"They've emulated Guy Fawkes and unsealed a tunnel beneath Whitehall," Narbonne interrupted. "I didn't dare ask for details, but from what one man said, I think they're using time-lock devices on naval barrel bombs, to give them time to escape. If they blow up the tunnel beneath Parliament . . ."

Duncan's stomach dropped. The tide must come and go without him. He had to find Windham, in whichever part of the British Isles his spymaster had gone in this inclement weather, and report this posthaste. "I'll look into this plot. That I promise you."

"I'm not finished," Narbonne said when Duncan stood. "What if it's only the start of their revenge, and they destroy Buckingham Palace, London Bridge, or the Tower of London to begin a collaborative Irish-Scots uprising throughout Britain?"

Duncan closed his eyes. Given Irish history, and the brutal abuse of power the English had used against the Scots and their lands since Culloden, it was horribly plausible.

". . . you've been scouring the Channel Coast. I want to know what you found there."

Too late Duncan caught what Narbonne said, and he stiffened.

"Yes, I'm an Irish-French Catholic with an ax to grind." Narbonne's voice turned gritty as he lay bare every reason for reticence on Duncan's part between them. "So I'll tell you

what you found. There were soldiers everywhere stopping entry to Boulogne-sur-Mer.
The area's flooded by spies of too many
persuasions and plots. You suspect Bonaparte
has more infantry — and possibly far more
warships — than the Treaty of Amiens allows,
and you need to find out why he's blocked
off every approach to Boulogne by land and
sea."

Duncan leaned forward. "You have royalist
spies inside Boulogne?" Narbonne's loyalties
had been obvious from the moment he gave
Duncan the information.

Narbonne whispered, "Not now. Nonresi-
dents without official permission have been
forcibly escorted outside Boulogne, and
newcomers refused entrance. My man was
killed."

Duncan's innards were going through the
Labors of Hercules today. Hell in a bloody
handbasket, he'd tossed a raw recruit like
Peebles into Boulogne alone. "Why? What's
going on?"

Narbonne shrugged. "Any proofs I have,
your government would want verified. My
speculations are useless to a government that
does not want to know what Bonaparte is up
to. It is convenient to them to suspect my
connections, and my religion," he said in a
wry voice.

Duncan waved that aside. Any Englishman
with a brain in his head couldn't trust a

French-Irish Catholic, especially one with a religious ax to grind. He wouldn't believe it now but for the evidence of his own eyes. "How long have you known of this?"

Narbonne's chubby face darkened until he was as purple as his gums. "I sent men across France after Bonaparte paid his thirty pieces of silver and the pope sold the faith there. Now Bonaparte gives bishoprics to his sycophants or those with gold enough to pay for his army!"

Narbonne didn't answer the real question. The Concordat had been proposed over a year ago, and a man of Narbonne's standing would have been warned early on from someone in the Vatican. Early enough to send spies throughout France to spike whatever guns Boney had set up. "You must have impeccable sources."

"I do." Grabbing Duncan's cravat, he pulled them face-to-face, blowing out the scent of rotting meat, and Duncan's stomach churned. "All Channel ports apart from Calais were closed this week. The coastal roads are guarded and blocked, and warships patrol all French waters from Jersey to Calais. I've heard whispers of a planned assassination of the first consul on the Channel Coast in late October. My sources say he's coming, but Bonaparte has no visit marked on his official agenda."

With a chill, Duncan remembered the

whispered *October twenty-ninth.* If royalist spies knew the date, it meant everyone in charge at the Alien Office also knew. Why hadn't he been told?

Narbonne spoke almost in a whisper. "So is this plot real, or is Bonaparte using the many previous attempts on his life to deflect us all from the truth?"

Duncan frowned hard. "Deflect us from what?"

The old man's gaze bored into his. "How do you hide a masked assassin? *Naturellement,* send him to kill during a masquerade," he answered the question. "How do you mask a conspiracy so large it couldn't possibly be missed if it stood alone?"

Duncan's mind pitched and rolled like his stomach did on his first day returning to sea. Assassination, betrayal of church, and international conspiracy, all in an hour. "Lose it in a crowd of other plots."

Narbonne nodded. "A hundred warships and a thousand soldiers surround Boulogne-sur-Mer. Bonaparte reads every dispatch he's given by day's end. He'd never go if he thought the assassination attempt was real, unless the plot comes from him, or there's something in Boulogne that makes his visit imperative. Either way, your government needs to know what's happening."

Narbonne's words churned in Duncan's mind amid a stormy sea of questions. Why kill a poor, silly king who spent half his life growing vegetables? Why was every entrance to Boulogne-sur-Mer blocked? Why was the entire Channel Coast manned by thousands of soldiers?

The scraps of conversation he'd overheard at the tavern . . . what did his enemies know that he didn't? How could he have missed the installation of a blockade while he'd been combing the Channel Coast — and how the *hell* had every member of his team missed it?

Answer: they couldn't have. One of his team was hand in glove with the French. God help them all if the rat was one of the sema- phore signalers.

Semaphore . . . the message about Eddie's daughter. If there was a mole, and he'd passed the message to the French, Delacorte might know they'd found her. Given what he knew, that boded very badly for Delacorte. How soon had the Frenchman known? Was *his* presence why she'd been attacked the first night?

"I'm afraid my usefulness ends here, Com- mander." Narbonne's sigh sounded like an admission of defeat. "Bonaparte's setting empires ablaze, and God help those who try to stamp them out. I believe the answer to your questions lies in what he is hiding in Boulogne."

The bow Duncan made this time was deep, filled with respect. "I would never have discovered this much on my own. Thank you, *Votre Éminence.* You spoke of speculations. I would hear them, if you'd care to share them with me."

For the first time since they met, Narbonne smiled. "Think how the Opening of Parliament will be after the attempt on Bonaparte — especially if he blames the English for it." The fatalistic shrug said it all. With Boney, it was always the Jacobins or the English. "If the attempt happens, Parliament will call the king to an emergency meeting. The conspirators will be ready for it, especially if they have an impoverished member of the House of Lords in their pockets."

As Annersley's legal representative and proxy since he'd turned twenty-one, Duncan had attended several sessions of Parliament. With every lord loudly abusing or pushing his agenda over whoever was speaking, it was lively and confusing enough in peacetime; but an emergency meeting with an addled king, a frightened Prince of Wales, a strident Duke of York, Irish and Scots landlords yelling about insurrection and a renewed threat of war — it made for a shambles that would cover any noise the conspirators made until it was far too late.

Narbonne murmured, "They must have a member of the House of Lords telling them about any changes in schedule — a man who wants a place of honor when Bonaparte takes power here. I believe those ranks are swelling daily. Bonaparte has many admirers."

Again, it was plausible. In the past two years, many of Bonaparte's fanatical spies had been British: night soil men and farmers, stable lads and housemaids, doctors and lawyers, sailors and high-ranking officers, naval and military. Even members of the aristocracy had been discovered to be in French pay.

He remembered a dream he'd had where he'd been tossed naked into the snow, and everyone he knew was there, laughing at him. Annersley stood at the front of the line, jeering. *Did you really think you could save the world, boy? You're pathetic.*

He said slowly, "You think they're aiming at revolution."

"Killing the king and many prominent lords will leave Britain with a gaping hole in its existing social system. It leaves the nation ripe for plucking by the *Grande Armée,* which is many times the size of its armed forces. I believe all this was planned before Bonaparte proposed the Treaty of Amiens, to give him time to create a means to bring his army across the Channel."

"An invasion fleet?" Duncan thought of the Liane, Boulogne's deep, wide river behind the shallow harbor, and all the new buildings erected on the seaside of the river, making it impossible to see anything from a ship in the

Channel.

In the light of the pillage of Parma and Piedmont, there was no hiding from Boney's intentions. He craved Britain's treasury, made fat on the wealth of its colonies — and to conquer Britain was to conquer Europe. His timing couldn't be better with the navy halved, not to mention a war-weary government and public. Addington would almost open the gates of London for Boney rather than declare war again.

Duncan stood. "Thank you for the risks you took to give me this information, *Votre Éminence.* I'll make certain our people investigate everything you've told me."

The old man bowed, his head dipped a shade deeper than mere acknowledgment or farewell. The implied respect lessened the cold clenching of Duncan's gut. So stupid to care what a stranger thought of him. About as ridiculous as the part of him that still feared Annersley's ridicule and craved his approval.

"There's a final message from Sir Edward." Narbonne's hauteur softened, giving way to an expression Duncan couldn't recognize. "He said, 'Bring my daughter home as soon as your work is done.' "

A sword tip of hated emotion ripped the commander's belly. Kings and consuls, plots and counterplots turned urgent in circles in his mind. But Narbonne's words injected the unwanted vision of a plucky young woman, a scrappy little fighter with a hidden fragility and quaint self-respect, so strange given her current status in life; but he assumed someone her age — little more than a girl — needed her mother.

Eddie wouldn't have asked him to leave France unless he believed the king *could* be assassinated, or dozens of lords were in serious danger. Given all he'd learned today, that his mentor, a King's Man to the end, hadn't come to meet the archbishop himself was telling — but he hadn't asked him to bring his daughter home straightaway. So how ill *was* Caroline? Why hadn't Eddie told him?

Suddenly he remembered Flynn's report. He *must* have a man in place at Le Havre by tomorrow's sunset, or the whole mission could fail.

If half of what he'd heard today was true, the girl was his best means to discover Boney's plans. Her need for reconciliation with the family must wait. The choice had slipped out of his hands. He'd bend the girl to his will if need be — and there was only one way to do it.

The archbishop murmured, "Go with God, Commander."

Indeed, God help him. He had the mission of his lifetime to set up, and a rat in his team. With Eddie, Leo, and Andrew unable to leave home, and Zephyr suddenly an unknown quantity, Duncan didn't have a bloody clue whom to trust. News of this caliber must be delivered to the Alien Office from a recognized King's Man, but he had no *time* to find one.

A face rose in his mind. A face that was like looking in the mirror, with scars in different places. He didn't like the man, but who else was there?

No matter how much you want to deny it, we are brothers, Duncan. If you ever need me, I'll come.

There was no help for it. He had to ask Alec.

CHAPTER 6

Outside St. Pancras Church, London
August 19, 1802

More than half an hour had passed since he'd tied and gagged the boy. He could start making a ruckus any moment.

From where he hid just inside the back entrance of the church, Lord Camelford tossed off the cassock he'd snatched from the unconscious underpriest and slipped out the doors. So that reprobate "Guinea-Run" Johnstone — no more than a common smuggler, despite pretending to be a reputable ship's captain — had at last come good with his information for sale. The archbishop had confirmed everything. Camelford knew he must get to France as soon as possible — but he'd been deported from Calais four months ago under the Rushworth false papers. He couldn't use his real name, since they'd put him on a "watch and deport" list.

He made a hissing sound through his teeth. Thomas Pitt, *Lord Camelford,* deported like a common felon . . . refused future entry into France. Bonaparte deserved death for that alone.

"Hie, you!" Camelford wheeled around. A sandy-haired boy with a freckled face and a black cassock stood twenty feet away, his face filled with suspicion. "What you doin' 'ere?"

Great God, the little guttersnipe couldn't even speak the King's English! But his sharp eyes bespoke intelligence — and unfortunately, with Camelford's height, harsh features, and hooked nose, when people recalled his face, they did so with accuracy.

It was as good an excuse as any. He was damned irritable with the heat in any case.

He loosed the knife from its sheath and flicked his wrist with the expertise of long practice. The frustration in his chest lightened as the boy gasped — but he staggered, pulling the knife out of his shoulder. *Damn it, he ought to be dead.* " 'Elp me, bruvvers!"

No time to think. Running so fast he stumbled over a crumbled headstone, Camelford jumped on the boy, stifled his second cry, snatched up the knife, and drove it into the thin chest.

Before he could enjoy watching the light fade from his eyes — the world was a better place with less rabble and Papists in it — the alarmed yell of another priest came. More missing of vowels and dropping of consonants. More east-end Catholic garbage! The lot of them were useful as only chimney sweeps, night soil men, or tuppenny whores. The whole district could do with a cleansing fire. Then their betters could do something useful with the area.

He sheathed his knife, ran to the fence, vaulted over and rolled down the embankment, got up, and kept running until his chest ached and his legs felt like rubber. *Reach the Thames docks.* This upcoming assassination attempt on Boney was a golden opportunity for a true English patriot to make certain the assassins carried it through. For the British aristocracy to retain its supremacy, and to stop this infectious disease of republicanism, Boney must die.

Within two hours Camelford was forty pounds poorer, but the three forgeries were in his pocket: identity papers and recommendations. By the time Commander Aylsham boarded ship, he'd discover his fourth lieutenant had decamped, but an experienced lieutenant had replaced him. In this time of demobbing, sailors and officers alike combed the docks looking for work. The letters of glowing recommendation for "Fourth Lieutenant Haversham," written by Camelford's own cousin, former Prime Minister Pitt, and Lord St. Vincent of the Admiralty, would ensure his place on the ship.

Cousin Will wouldn't give him away . . .

and in a few short weeks, Boney would be dead.

The Isle of Bute, Southwestern Scotland
August 22, 1802

The first shot whizzed beside the boy's ear like an angry bee. Puzzled, the messenger swatted at it. He didn't connect the bee to the bang seconds before; why should he? But the second bang came from right nearby, and he fell to the ground with a terrified cry, groveling on the wet ground with his arms shielding his head.

"That was yer warnin', Sassenach boy. You been askin' where the Black Stewarts could be found? You found us. Now get off my land!"

The voice came closer by the moment. A native Londoner, the boy barely understood a word the old man said, but he got the danger right enough. He curled into a ball and lifted an oilskin packet with a shaking hand. "I'm just deliverin' a letter! Commander Aylsham sent me!"

For long moments, only the sound of the howling wind and pounding rain filled his ears. Then the man spoke, his accent clear and sharp. "Did you say Aylsham, boy?"

"Yes, sir! Me mam diden want me comin' all this way, but the commander promised *five pound* if I put this into Alec Stewart's hand, an' more if I bring 'im back to Lunnon quick-smart. *Five pound and more,* sir! It'll keep me family fed fer months!" The boy dared look up to the face now right in front of him and blurted, "The commander, he looks awful like you, sir, he do, but his hair's black, not silver. Sir, me mam need that five pound, she do!"

"I'd say she does — and she'll get it all and more." The voice was softer, clearer, as was the old man's face. "Take this to Master Alec," he said to someone inside, passing the packet along. He turned back to the courier, smiling, and pressed a coin into the boy's hand. "Ye've only an hour to make today's last ferry, but dinna fash yersel'. My grandson's a quick packer."

CHAPTER 7

Trouville-sur-Mer, France (English Channel)
August 25, 1802
The sturdy young man with light-brown hair tied back in a queue and worried eyes stood perfectly straight in front of his commander. "What if he doesn't fail tomorrow, sir?"

Despite his growing impatience to be gone to Abbeville, Duncan lightly cuffed his first lieutenant on the shoulder, with a smile. "He will fail, Flynn. He's not ready yet. But *you* are. I have every confidence in you. When you complete this part of the mission, follow him to the house . . . and make certain he can't hire any assistance at all." He dropped a heavy purse into the younger man's hand. "Hazeltine will be in place. You just do your part."

"If Mr. Fulton sees me around the new house, he'll know —"

"You don't go near the house, Flynn. Leave that to Hazeltine, and to me. Do your part, and by the time you have, the ship should be anchored off Ambleteuse, a manned rowboat in the river mouth between Ambleteuse and Wimereux after sunset every night after we arrive. Just hire a coach and return to ship."

"But sir —"

"A horse awaits you southwest of the river mouth, at Les Planches. Take the Deauville road. You should reach Le Havre just in time for the test."

Obviously recognizing dismissal in the note of impatience Duncan couldn't quite mask, Flynn snapped to attention and saluted. "Aye-aye, sir. I won't let you down."

"I know you won't." The torpedo testing in the morning provided a gilt-edged opportunity that might not return for months. Their mission had a good chance of success . . . as long as Robert Fulton failed.

The moment the launch that took Flynn to the river mouth at Trouville was back and lashed into place, he ordered, "The marshes of Le Crotoy near Abbeville, before sunrise."

His remaining lieutenants began snapping directions, and tired sailors ran to their stations.

Le Havre, France
August 26, 1802
The sun had barely risen above the hills behind the town when the sleek, fish-shaped underwater boat *Nautilus* came to the ocean's surface two hundred feet from shore.

American inventor Robert Fulton murmured a prayer. This was the culmination of years of hard work. Minister of the Marine Decrés had sent his secretary for this demonstration. Just weeks ago, he'd demonstrated his steam-engine could work on a small boat when the boat had traveled two miles down the Seine River near Paris. High on the excitement of official interest, he'd bragged that he could use a spring-propelled chamber inside his submersible boat to shoot the barrel bomb fifty feet in front and sink a ship. But the minister of the marine had sent his man at least two months too early.

After a failure off Brest to attach his little porcupine-shaped bombs he called *torpedoes* to a British warship, he had this last chance with the barrel bombs he called *carcasses*. If he could do it, the first consul himself would come for a private demonstration.

Even though he was stooped over, Fulton's head filled *Nautilus*'s observation dome. Though he'd locked the hatch of the submersible boat only eight minutes ago, with the spring-propulsion equipment beside the pole down the center of the craft's belly, the usual propeller and rudder cranks and the pump on each side, it was an overly snug fit for three men. Fulton's clothing was already limp, and the stench of nervous sweat filled his nostrils.

Only a small lantern lit the gloom, easy to

extinguish in case of fire. As they broke surface, the late-summer sunlight hurt his eyes. Through the tiny observation dome's window, he saw his target. The long-retired frigate provided by the Ministry of the Marine sat on the calm tide like a ghost scow about fifty feet away. He scowled at it, his enemy of days. He'd been practicing since he'd received word of Decrés's interest.

"Blow up this time, you — dog." Harsher words didn't come naturally to him. Though he was now a famed scientist, the child in him still wanted to check for the lightning bolts his childhood pastor in Pennsylvania vowed would hit him if he broke any of the commandments.

So why are you creating this instrument of death?

Thou shalt not kill, Robert, his minister's voice whispered in his head. *Those who take up the sword will perish by the sword. Gaspard Monge is an atheist, Robert! Remember what St. Paul said: bad associations ruin good habits . . . do not become inventors of injurious things . . .*

Fulton thrust out his jaw. If his demonstration was successful, the English spies that dogged his steps would report to their masters, and England wouldn't dare resume war. God must surely smile on that? "Light the fuse, Nathaniel, and seal it. Release the carcass on my count, Fleuret."

His assistant Nathaniel Sargent lit the two-foot-long fuse wick — three minutes burning time — pushed it inside and sealed the slender bomb with a thick cork. The entire bomb had been dipped in tallow to keep everything watertight. Sargent dripped hot tallow over the cork and pushed it in hard. A minute later, he pressed the wax and nodded. "It's ready."

His bomb maker, Fleuret, pulled back the spring of the propulsion chamber as far as it would go — three feet, no mean feat in a craft so small. The spring gained strength. *One two . . . oh, please, Lord, don't let the fuse burn too quickly, it will kill us all . . . three four —* "Now!"

The spring hit the square of steel at the far end of the chamber, propelling the bomb-release catch. The bomb flew out of the chamber into the water — but it acted on *Nautilus* like the recoil of a pistol. All three men flew backward, trying to grab at the pole Fulton had soldered lengthways throughout the craft. He scrambled to his feet, looked through the window, and began the count. "One hundred, two hundred, three —" Long before he'd made it to ten, he saw the little bomb bouncing to surface. "Back up and submerge as fast as you can!"

"How close?" Fleuret leaped across the craft to reach the pump after being thrown back. Sargent jerked the propeller cranks with the haste of terrified knowledge — disaster was imminent. Again.

"It surfaced by driftwood, only twenty feet away!" As Fulton dove toward the rudder, blinding light and a boom filled the submersible. The harmless driftwood became spear-shaped shards flying right at them. The windows shattered. A torrent of seawater cascaded in.

James Flynn watched as twelve men rowed to retrieve what remained of *Nautilus* and its crew. Four men were pulling diving bells over their heads, attaching them to the underwater suits they already wore. Another two were tying grappling hooks to the launch boat.

Crowds milled around the shore, laughing at the American's latest disaster. Fulton had had many successes, and they'd been spectacular; but his failures, so ridiculed by their first consul, really were funny. But failing before Minister Decrés's secretary had killed any hope Fulton had left of funding from the first consul.

By the time an hour had passed, the shoreline was almost empty. The divers had found the sunken submersible, and it was being rowed back to land with the grappling hooks. The minister's man was long gone. Sundry spies — Flynn had noted royalist, Jacobin, and Bonaparte's and Fouché's ghosts in different places around the harbor — had left to report to their masters.

In his disappointment, Fulton seemed to need an outlet for his fury. Having draped a blanket across his friend's shoulders, the famous scientist Monge stiffened when Fulton spoke. Moments later Fulton stood frozen as Monge left, taking what was probably Fulton's last hope of gaining French funding with him.

Monge spoke to Fulton's assistants. Fulton stormed away when he saw the two men follow Monge to the carriage, trailing their wet blankets.

If there was ever a time to fulfill his mission, it was now. Flynn slipped down the docks, toward the inns, rather than the taverns and whorehouses behind the warehouses, in Fulton's wake. The man was too fastidious to consort with harlots, too religious to drink laudanum or frequent taverns. He'd guess it likely the American was drowning his sorrows in a coffeepot.

He ran the man to ground in a coffeehouse as expected. Looking like a bespectacled drowned kitten, Fulton was grumbling into a pot of chocolate. So Fulton had a sweet tooth — but his air of gloom told Flynn the chocolate wasn't giving much comfort.

Flynn approached as he'd been instructed, his released curls both halting any thought that he was a sailor and emphasizing his youth. He bit his lip over an eager smile, with the air of a puppy. "M'sieur Fulton, I am a great admirer of your work."

With quiet precision Fulton put the cup down and refilled it from the pot keeping warm on a contraption over a fat candle stub. "I'd prefer to be alone, if you don't mind, monsieur. It's been a trying morning."

"I understand," Flynn said, sounding downcast. "I was there this morning, m'sieur. I was so hoping you'd make it. I wanted to say, *don't give up.* You're so close now — and it's obvious by what that man said as he climbed into the fancy coach, he thinks so too —"

Fulton's eyes blazed behind the goggles. "What did he say, and to whom?"

Flynn blinked. "I'm not certain who the other man was, m'sieur — he remained inside the coach. But the important man said your invention could most likely work in the hands of experienced naval engineers —"

Fulton whitened, and he huffed in choppy breaths. "Not until I am dead, Monsieur Decrés," he muttered, his gentle eyes hard, "and you can bank on that, as surely as you banked on taking my inventions without payment!"

The inventor downed his chocolate and stormed out.

Left to pay the reckoning, Flynn chuckled. Mission accomplished, and far easier than he'd hoped. Fulton's paranoia had grown to legendary proportions as First Consul Bonaparte became more important, and less inclined to pay for what he wanted. The American's excellent mind would ensure he disappeared before Boney's men came to confiscate his life's work. One of their French recruits awaited the inventor at home to make Fulton an offer he couldn't refuse.

Stage three was up to the commander, and the girl he'd found.

CHAPTER 8

Tavern Le Boeuf, Abbeville, France
August 26, 1802

The stranger was back.

For the past seven nights a different man waited outside Le Boeuf beside the horse. When she'd backed away the first time, he'd said the words *tide watcher* and handed her a note.

Madame, please accept John's escort for a few days. I will return soon.

This John was a man of few words but kept his pistols ready. As they walked home, he constantly watched for signs of trouble, but there had been none. At the door of the *pension* he'd helped her off the horse, bowed, and vanished into the night.

But tonight *her* stranger sat at a well-lit table by the fire. He'd left his cloak on, probably so she could identify him. He couldn't know she'd already recognized him by his height and breadth, and the slight hunch of his left shoulder she'd noticed the other night.

Seeing her watching him, he moved his cloak to reveal the knee breeches, waistcoat, and cravat of the socially conscious, up-and-coming businessman. His waistcoat had too much embroidery on it. He ate ragout and swallowed ale with seeming gusto, yet the effect was the same: no sense of belonging. A purebred Arabian in a peasant's stable. Nothing but the cloak sat right on him.

Why was he showing her his face? What had changed?

Though she sensed a trap, she kept looking whenever she passed. She held him feature by feature in her memory, as if putting a puzzle of the world together.

He was younger than she'd supposed, perhaps thirty. His black hair was thick and tumbled, caught back in a naval riband. In the shadows cast by the warm, dark room and his hair it was hard to tell, but she thought his heavy-lidded eyes were brown. His brows soared toward his temples like raven's wings. He had a heavy nose, sharp-defined cheekbones, and a tense mouth above a chin with a cleft.

It was a striking if not handsome face. The scars on his cheeks drew her gaze. The left side had the worst injuries, with slashing cuts and the melted flesh of imperfectly healed burns concentrated near the ear. The other side had older cuts close to his mouth, and one by his eye.

A brave face with haunted eyes. Did all King's Men have that on-the-road-to-damnation look? How many times had she seen the self-loathing and desperate need to forget on her father's face whenever he came home? She'd never understood the expression until she married Alain. Until her first beating. Until she came to France and saw her first beheading. Until she could give no more than a pittance to hollow-eyed soldiers' or guillotine widows and their begging children because, if she gave more, she'd have to whore herself to survive.

Until Alain took Edmond from her, and in the mirror, she'd found her father's eyes in her face. Now she saw Papa reflected in the eyes of a stranger with lies on his tongue and suffering in his soul.

Her gaze flicked left. LeClerc and Tolbert were still at their table. During the past week they hadn't approached her, hadn't insisted she serve them, or even attempted to touch her. But they watched her, and the encore of their attack crept up on her from behind. She'd felt it all week, even with John in the tavern, or walking home beside her.

As if they'd waited for the stranger's return, she knew it would happen tonight.

After his meal, the stranger sat back in his chair, drinking ale, in no hurry to leave. Louise flirted as she served him, but his gaze remained on Lisbeth. Fear slow-dripped down her back, tossed from the guarded expression in his eyes. Whatever he wanted from her in exchange for his protection hovered on his tongue.

Not without Edmond. Never without Edmond. The thought strengthened her.

At closing time he put a handful of coins down on the table, pushed back his chair, and crossed the fire-warm taproom to her. "I'll wait outside for you, *ma chère.*"

The low tone had a carrying quality, again spoken with the subtle Spanish accent.

She heard chairs scraping back. Without hurry, he turned to LeClerc and Tolbert. She couldn't see his expression but could visualize him smiling, fingering his pistols.

They hurried from the tavern.

"They're planning something," she murmured. "Be on your guard."

He looked down at her, conveying something with those shuttered eyes. "I'm glad your throat has healed." Still without urgency, he left the tavern.

Louise came to help her with stacking glasses. "So that's why he wouldn't look at me." The buxom, dark-haired girl grinned at Lisbeth and winked. "Smart girl, keeping yourself for him. There's something about big, fighting men, isn't there? And his accent . . ."

It came to this. Either she accepted his

protection or fought the likes of LeClerc and Tolbert alone. Either she accepted his proposition, whatever it was, or waited for Alain to find a way to kill her. She smiled at Louise, quick and unhappy, and kept stacking the glasses.

An hour later, she stepped out into the cool air of a dying summer night. Within seconds the stranger appeared on the path beside her. "Good evening, monsieur." Since marrying Alain she'd learned to sheath her sword. She still had Alain fooled that she was her mother's daughter, a gentle and refined lady well out of her depth, lacking intelligence and strength.

It was time to test this man out. To learn what he saw in her, what he wanted.

"Good evening, madame." Again, as soon as they were alone, the Spanish accent vanished. "Allow me." With cupped hands he lifted her onto the horse, now equipped with a sidesaddle. She settled onto it with an odd sense of happiness. It felt nice. Almost like she'd returned to the girl she'd been before she'd run off with Alain — Mama would say, the girl she *ought* to have been. A low-lit lantern hung from a short rope tying it to the pommel. A rifle hung beneath that. He was well prepared. "They've gone?"

"For now." After fishing in his cloak, he held out his hand. "I believe you know how to use this."

Not startled by this knowledge of her, yet disturbed, she glanced at the pistol. It was the daintiest she'd seen, with pretty swirling patterns engraved on the handle. "Is this — ?"

His smile sat oddly on him, a door where a window should be. "A lady's muff pistol, yes. It's for you."

The sense of wrongness reached down into her heart like an ice blade. Testing him was no longer an amusement. "Monsieur, while I am grateful for —"

He shook his head, with an imperative air that made her indignation wither half spoken. "If you cannot name me Gaston, call me by an endearment. We want people to believe I'm your protector." When she opened her mouth again, he lifted a hand. "*Protector* is a word with two meanings, madame. Be sure I will never ask you to be my mistress. I will only protect you from the likes of them." That dark, heavy-lidded gaze met hers, older than his years: the wounded warrior enforced her reluctant belief. "It's primed. You have only one shot. Make it count."

Unsettled more than she cared to admit, she nodded. Last time, he'd saved her from the unspeakable. Tonight he led her on an unseen dance into a storm. Riding while holding a pistol and looking out for attackers — what had happened to her? Every time this man came near her she fell into emotional and physical quicksilver.

At a crossroads, she had a choice: to follow his lead, to fall in with him, or to back away from the poison. She had the right to say no — and she would, if he asked the wrong question.

"Be prepared," he murmured as he led the horse toward the town.

"Nobody will believe you're my protector if I know nothing but your name, monsieur."

"That's reasonable." He sounded restless, dissatisfied. "I am the son of Abbeville's former mayor. My parents and sister were beheaded early in the Revolution. I escaped to Spain and served in the naval forces. I rose to the rank of first lieutenant. I returned to France a few days ago. I plan to become involved in local government like my father."

"An interesting history," she murmured in polite disbelief. "Do you know local politics?"

His gloved hands moved like a shrug. "I haven't lived here since I was a child. Any ignorance on my part will be excused for a few months. In any case, I won't be here long."

Everything he said tonight left her unsettled. "How many times have you needed to adopt another life?"

"Choose your endearment, *ma chère.* I believe our furious friends are watching us from the alley to the left." His hands held his pistols, straight and steady.

She glanced over and shivered. "Does this pistol throw at all, *mon coeur*?"

He glanced up, the hood falling back. His eyes gleamed with approval in the light of the fuller moon. "A little to the right, at this distance perhaps two inches. Can you compensate?"

"I hope so, *mon coeur.*" She let the reins fall. Holding the pistol, she used the left wrist as balance as she took aim at the men, controlling the tremors in her hand.

He aimed both pistols with his feet planted apart, left in front of the right. "Annoy my woman again at your peril, messieurs." The words rang across the street, Spanish accented.

LeClerc stepped into the light. "You won't shoot us for the sake of a stupid English bitch —"

The pistol dropped, aimed. The stranger pulled the hammer, tensed his body, and fired.

Lisbeth rocked back in shock with the explosion. The horse didn't flinch at the sound or rear when the air filled with acrid smoke. Obviously a trained battle horse. Was the stranger cavalry, then?

A scream split the night. When the smoke thinned, she saw LeClerc sprawled on the cobbled street, holding one foot and howling.

Candles lit in windows all along the street. Silhouettes appeared at windows, but in seconds the curtains pulled back together. Memories of the Terror were slow to vanish. Nobody would risk becoming involved.

"You're crazed!" Tolbert shouted. "Why did you shoot him? We only wanted some fun with the girl. If you're happy to share, we can —"

The stranger dropped the second pistol to Tolbert's feet. "Find your fun with a willing woman. This one doesn't like you."

Tolbert bolted, leaving his friend on the ground, moaning and weeping.

The stranger strolled toward LeClerc. "Are we done, m'sieur?"

"You wait until I . . ." When he saw the pistol turning to his other foot, LeClerc cringed further into the road. "Yes, yes — take her, I don't want her!"

"Good choice." He stooped, pocketed LeClerc's pistol, and returned to where Lisbeth waited on the horse, openmouthed. "Take the reins, *ma chère.*"

Lisbeth scrambled to obey. Again he led her on a dance too intricate and changeable for her to follow with any grace, let alone attempt to change direction; but she hadn't agreed to live the lie yet. *A lady must always be honest.* Somehow she couldn't separate herself from Mama's little truisms. He stubbornly remained *the stranger* in her mind. She couldn't think of him as Gaston when it sat on him as ill as the overdone, merchant-class clothing.

"If they hadn't told Delacorte about the other night, they will unquestionably tell him now," he murmured. "Will he object to your having a protector?"

She blinked. "I don't know." She didn't know how Alain would react to anything, because she'd never known him. She'd only seen the pretty façade he'd chosen to show her before their elopement, and the violent, angry man after.

He kept walking beside the horse. "You're not safe here."

Her heart took off at a gallop. "I told you, he burned my travel papers. Soldiers patrol every road in and out of town. The *gendarmerie* keeps watch on all foreigners."

"I have travel papers with a name no one will connect to you. I can get you out of town. You can be in our homeland within the week."

Our homeland. Although he'd slipped into his role hand into glove, *this* was why she'd felt such a sense of wrongness seeing his clothing, watching him eat, even hearing the name he'd given her. Whatever his name was, Gaston Borchonne was not it. This man was thoroughly British, and a gentleman.

Whatever he wanted from her, it was time to push her own agenda.

"Is this my father's plan? Where have I been the past year — Scotland? That's where the fallen girls go during their nine-month ill-nesses, isn't it? You know I have a son, don't you — *Gaston?* You seem to know everything else about me."

"Yes, I know about your son." He didn't say anything else. The sounds of booted feet and slow-clopping hooves filled the silence until she wanted to scream. "Perhaps I presumed too much, too soon. If you wish for your husband's return —"

She shuddered. Alain might appear like a medieval troubadour with his blond curls, blue eyes, and dimpled smile, but there all resemblance ended. God knows his absence from her life was a blessing; but while he had Edmond she'd play the cowed girl, the help-less lady, the tavern wench, even the sup-plicant — anything to stop him from taking her baby beyond her reach. "I won't leave without my son."

There was a smile in his voice. As if he ap-proved. "I rather thought you'd say that."

She didn't know how to answer. Waiting for the terms to come.

When they reached the *pension,* he lifted her off the horse. As they stared at each other after the awkward intimacy of strangers, he dropped his hands from her waist. "I hope John gave you the tincture of arnica for your bruises."

"Yes, he did, thank you. Why do you bother with me, monsieur? Why do I matter?" In her

101

experience, altruism didn't exist. He was here because either Papa sent him or he needed something from her, and she was tired of waiting.

"I told you, I protect you only in the physical sense." He didn't speak sharply, or with anger. He merely said it, and she hated how much she wanted to believe him.

She was the one who held the dagger in her speech. "Then what *do* you want from me?"

He bowed over her hand. Soft as a breath of wind touching her ear she heard, *"Not yet."* Then he left her, walking the horse through the marketplace toward the river.

The sound of his horse's hooves echoing slow and unhurried in the deep night was a wordless gauntlet thrown down. He was daring her to follow.

It killed the cat, they said. Papa said it would kill *her* for certain. More than a year ago her intense curiosity had led to her downfall, wanting to understand Alain, the poetic, sorrowful young émigré who worked in the local village as an apothecary's assistant.

Now that curiosity had returned in full measure, and again, she couldn't resist. Whoever this man was, she had to *know* — and she needed some of the high ground in their invisible battlefield. She'd do more than follow his lead in the dark dance he'd orchestrated. He needed to understand she was more than his pawn. He'd tell her the truth, give her his real name, and explain why he needed her before she'd agree to help.

In moments she'd grabbed the candle burning in the hall of the *pension.* Swift and silent, she left and locked the door behind her.

She moved against walls until she'd crossed the market square: a creature of the night like the whores, spies, murderers, and criminals, filled with calm certainty. He knew she'd follow him; he'd lead her in that dance into darkness, the mystery glimmering like a jewel in the night, irresistible. And he knew that, too. But she had her own methods of control.

The stranger continued northwest toward the part of town where the affluent lived, the business owners, politicians, and magistrates. Never once did he look around or behind: the quintessential man with nothing to hide or fear.

More unheard whispers in the night. *That's it, follow me. Trust me.*

Men could be such fools. If she didn't know him, he didn't know her, either.

When he reached the Somme River, he turned right, and the beginnings of the morning mist rising from the water swallowed him. There was no trace of him by the time she walked into its coils. Though she bent low and shielded the candle with her hand, all signs of hoofprints or boot prints ended at the edge of the mist, the cloaked specter vanishing into the night.

Jaw set, she trudged into the mist. Even walking bent and holding the candle close to the ground, the stony trail was too dark for her to see anything but rocks. At the first row of houses, she searched closely for signs of recent entry, but found nothing.

Then a cat bounded onto the top of a lime-washed wall. As she jumped in surprise and dropped the candle, the cat leaped into the tangle of neatly trimmed bushes in the next property. Its slight air of alarm awakened a core of excitement in her, a humming certainty. Moving to the gate — a polished wooden affair with a simple latch — she pushed it inward. Smooth and silent, the gate had well-oiled hinges.

This must be it. Excitement expanding with each step, she crossed the garden.

At the door, a moment's doubt. If she was caught — "Nothing ventured," she whispered, and tested the door. Noiseless, it swung open —

A massive figure stood behind the door.

CHAPTER 9

Six Miles Off Le Crotoy, France (English Channel)

August 27, 1802 (early morning)

One of the night watchmen had gone to use the head; the other was taking an enforced nap. Since they were anchored in quiet waters, surrounded by rocks where few deep-hulled French ships could venture, all was quiet. With fifteen minutes between third and fourth bells, Camelford counted on the first watchman making a bet on the cockroach race in progress belowdecks and watching the outcome before he returned.

The ship was in darkness. Nobody else was topside this time of night, despite being in French waters: the result of the commander and first lieutenant being on assignment, the others too young, and the ship's master too bloody old. If *he* was commander, he'd have ordered four men on the watch day and night — watching one another as much as the waters surrounding them. Something wasn't right on this ship — something, or some*one.*

Which was why he had to get away tonight.

As quietly as possible, he sawed the ropes holding a small rowboat inside two larger boats in the center of the ship; but how he was to get it over the side in silence God only knew.

"Me lord, let me 'elp you."

Camelford swung around. In the lowered light of his lantern he saw a red-haired boy behind him. The cabin boy, if he remembered rightly. Even in the night gloom he could see the impertinent freckled face looking at him as if — as if they were equals. Or co-conspirators.

As he was about to swing his cane at the boy's face, the boy stepped back, grinning. "Nah, you don't wanna do that, Lord Camelford, 'lessen you *want* everyone to know where you got off the ship and what yer doin' next. I'm *really* loud when I'm hit."

The dropping of the boy's voice on saying his title made Camelford stiffen. "What mean you, boy? I am Fourth Lieutenant Haversham —"

The boy sneered. "I ain't stupid. I seen your picture in the news sheets when ya got nicked in Calais. You ain't got a face a bleeder forgets. You been smart to keep yer head down, but more'n that, yer bloody lucky the commander's too worried about summat to notice yer. But he will when he's back. Guess-in' that's why yer headed out now. But yer gunna need me help."

He stared down his nose at the boy. "What possible help could the likes of *you* give me?"

The boy's grin only grew. "I been scorched by worse mouths than yours, me lord, and prob'ly hit by harder fists. Now stop wastin' time — 'less o' course you *got* someone to help you put the boat over, or a coach driver what speaks good French and knows how to get about. If a toff like you goes about demandin' a coach and driver, they'll remember you. Don't matter what you wear, yer face'll give you away since yer deportation was in all the news sheets — and soon's you open yer mouth, you scream 'toff.' "

The boy had a strong streak of common sense. Camelford's hand twitched, wanting to belt that impertinent mouth closed. "Well, go on. Don't be all night about it."

"All roads are blocked by soldiers demandin' Frenchie papers. Have you got any? *I* have — and what's more I can get you some too."

"How?" Camelford demanded, furious. The boy actually *winked* at him.

The boy cocked his head backward. "Them Frogs what're on board? I can nick a set o' their papers in five minutes flat."

"The authorities will want your papers, too."

"Lord love ya, m'lord, I *told* you I have 'em."

How *dare* the little guttersnipe roll his eyes at his betters? "You're wasting my time with all this posturing and bragging. Get to the point or I'll kill you now."

The boy sobered and lowered his voice. "I'm commander's fetch-and-carry, me lord. I got me Frog papers. Marcus René Balfour, I am, a coach-for-hire's lad, which is why I can travel."

"Why do you want to help me?" If the commander had set the boy on his trail —

The boy's lip dropped. "I'm as clever a cove as you'll find in all Lunnon, but the commander only uses me to fetch and carry acos I'm little an' low-born. It ain't right."

In the boy's eyes, seething with frustration, Camelford saw the ambition and drive he needed. "If you're not back in five minutes, I'll go without you."

The boy ran off, his soft chuckle floating back to Camelford on the wind.

If the boy survived a week in his company, it would be a miracle.

Abbeville, France
"Forgive me, madame. I didn't mean to frighten you."

She'd dropped her candle. Picking it up, she murmured, "I'm not frightened. You startled me, that's all."

"I see." He sounded amused. A scraping sound, flint on tinder, and a candle stub lit the narrow hallway with mullioned walls and wide, scraped floorboards. "My felicitations. You came to the right house, and I didn't make it easy for you." The stranger pulled off his cloak and smiled with an approving air.

"The cat was a nice touch. Subtle. Did you send it running?" She stepped inside, feeling as if she'd been congratulated for coming in last in a race. She wouldn't be tame. No, for her sake, and her son's, she'd fight all the way.

His nod matched his smile: more elliptical. It suited him well. "It's the ability to recognize and track the small signs that impress me the most."

Her brow lifted. "Impressing you is always my sole aim, of course."

He chuckled. Began to say something. Stopped.

Ice gelled in her stomach. She whirled around, heading for the door.

"It seems my silence is clumsy. Beg pardon, madame. You are free to leave at any time."

She stopped. Asked the question burning on her tongue, even though it put her at a disadvantage. "How did you leave so little trace on the path? I couldn't find a single hoofprint."

"A broken tree branch covered with leaves. I left it at the edge of the path for you to see."

"Ah." She smiled a little. "I didn't think of it. Next time I'll do better."

"I'm certain you will." Again she heard the odd note in his voice.

She tilted her head, narrowed her eyes. "You're testing me."

He nodded, with approval in his eyes. "I had to know if you were ready. You met every trial with curiosity, intelligence, and courage — the exact combination I need."

Ah, that damned curious cat — her soul sister. She was drowning in the quicksilver he'd laid around her, and still she couldn't stop. "You shot LeClerc to *test* me?"

"Tell me why." He lifted the candle a little.

In some indignation for the help she didn't need, she said coolly, "The same reason you showed me your face at the tavern tonight. The same reason you let me know the name you gave me was a lie. To see if I'd be a liability by my reaction to your scars, and to shooting LeClerc."

His sound of applause was a bare whisper. "Well done."

"I don't need applause," she muttered, but he only grinned.

They hadn't moved from the hallway. Clever of him. She'd feel threatened away from the easy means of egress.

Finally, she murmured, "Are you one of my father's men?"

"My department deals with foreigners at home, and with more delicate matters on both sides of La Manche."

110

La Manche was the French term for the English Channel. Unsurprised, she nodded. "You know my father."

Ten seconds passed before he answered. "I was at school with Leo and Andrew."

"You have the Harrow accent." Curious, the way he'd put it. Andrew was three years younger than Leo. He should have been to school with only one of her brothers. There was something in that, a story shrouded in the night. "I thought Papa worked for Military Intelligence. Did he or my brothers send you to find me?"

And why hadn't *they* come to her?

"Our mutual enemy knows every member of your family by sight," he replied to her unspoken question. "I'm still anonymous. And it's best not to mention specific places of our homeland aloud while the door is open."

Then she realized why his mentioning her brothers felt off. He'd called Andrew by the French André. She nodded, assimilating the order almost absently. So her family still cared, at least enough to send him to her. "How is my mother?"

"She misses you."

Her head snapped up. He'd hesitated, weighing his words before speaking. "What's wrong? Is Mama well?"

He looked around. "Not so loud. You're the only woman here fluent in our native tongue.

If a neighbor hears you, they'll inform the gendarmes — or your husband."

A chill seeped into her blood. She'd lapsed into English without noticing, her second mistake in as many minutes. She murmured in French, "Nicely deflected, monsieur. A subtle touch of fear to turn my mind, hoping I'll forget my question. Or perhaps you're hoping my curiosity will prevail, and I'll close the door."

To her surprise, he chuckled again. "You're right. Yes, I want the door closed."

It was time to fish or cut line, as Andrew had said to her whenever she was in trouble — when he was home, that was. She closed the door and, in strange defiance, locked it.

The stranger smiled. "Eddie would be proud of your courage. Your French is superb, madame. You have no accent at all."

She drew herself up. "I'm sure you know Mama's mother was French. Grand-mère taught me several accents. It was a favored game of ours. So, is my mother well?"

A second slight hesitation. "Eddie mentioned nothing in his most recent letter to me."

If he called her father *Eddie,* he must be a social equal, or Papa wouldn't allow the intimacy; nor would Papa correspond regularly, as the stranger had implied. Was it at Harrow that Papa had recruited him?

How young had he been? Why had his family allowed it?

"Several accents, eh? An accomplishment indeed," he said, returning to an earlier point with spurious politeness. Another challenge masked by good manners.

Proud enough to be distracted, she pursed her mouth, smug. "I can be a Parisian lady or Breton fisher lass" — she used that particular accent — "or use the Occitan or even Alsace without difficulty. Grand-mère and I found the game quite amusing." Using even the semi-Germanic Alsace without a trace of false accent. "I also speak some German and Italian."

He nodded. "You'll do."

Her brows lifted. "I'm certain I shall, once you tell me what it is I shall do *for.*"

But he only grinned. "You proved yourself to be a true daughter of our homeland when you refused to return to the house to spy on your father."

She gasped. "Papa knows about that?"

"You disappeared as we were planning to take you back. Your father . . ."

So somber his voice: the specters of his past only putting a tentative foot out of their cages. But she only heard one thing. Papa had tried to rescue her. "Did he send you here?"

"I searched almost a year before I found you."

Not once had he answered her questions

directly about Papa. She let it go — for now. There were many ways to skin a cat. "So we return to the point. What do you want from me, monsieur? With no more roundaboutation or false names, if you please."

Though he nodded, she noticed his words came in clear reluctance. The man hated parting with information. "In my dealings with you I've seen courage, intelligence, curiosity, loyalty, and a well-developed moral code."

"A ruined woman who eloped with an enemy spy?" she mocked, shearing away the compliment. "Somehow I can't see my morals shining for any stranger to distinguish so easily."

"It's because of the woman others perceive you to be — what you've had to do to survive — that I need you." He took a step toward her, and another. Lisbeth held her ground, chin lifted, eyes calm — she hoped. But holding herself so stiffly, she felt every one of her fading bruises.

He stopped a few feet from her. "Good work, madame. If I had not met you the way I did, I'd assume you had no fear of my approach."

Again, the compliment felt wrong: a vision of how he'd first seen her stripped away any pretensions to dignity. "I'm tired. Can we dispense with the compliments and reach the part where I discover what I 'shall do' for?"

A startled moment, and then he chuckled. "Eddie said you weren't the common run of well-bred female."

She suppressed the childish urge to retort, *And how would my father know?* "It's late, monsieur. I realize you're enjoying this game you're playing, but I've worked all night. Either you tell me what you want now, or I unlock that door."

In the half gloom she saw the flash of his teeth, acknowledging her accusation. "I overheard snatches of conversation at Le Boeuf the night we met. Tonight those same men left when I entered. I stand out, as you see." He motioned with his hands, a reference to his height. "You, however, do not." When she stared at him, eyes alight with amused incredulity, he amended, "I mean, you have reason to weave among the tables and patrons, and if you hear something, you can legitimately approach those men . . ."

She drew a breath. "I won't get pillow talk for you," she said, with needle-fine anger.

"I won't ask it of you." His restrained reproof made a blush mount her cheeks. "Indeed, the woman I've seen at the tavern is just what I need. Intercepted dispatches show Bonaparte has warned his spies against frequenting whorehouses or confiding in their mistresses, or women who flirt or attempt to seduce them. But a woman who works without a smile, won't flirt, won't tug her décolletage down or linger at tables — and that must be your inflexible rule, never flirt or linger, no matter what — you won't even be noted as a threat."

It seemed sensible, yet felt unfinished. Something about it was too *wrong* to not object. "Not if they know you and I have come to know each other — and now you've publicly claimed me, Monsieur Marron will know. He's already furious that I won't entertain the patrons. He'd see our, um, friendship as a threat." She made a rueful face. "Quite a few of the regulars have wagers as to who will be the first to break my resistance, and they come every night to either charm or molest me. You've destroyed their hopes. They may change taverns — and M. Marron is very attached to his profits. I'll probably lose my position."

Expecting anger, his nod took her by surprise. "Well thought out, madame. Do you have any suggestions?"

She put her hands on her hips and stared him down. "How can I, when you haven't told me what you really want from me yet?"

Again, there was no anger — and too late, she realized she'd played into his hands. He'd counted on her to say it. "You're a quick study, madame," he replied, with approval in his voice. "You have one other unique position that makes you invaluable to us."

"If you want information from my husband," she snapped, "stop pouring the butter boat over me. He left me three months ago."

"But you know where he is. You've been there."

Her mouth fell open.

"I've had John follow you to protect you. You went to Eaucourt six of the seven nights he escorted you home, stayed twenty-five minutes, and left. You have an arrangement with the older Madame Delacorte, it seems."

Tongues of fire licked at her, hot, furious. "Does it occur to you that knowing my most private business won't endear me to your cause? I don't like you ferreting out my secrets, monsieur. And I won't have you near my son, or using him to ensure my co-operation!"

A long silence. The shadows of the candle-light played over his face, revealing nothing. "Is it using your son to tell you I already have three men watching the house to ensure, not your cooperation, but his safety?"

She blinked, once, twice. Her mind blanked. Only one word came to her. "Why?"

And he smiled. Yes, the fish had taken the worm, was on the hook — and if she resented it, the almost sick hope swamped the anger like storm waves over a small boat. "Because I will return your son to you."

CHAPTER 10

As a girl, Lisbeth had read Mrs. Radcliffe's lurid novels at night, keeping them stuffed beneath her mattress, lest Mama found out. In her beloved books, a shocking discovery or joyous news made the heroine freeze in place, her heart pound or throat tighten, or she'd faint in the hero's arms.

I will return your son to you.

No such pretty reactions for Lisbeth. Bile flew up like a flock of birds desperate to escape, and she vomited over the hall runner, and the stranger's boots before she fell in a huddle against the wall, gasping and hiccupping.

So typical of the disastrous tomboy she'd been. In two meetings, she'd managed to show this man everything that a woman of pride and social position would never reveal.

He turned and walked off, and she couldn't blame him for it. She disgusted herself.

But he was back in moments. "Here, madame." He pressed a glass into her hand.

"Breathe normally, in and out slowly for the next minute, and then drink."

A massive hiccup emerged when she tried to thank him, so she followed his instructions.

He cleaned the vomit with some rags while she recovered. When her body was behaving itself again, he said, "Come into the sitting room. I apologize for the dust. I've barely stayed here, and I haven't yet found a house-keeper."

Weakly she nodded, not caring what state his house was in. *Edmond . . .*

When she was pregnant, all she'd seen was Edmond's violent conception. But one look at him and his conception made no differ-ence. She loved her baby heart and soul, and from the moment Alain took him, she'd ached with his loss. A half hour snatched with Edmond whenever Alain was away in no way lessened the hunger. The only way to not give into madness had been to show Alain that no matter what he did, he couldn't break her. One day he'd have to leave town for longer than a few hours, and she'd take Edmond —

That was as far as her plans went, driving her to silent despair.

But this ruthless stranger had sworn to rescue her son, and every emotion rose from the icy grave she'd buried them in, alive and burning. She didn't care what he wanted from her, or what it took to get her baby back, she'd do it.

The stranger helped her to her feet, led her to the wide front room, and seated her in a red wing chair before the empty fireplace. Dust flew up, making her sneeze. "I beg your pardon. I can't afford to open a window. You know how it is here. You've lived here long enough."

She nodded. How many people had lost their heads through an indiscreet word overheard by neighbors . . . or through enemies listening at open windows? Envy, lust, or covetousness had led to thousands of false accusations during the Revolution, and the Terror. Her poor parents-in-law were proof of that.

He lit a lantern, sat on a horrible mustard-yellow chaise facing her, and spoke in a dispassionate tone. "We suspect the numbers of French infantry and ships grow weekly, despite the terms of the peace. This comes at a time when our naval superiority is severely depleted. The British people want peace, so the government refuses even to wonder if First Consul Bonaparte has broken the Treaty of Amiens. We must prove the truth, or face the consequences."

Fighting the urge to hiccup she nodded, waved at him to go on.

"Both nations are flooded with enemy spies, and Delacorte is very highly ranked." His arms spread out. "So why does he remain here?"

Lisbeth blew out a breath. With every pore of her dying to ask about Edmond's recovery, she forced herself to follow the conversation, to prove herself to him. "Alain's father was of the nobility. He was guillotined early in the Terror, and his mother was brutalized two days later. It affected her mind." *And my three-month-old son is in her care, maintaining her fragile hold on sanity.* "Alain comes and goes, but he never leaves her, or my son, for long."

His silence screamed in protest of her half explanation. "His brother Guillaume stayed with her when he was courting me —" She skidded to a halt before saying, "*In England.* Guillaume died of consumption nine months ago. He was dying when Alain brought me here."

"Sadly, it's a common story since '89. Robespierre was a self-righteous fool, and the Directory a toothless lion. No wonder people flocked to the first consul's banner. He's proven himself an effective leader, unlike the others." He frowned. "But it doesn't answer my question. Why does a man so ambitious and ruthless as Delacorte stay in this backwater? Why hasn't he moved his family to Paris, or back to Britain, where they could pose as émigrés?"

"That I cannot tell you. Though it would be rather hard for him to indulge his amusement at my degradation from that distance," she answered with a careless shrug. Not for her life would she show this man any weakness, when her son's rescue was being discussed.

"He wouldn't need that if he was on assignment — unless he already is. What's happening here, madame? You said he comes and goes. Surely you've seen or heard something."

Despite her will, when he leaned toward her, she jerked back, and the hiccups began anew.

"I beg your pardon, madame. I forgot." He moved back on the chaise. "Breathe slowly and take another drink."

His empathy disarmed her, as did his lack of judgment at her overreaction. But she couldn't even take that at face value. It might only be an indicator of how much he needed her. Which would be excellent if she had anything she could bargain with — but with her father's seeming blessing on his mission, and his men already watching the house where her son lived, the stranger held all the cards. Curious on that point, she decided to test it out. "I'm well aware of what I owe you —"

"I have told you many times that you owe me nothing, Madame Delacorte." The words held a strange bitterness, directed not at her, but elsewhere: another time, another woman. "Whether you help me or not is your choice."

Not when you hold my baby's rescue in your

hands. She had no choice but to move with his unseen dance. He controlled the conversation, information given and withheld, allowing her to come to the conclusion he desired.

But she'd done that once with Alain. She refused to repeat her mistakes with any other man, no matter what he promised. "Tell me, why is Tavern Le Boeuf important? What was said in those conversations you overheard?"

Another slight smile was her reward for her insight. "I told you, I saw certain agents — of varying political groups — discussing matters of deep interest to us. I believe Le Boeuf is part of an espionage hub from here to Boulogne-sur-Mer. Perhaps it goes as far as Calais or Paris. We think there's a connection to Alain Delacorte — and to his master."

She lifted her chin. "Napoleon, you mean?"

He shook his head, mouthed, *Fouché.*

A sliver of ice pierced her heart. In France there was only one Fouché. A former religious schoolteacher who never took full monastic orders, Joseph Fouché had encompassed France's radical political change with all its rabid self-interest. It was whispered that in the thirteen years since the Revolution began, he'd killed more people than the most sadistic of Inquisitors had managed in a lifetime. In Lyon he'd watched a massacre of innocents with a pair of severed human ears dangling from his hat. Quiet, emotionless, he lived in the shadows; yet those who attempted to lower his political dominance ended up headless, their bodies floating in the Seine.

Alain had embraced the enjoyment of torture with sickening enthusiasm. Lisbeth's body still bore the marks of his abuse, which occurred even during her early pregnancy, until the doctor had hinted that any further . . . *um* . . . clumsiness (turning pale and twitching) . . . could hurt the unborn child.

That was the reason she'd never leave France, why she risked her life to go to the house in Eaucourt. Edmond was in the care of a nervous wreck and an aficionado of the new de Sade. She had to keep her baby safe.

The stranger walked into her thoughts as if he saw the point she'd reached. "You said he comes and goes?"

His tone brooked no denial. Aching for her baby, she nodded. "If you want dates and times, I can write them down. But if he found out . . ." Suddenly she understood why this stranger had publicly claimed her as his woman. "No. I won't go back, or ask him questions. The last time he was displeased with me . . ." A wave of nausea hit her. "No. I can't do it."

The stranger looked in her eyes, his grim. "It won't happen again. I will ensure it."

She must regain her calm, for Edmond's sake. "That might be difficult when the whole town believes I'm a whore, even the gen-

124

darmes. When I laid a complaint at the prefecture, they suggested I put my price up. If LeClerc and Tolbert could afford me, even the poorest-paid police among them might come for cheap nocturnal visits."

His face closed off, but a faint scent of violence hung in the air. "Was it Delacorte that invented and spread the story about your soiled virtue? It's obvious he set those men onto you."

Unsurprised by his perception, she nodded.

"That's why I'm certain he'll return when he knows you have a 'protector' — but I can and do swear he won't hurt you again. You won't be alone, madame." In his expression, in the respectful tone he used, she saw his knowledge of the kinds of abuse Alain had inflicted on her. "I want you to remain at the tavern as long as possible. Can you listen to the conversations as you pass, and if you learn anything you feel will be of interest, report to me?"

No longer did he sound so confident, and that tipped the scales in her favor. "Yes."

His shoulders dropped a little. In his tiny show of relief, again she felt more in control, even as she noticed that slight unevenness to his body. "Leave a note inside a red rag that will be tied in the shrubbery on the road south. I'll show you where."

Judging an answer to be unnecessary, she waited.

There was a smile in his voice. "I'll train you. Are you willing to forsake a little sleep?"

She wasn't particularly worried — yet; she had already worked ten days on and two days off, in twelve-hour shifts, and covering for the other girls when they entertained upstairs. But for her baby — "Certainly."

"Mine are no empty promises, madame. In return for your help, you and your son will go home." His voice was neutral; his eyes were not. *Compassion.* "Your son's papers are ready with a new surname."

"What name? You can't use Sunderland."

"Obviously not," he said, but he softened the slight sarcasm with a bow. "His birth will be registered at a church in our county with a different father, a member of the nobility: a man Delacorte cannot trace to your family."

"Why?" This time she wouldn't take a deflection. "Why do you care about my son?"

"A workman deserves his wage," he said with a strange smile, quoting the Bible. "Besides, no innocent should be raised by that man." The depth in his tone went beyond sympathy for her situation, beyond pity or promises. The haunted eyes spoke to her.

Moved by it, she grabbed his gloved hand and kissed it. "*Thank you,* monsieur. I will call you *mon coeur,* Gaston, anything you wish. I will make no more errors. Anything you ask —"

He snatched his hand away. "I need no

thanks from you. Until I tell you otherwise, I *am* Gaston Borchonne to you and the world, as you are Elise Delacorte to me."

Her head drooped. "Certainly . . . Gaston."

Her meekness seemed to exasperate him further. "*Gaston* sounds too much a lie on your tongue. Stick to monsieur when we are alone, if you can't do better than that."

"I'm sorry if I'm uncomfortable with lies," she snapped, despite her fear for Edmond. "I suppose I will learn the way of it soon enough, but I'd prefer it not to be my way of life."

His eyes softened, but she saw the reluctance — the *thinking* of ways to reassure her. "It's like that for us all at first, but don't be afraid of me. I might lose my temper, but I'll never hurt you. I will see your son rescued, no matter what happens."

She was so necessary to whatever his real plans were, then.

"I will see you home. You'll need rest for what comes next. You have a lot to learn."

He rose to his feet. Shutters slamming down. Obviously, the conversation was over. Torn, she followed him to the door — but he blocked the way, with a smothered curse. "Don't look, mada— *ma chère,* for God's sake, don't look."

CHAPTER 11

Still blocking the doorway, Duncan stared at the body of LeClerc, sprawled across his doorstep: a mouse left by Fouché's cat. A crude bandage covered the foot he'd shot a few hours ago, but that wasn't the fatal wound. There was a new hole through his heart. His face was a ghastly gray, his eyes bulging, highlighting the violent bruising down one cheek and a broken nose. Blood trailed right down the garden path. Delacorte had dragged the body here while they'd sat in the parlor making their bargain. It had to be Delacorte. He wouldn't trust a minion for this, and the self-indulgent, unnecessary violence on a helpless man was characteristic of him.

Something moved off to the left. Torches were bobbing in the distance, coming toward them. More gendarmes would be closing in via the back lane.

Delacorte had overtaken them too fast. Duncan's velvet fist challenge had been answered with an iron glove. The manned rowboat on a disused dock only half a mile north was useless when they couldn't escape the house. His plans for removing Lisbeth and the child discreetly from Abbeville were in the dust.

Check and mate. *Vive le France.*

Lisbeth pushed past him and gasped. He shoved a hand over her mouth to smother the rest of her shocked cry. He held on until she bit him. "Did you see the torches?"

Glaring at him, she nodded.

"He's bringing gendarmes to arrest us both." He released her. "I hope you didn't have anything of value at the *pension.*"

She rose in his estimation by her simple shrug, but there was fear in her eyes, and youth. She was still so young. "Just protect my son."

Pulling the door shut, he took her hands in his and looked into her eyes. "I swear it."

Her face changed, softened. "Then we'd better get out of here."

Duncan considered the options in seconds. "The back way will be covered. If we —"

He spoke to the air. Lisbeth wasn't there.

Bolting the door, he ran through the house to the back. Still locked and bolted, thank God; so she wasn't panicking. In the minutes they had before the gendarmes broke in, he searched the lower floor of the house.

He found her in a little, triangular storage

room at the end of the hall beneath the stairs, a room with an odd-shaped door and no windows. In the shadowed light cast by the lantern set behind the door, she was tugging at a corner of a carpet that shouldn't be in such a tiny room. "Pull the curtains closed in as many rooms as you can. Alain will have all known escape routes covered, but the house is very old —"

He ran out and drew the curtains everywhere he could. "You think there's a tunnel." He dropped to his knees, tugging at the carpet with her, making dust fly in all directions.

She nodded as she kept pulling. "Grand-mère's ancestor was a Huguenot in Catherine de' Medici's time. Tunnels beneath the stairwell cupboards were a favored means of escape from the wrath of the Church, especially in areas of soft soil like here, near the river. It meant easier digging, and Caen stone was used to reinforce the walls of the tunnels."

He lifted his brows, impressed that she thought so fast in a critical situation. "If there's one here, it hasn't been used in years. The carpet's been laid on top."

"I realize it's a risk. Lock the door, and don't make any tears in the carpet," she hissed.

Bent almost double, he spread his hands wide at each edge of the carpet and tugged.

It took repeated pulls and tugs before the dirt of a century began to give. A final tug, and it fell back in his hands.

Lisbeth peered over his shoulder and made a soft, hissing sound of victory as they saw the square cuts to the floorboards, and a handle resting in its carved-out place in the wood.

"Don't get your hopes up," he warned her. "The tunnel could have collapsed or filled with water a hundred years ago."

"You're objecting because you didn't think of this plan," she snipped, and he fought a grin. Bloody impertinent chit was right. "The tunnel *will* be clear because it's the only way you can save my son." She stuck her knife in the cut floorboard in the farthest corner against the wall, sawing at the dirt. "Lay the carpet back over itself without making a crease. We want it to fall back in place when we go. Get one of the knives I'm sure you have hidden in your boots, and help me loosen the dirt."

With grim humor he wondered who was the seasoned spy, and who the pupil. "You really are your father's daughter."

Is it surprising? At her age you were in France, gathering information for Britain. Yet though he'd been thoroughly trained, he doubted he'd have been so coolheaded on his first mission. Far more than Leo or Andrew, she'd inherited her father's phenomenal memory, and natural talent for espionage. Though Eddie would hate it, being a traditionalist when it came to women, right now Duncan would take whatever advantage he could get, and be bloody grateful for it. He took a knife from his boot and began working on the crevice on the other side.

"Hurry." He looked up; her face was gray and creased with dust. "Patience isn't Alain's strong suit."

He finished one side and dug the knife in around the corner.

A noise came from outside. "Turn down the lantern!"

"This will be the last place they look," he whispered, to reassure her. Panic would kill them both.

Another noise, closer. They were checking windows. The closed curtains in the other rooms would create a delay while they worked out where to break in first. Clever girl, thinking of that. He got the last of the dirt loose. "Move back." He pulled the knife from the crevice, grabbed the ring of the trapdoor, and put his whole force into yanking upward. Nothing. After twenty seconds, he drew in a harsh breath. "One, two . . ."

Again, it didn't give. He watched Lisbeth work the knife, stabbing along the crevices. Then she pushed both knives right in and wiggled them around. "Try again."

He set every muscle in his body tense and

hard and pulled with everything he had.

A deep voice yelled, "Gaston Borchonne, open up, in the name of the first consul!"

Again! she mouthed without sound. She dug the knives in while he pulled.

With a groaning sound and a crack, the trapdoor at last lifted. "Hold your breath and move back. The air could be a hundred years old."

Pounding on the front door. Muffled yells from the back.

"We can't wait." She pulled the edges of the carpet up. "Hold the carpet at the corners of the trapdoor, so they fall back together." She picked up the lantern, wrapped the edge of her cloak over her nose and mouth and around her head like a Bedouin woman, and stepped into the hole. "Follow me." She swarmed down.

A shriek of cracking glass — the front sitting room. A muffled yell. "Gaston Borchonne, open in the name of the first consul!"

Holding his breath, Duncan turned and found the steps with his feet.

Thuds came harder, faster. Glass crashed inward. The fifth stair down was cracked partway through, sagging in the middle and he swayed, leaning forward to stop from falling. Seasoned sea legs helped him hold balance.

Lisbeth was at the base of the old ladder. "Grab the rope to pull the door down. Make sure the carpet falls with it." She turned the lantern up, and he saw she'd dropped her cloak from her face. "This seems to be a side tunnel leading to a wider one. The walls of both tunnels are bricked, and they've been mortared recently as well. There's fresh air circulating here."

He found the rope hanging beneath the trapdoor. "Thank God for that. Lift the lantern higher — yes! Here's a latch." He pulled the door down and shoved the rudimentary bolt-and-latch across. It was rusty and groaned in protest, but it moved. "Thank God for that, too. An inch is all we need. Hopefully it will take hours to find another entrance to the tunnel."

"Do you attend church, mon— um, Gaston?" she asked softly, a little laughter in it.

"I do at home." He joined her at the base of the ladder, grinning. "I've learned to be grateful for unexpected miracles in this line of work. And no need to call me Gaston. Delacorte's ended any chance of my passing as Borchonne. We can't stay in Abbeville."

"My son," she murmured, in sharp anxiety. "I won't go without him."

"I understand, but we have no choice. Delacorte will kill us both. Best if we disappear and leave my men to it. My orders are already in place to take Edmond."

She must have understood there was no choice. Her face hardened, but she nodded.

"Which way?" she whispered, standing at the fork of the two tunnels. "There's no difference between them."

"Which way has more air circulating?"

She turned her face this way and that. Lifting the lantern, she strode to the right.

A glimmer of a plan lit in his brain as they walked. "Let's hope we don't run into whoever made the tunnels their playground."

"So long as it's not Alain and his gendarmes, I'll shake their hands in thanks."

No hesitation in her voice or uncertainty in her walk. Thank God. He couldn't abide wailing females who expected a man to protect them from every little thing. "Can you see anything ahead?"

She frowned. "Not yet." She kept looking right and left as she walked. "Do you think smugglers are using this? Or some religious group?"

Perhaps she kept asking questions from a need for reassurance. He didn't care. Whatever kept her going, he'd do. "We'll know when we see altars and icons, barrels, a fleur-de-lis, or the red caps of the Jacobins."

"If Fouché's his master, Alain's a Jacobin."

Right now she didn't need to be reminded Fouché owned every spy group in France, and they could be facing any kind of violence or weaponry at the other end of this tunnel. So he grinned. "Then we pray it's not them, and thank God when it's someone else."

"I think I'm learning the religion of espionage." Her soft laugh had the Norfolk lilt. It sounded nice. Like home.

The candle in the lantern sputtered. She turned, her eyes wide. "We need candles."

"I have one." He spoke with deliberate coldness. "Don't panic."

She didn't reply, but her eyes flashed and her chin lifted, like Eddie when he was angry.

Opening the lantern door, he grabbed the candle stub and held it out to her. "Take this. It seems you need the reassurance." He spoke with deliberate coolness.

The resentment in her eyes grew, but she took it.

He put his last candle inside the lantern. He'd have to find a way out, and fast. If she was nervous now, God knows how she'd be when they lost the light. "Would you like me to lead?"

"No." She spoke through gritted teeth, and he fought laughter. At least she was a fighter.

They'd gone at least a mile, unless he'd lost his sense of distance. Were they even heading north? He didn't think the tunnel had turned. The bricks were no longer holding the walls up; the tunnel grew smaller, until they were on their hands and knees.

"Give me the lantern," he said when she lost balance. She handed it to him without a word — but within a minute there was nothing but natural soil and rock in front of them.

"It ended. It just stopped," Lisbeth cried. "Turn around. I have to get out. I-I think I'm-I'm going to be sick —"

"Lisbeth," he said quietly. "Can you still feel fresh air on your face?" She made an odd sound. "We're still near an exit. Take a few breaths, you're exhausted." He maneuvered himself so he sat, then he took the lantern and set it down between them.

She sat beside him, leaning against the damp wall of the tunnel. "I went past *exhausted* hours ago," she said eventually. "You called me Lisbeth."

"Yes, I did." And in doing so, he'd proven his closeness to the family. Leo had told him they'd given her the nickname "Lisbeth" when she was little. She couldn't pronounce her name properly, but she wouldn't let anyone else introduce her. At first using it to tease her, they'd soon forgotten she was ever Elizabeth. Few outside the family called her that. Still less did anyone use her intimate nickname of Lizzy.

Last week, calling her madame had given her back her dignity, and the power of choice. Elise would be her cover name, since it was common in France. But she needed a friend now, and following her wiggling bottom for the past ten minutes mocked his attempts at distance. "I am Duncan, Lisbeth. I'm pleased to meet you." Unable to bow, he held out a hand.

Her eyes were quizzical. "Is that your real name?" It was less a question than a demand. Needing something or someone to trust, to believe in.

"It's the name I prefer," he said, giving her what truth he could.

She relaxed, smiled, and took his hand. "I'm pleased to meet you, Duncan." Then she chuckled, again with that soft Norfolk lilt.

He grinned at her. Even pale and covered with dirt, the blind distance had vanished from her eyes; she looked vivid, alive, and strangely contented. "It is rather absurd. We were beyond politeness the moment we met."

"But you made me laugh and stopped me from panicking," she whispered, laying her hand on his. "Thank you for trusting me with your name at least."

Odd that she'd seen his greatest flaw, when they'd only known each other a few hours all counted; absurd that a simple touch on his hand felt so intimate. He should have taken up the girl's offer at Le Boeuf. He'd been without a woman too long, and he couldn't afford weakness with this one. "It's past dawn. We have to leave the tunnel. Can you last a little longer?"

"I could sleep sitting up" — she yawned — "but to have my baby, I'd stay awake a week."

He believed it. She'd do whatever it took to have her child safe with her.

"There was a tunnel branching off a short way back. We'll have to take the chance."

"Yes," she said, sounding small and frightened again.

"The boat's waiting for us. I sent three men to Eaucourt. They're awaiting their chance to rescue your son," he said, fumbling to say the right thing to calm her down.

When she turned back and smiled at him, it was like the sun rising. "Thank you, Duncan." She touched his face, right where the scars were.

Slowly he moved his head back, trying not to offend her at this critical moment. Had he said or done something to invite that kind of unwarranted intimacy? He'd thought he was safe from that kind of thing, given Delacorte's treatment of her, and the attack last week. He'd have to establish the boundaries of commander and team member when they were out of here. If she got silly, romantic notions about him, the mission would fail — and he'd never had a mission as vital as this one. "It must be daylight now. My men won't wait forever." He wriggled around in the cramped space, picked up the lantern and took the lead in a two-knees-and-one-hand crawl.

The tunnel widened again. When it reached the branch, the bricks resumed. "We ought to have followed the side path in the first place, but it was heading away from the river instead of to it. Now we have no choice."

Soon they could walk again. A natural light source came from the left, weak as sunrise in cloud. He snuffed the lantern. "The exit's close."

Again, she didn't answer. She hadn't spoken since thanking him; he kept filling the strained silence with awkward comments. So she *had* taken offense over his small rejection. He supposed he'd have to beg her pardon for not wanting her to touch him now. It didn't matter. His only pride was in his duty. Whatever got the mission done, he'd do.

He moved forward, noiseless even in his riding boots, until the light source was evident. He turned, whispering in her ear, "Be careful, the stairs are steep and carved from sandy rock. They could crumble."

She nodded, her body stiff and taut. Yes, she was offended — but what mattered was that, so new to the game, and just having seen a dead body, she'd taken the time to calm herself. She was quick thinking and mostly slow to panic. She'd been the one to save them in the house. She had all the makings of a fine team member, if only her presence wouldn't disrupt his men. A pretty girl like this was bound to turn heads, make for fights . . . but it seemed she was easy to direct, at least. A small rejection and she wasn't touching him, or even talking to him.

He could deal with his men when the time

came. Turning back, he began climbing.

There were a dozen stairs leading to a trapdoor, similar to the one they'd escaped through. It was roughly made, an imperfect fit, which allowed the weak light of sunrise to come through — but about to push the door up, he heard a hard voice lifted in anger.

Behind him, Lisbeth stiffened and stilled.

It wasn't long before he knew who was on the other side of the trapdoor. Nobody said *rivers of blood* with such relish. "Jacobins," he said softly, hoping to God she wouldn't panic. He checked his fob for the time. "Something big must be going on for them to meet so early in the morning. It isn't like them to meet at sunrise."

"If Jacobins use the tunnel, Alain knows how to get here — and he'll know where we've come," she returned calmly enough, but her eyes sang a familiar song. She didn't need to accuse him out loud. He'd failed in his promise to protect her from Delacorte, and they both knew it. From frying pan to bloody conflagration, and he had to think quickly.

The Jacobins were the most volatile organization in France. The Jacobin Robespierre had led France into the deadly Reign of Terror. Since Robespierre's execution in 1794, the group had been hiding in pockets. Then, with the rise of their new favorite son Fouché they'd enjoyed a vocal resurgence — one reason the first consul removed Fouché from office.

But it didn't matter if he held the title or enjoyed Boney's favor. Everyone knew he still ran every espionage group worth knowing in France, and it was suspected he was the source of the attempts on Bonaparte's life since the infamous "infernal machine" in Paris that killed fifty people. It was also obvious who was behind every attempt in return to lessen Fouché's power base and had the news sheets mock his fearsome reputation. Bonaparte and Fouché were locked in a power struggle that was fiercer for its being unacknowledged, the glorious hero and the brilliant puppet master.

Throughout these thoughts, Duncan's mind raced with plans. He bent to her, mouthed *Follow my lead,* and tried the door. It didn't move. With slow deliberation he knocked, in the intricate musical pattern he'd been taught when he'd infiltrated the Jacobin Club in Paris in '93.

Sudden, utter silence. Then sounds of hasty shuffling, and the trapdoor opened. Several faces peered down. One man was smiling as he greeted, "Welcome, brother, we've been —" But then every man blinked as they looked at him, and half a dozen muskets were pointed in his face. "Brothers, we've been betrayed. Kill him. Kill them both!"

CHAPTER 12

Simultaneous musket hammers clicked into place. "Wait," Duncan whispered to the men with muskets. "You've been waiting for someone to come with news, haven't you? I have news for you. Delacorte has arrived, but he's brought a dozen gendarmes with him."

At the worst moment, Duncan felt a tug at his cloak. "They're coming."

The Jacobin leader pointed his musket in Duncan's face. He'd seen the man before, but where? "He'd never betray us to the gendarmes. He knows Bonaparte would behead us all! And your face proves what you are!"

Dust wandered up Duncan's nose. As he fought the urge to sneeze, his mind raced. The Jacobins were a dramatic, paranoid bunch when things were going well, but that they suspected him because of his *face* . . . then he understood. He was going to *kill* whichever Stewart brother was interfering in his life this time.

They were in a disused barn with broken stalls and rotten hay, but the barn doors were new and solid, and the windows had iron shutters. The trapdoor had a heavy iron manger cemented on its upper side to weigh it down.

If Fouché was feeding money to the local Jacobins, it explained Delacorte's continued presence in Abbeville. It also meant Boney *was* up to something important on the Channel Coast, if Fouché was sending his major players here to keep his eyes on it.

Looking at the leader's face, a memory clicked. "See who's with me, and tell me again that you'd trust Delacorte with your lives." Taking advantage of the momentary confusion, he pushed his way up and into the barn. Lisbeth scrambled up after him.

The barkeep and son of Tavern Le Boeuf's owner gasped, "Elise?"

"They're coming, Marron," Duncan said urgently. "Are you so certain of his loyalty over and above his hatred of his wife? Was he not mentored by Fouché?" All the world and his aunt knew spymaster Fouché's well-deserved nicknames: "The Butcher of Lyons" for the mass murder and destruction of that city, and "The Weather-Cock of Saint-Cloud" for changing loyalties with every passing political wind. How he always emerged unscathed was the mystery.

Without consultation two of the men

slammed the trapdoor down, shoved three massive cannonballs inside the manger, and sat down hard.

Duncan kept his gaze on Luc Marron's face and his hand on the primed pistol in his cloak pocket — but Marron was no fool. With a waved hand, his men searched their guests and took Duncan's weapons.

The tavern owner's son turned back to Lisbeth. "Elise, why are you here?"

Hair and face covered in grime, Lisbeth faced Marron, biting her lip, eyes pleading. "Alain discovered my . . . friendship with Monsieur Borchonne. He came to Gaston's house, where I was, ah" — she looked down, fiddled with her fingers — "talking with him . . ."

Sniggering sounds came from all around. Bloody clever of her to play the cowed girl and make excellent use of her bad reputation at one time. She'd be a fine asset to his mission.

"Within a minute of finding LeClerc's body, gendarmes were at the doors. My *grand-mère*'s great-great-great-grandfather was a Huguenot. I found the tunnel in a storage room of the house." Grimy hands fluttered in a helpless gesture. "The tunnel was the only way, Luc. I'm sorry to have brought this upon you. We only wanted to escape Alain and the gendarmes."

A thudding sound came from beneath

them: a series of musical knocks, just as Duncan had done. "*Frères,* brothers! It is I, Alain. Let me in!"

The other Jacobins looked to Marron. His body twitched, his face torn by indecision. Too long the silence. After less than a minute, Delacorte snarled, clear for them all to hear, "Shoot the door at the edges. The center has lead weights."

Lisbeth was right; patience was not Delacorte's forte and could be his downfall, if Duncan could make use of it —

"You brought this on us!" Luc Marron's kind face turned dark with accusation. He glared at Lisbeth and lifted the musket. "If I leave you here for him, he'll be satisfied."

"You'd kill me for an accident?" she whispered, her eyes big with pleading. "If we hadn't come, Luc, where would you be now? Facing the gendarmes yourself after Alain betrayed you. If I had been Genevieve — is she not my age? — would you allow anyone to shoot your daughter?"

Marron's gaze dropped. The musket wavered in his hands.

Another thud came; an explosion sounded from below. The trapdoor's farthest edge blew apart. The Jacobins yelped and jumped off the trapdoor as a high-pitched cry came from beneath, in jagged harmony. Back-shot could kill in enclosed spaces.

Marron paled. "The wood won't hold for

long. Load it down with the old cannonballs in the corner!"

Three men ran to do his bidding. Duncan snarled, "You know it won't hold them for long. They'll kill us all. Run!"

Marron grabbed Lisbeth's arm. "Bring him, and Raoul. Come to the boathouse via the south. I'll take her by the north path and meet you there."

One man ran for the weights while the others looked around. One cried, "Raoul's gone!"

"This proves the treachery. Bring Borchonne to the clearing by the boathouse. Question him there." Marron dragged Lisbeth out the door.

She looked at Duncan, with all the irony he felt. *You won't be alone. You're safe now.* Within hours, his promise had become fool's gold.

Weaponless and surrounded by five armed men, Duncan had no choice. He let the men tie his hands and drag him out of the barn, running for the unknown boathouse. This Raoul who decamped so suddenly must be Alec or his twin, Cal, or some other damned Stewart he hadn't yet met; but for the first time, he prayed for some Stewart meddling in his life.

CHAPTER 13

Somme River, North of Abbeville
August 27, 1802

At the decrepit boathouse a few miles north of Abbeville, Luc had dumped a rickety chair in front of the only window in the building, plumped Lisbeth down on it, and tied her hand and foot with boat rope; he had been questioning her for over an hour.

It was one of those rare crystal-clear late summer days. Brilliant morning light penetrated the thin forest and poured through the dirty windows, searching out shadows, exposing secrets.

If Alain were outside, he'd see her in seconds. *Easy pickings,* he'd say in a sneering tone.

"Who's the man you came with? What does he want with us? How long have you known about me?"

Telling as much truth as she knew must be her best course, less chance of being caught in a lie. "His name is Gaston Borchonne. I

148

met him last Tuesday night, when he stopped LeClerc and Tolbert from raping me behind the belfry of St. Vulfran's. Then he became . . . a friend. You saw him last night talking to me at Le Boeuf?"

Luc interrupted her in a harder tone than she'd ever heard from him. "Your private life is of no consequence to me. What does he want with us?"

Even without her cloak, sweat trickled down her neck. *Where was Duncan?* "I told you, we only wanted to get away from Alain."

His hard slap rocked her head sideways. "I want the truth! What does your *friend* know about —" He closed his mouth, gaze darting to his compatriots.

She almost laughed. After a year with Alain and working in Le Boeuf with some of the worst of the male species, did he think a piddling slap would break her? *Make use of it.* She forced a humble tone with fear pulsing through it, to make Luc despise her weakness and underestimate her. Just as Alain did. "Please don't hurt me. I knew nothing about your group until we came up through the trapdoor this morning. We found LeClerc's body on Gaston's doorstep last night and escaped through the tunnel, which led us to you."

One of the other Jacobins who'd just walked in stopped and gasped. "LeClerc is dead?"

She nodded. "His body was brought to

149

Gaston's door. I was with him the entire time. I know he didn't do it."

Luc waved that off. "You ask me to believe you found a door to our tunnel, and it opened like magic?"

The morning sun slanted in through the northeastern-facing window. Lisbeth watched the dust motes dance around her, trembling with exhaustion and apprehension. As a Jacobin — which he must be if he was Fouché's man — surely Alain knew to come here as well as to the barn. How long did they have? "We dug an inch of dirt out of the crevices with knives and pulled hard before it opened. Gaston didn't know it was there —"

"He is not Gaston Borchonne, woman," the Jacobin who'd entered the boathouse snarled. "I am Gaston's second cousin. He has similar coloring and height, but Gaston's ears stuck out from his head."

Luc's arms folded over his chest. "So who is this man, and what does he want with us?"

Her head pounded from lack of sleep. Her fingers and toes were numb from their bonds; she wriggled them, keeping ready for escape. "I only met him last week. He saved me, gave me the Borchonne name, and said I'd see him again. Tonight he came back. He told me he'd been in the Spanish navy, was a first lieutenant."

Luc peered into her face. "Do you know how I can tell you're lying to me?"

Play the helpless girl. Obey him. She shook her head, eyes wide.

He smiled, cold and thin. "The same way I know you sometimes wonder if it would be worth it to go upstairs with the men who throw money at you. Your head drops a little and you blink when you say no."

Compared to Alain, Luc was a novice in the art of interrogation. Sighing, she met his triumphant gaze blankly. "I'm nineteen, Luc. I've been awake almost a whole day. I've seen a dead body, escaped gendarmes and Alain, thinking I was safe at last, only to fall into your laps. I'm falling asleep sitting up, my eyes are burning, and I'm too close to the window."

"The window?" one of the other Jacobins asked when Luc only scowled.

She blinked again. "If Alain and the gendarmes are close by, they'll shoot the window."

"Why?" Luc asked, sharp. "How would you know this?"

She cursed herself for forgetting to play the ingénue. Men were only easy to manipulate if they believed she was a silly girl. "In the past week he's had me beaten, tried to have me raped and accused of murder. I think Alain wants me dead without being implicated in the murder. In shooting the window, he could blame the gendarmes for killing me, or perhaps any of you here."

151

"He's our brother. He wouldn't betray us," Luc snarled, not bothering with the rest of her tale. In post-Revolution, post-Terror France, violence was still so commonplace it was rare if a woman *hadn't* been beaten or raped and beaten at least once; and with Lisbeth being English, and of the aristocracy, of course she was a prime target.

A helpless smile was her best weapon. "I'm sure you know best." She let her lashes droop. A foolish mistake: a warm blanket of weariness covered her, whispering *sleep.*

With a growl of frustration, Luc shook her and asked about the tunnel again, how she'd known to go looking for it.

"Grand-mère told me about the tunnels created in the time of the battles of Rouen and Dreux. The Huguenots used them to escape from Catherine de' Medici's Inquisitors. Many of those escape tunnels began in the storage room beneath the stairs." She yawned, making her eyes water. "I'm sorry, I'm so tired." Since she was half asleep, she'd make use of it.

"Where does the imposter live?" Luc demanded.

She frowned as she tried to remember the number on the gate. Where had she gone?

Damn her self-pitying stupidity the past year, a tired ghost drifting through life without a fight! Damn everyone in Abbeville, and *damn* Alain most of all. She wanted her baby. Whatever it took, she'd have Edmond. She'd play any part — she'd kill if she had to; but she refused to die.

The creeping sense of being watched returned. She moved her head again, listening for any sound or movement. She tightened her body, ready to flip the chair.

"Answer me, Elise! Where does the impostor calling himself Borchonne live?"

Lisbeth shook herself, thinking hard. "It's on the Quai de la Pointe — twenty-eight, I think," she answered, but now the exhaustion wasn't an act. Her head had turned dull and stupid. Every blink made it harder for her to open her eyes again.

"He stayed in my family's house," the real Borchonne's cousin muttered angrily.

"Never mind that! Did your family build the house, and were they ever Huguenots? Is there a tunnel there?" Luc demanded of the other.

As they argued among themselves, Lisbeth's head drooped again. The Jacobins' quarrel came warped, as if through water. Sleep beckoned her, a shepherd calling to his sheep. Though she tried to remain ready for attack, her chin touched her chest, and she drew a quivering breath. Cushioning darkness whispered its haunting tune.

Boom! The window exploded. More musket fire came from the other side of the boat-house. Lisbeth flung the chair sideways a moment too late. Though the ball didn't hit her, glass shards followed like a faithful lover. She cried out as broken glass embedded in her cheek, arm, and shoulder, near the neck. Blood ran down her face and arm, and there was a horrible, painful pulsing at her shoulder.

Luc yelled, but she couldn't understand him over the whooshing arcs like rushing water inside her head. Then the pulsing and the pain took her to blessed blackness.

Tied hand and foot, Duncan was on the ground in a small clearing not far from the boathouse. This northern forest was thin, with several clearings. After being up all night and spending hours in the tunnel, the bright sunlight nearly blinded him.

He'd endured an hour of their questions, slaps, and punches. They rapped out questions without giving a thing away — but they kept returning to one subject, harping and haranguing him about his face, and his family.

That word gave away the reason for their paranoia. Alec must be here, but how he'd infiltrated the Jacobins so fast after dealing with Windham and the plot against the king . . .

You fool! It's not Alec. It must be Cal.

The Jacobins had just brought out their knives, ready to cut, when the boom of muskets filled the air. Curse the Jacobins' paranoia, separating him from Lisbeth! Duncan snarled at his captors, "Sounds like Delacorte reached the boathouse."

"Luc could be shooting your lady friend, *Gaston Borchonne.*" The man used his cover name mockingly, but his gaze shifted left.

Acrid gunpowder smoke drifted over and around them. "All this smoke is coming from *inside* the boathouse? All those shots to kill one woman? I only met the lady a few days ago. I won't miss her if she dies. I assume your attachment to your friends is strong enough to find out what's happening?"

The noise of exploding shot filled the dell, coming from the boathouse. The one in charge jerked his head; a young man ran off, crouching, holding his musket in front of him.

All the Jacobins were on their feet, making sure their muskets were primed, the shot dry.

One of the first maxims Duncan had learned as a spy was not to kick his enemy when he was down; the other was, *show no weakness.* He watched those watching him, working at his bonds, waiting for the right moment.

The young man ran back in. "Delacorte and the gendarmes are shooting our brothers!"

The men ran off, leaving Duncan alone to work on the triple-tied knots at his wrists.

When Fouché hears of this debacle, Dela-

corte's a dead man. To save his skin, Delacorte would have to kill every Jacobin here,
kill them all, including the gendarmes left
alive, and blame another group for it. Even
then he wouldn't have long to make himself
worth keeping alive —

Oh, the clever bastard. Delacorte would
denounce Lisbeth as a British spy . . . and
because she was Eddie's daughter, Boney
would give the story credence. Especially with
Duncan here — his description had been
given in a dozen or more plots through the
years, only dropped because of the public
alibis his half brothers Alec or Cal Stewart
had given him.

He pulled and tugged his hands, but though
his skin ripped and bled, the ropes remained
tight. He cursed the Jacobins in every language he knew for being so bloody efficient
for once.

"Here, lad, let me."

Duncan twisted around. A face hauntingly
similar to his own was right behind him, with
a mess of black half curls tied in a careless
riband at his neck. Yes, he'd been right about
why the Jacobins had treated him as an
enemy at first sight of his face. But there were
no scars on this man's face. "You're Cal."

"Aye, lad," Alec's twin said in a voice
devoid of emotion as he cut Duncan's bonds.
"Good to meet you at last."

Duncan's eyes narrowed. "You're this

Raoul the Jacobins talked of."

The Black Stewart handed Duncan a rifle. "I saw you come up from the tunnel and hotfooted it out of there. I found your men on the northern dock. They're beneath the boathouse now, with a cache of handy weapons. I took these for us."

His hands and feet numb from the tight bonds, Duncan dropped the rifle Cal tossed at him. Seven barrels looked up at him, wedged tight together. "You can use a Nock? And what are you doing in Abbeville with the Jacobins?" After wriggling his hands and feet, Duncan checked out the barrels, bracing himself for the same kind of mummery Alec enjoyed.

Cal shrugged and hauled Duncan to his feet. "Of course I can use a Nock. I wouldn't have brought them otherwise. I infiltrated this group months ago. I found Delacorte a few weeks back, notified Zephyr, and gathered as much intelligence on Delacorte as I could."

Duncan's eyes narrowed. "When did you receive your orders to come here?"

"You'll have to ask Zephyr about that."

Expecting more information was useless. Cal and Alec were as well trained as he.

Heroes of the Glorious First of June sea battle in 1794, the Black Stewart twins had come to former spymaster William Wickham's attention. Once Eddie gave his commanding officer the family history, the rest was inevitable. Three brothers with a close enough resemblance to give each other an alibi — one not known to be family, therefore even giving *both* the known twins an alibi — was too grand an opportunity for Wickham, and now Zephyr, to pass up.

Alec, Cal, and Duncan: the three sons of Broderick Stewart, the last Jacobite hanged at Tyburn in 1772. Laird and Lady Stewart, stripped of home and title after their son's disastrous participation in the Pretender's claim to the British throne, had raised the twins Cal and Alec by any means possible. They were proud Stewarts with full heritage. The bastard Duncan was Baron Annersley's heir, bought and paid for through marriage to their father's straw-damsel sweetheart, a chambermaid swollen with child. An English aristocrat to his fingertips, Annersley had his heir but treated Duncan as a necessary evil. Why were the Stewart brothers always protecting him? His birth had killed their father. What the hell could they possibly want from him?

"I like the modifications you made to the Nocks, lad," Cal said, inspecting them. "I've seen the full-bore pieces set ships on fire or break the shoulders of the shooters."

Duncan realized in resignation that Zephyr *had* found Lisbeth before he did. Could he never do anything simple, such as notify Duncan of the girl's locale? "With only one round of shot in each of the barrels instead of two rounds, half the amount of gunpowder, and the wadding at the butt of the stock, it lowers the danger considerably. The wadding has India rubber for softer recoil." He watched Cal bounce his hand against the rifle butt, wishing he was anyone but one of the twins that reminded him of his ancestry, the background Annersley had taunted him about all through his childhood. *Only a royal bastard is acceptable, and Scottish royalty no longer exists, boy. You are nothing except what I make of you. Nobody else wants you.*

"Let's go." Duncan tossed the enormous rifle over his shoulder, the leather strap across his chest, and ran north along the river, in the wake of his former captors.

The river carried bobbing pieces of walls, broken glass, and roof shingles on a sluggish tide. He ran faster. Another fifty yards, and a small, uneven dell opened up by the river. Standing at its southern edge, he took in the scene. What remained of the boathouse at the northern rim of the dell was a smoking ruin. Rocks and trees formed an odd semicircle around it, warm sunshine and the pall of shot lighting it in a ghastly halo. Parts of the walls on two sides exploded as he watched. The men who'd taken him were halfway to the hut, dead or dying, lying in dirt and pools of their own blood. Closer to the hut were the bodies of gendarmes. More bodies — presumably other Jacobins, he couldn't identify each body at this distance — sprawled around where the walls and door of the boathouse had been.

He couldn't rush into the place with a shooter still alive outside. His gaze darted around, checking out the forest. "Halfway down the path I'll shoot the Nock. Then you cover me while I run for the boathouse."

"She was alive ten minutes ago when I looked in. The rowboat is beneath the trap-door in the floor of the boathouse, with your men waiting."

"She was alive and you didn't save her." Duncan watched the glade for more shots, and their direction. Every second gave him more information on who was where.

Cal answered without heat. "She was tied to a chair and injured, but still breathing. Odds were too long on my own with three Jacobins alive and firing at anything that moved. We'll need your men unharmed to take the oars. So I came for you."

Duncan ran, but the thirty feet between him and the boathouse seemed as endless as Chaucer's ocean. No time to think of what could go wrong. At the halfway point, he bundled his cloak on his shoulder and lifted the rifle into position. He squinted for the best aim and pointed at two trees close together. Standing wide and leaning as far forward as he could, he dropped his elbow, wrapped his fingers around the smoothbore barrels, and fired.

The flash pan blew to the right. Fire exploded from the barrels, burning his fingers, and the stock butt walloped him in the shoulder. Even with the wadding and rubber, pain ripped through his body. As he fell back, the trees split apart, bursting into flame. He scrambled to his feet. No broken collarbone or dislocated shoulder, but it throbbed like the dickens. Two screaming gendarmes bolted for the river, hair on fire, jackets burned. Another two ran off into the forest, diving behind whatever cover they could find.

Delacorte was losing allies fast. Duncan shoved the rifle over his back, pulled his knives from his boots, thrusting them into his cloak pockets, cocked his pistols, and ran for the boathouse.

"Get down, brother!" Cal yelled. Duncan ducked, wondering how the hell Cal knew he'd learned Gaelic. Then he was rocked off his feet by the explosion of the second Nock. He stumbled into the boathouse and dove to the ground.

The wall facing their attackers had but an arm's length of height left, the floor strewn with glass, wood and plaster, bodies and blood. A pall of acrid smoke lay over the ruined room, the stink of river mud and blood and piss on the floor. He couldn't feel any sign of life.

Lisbeth was sprawled on the dirt floor tied to a half-broken chair, more flotsam from the battle. Her face was sliced open. A pool of blood surrounded her, more smearing her body. Even through the grime of the tunnel floor, her skin looked as white as the daubs of shattered plaster on her face. If she was breathing, he couldn't see it.

His pulse pounding against his skull and chest, he crawled to her.

CHAPTER 14

The Tuileries, Paris
August 27, 1802
"My lord Consul, Monsieur Fouché has been located and brought here."

In his study, seated at the mahogany desk that had once been the king's — France was just emerging from the terrifying amount of debt he'd inherited two years ago, and refurnishing would be a waste — First Consul Napoleon Bonaparte glanced up at his third secretary and nodded. "*Bien,* Barteau, *merci.* Send him in." He made a point of knowing the names of everyone who served him, and always thanking them. Such small honors created loyalty.

As he waited, he hummed to himself.

Non, non, z'il est impossible,
D'avoir un plus aimable enfant.

If his valet Constant were there, he'd have heard the small Italianism inserted — a sign things were going his lord's way — indeed, his master was a happy man.

When the doors opened again, Napoleon became expressionless, watching the minor spectacle. As expected, his sometime ally Fouché came in between two soldiers, dressed in a shabby coat and breeches; his thinning pale brown hair was unkempt, his skinny frame hunched over in a cringing kind of subservience. From long experience, Napoleon knew it was but a ruse, and worse than useless. Repulsive at the best of times, Fouché had a resemblance to a miniature greyhound when he wanted to appear humble.

A ridiculous disguise today, unless he'd spent the one million two hundred thousand francs settled upon him earlier this year and run through the moneys coming to him above that from the senatorship of Aix. Never in history had a minister been dismissed with more honor and more lush payment than Joseph Fouché, and everyone knew he still ran every spy group in France worth knowing about. So what was the point of this little performance?

Bonaparte hadn't reached this current pinnacle of power by being stupid; yet there was no brain to match Fouché's, in terms of pure cunning. A human phantom, he manipulated all the major players in France without the public ever being aware that he'd even done more than play a very minor part in the pageant . . . but since the near loss turned into stunning victory that had been the Battle of Marengo in 1800, Napoleon had Fouché's measure. He might make use of the man's mind, but he would never take his loyalty at face value. So what was this little pageant about? Why was he playing the supplicant?

"Ah, Monsieur Fouché." Bonaparte greeted his former minister of police with a smile. "It is good to see you so well, and flourishing."

Fouché's answer to this sally was a thin returned smile. Since he'd been deposed as police minister he had to know his disguises were transparent to his leader, yet still he put them on. By now, even he probably didn't know who the true Joseph Fouché was.

With a brief salute, Napoleon's soldiers left the office. Bonaparte swept a hand to a chair. Fouché sat on its edge, as if expecting a sword to pop up through the cushion. "My lord, it is such a pleasure to return to your presence," he said when it was obvious his lord wouldn't give him an opening to see which way he ought to jump. "In what way may I have the honor to serve you?"

Whenever he was in the same room as Fouché, Napoleon felt as if he'd been drawn into a dark alley with pistols and knives aimed at his back. "You may tell me why your Jacobin and royalist spies have flooded the Channel Coast, and most especially why they attempt to enter Boulogne-sur-Mer and ingratiate themselves with M. Robert Fulton in Le Havre."

Fouché's narrow eyes widened as a hand fluttered up, like a maiden's. "But my lord, even though I am no longer the minister of police, which office you disabled in your wisdom, you must know I separated myself from the Jacobin party many years ago. I have not returned to them. And I was never a royalist, I assure you. Indeed, in the assembly, did I not vote *la mort*?"

After assuring royalists the night before that you would vote to keep the king alive. And one day you'll swear you were forced to vote "la mort." Napoleon kept the thought to himself. He did not jump about when snakes hissed, but waited to see which way they'd slither. His was the power in France, and Fouché responded to its warmth like a sunflower.

Eventually, Fouché murmured, "One hears rumors, my lord . . . one has friends. The Channel Coast is far, and the weather there is insalubrious to my weak chest. So I sent some friends to verify those rumors, for the protection of France."

Napoleon wasn't about to ask anything. If he gave Fouché any indication, the man would know which lie to tell, what poison to whisper.

Fouché sat watching him, like an expectant dog at table, waiting for that one crumb that would give away his master's current mood.

But Napoleon hadn't survived two years as France's leader by being stupid. His smile didn't shift as he continued to wait. He knew who would break.

"Pernicious rumors," Fouché said at last. "Always there is chatter about conspiracies —"

"But were there anything serious, you would soon see the evidence in the Place de la République," Napoleon finished Fouché's own quote of a few years before, alluding to death by guillotine without a trace of emotion. Nor did he remind Fouché that he himself had said those words to President Gohier the night before the coup d'état of 18 Brumaire.

Though he'd showered Fouché with honors for a while, he'd known what kind of man he dealt with. Fouché had betrayed Robespierre, Barras, and Gohier in turn and had almost done so to *him* when the false rumor reached Paris that there had been disastrous losses at the Battle of Marengo. Fouché's had been the highest praises when he'd returned the victor; but the conspicuous silence until then taught Napoleon that a chameleon always changes hue under fear of attack. "Tell me what you have learned."

With a swift sidelong glance that made Napoleon suppress a shudder, Fouché tested the first water. "I've heard vile rumors that you will put aside your wife to wed a Bade-

167

nese princess — that, I beg your pardon, my lord, your family still wishes you to found a royal dynasty —"

"Facts, not rumors, if you please," Napoleon interrupted, without expression. "As none of my family currently resides on the Channel Coast, this information is somewhat redundant."

Fouché's pale cheeks touched with color; his eyes flashed at being stopped midstride. He thrived on the cunning of Iago, watching the poison take root and flourish. Manipulation through secrets and innuendo was the breath of life to him.

But Fouché would dance a Corsican two-step today. He must become too incontinent with fear to dare be seen showing loyalty to any but the first consul . . . at least until the Louisiana Purchase was signed, the payment sent to Paris. Then the snake could send his spies anywhere he wanted. Napoleon's spies in Fouché's camps kept him very well informed, and *his* men's loyalty couldn't be bought.

After three more wearying tries to interest him in malicious rumors about his family or his more loyal generals, Fouché said at last, "British spies have been seen in the region."

Though Napoleon didn't move, inside he jerked to attention. He waved a dismissive hand. "Ah, your favorite egress from my blaming your beloved Jacobins — the British.

You have been trying to interest me in their doings since the Christmas Eve killings. I say bah to the Red Rose Team or the White, Mr. Windham's famous teams with their pretty names: d'Assas, Lemaire, Tamerlan, and their fancy Pimpernel. They and Captain Wright, and the so-famous Sir Sidney Smith, they release minor prisoners we leave for them and gather only information we want them to know."

Ah, those heavy-lidded eyes flashed. Fouché hated his choice nuggets of knowledge being rubbished, but he replied meekly enough. "This is a new team, my lord. They've infiltrated Le Havre, Rouen, and Audresselles. A young Englishwoman works in a tavern in Abbeville that is a haunt for spies of every persuasion. Another Briton has just situated himself in Boulogne-sur-Mer, at a time when you are setting up the semaphore tower there —"

Ah, here is the information I need. But instead of pushing, he smiled. "Ah, is not this young woman in Abbeville the wife of your protégé, thrown aside the day she gave him a son? Nicely trained by you, *Citoyen* Fouché. Perhaps he ought to be sent to Guiana with the others?"

Another jolt of anger seared those repellent eyes. If there was one thing Fouché did care about, it was his family, his ugly wife and unattractive sons. He'd truly grieved when his children died. Though Napoleon despised underhand tactics, Fouché never cared when he left a family other than his own in grief. "If you will forgive me, the woman must be interned, my lord. My man repudiated her when he discovered that she's a spy, a danger to loyal men of France."

Napoleon lifted his brows. "A girl reared in the country by her mother is a spy? A girl who spent the year pregnant and is working in a tavern? Now a boy perhaps I could credit. Sunderland's sons are in the game, I know, but this chit? When did she find the time?"

"She lives on a tavern wench's wage," Fouché murmured. "She must be receiving funds elsewhere, for she refuses to sleep with the tavern's patrons to fill her coffers."

More poison Napoleon refused to swallow. "I see you believe it at least. Leave her, intern her, I care not, but a nobleman's daughter is not to be killed. I will not hesitate to implicate you with the European Tribunal in anything you do."

"I do not have the power to do anything with her, my lord," Fouché was quick to say, with no seeming resentment. "I am your humble servant alerting you to a danger I see."

"Then why did I need to send soldiers to bring you here before you informed me?"

Fouché sat still and calm, but his cheeks

had turned the sallow color of a good Brie. "I would not dare enter your presence without an invitation, my lord — ah, *Citoyen Consul,*" he added, in a seeming innocent slip. "I know my place."

One sneaking allusion to his family's ambition he'd allowed; but no one, but *no one* insulted his sainted mother! Of course she wanted her son to rise above the rest, to have the honors given to him. Had he not more than earned it? "Did you not say that to your friend Gohier just before 18 Brumaire — or was it Barras?" he asked, not bothering to sheath his verbal sword. "Answer my original question, Monsieur Fouché, and not with an allusion or an attempted distraction, but with truth."

A rat in a trap, Fouché, with eyes blank, thought quickly. "I needed a final piece of information, my lord. I'd heard of a nefarious Jacobin scheme planned against the gendarmes of Abbeville by this English noblewoman and her British cohort, pretending to be a . . ."

As Fouché went into his usual colorful detail, condemning this English girl and naming each of the local Jacobins — his former sworn friends, whom he now led to their deaths without a single regret — Napoleon let his thoughts drift. If a British spy was indeed in Boulogne, they couldn't be allowed to leave or to send a message. He must get his best people onto that —

"The man has a connection to Fulton, and to the Infernal Machine plot. I believe he has proof that the British gunpowder and shrapnel were supplied by Messieurs Pitt and Windham."

Napoleon snapped to attention. The infamous bomb on the rue Saint-Nicaise that killed and maimed so many people in 1800 haunted him still. That they had died in his city, under his rule, by a bomb meant for *him*, made him the soldier on watch who'd let the enemy sneak behind battle lines. He'd beheaded two Jacobins and sent many more to Guiana; but it wasn't enough. It never would be.

What had Fouché said? It took but a moment to remember the details. The Briton at the tavern — the Sunderland girl's seeming cohort — had a connection to Robert Fulton, whose inventions were far more interesting than he'd so far let on. "If that's so, I expect you would already have brought them both to me for questioning."

Fouché smiled, thin and satisfied. Iago indeed, happy to find his version of control. "My man is, shall we say, forcing the issue at present."

So he had no confession or proof as yet. "Neither is to be killed until they're interrogated and identified. Tell Monsieur Delacorte that his unwanted wife is to be left alive." He saw the eager flash pass through his former minister's eyes. "No, it is best if you do not involve yourself. I will send a semaphore myself on the subject — as you say, there is now a tower in the town. I will let Delacorte know my men will be sent to the region. Any men you have there may retire when mine arrive. Your cooperation is appreciated, *Citoyen* Senator Fouché."

A moment's darkness in Fouché's eyes, then he smiled again. If there was one thing Fouché understood, it was patience. He would be raised again; they both knew that. His brilliance would ensure it. He stood, bowed, murmured some praises, and left Napoleon's presence.

When he was alone, Napoleon smiled, having got the information he'd sought.

Fouché kept his face completely impassive until he was back in his charming château on the Île-de-France, where none could follow or watch him. Then he smiled. He'd planted the seed; Bonaparte's paranoia would water it, and the British spies on the Channel Coast would make it grow. They'd find the clues he'd left for them and foil his lord's mighty plot.

He had a prince ready to step into the excellent financial condition in which Bonaparte had left France. Unlike the arrogant Prince de Condé or the stupid Louis XV III, *his* prince had learned the lessons of Louis's beheading and would end the threat of war that the kings and lords of Austria, Russia, and Britain, burning for revenge and terrified of rule by any but those born and bred to power, would declare on France before long.

And Fouché would be the one holding the strings to make the new king dance.

CHAPTER 15

Somme River, Abbeville

"Bring her to the trapdoor. I'll cover you."

Cal's voice right behind his ear startled Duncan. He moved faster, ignoring the glass digging into hands and knees. Cal went to the only possible exit, now that the walls were gone: the trapdoor over the river. He lifted it for Duncan, and then piled up wall rubble around himself for protection.

As Duncan passed a sprawl of bodies, one head lifted. Luc Marron's bleary eyes met Duncan's, and saw the knife in his hand. "I have four daughters. Please. I wouldn't hurt Elise."

He ought to question the man — but if Cal had been part of the group for months, there would be little he didn't know. He glanced at Lisbeth lying in dirt and blood, and saw the mark of a handprint on her cheek. He turned back in time to see Marron wince. With cold precision he pulled the Nock off his back and whacked Marron on the head with the side of the stock. If the Frenchman's slump were a ruse, he wouldn't stop him from taking the girl.

His gloves and breeches shredded on the broken glass as he crawled; little shards lodged in his skin. Shots whizzed past him. Cal answered with shots. "Hurry, lad."

An eerie silence fell as Duncan reached her. Not even a bird chirped. Delacorte must be alone now, either looking for discarded weapons or reloading. Or he was watching, waiting to shoot.

Lying flat, Duncan cut her bonds. A tiny exhalation came from her lips; blood pumped from her shoulder, sluggish. The glass had gone in so deep he didn't dare pull it out. With his arms beneath her back and legs he strapped her to him, but every movement he made caused fresh bleeding. Rolling onto his back, he laid her body across him, feeling her blood drip on his skin.

Cal hissed, "I'm out of ball shot. Give me yours."

"She has glass in her shoulder. If I don't hold it together, she'll bleed to death."

A new volley of shots began. Cal lifted the trapdoor, ordered, "One of you, arm yourself and get up here. The other, throw me a weapon!"

Duncan laid Lisbeth's head on his shoulder, keeping her neck motionless with his hand. Her breaths were shallow and fast against his torn shirt and chest. He inched toward the trapdoor on his back. Glass shards tore his layers of clothing and lodged in the skin of his back as he inched on. Every twenty seconds he halted, waiting to feel her breathe again.

"Move left, lad. Less glass and fewer bodies. That's it." *Boom.* An answering shot, and Duncan coughed out the acrid pall from his lungs. One of his men had joined Cal. "Come around to the right, back toward me. Aye, head straight now and you'll make it."

Without time to think, Duncan followed Cal's advice.

More shots, closer. Delacorte was moving in. Cal fired off another shot. "I've only enough powder for two shots. Hurry."

Duncan found the trapdoor, inched his way around as fast as he could, swung his legs into the hole, and slowly sat, cradling her the whole time. "Help me," he ordered down the hole.

"I'm here, sir." His third lieutenant, Hazeltine, put his hands at Duncan's back.

He felt his way down another ladder with booted feet. Hazeltine helped him settle on the bench, with Lisbeth cradled like a babe against him. Looking down, he saw the pale, peaceful blank that presages death. He whispered fiercely, "Don't let go, do you hear me? You have a son to raise. Damn you, girl, fight!"

Cal and Burton stepped down into the boat.

"She needs a doctor," he said as Cal sat across from him, searched Duncan's pockets for pistols, laid them on the bench beside him, and grabbed two oars. He nodded, and Hazeltine and Burton pulled oars in time with him. "There's one aboard ship, but there's no time. I hear there's a midwife in Fontaine. We could be there in half an hour."

"I know her," Cal said shortly. "What of your ship, lad? Where is it anchored?"

Duncan stared at this man who called him "lad" and "brother" so easily and seemed to know all his secrets. What was it with these Stewarts? They interfered in his life with total ease and no conscience. "I gave orders to anchor off the marshes by Le Crotoy every night at first watch, six bells, until mid-watch, eight bells — two hours before sunrise."

"I was in the navy, lad. I know the terms," Cal said mildly.

Duncan looked at the man who was almost an unscarred mirror of himself and said, "So who were the Jacobins waiting for in the barn last night, and what are they planning? And how did Delacorte know exactly where to come to be able to accuse us of working with the Jacobins?"

The boat jerked left toward the riverbank. Before they could right it, a shot rang out. Duncan forced himself to remain still, shielding Lisbeth with his body —

Bloody virtue was not its own reward this time. The ball ripped through the top of the rowboat and into his thigh. He flinched. "Aaargh!"

Lisbeth moaned as the boat rocked, and he couldn't hold her still.

"Commander," Hazeltine cried, jumping toward him.

"Stroke," Cal snapped in French. "We must get out of here! Faster!"

Duncan glared at Hazeltine, gritted teeth, low voice. "Not . . . commander here."

Another shot hit the boat near Duncan, embedding in the bench.

"The shooter stands seventy degrees northeast of you, monsieur." Burton handed Cal two pistols. "I primed every remaining pistol while I waited for you."

"Good man. It's Delacorte, Duncan," Cal said softly. "He's trying to sink us. Are you well enough to keep going?"

"I'll make it." Duncan turned his head. Even in a mist of pain he could see the man on the riverbank. The height and breadth, the blond curls . . . he could almost imagine the bright, cornflower-blue eyes. Such angelic beauty was rare in a man without appearing effeminate.

No wonder Lisbeth had run off with him. He was the epitome of physical masculine splendor. With a poetic tongue feeding her sad tales of his youth in revolutionary France, he could easily turn a young girl's head.

Still less was he surprised that, after a year of experiencing Delacorte's dirty peccadilloes and his painful methods of control over women, she'd trusted *him,* Duncan, so easily. If he was Vulcan to Delacorte's Apollo, mongrel bastard to the other's purebred, Delacorte had shown his soul within hours of Eddie refusing him entry to the house. Why he'd joined the Jacobins was no mystery. He might be of the noble class, but ambition and paranoia, the love of violence and need to blame others had dominated everything he had done since the death of his father.

Sweat broke out with the effort of holding Lisbeth in his pain. "He's reloading."

"Pull faster!" Cal aimed and fired one pistol and the other, right-handed and left.

A scream rang out in the fading sky. Cal nodded in satisfaction. "I thought hitting his leg in the same place an appropriate farewell, plus it will slow his pursuit of us. Seems he likes receiving pain less than giving it. He won't be chasing us for a while."

Lucifer, son of the morning, how thou art fallen. Duncan watched Delacorte's perfect face twist in anguish and redden in unbridled rage. Again he forced his mind from his own pain, checking the glade and surrounds. "Looks like no one's with him. To Fontaine, double time." He wanted to tell Cal to kill the bastard, but if Cal hadn't done so already, it was because he had orders to keep him alive. Only Zephyr had that kind of authority — but why would the spymaster want Delacorte kept alive? He'd find out before he was much older, that was bloody certain.

"How will we reach Le Crotoy? Isn't Valery-sur-Somme guarded also?" Cal asked.

"Not so thoroughly as Boulogne." Duncan forced himself to think through the pain that was making him light-headed. "My fourth lieutenant should meet us with a coach and four horses, plus horses for us as outriders. He'll meet us at the crossroads above Fontaine."

"Actually, sir, Hill's doing that," Hazeltine said.

Duncan gritted his teeth. Hazeltine was both physically clumsy and with a mouth that tripped over itself, and he wouldn't have kept him on his team if he'd had the choice. But Hazeltine was cousin to a viscount who steadily voted for the continuation of the Alien Office on the occasions such debates returned. "Don't use surnames. Why is a midshipman doing this?"

Hazeltine's hesitation was pregnant with tension and fear. "We're here with you, the first lieutenant fulfilled his mission and is returning from Le Havre, and the fourth lieutenant — well, he's done a runner." Hazeltine peered at Duncan, his honest eyes alight with anxiety. "He took a rowboat and disappeared about two hours after you left ship. He stole the Jaulin papers. It seems Mark — uh, Marcus René went with him."

When Lisbeth moaned, Duncan realized he'd squeezed her in his fury. He softened his hold, but his mind whirled. His new fourth lieutenant had joined them *after* he'd been with Archbishop Narbonne. While he was waiting for Alec to come to him, Narbonne sent word that a young priest had been killed outside the church as they'd spoken, another tied up.

Idiot! He should have been suspicious when his fourth lieutenant had disappeared, with Haversham conveniently at hand to replace him. But in the peace, too many ships had been decommissioned, with hundreds of sailors and officers hanging about the docks desperate for paid work. Lost in the archbishop's information and fear for Lisbeth, he'd let Flynn hire the replacement lieutenant. On board ship with him for one night, he'd never looked at the man.

There must be good reason why both Pitt and Admiral St. Vincent had given Haversham such a thorough recommendation. The imposter must be a man of birth and means to have their interest — or were the papers forgeries? If so, they were expensive ones to fool Flynn. Why would the man risk death . . . to join *his* ship? If he'd wanted to get to France so badly, why not just take the packet at Dover?

The next shot hit the end of the launch an inch above the water line. "Faster, damn you!" he snarled. "We can outrun —"

Then he froze. Someone had to have been listening in on his conversation with the archbishop: a man who'd killed a priest without thought for the consequences.

This missing lieutenant, an efficient seaman, had given him a recommendation by *Pitt.*

Only one man was stupid enough to forge the former prime minister's handwriting and believe he could get away with it . . . because he probably would.

Duncan didn't know he'd tensed until pain tore through his injured leg. But damn it, by his inattention he'd let the Mad Baron loose in France — a violent man who hated everyone born beneath him. And Mark, the ambitious Cockney cabin boy far too smart for his own good, had decamped with him.

Dropmore House (Lord Grenville's Residence), Buckinghamshire, England
Alec Stewart arrived at Dropmore House at six, the country hour to dine.

He'd learned Zephyr's whereabouts by visiting the British Alien Office in Whitehall, pretending to be Cal. From an undersecretary unfamiliar with the Stewart brothers, Alec had learned that Zephyr was staying at his cousin Lord Grenville's home in Bucking-hamshire, only twenty-five miles away.

Alec had stayed in Duncan's rooms on Jermyn Street, where Duncan's finicky valet gave him a bed and nightshirt, fussed over his hair, insisted on a night shave and having his clothes pressed. "Commander Aylsham always does so, sir."

Alec gave in. He supposed this namby-pamby would faint if he saw Alec sleeping naked. No wonder Duncan didn't take him aboard ship.

The next morning the valet took him to buy the latest in evening attire before he left for Buckinghamshire. "Lord Grenville is a stickler for the observances where home and ladies are concerned, sir," the man said, eyeing Alec's clothing with ill-concealed distaste.

A suggestion that he could wear something of his brother's made the valet stare in shock.

So Alec forked out a hundred pounds for ridiculous London wear: bloody uncomfortable knee breeches and waistcoat under a tight cutaway coat. His hair was artfully arranged in curls instead of simply tied back with a ribbon, dropping over his face enough to annoy him. With his height and breadth, the frills on the shirt cuffs and the intricacy of the cravat made him look like a giant dandy. To top it off, he had to bring Duncan's man for dressing. "Lord and Lady Grenville would be shocked if you didn't bring me, sir," the valet insisted.

Once admitted to the magnificent house, the butler led him down a wide hallway into an anteroom. "Please wait here, Mr. Stewart." The butler closed the doors behind him.

Lifting his brows a little at the exquisite rudeness, Alec looked at family portraits, the highly decorated doors, walls, cornices, and shelves. A ridiculous-sized house for two people, but probably they'd still expected to have children when it was built twelve years ago.

He'd been cooling his heels for ten minutes. He'd expected better manners than this. Twelve minutes . . .

Then Lady Grenville pushed the doors open. The plump, pretty woman curtsied to his bow. "My dear Mr. Stewart, I do beg your pardon! You have come in this horrible weather! So naughty of Lord Grenville not to have told me you were coming! Never mind, it can be fixed in a trifle. You'll stay the night, of course."

She told the butler to make up the second-best guest room and take the valet upstairs. Bustling Alec through the Blue Room and the creamy-colored morning room, Lady Grenville entered the dining room. Two thin men sat talking in low tones. Both wore old-fashioned wigs and de rigueur knee breeches, cravats, and exquisite fitted jackets for a dinner of ten years ago. Although they had a basic familiarity of features one could expect from cousins, one man had a contented face and pleasant eyes, but the other — William Windham, Zephyr — was sharper faced, his gaze constantly inquisitive. A little lady sat beside him, either a paid companion or a poor relative, well dressed but without jewels, frills, or furbelows. She sat quietly, smiling and nodding at appropriate places.

Alec drew a sigh of relief. By the shrewd look in both Zephyr's and Grenville's eyes, he knew a meeting would take place over port. He smiled at Lady Grenville as the footman seated him.

He'd forgotten how long a "country dinner" took among the English aristocracy. At home, nobody knew who'd turn up on any given night, children ate in the Great Hall with the family, and Granddad liked hearing the pipes played as he ate, so mealtimes were loud and fun. Here, everything was done with decorum. Four courses at least — the soup, the salad, the main course, and dessert all took their time. The servants at least worked with efficiency.

Good old stodgy England, with her long-winded rituals and addiction to appearances by the ruling classes. Bonaparte would have to shove war in her face before she realized he was up to something. Then the government would have dozens of meetings to discuss the *possibility* of war before they made a declaration. By then Bonaparte would have his Grande Armée marching across the fields of Hastings on its way to London — but naturally, England couldn't be expected to respond to that threat until the fourth course was complete.

At last the covers were removed. Lady Grenville and her companion retired to the withdrawing room while the men drank port and spoke of things ladies didn't want to hear.

The butler returned with the port on a silver tray, poured three glasses, and left with a bow. Then Windham spoke. "Well, Apollyon, trot it out. It must be big to bring you from your self-imposed retirement in the wilds of Scotland. Who sent you — Abaddon or Tidewatcher?"

Of course Zephyr knew which of the Destroyer Twins he was; the scars he'd received during the Glorious First of June sea battle gave him away. Cal's scars were less noticeable: stains on his mind, sword cuts on his memory. Hating the code name as much as ever — from the Bible book of Revelation, Apollyon and Abaddon both meant "destroyer" in Greek and Hebrew, Zephyr's nasty little joke — he said, "It was Tidewatcher, sir. He has vital news."

"Well, don't waste time. The ladies await us."

Grenville sat quietly, port in hand. Grenville was not only Zephyr's cousin, he was also related to Pitt: a former foreign minister who'd resigned with Pitt on conscience matters. He was privy to every *on-dit* passing through the Alien Office.

Alec spoke of Duncan's meeting with Archbishop Narbonne, what he'd discovered on the Channel Coast: the reason he'd returned to active duty without asking Zephyr's permission. Then he handed Windham a packet filled with letters, notes, and drawings. "His team gathered this information over several weeks."

After reading a page, Zephyr passed it to Grenville. "If it wasn't you bringing me this, I'd think you'd filched it from the Greek tragedies. I'll need to think on this."

Grenville put the information in his jacket pocket. "The ladies await us."

Zephyr nodded. "Quite right." The piercing glance at Alec was punctuated with a frown, but it was to his cousin that he spoke. "Hell and damnation, Will, the navy's a mess, our best ships in the Caribbean . . ."

Grenville shook his head. "Anne must see no sign. It would distress her, especially with Thomas —" He stopped, flicking a glance at Alec.

Alec kept his face neutral; but even in remote western Scotland, Lady Grenville's little brother had become a byword. All the world and his aunt knew the Pitts had shelled out enormous sums to keep Lord Camelford from prison. His ungovernable temper, his expert use of all kinds of weaponry, and his belief in his superiority to the rest of the world would see him shot or hanged one day. What had the unbalanced baron done this time?

When one was in England, one played the game. If everyone pretended all was well, then it was. Lady Grenville wasn't barren; her brother shouldn't be committed for insanity; Bonaparte wasn't preparing for war or invasion; and someone wasn't about to kill the king. At least not until the ladies retired for the night.

Alec held in the chuckle, imagining Grandmamma's reaction, should any of her male relatives attempt to keep such important information from her.

The cousins passed through the western-facing door to Lady Grenville's sitting room. Alec followed, ready to keep country hours. If he knew Zephyr, the spymaster would wake him around 3 A.M. with his instructions, and he'd expect them to be carried out immediately.

When he reached the room, he sent Duncan's horrified valet off to London to the western Thames docks, to give a note to the captain of the fishing sloop he'd hired to take them to the usual dropping-off point. They'd be leaving for France at first light.

CHAPTER 16

*Rue de Miromesnil, Faubourg Saint-Honoré,
Paris*
August 27, 1802

The day that had begun clear and bright was turning oppressive in its heat and the threat of an oncoming summer storm. Lady Georgiana Gordon, youngest daughter of the Duke and Duchess of Gordon, looked up at the threatening clouds and hurried with her maid from the coach to the opulent house Mama had rented from the cousin of the Duc d'Orléans before they'd come to Paris. "A bath, if you please, Prunella," she said to her maid, handing the collection of bandboxes to the footman. "I will take tea in the afternoon room."

"You have visitors, m'lady," the footman said, before he followed in Prunella's wake. "An English gentleman and a . . . lady."

Intrigued by the little pause that spoke volumes by servants, Georgy felt her brows lift. The smile her admirers assured her turned her into a goddess, despite the buckteeth she so hated, came alive. Not that much had made her smile since Francis had died in March. She might not have loved him, but she'd liked and sincerely respected him. Marriage to him would have been no hardship — and since her friend Lizzy Sunderland's defection she'd needed someone to replace her. Francis had been that, a gentle soul with an unexpected streak of mischief, sweetly poking fun at their world — and being a duke, he was a friend her fastidious mama had approved of. She'd become even more vigilant since Lizzy had run off with the "wrong sort" of man last year, ruining her family's good name and her reputation. It seemed Georgy had been tainted by association.

"You ought never to have looked below your station, even for a friend." Mama had scolded her so many times Georgy had long since gotten over her impish desire to say, *But, Mama, you're also a baronet's daughter.*

Two days before their engagement was made official, Francis had died suddenly of a mysterious illness. Nasty whispers circulated that he'd died of an overdose of the Duchess of Gordon's ambition. Mama, in her duty visit (as she'd put it) to the sixth duke, Francis's brother John, had been told in no uncertain terms not to expect him to step in for his brother to make her daughter a duchess.

The Polite World had spent weeks laughing at the silly, ambitious Duchess of Gordon and the daughter no duke wanted . . . so here they were in Paris. Had been since June, without a single offer in sight. The attention of the Vicomte de Beauharnais, Napoleon's own stepson, was a balm, but even to Mama it was obvious Eugene wasn't serious.

Georgy shook herself from her reverie and went into the afternoon room to greet her visitors. She turned to the gentleman, leaving the . . . lady . . . obviously more worthy of her interest, for later.

But the gentleman sitting on her chaise longue took her aback. Harsh featured, hook nosed, and a known woman hater, he jerked to his feet with his customary objection to manners, refusing to admit that a Gordon could outrank a Pitt. "Lady Georgiana," Lord Camelford greeted her, with a bow bordering on insolence. "I know we haven't been formally introduced. I hope you don't mind that I've called on you."

His voice said clearly that she should acknowledge the honor he'd done her in coming — but the words popped out of her mouth before she could stop them. "Good gracious, surely you of all men aren't here to propose to me. You don't need my money, do you?" Then her hand almost slammed over her mouth. If the Mad Baron took offense —

To her relief, Camelford chuckled. "I like the word without any bark on it. I don't need your money, nor do I want you. I do need something from you, however."

She sighed. "Thank heavens for that. But I am intrigued to know . . ." Suddenly recalling Camelford wasn't her only visitor, she let her gaze shift to the right — and she gasped.

She'd never seen or imagined a woman so — so, well, *beautiful.* Truly, a poem could be written to her sylphlike loveliness. She was Venus arising from her shell. Small and gently curvaceous, skin like real peaches and cream, hair of a perfect strawberry blond with a subtle overtone of moonlit silver through it, so glossy — melting blue eyes, a classic nose, and even dimples in the creamy skin . . . a luscious peach-pink mouth that truly tipped up in that mysterious half slant that men called "the signature of Venus."

For the first time in her social whirl of a life, Georgy had seen a young woman who fit the clichéd soubriquet of "The Incomparable." She was certain that, once seen, this perfection of face and form would never be forgotten.

"Lady Georgiana?"

Oh, heavens, even her voice was soft, as lyrical as music! This woman would set London on its ear. She couldn't believe Camelford wasn't even looking at the woman . . . Georgy knew she was being horribly rude, but she couldn't stop staring. Belatedly she pulled herself together. "Yes, I am Georgiana Gordon. How good of you to call, Madame . . . ?"

"Recamier," the other murmured, smiling: a Botticelli come to life. "Jeanne Françoise Recamier, my lady. I hope you'll forgive the impudence of my calling when we've never met."

"Certainly," Georgy said stupidly, holding out her hand, then retracting it and curtsying as good manners required. In a lemon silk day gown, when Madame Recamier also curtsied, she looked like liquid sunshine. "You're most welcome. I've already called for tea for us."

"Tea is pap," Camelford snarled, breaking in on the dreamlike state Georgy had fallen into. "I need to talk to you without this woman here, and I'd appreciate it taking place now."

"I'd heard you were eccentric, but I assumed you'd been taught the manners of a gentleman. It seems I was wrong," Georgy said, using the gentle but chilling tone she turned on impudent tradesmen or social climbers. "If you will return tomorrow at two, my lord, I will see to it that my mother and I are at home for you."

Camelford jerked to his feet and stormed out.

Madame Recamier winced a little as the

door slammed behind him. "Well, one cannot say he doesn't know how to make a lasting impression," she said, mouth quirked up, eyes glimmering with fun.

Impressed by both the humor and the discretion — not speculating on what Camelford wanted from her — Georgy smiled back. "Madame, I can only —"

"No, my lady, do not apologize for Camelford's appalling manners, when it was I who ensured he would make such a request, and that you would, ah, ask that he leave. I have, as you might say, a way with men . . . either for good or for bad." Her eyes still twinkled. "I annoyed him greatly by not respecting the grand name of Pitt."

Georgy blinked, but found nothing to say.

"I'd heard you appreciated pound dealing," Madame Recamier said, in unaccented English. "Is that not so?"

"Um, yes, I do like plain speaking." Georgy blinked again, frowning as she looked again at the vision of feminine perfection before her. *Not so much as a smear of rouge,* she thought in wonder. "Since we are being open, I will ask: who are you?"

The woman leaned forward, hooking a finger toward her. Georgy too leaned in. Then the woman whispered, "In certain circles I am known as The Incomparable."

Georgy almost laughed aloud at the appropriate soubriquet. "By whom?"

The lady looked in her eyes: message or warning. "I have the honor of training certain important people who love our nation to gather intelligence for us. The cousin of the gentleman who just left us would deeply appreciate your help. He believes you may help with the, ah, small issue of that gentleman's current geography, and with other delicate matters of state. You are also in a position to help your friend Elizabeth Sunderland, who is also working for us."

Somme River, South of Abbeville

Duncan counted getting through Abbeville alive as another minor miracle. "Delacorte's allies have deserted him," he said to Cal. Anything to keep from focusing on the burning in his leg or Lisbeth's fragility. He'd covered both their injuries with a blanket stored at the boat's stern. No point in giving the evening fishermen a view they could describe to the gendarmes.

"I counted on it." Cal kept the stroke shallow, propelling the boat along. The men followed his lead.

Fifteen minutes later they reached Eaucourt, with its crumbling fortress castle at one end of the village, a small farm prison at the other. They passed the house that held Lisbeth's son, and Duncan saw nothing out of place. Delacorte's men were hidden well.

The next town, Pont-Remy, was a sleepy

village consisting of a scruffy inn and a few farms, and a half-built shipping canal going nowhere. A candle lit a window here and there as night fell like a heavy curtain dropping over the land.

Again all seemed quiet, but barely seven miles from Abbeville, it would be easy to have gendarmes awaiting them in the darkness.

As if in answer, he heard hooves in the distance. "If Delacorte sent riders ahead . . ."

Cal answered through puffing breaths and pulling strokes, "How could he? After this afternoon, he's lost the gendarmes. There are Jacobins enough in Abbeville to be related to half the population, so he's lost the townsfolk. He's injured and on the run, and knows Fouché will soon be on his trail. We're safe until he finds the funds to buy new men."

Duncan's fury at Cal's being sent to watch over him subsided. The pain was clouding his mind. "I suppose you know where he keeps his son, as well?"

"Oh, aye, we passed it not long ago — but you knew that." A small smile touched his face, lighting nothing within. "The lassie's right to want her bairn back. No child should be raised by that man and his mother. Cruelty is his amusement, and the poor lady barely knows her name. It's said she dropped the bairn recently. Luckily he fell back into the cradle."

Duncan sent up silent thanks that Lisbeth

wasn't awake to hear that.

By the time they reached the farming hamlet of Fontaine, the wider canal turned pewter in a sullen sunset. The scent of rain was in the air. Halfway up the hill, the spire of Église de Saint-Peter pierced the low-hanging cloud. Candlelight dotted windows of small farmhouses as women worked in the kitchen, and men in barns or sitting rooms. Cockerels split the air with their last calls of the day. Cows lowed, needing relief from full udders. The yowling of copulating cats came from nearby. Somewhere a dog barked, but only once.

Everything seemed undisturbed; neither the rumbling of wheels nor suspicious silence to break the tranquility. He looked at Cal. "Seems safe enough."

The Scot nodded. "D'ye have a dislike of natural healers? This woman uses herbs and the like. Some of her neighbors call her a witch."

In Cal's eyes, Duncan saw knowledge of the labyrinth of unbalanced prejudices he'd been forced to accept during his youth, lest Annersley whip or throw him in the cupboard again. "No." Lisbeth was shivering even with his cloak around her. "Land here." He pointed at a tiny punt, barely an indent in the canal with two dories tied to it. "Push the boat under, then find the midshipman and help him bring the coach to the house. Even after treatment, Miss Sunderland won't be fit to be carried far."

"I can do it, sir," Burton offered, with a significant look. Though as brave as a lion in battle, Hazeltine was a disaster on two feet, often with one of those feet in his mouth.

Duncan shook his head. "Just do it, Hazeltine. Help me up first."

Cal leaned forward. "You can't carry her. I'll get her there sooner, lad."

He hated to admit Cal was right. "If the glass goes in any farther . . ."

"I'll care for her as if she were my own sister." Cradling her like a babe, Cal stepped off the rowboat with caution and strode up the pier and onto the path.

Duncan turned inward, concentrating on his own pain. In any case, she was probably safest with Cal. Within a week of their first meeting Lisbeth was half dead, her life in tatters. Like father, like son. No matter which father — Broderick Stewart or Charles Urquhart Aylsham, thirty-fifth Baron Annersley — they had both destroyed everything they touched.

Eddie would tell me to stubble it. Guilt and fear are time-wasting indulgences. Just do your duty. "Help me out of the boat."

His men held his elbows, but even straightening his leg made him gasp. "Burton."

Burton slipped his arm under Duncan's to keep him up. "Go, Hazeltine," he ordered, panting through the pain by the time he was on the pont.

By the midwife's gate he was nauseated, his head pounding and his leg in agony. "Thank God." The two men made their way down the muddy, rock-strewn path to the farmhouse. There was light at the rear left side of the house. "That way."

The midwife lived in a country house of ancient wattle-and-daub plaster, with wooden beams crossing every which way to hold the structure up. The windows were small and shuttered, facing away from the punishing Channel winds. The door was thick oak, expensive and modern, likely replaced during the Revolution or the Terror, after what he didn't want to think.

"Come," a feminine voice answered when Burton hit the door. Burton pushed it open with his foot, half carrying Duncan in. The room was big and wide, with a cavernous fireplace that had a bubbling copper pot of some stew that smelled delicious. Even through the pain Duncan's stomach growled; he hadn't eaten in a full day. Several hooks hung from the ceiling, dried-grass ribbons holding drying herbs and flowers together.

A strange structure stood near the fire, a thin, waist-high bed. Lisbeth lay on it on her back while a woman worked on her wounds, Cal assisting her.

Duncan blinked. He'd expected a comfortable woman of ample proportions, or a scraggy woman muttering incantations like the witches in *Macbeth.* This woman was lovely. In her forties, she was tall and curvaceous, with dark hair touched with gray in a neat chignon. Her cotton gown fell over gracious hips, feet encased in slippers. Her small nose twitched, as if smelling for changes in her patient. Her lips were lush, her top lip curved up as if she found the world amusing. Wide and brown with thick lashes, her eyes were fixed on Lisbeth as she worked.

Holding Lisbeth's cheek wound together with his fingers while the woman worked on the shoulder injury, Cal indicated a padded wing chair by the fireplace. "Take care, Burton, his back is likely scored all over."

As Burton settled him in, the woman glanced at Duncan. "Your brother needs tincture, Monsieur Stewart, twenty drops in brandy. Mind the time," she added as Cal moved over to a solid table away from the fire. "If I can't tend to him within an hour, dose him again." She smiled at Duncan. "You must be hungry, m'sieur, but I can't take the risk you'll be sick."

"I'll be fine, thank you, madame." He took the glass from Cal and tossed it off.

"If you have any left in your mouth, roll it under your tongue." Tolerant amusement laced her tone. She threw him a wry smile. "I'd offer you a bed, but I doubt you'll take it. Young man" — she indicated Burton — "fetch the footstool in the next room, and bring the pillows. His leg will do better lifted, and warm. Is the wound tied?"

As Burton left the room Duncan asked in hard anxiety, "Will she live?"

The woman frowned. "This wound is deep, and the glass has left dirt inside. But she is young and strong. I'll do what I can."

He sighed and nodded. With his leg up, his body warm, and Lisbeth in honest, skilled, and sensible hands, Duncan's body dictated its need and he was helpless to fight it.

Fontaine, France

He woke with a start in deep night. The woman had peeled back the blanket covering his leg and was cutting his breeches. "This is the best way," she said when he stiffened. "I'll sew up your leg once the ball's been taken out. I can sew your breeches after I've finished your back, but your shirt's torn beyond repair."

Something in that struck him as funny. He tried to laugh, but it was too much hard work. He closed his eyes and let the woman perform her tasks unhindered.

"He needs more tincture, Monsieur Stewart," she said when he hissed in a breath.

Cal brought him the glass again. "Hold it under your tongue, lad. It works faster."

Duncan obeyed, because his leg was afire

again. The knife's point dug deep into his muscle. His head spun. Cal put a stick between his teeth, a seaman's trick to hold in screams.

"Did he complain of pain on the way here, or tell you how deep the ball went?" The woman's voice sounded weary.

"Nary a word." That was Cal.

A final dig into his leg muscle; a harsh growling sound escaped him with the long pull that followed, and a dull metallic *clang* told him the worst was over. He sighed — but then he felt the warm gush of blood, and his head reeled anew.

A cold splash, a sharp sting, and dull, hard pain and the overwhelming smell of herbs and flowers filled his head. Wasn't lavender for headaches . . . ?

A cloth wiped his thigh. Then he felt the short, sharp stings of a needle, over and over. He gritted his teeth, but one groan escaped him, and sweat rolled down his face.

"More tincture," the healer said tersely. "Just put the drops straight into his mouth, and then another full dose with the brandy so he will sleep. You won't have to endure the pain much longer, Monsieur Stewart." The woman's singsong voice was soothing. "I'll work on your back once you're asleep."

Cal removed the stick from his mouth. "Aylsham," Duncan muttered though a clenched jaw.

"Pardonnez-moi?" the woman replied, sounding puzzled. "What does this word mean?"

He'd surely lapse into unconsciousness any moment. "My name . . . is Aylsham."

"*Bonsoir,* Ill-shame . . . it is a pleasure to meet you. My name is Clare. I have said something amusing?" she demanded as Cal chuckled, and Duncan seethed in silence.

"Not at all," Cal said. "My brother's making little sense right now, I fear."

Clare said, "He has had a hard evening and borne much pain with no complaint."

"It's not his way," Burton put in. "Last year he fought for an hour with a knife in his belly. It wasn't that deep, he said, but he left it for the ship's doctor to pull out."

Soft probing at his belly. "Ah, I can see why," she said moments later. "In that position, pulling it out without a doctor's skill might have killed him. Your brother is a sensible man."

His world descended to the pinpricks behind his eyes. He wanted to say, *Stop calling me his brother. I just met him today.* He frowned, blinked, opened his mouth —

"Ah, *non,* he bleeds again. Cal, help me," Clare said tersely. It was the last thing he heard.

CHAPTER 17

The Road to Valery-sur-Somme, France
August 28, 1802 (Afternoon)
The jolting of the coach yanked Lisbeth from
the black shroud enveloping her. Though she
was cushioned on a pillow and wrapped in
blankets, even her lips ached. Her skin had a
hundred needles piercing it. The headache
was like nothing she'd had —

Yes . . . it was like the first day she'd awoken
in France. Alain had drugged her when she'd
tried to leave him and run to Grand-mère.

She struggled to sit up. If — what if Alain —

"Rest, madame," said a soothing feminine
voice. "You are safe, with friends."

Her mouth and throat felt rubbed by sand,
but in her mind things clicked into place. The
strange woman was shielding her from the
worst jerking of the coach with her arms and
— yes — her bosom; that was the pillow.
"What . . . happened to me?"

"First you need this drink — no, don't try
to sit up, it will make the pain worse."

Lisbeth pushed herself away and learned the truth of the woman's words. Painful nausea; she almost threw up all over her. Aching to take it, she croaked, "No. I won't take your laudanum."

A masculine voice came from the other side of the coach. "I know Andrew and Leo. I also know your friend, the man you call Gaston Borchonne, or perhaps you know him as Tidewater."

The French was delivered in the lilting accent of the Scot. When she didn't open her mouth, the man kept speaking. "Lass, look at me. We've never met, but I can prove your friend trusts me."

In the uncertain light of the curtained vehicle and another light source — was it a lantern? — she saw only a blur. Blinking, she saw an outline that crystallized into a bulky — no, there were two men — two heads —

Two almost identical heads. Two men with harsh-featured faces, dark hair, full lips, and dimples in their chins. One face belonged to the speaker; one was the pale, scarred face of her stranger . . . Duncan, if that was really his name. He was sleeping, his head on the Scot's shoulder.

It seemed everyone was unfamiliar in this coach. But in the past year she'd learned strangers could be kinder than people she thought she knew.

The Scot watched her. Like her stranger,

his smile didn't touch his wounded eyes. There were slight differences — the Scot had no scars on his face. He was darker, his cheekbones harder, and his nose more classic — but the resemblance was too strong to deny. "Aye, Duncan's my brother — my half brother, you English would say. My current assignment is to help him, but when Leo and Andrew discovered I was coming here, they asked me to watch out for you. I've been doing that for weeks now, but wasn't in any position to take you or the child out of Abbeville. I had to wait for Duncan."

In those damaged eyes, she read truth. How odd. She'd supposed her stranger to be alone.

It seemed he read her other, unspoken question. "I became friendly with Leo in particular over a shared liking for euchre, when we were in Neuchâtel. He spoke of you often — they both did. Lizzy the little rebel, they called you. Said you even named your horse Rebel."

That he knew her nickname, even the name of her horse, soothed her suspicions. Too exhausted to speak, she opened her mouth.

"Take care," the woman said. Moments later, water dribbled down her tongue, and she reveled in the wetness in her mouth and throat. She tasted slight bitterness and closed her mouth.

"Tell her what is in it," the woman said. "She has no reason to trust me."

"It's not bad, lass, I promise you. The drops in the water are herbs for pain, and to help you sleep," the Scot said over the loud rumbling of the coach. "Duncan took it willingly when he woke up. Before long you'll be anxious to take it, but it will take longer to dim the pain."

Duncan. Is it his real name, then? But the drumming on her skull grew insistent; the sharp pains on her face, arm, and shoulder added to the jagged orchestra.

Duncan slept on the Scot's shoulder, indicating trust.

She opened her mouth again and took as much of the laced water as the woman would give her. Eventually her eyes closed again, returning to the welcoming blanket of oblivion.

When Duncan awoke, he was resting against the squabs. The coach door stood open, showing a vista of rivulets and scummy ponds twining through marshy land to the sea. It was late afternoon. The sun was low in the sky, throwing a metallic light on the churning ocean. Thick leaden clouds flew on wings behind, a storm anxious to show its power.

Men rushed around his biggest rowboats. Cal was barking orders, which everyone obeyed without question. Duncan's men were setting up makeshift beds between the boats' benches with spare oars and blankets.

Too tired to take command, he turned his head. On the opposing squabs, Lisbeth's head lay on the healer's breast. What showed of her face around the bandages was porcelain white, her lips pale. Her half-unbound hair tumbled over her shoulder but didn't disguise the wad of padding beneath. Her arm was under the blankets.

The woman saw his glance. "We had to leave my house. A neighbor came around, one I do not trust. But your lady has made it so far. I think she will recover."

He let out a breath of relief and smiled a little. "Thank you, madame."

"You're in pain." In the light of day, she was still beautiful, in the calm, ancient manner of a woman familiar with suffering. "Your brother has everything in hand. Makeshift beds are in place for your lady and yourself on the rowboats. Take this if you wish to make the night tide, Monsieur Stewart."

Considering she'd been awake over a day treating himself and Lisbeth, the woman's serenity was remarkable. He took the medicine without argument, thanking her.

"I shall visit Valery-sur-Somme in the coach, procuring herbs. This is why I hired the coach. A broken coach wheel lies on the road to Valery to explain my late arrival and decision to stay the night."

It was a good plan. Unable to think of

anything to change he said, "The name Stewart . . ."

The woman seemed to understand. "The Bonnie Prince and his cousins left behind many children with his name who never returned to Scotland. It's safe to use the name here."

Unsure how to answer, his gaze drifted back to Lisbeth.

Again the woman said, "Your lady will recover. She has survived the rowboat, the sewing I performed, and this coach ride, which says much for her constitution, and her courage."

She's not my lady. It was too much to explain. He was just glad she was alive.

"Your brother has the tinctures you'll need, including lavender to prevent infection in your wounds. I advise you to take everything as required, monsieur. The sooner you recover, the sooner you can take command of your ship."

"My sincere thanks for all you've done," he said, finding his voice at last.

"I'll have herbs to last the winter, and my cellar will be full of vegetables." She grinned, and that mature loveliness sprang to life. "Your brother has been generous with your purse."

"I'm certain he has been, madame . . . and you deserve it all and more."

"I'd have done the same without payment,

monsieur. I know of this poor girl — and her husband. I've treated some of his victims." As Clare looked at the girl, Duncan saw Lisbeth through the older woman's eyes: delicate porcelain, ready to shatter with a touch. When had she last had a good meal or been able to just rest through the night without fear?

"Delacorte's father was loved in Abbeville. He would be distressed to see his son's fall." A curious heaviness rested in her eyes: the ageless grief of the Madonna portraits. "Do not let him raise her child, monsieur. I've seen his descent since his father went to the guillotine."

He didn't know what to say, what promises to make.

Suddenly he remembered his contempt when Alec told him the Stewarts had tried to rescue him from Annersley's clutches. For the first time he realized the sheer enormity of what he'd expected the Stewarts to do — to steal a little boy in a medieval stronghold filled with servants. His men had it tough enough retrieving Lisbeth's son from a much smaller place.

Clare peered out the door. "If she wakes on the journey to the ship, dose her with this tincture. Do you have a nailed-down bed in your quarters?"

Fighting an urge to apologize, he shook his head.

She frowned. "Ask your sailors to nail down some high-backed chairs either side of the hammock, wedging it tightly, and cover her with blankets tucked between for extra tightness and weight. You and she both must be as still as possible for at least a week."

Cal stepped halfway into the coach and put his arms out for Lisbeth. "I've already given your orders. Don't worry so, Clare . . . uh, Madame Faîchot."

There were definite undercurrents in that verbal fumble. Flicking a glance from one to the other, Duncan knew where Cal had spent his lonelier nights during the past few months.

After Lisbeth was in his arms Cal said, "Burton will help you to the launch, lad. I'll get the lass settled on the ship." He stepped down to the ground, cradling Lisbeth in his arms like a newborn babe. "I'll join your men in Eaucourt while you take her home. Tell her the boy will be with her in England as soon as I can rescue him. I wouldn't leave a dog with Delacorte and his poor mother."

Duncan nodded. There was no point in telling him Lisbeth wasn't going home yet. "My thanks, Cal — and from Lisbeth, if she knew."

Lisbeth hasn't agreed, the voice of his long-dormant conscience nagged. *But she will,* the agent answered himself. *She'll have her child. Whether she hates me or not doesn't matter.*

"No need to thank me, lad," Cal said

crisply, as he bore his burden toward the launch. "It's the Black Stewart way. You'll learn in time."

Duncan fought the urge to growl. What was the point? No doubt Cal was like his twin in the deafness that overtook Alec whenever Duncan said something he didn't want to hear.

With Clare's hands at his back, he hobbled down the stairs. Leaning heavily on Burton, he made it to the launch without breaking open his wound. He hoped to God Lisbeth made it, too, or the mission would end in disaster. Everything was in place except her.

He had to force the issue now.

CHAPTER 18

Rue Saint-Nicaise, Paris
August 28, 1802

Camelford had known that woman was trouble from the moment he'd seen her in Duchess Gordon's house in Faubourg Saint-Honoré yesterday. He'd tipped the footman well to let him listen outside the door for a few minutes. It had been enough. The Recamier woman worked for dear Cousin Will, who had set up the Alien Office back in '93.

He'd been following the Recamier woman since she'd left the Gordon house yesterday. By now he was certain she knew it and was leading him a merry dance across Paris, shopping, meeting friends, riding in the park. He was even more sure that the meeting she'd had with Will's precious Alien Office agents had already taken place under his nose.

No chance of blackmailing her for information, then. He didn't let it worry him. He'd find a way. He always did.

Crossing another bridge, they were in the

rue Saint-Nicaise, by the Tuileries Palace — the seat of Boney's power. In dangerous waters now since he'd been deported in April and told not to return to France, with posters of his memorable face to prove it. He felt no concern. He knew his worth, what he could do, the lines he could cross with impunity. They turned into the side alley, the rue de Malte, cramped and dark, with buildings overhanging the cobbled alley like a threat. This was where fifty or more people had died two years ago: the infamous Christmas Eve assassination attempt. More power to whoever did it. It was a shame they hadn't killed Boney and his trash wife along with the guttersnipes who played in the street late at night.

Halfway down, Madame Recamier turned. "I believe we've played this game long enough, Lord Camelford. What is it you want of me, and why should I give it to you?"

Camelford grinned down at that exquisite but lowborn face, unmoved by anything but amusement. She played the French noble lady very well, but like an ape taught to imitate its betters, he sensed something just a little off in the performance. He drew her to the side of the alley beneath a sagging old extension of a medieval row house. "Have you informed my cousin as to my current whereabouts yet?"

She nodded, smiling. "Is there anything else

you need to know?"

She didn't seem in the least intimidated by him — a novel experience. Since it was obvious by his continued freedom, he asked, "Why hasn't he given orders to take me?"

A simple Gallic shrug. She must have been in France some time, then. She knew why Will hadn't had him taken, but she wasn't about to tell him. The air around this woman shimmered with well-honed talent. Whoever she was, this Incomparable, she had Will's confidence — and that was hard to obtain. He had proof of that.

Hiding his irritation, he asked, "Where have you hidden the real Madame Recamier? Or did you marry the poor fool for protection? Does he believe you're a real lady, or does he look the other way for gold?"

The shot went wide of his intended mark. She merely smiled.

Ah, this woman would be a small challenge. She'd won the first round and was pushing her power today; but breeding always won out in the end. Without warning, he murmured, "Have you yet discovered what day the Corsican will be in Boulogne-sur-Mer?"

Again, he was disappointed by the simple shrug and smile. "I have no interest in it, Lord Camelford. My work is here in Paris."

"Liar," he returned, wanting to strangle the pretty whore. "I know who you are — Sylvie. I saw papers in my cousin's study."

The pretty bitch laughed, waved, and walked away, with no fear that he'd follow or hurt her. Caring not the snap of her fingers for his threats.

Why that convinced him to leave her alone, he didn't know.

He turned, left the rue de Malte and went out of the rue Saint-Nicaise to the rue Saint-Honoré, straight and wide, where he hailed a hackney. "Rue de Miromesnil, Faubourg Saint-Honoré," he snapped, after he'd wiped the dirty seat with his handkerchief.

He'd get the information he needed, one way or another. Lady Georgiana, so new to Cousin Will's game, would be easier to pump. He needed the date, and he needed it now.

Fontaine, France
August 31, 1802

In the glimmering mist of a river valley sunset, Clare alighted from the coach at the crossroads halfway up the hill above her house and asked the driver to leave everything outside the door.

Only when he'd gone did she open the door of the farmhouse nestled deep in the valley.

She'd sent Cal to Eaucourt to meet his brother's men. Unlike the child, she could look after herself, she'd said — and Delacorte wouldn't be coming this way until he'd healed.

The truth was simpler. She *knew* an injured, furious Delacorte would be here and would kill Cal the moment he walked in. If Cal died, his brothers would start a private war of vengeance; and if the Stewarts lost, the English girl's son would grow up to become a monster.

Or maybe, like her child, he wouldn't grow up at all.

She'd lived, loved, lost a child, made mistakes. Lisbeth's son deserved the same rights.

There was no sign of light in the wattle-and-daub house built by her ancestors; all was silent. After bringing in her packages, she closed the kitchen door. A slight rustling sounded.

She lit the lantern on the wide, polished mantel and opened the wick for more light. Then she turned to look at the man standing behind the door. "*Bonsoir,* Monsieur Delacorte."

In reply he gave her a blinding smile. "Clare, *ma chère,* must we be so formal?"

He must be desperate for information, if he was playing the angel with her. "Alain," she conceded in a reluctant way, as if he had the power to hurt her. He liked that — and he never understood why he lost that power so easily with his lovers.

Five years ago she'd thought herself in love. Then he'd lost patience with her canary's twittering and broke its neck. Sickened, she'd ended it; but when he saw she'd lost her blinders about him, he'd beaten her until he'd taken their unborn daughter's life.

"I hope you haven't been waiting long," she said now.

"Long enough." Bright eyes touched with turbulent clouds. "May I sit?"

Cal had told her that he'd shot Delacorte in the leg. "Of course."

"I have no desire to crick my neck looking up at you." He waved a hand at a second chair as if it was his permission to give. He fell into the chair, slow and awkward.

She'd better tread with caution. A poor loser with a propensity for hurting others made a formidable enemy.

"You've been away overnight. So many purchases?"

She smiled at the sacks she'd brought in. "I needed these things for women in travail."

His brows lifted. "*Ma chère,* whom did you treat to gain so much coin? Who accompanied you in the coach, and where did you take them?"

Her gaze lifted to his. He wasn't even taking the time to play with her, to make her afraid. He truly was desperate. "An injured Jacobin. There was some kind of confrontation with the gendarmes three days ago. It took so many medicines to save him, I needed to replenish. He was from Valery, so I accompanied him and stayed the night."

He smiled. "Madame Fournier told me she

heard many voices in the coach — including a woman speaking in English. A woman who I hear has a strong resemblance to my wife."

Expecting something of this kind, she made no answer. Delacorte's wife had cried out in English when the jolting of the coach hurt her — but her neighbors couldn't possibly have heard it from the road. Nor could they have seen the girl, bundled up as she was in a blanket.

One of Cal's brother's men was in Delacorte's pay . . . or worse, a French patriot. That kind — like Alain — betrayed and killed their fellow man without the slightest twinge of conscience. They believed in whatever cause they had with the same fervor as the old Inquisitors.

Alain was using her neighbors' coveting of her land to protect the man.

Clare knew from that moment. Alain couldn't afford to let her live — but then, she'd known he'd kill her as soon as he found out she'd saved his wife and his enemy.

"Did you see the Reynard trap passing you as you headed for Valery? Farmer Reynard saw you with two dark men and a blond young woman," Delacorte said. "Who were they, *ma chère*? Did they give you their names, or did you not need to ask?"

He wasn't approaching the point slowly as he always had before, enjoying the cat-and-mouse chase. He'd betrayed Fouché; he must be frantic to clean the mess he'd made, to rid himself of everyone who could tell the truth. He'd have to start running, and soon.

Her head was jerked back by her hair. "You've been thinking too long."

When had he risen from the chair? How had he moved so fast?

Alain was smiling down at her, almost fondly. "*Oui,* I fooled you with an exaggerated show of my injury. Your friend didn't hurt me as much as he'd hoped." He sighed. "It's a shame. I quite liked you, if not your stupid canary." The touch of cold on her neck was too rounded to be a knife. A pistol. "Tell me where they went, the people who traveled with you, if you don't want your head left in pieces around the room."

Two Hours Later

Delacorte was too intent on torturing Clare to notice the shadow at the kitchen window.

A glance told Cal it was too late to save her. She had dozens of cuts to her face and body, two black eyes and a broken nose. Her hair was hacked off on one side, her dress in shreds. God alone knew what else he'd done to her before making the cuts — and there was a deep puncture wound in her belly. Unlike Fouché, who was devoted to his ugly wife, Delacorte enjoyed inflicting pain on women who'd once loved him.

Clare lifted her head. Cal drew back before

Delacorte's gaze followed hers, but she mouthed one word. *Please.*

He'd seen the same look in Rose's eyes when he'd begged her to live. Sweat trickled down his face; his muscles ached and his stomach cramped.

She screamed, and Cal's eyes snapped open. Delacorte had sliced her stomach. He asked another question. Cut her belly farther open until her innards spilled out. Though her eyes were shut, her mouth moved. *Please.*

Forgive me for making you wait, Clare. Forgive me for leaving you in the first place. He lifted his pistol, pressed it against the glass, took careful aim, and shot her in the heart.

Clare died before the glass shards cut into her face — and Delacorte turned in time for shattered glass to rain over his face and arms. As the dirty bastard screamed, Cal fired another shot, this time at his other leg, in the knee. Delacorte fell to the ground, clutching his leg and holding his face, which had several deep cuts. From now on, he wouldn't be so pretty. Nor would he be chasing Duncan's lass for weeks to come . . . if he lived.

By God, Cal wanted nothing more than to kill him — but his orders had been reinforced by both Zephyr and Pitt himself. *We've learned he's a go-between in the war between Bonaparte and Fouché — and he has vital knowledge. He doesn't die until we know what it is.*

He could do it now, get the information through the same kind of pain the bastard had just inflicted on Clare — but that could put Duncan's mission in jeopardy through their resemblance. Both he and Duncan had been seen with Clare. Remaining hidden for now meant the finger of blame for the shooting would likely fall on the Jacobins, or the gendarmes — but the days of the Stewart brothers giving each other an alibi were over.

Cal hoped the knee injury turned septic and poisoned Delacorte, except that dying of wound fever wasn't enough. If ever a man deserved to be hanged, shot, beheaded — all three would be better, with his head left on a bloody pike — but Delacorte didn't deserve such a quick death.

Shaking, Cal turned away. "One day, I'll kill you."

Norfolk, England
September 2, 1802
In the light of the blazing fire, Sir Edward Sunderland held his wife's hand. "You look lovely today, Caroline."

Caroline's face lit with a ghost of her crooked half smile. "Thank you, Edward."

Was it a lie, when she looked as lovely as a memory lost in a pale winter morning, a flower wilting in unending frost? The wasting disease was inexorable, stealing piece by piece the crooked beauty he'd loved for thirty-five years. The profusion of hothouse flowers in the room and the lavender water sprinkled over the cushions and bedding didn't stifle the faint scent of decay.

He'd taken her to the best doctors in Harley Street, but nothing any of them tried had reversed it. "It's in the bones, Sir Edward. It's just a matter of months."

Caroline saw him thinking again. Her smile faded, and with her fair skin and white hair, she was almost lost in the pillows. "You didn't write to her, did you, or tell Duncan." It wasn't a question. She knew.

He couldn't look into his wife's face and lie as he always had before, not when every word they spoke could be the last. "No," he said hoarsely.

Her hand trembled in his before she tried to squeeze his fingers. Tried and failed, just bent them over his. "Please, Edward. Please."

For nearly forty years the King's Man had put king and country before life, love, and family. When Delacorte outwitted him, he'd even sacrificed his only daughter to keep the country safe. But looking into Caroline's eyes, he knew that Lizzy hadn't been the only one to pay the price. Lizzy's ghost was killing Caroline with her loss.

"Leo and Andrew are coming tomorrow with Marian and Rachel," he said in a bright voice — but though Leo and Andrew visited regularly with their new wives, they could hardly bear looking at the ruin their mother had become.

Her eyes closed. Tears trickled from the outer corners. Her hand went limp in his. "I'm tired now."

Caroline's dying, and I refuse her the only thing she's asked of me in years. What sort of husband am I? What kind of father, to leave my child in France unprotected?

Again the temptation ate at him to bring Lizzy back. Again he saw thousands of innocent faces, and his wife's dear face struggled to be seen in the crowd of soldiers and sailors who'd die. Wives and children left destitute by war. How could he choose a few days of happiness for his wife, balanced against the wives, mothers, and children who'd lose much more? Lizzy had made her choice. It was too much to ask tens of soldiers to go and retrieve her, to allow their wives and children to suffer. At least Duncan had no one to mourn his loss —

Good God, what sort of man have I become, to sacrifice the lad who's like a son to me?

All he knew was that he couldn't go to France. If Lizzy's loss was killing Caroline, his wife's loss was killing him in turn. Why had he never realized how much he loved Caroline until he knew he was going to lose her? Why was it only now he sacrificed everything to be with her?

It was glorious retribution, looking at the wraith his wife had become. He no longer knew if Caroline accepted his higher calling, or believed he too had made sacrifices. He didn't even know if Caroline still loved him. For years, all Caroline wanted was for him to be home; but since Lizzy had gone, all she'd wanted was for him to go. Since Caroline became sick, all she'd wanted was for him to take himself, his love, and his guilt off to perdition elsewhere.

Damn it, Lizzy, if you hadn't scarpered off with that piece of French trash —

When he reached the door, Caroline said in a weary voice, "Stop it, Edward. Alain Delacorte is as well born as you or I, and I knew I was ill before Lizzy left."

A knife twisted in his guts. Another fact the brilliant King's Man hadn't known about his own family. "Why didn't you tell me?"

"You didn't want to know," she whispered. "You never wanted to know."

The old brass doorknob was suddenly fascinating. He couldn't look away from it.

"You'll need her when I'm gone. If you don't tell her now, she won't forgive you."

He didn't know how to answer. The daughter he barely knew had become the invisible barrier between them. Lizzy the charming rebel, daring and self-willed, always refusing to become a lady; a fearless, honest girl, too damned clever for her own good. But Caroline adored her, and his wife had no one else. The boys overindulged and petted Lizzy when they were home, so it was up to him to punish her in some half-cocked manner on the rare occasions he was home, seeing she was becoming spoiled.

Well, Lizzy had turned out to be her father's daughter, and no mistake. Despite numerous beatings, she'd refused Delacorte's demands to return home to spy on her family. No matter how Delacorte abused her, her loyalty held true.

But Duncan's letter of yester eve had truly shocked him.

Her baby taken from her, working as a damned tavern wench, attacked and set up for murder, and still she'd found an escape tunnel and outwitted the notoriously paranoid Jacobins. Leo and Andrew were loyal and solid operatives — but it had to be Lizzy who'd inherited his talent for espionage, coupled with her own reckless courage and unpredictable brilliance; and because she was a woman, she was suffering for it.

Why couldn't she have stayed home, married well, and remained safe, like her mother? All the pain and trouble she'd caused . . .

He sprawled on his favored chair in his library, mouth-breathing in the first sip of his fine brandy purloined from France during his last mission. A scratch at the door; his

227

butler Conway came in, bearing the customary silver salver. "A note has come from France, Sir Edward."

He stood, holding out his hand. "Give it to me."

The note was short.

For God's sake, Eddie, tell me if Lady Sunderland is seriously ill. I'm currently anchored by Portsmouth but must return to France. I can put Lisbeth to port for you to collect her. I need a young, pretty woman of her strength and intelligence for my mission, but she's badly injured, as yesterday's missive informed you. I'm waiting on your order. If I don't hear by return post within three days, I'll take it as permission to make use of her.

His stomach clamped. He hurt from his eyeballs to his toenails. Little Lizzy . . .

When had he moved? He felt his face heat to burning point, watching the letter curl and shrivel in the heart of the fire before he realized he was leaning on the mantel.

CHAPTER 19

The English Channel
September 3, 1802

Lisbeth woke in the middle of a dry retch.

The cabin was warm and airless. She longed to get up, run outside, and just breathe; but every time she tried to get out of the hammock the ship rolled, pain ripped through her body, and she fell back, defeated. Every so often in the past few hours — or days, she didn't know — someone had dribbled a small amount of fluid down her throat, fed her soup, or helped her to the water closet before she fell asleep again.

But now it was air she needed, craved, and —

"Ah, you're awake."

She frowned with the sense of the unfamiliar, until she realized it was because he'd spoken English. It had been so long since she'd heard her native tongue. After a moment she murmured, "Scottish man . . . said he was your brother."

"Yes, he did." Three stark words, no confirmation, no denial.

Ah, the keeping of secrets, that at least was familiar. He'd become the stranger once more, obviously for some purpose.

She turned her head. He was lying in a hammock beside her — but clad in the stark, neat clothing of the naval officer, his hair pulled back in a riband, he'd taken on yet another persona. Who was he now? Did he have yet another name to give her?

She swallowed. "I need, um . . ."

"Of course, but we have only a chamber pot in a rigged water closet. I'm sorry for the discomfort." As he swung out of the hammock the ship rolled. He staggered, gripping the chair.

To her surprise, it didn't tip over, or even move. She tried to peer over the edge of her hammock, but pain tore through her, and she fell back with a gasp.

"Move very carefully at all times, madame. Your left arm's strapped to your body. Your shoulder must remain immobile until the wound heals. You're recovering from wound fever."

Refusing defeat, she turned her head until the discomfort bordered on pain. She saw two chairs on either side of his hammock, still even with the ship's rolling. "Why are the chairs nailed to the floor?"

"We need to be still until our wounds heal,

and the ship's surgeon can cut the stitches." As he stepped toward her, he picked up a cane from the nailed-down chair.

She frowned, trying to think. "What happened? I remember the tunnel . . . the Jacobins . . ."

"Delacorte shot the window in a boathouse where you were being held. You were injured by broken glass. You've been very sick the past week." He put the cane down on one of the chairs. "Stay on my left side."

Absently she lifted her good arm as she absorbed what he'd said. "Is he still chasing us?"

"Thanks to Cal — the Scot — he'll also be abed a few days yet, I suspect." He swung her from the hammock, but he winced.

The ship pitched again, and he leaned hard against the nailed-in chair, his legs splayed. His brow broke into a sweat as he held her still. "Don't move, madame. If we fall, we could both return to where we were the other day."

She stilled against him. Through her pain, she became aware of other things . . . his heart pounding against her undamaged arm, the warmth of his skin against her shoulder. Uncomfortable with it, she moved away a little. "How did we get onto this ship? Who owns it?"

The motion of the ship steadied. He settled her on his arm and turned her, leaning on his cane. "Do you think you can walk to the corner of the room?"

He'd called her madame. It seemed they were back to the beginning. "I'd better. I doubt you could carry me."

He chuckled in reply to her little joke. "True, but I have stout sailors at my command."

Even through a throbbing head, her brows lifted. "So it's your ship? Are you a captain?"

A bell sounded, deep like an echo off a cliff. "It's the ship's bell," he said with a smile when she started. "It chimes on the hour and half hour. I can call for food, if you're hungry?"

"Yes, I am — for food, and some truth at last," she snapped, too overcome to think of tact.

With a glimmering smile, he kicked the door with his undamaged foot. "Food for the lady to be brought here, West," he told the burly sailor. "Return as soon as possible."

"Aye, Commander." The man strode down the small passage.

He shut the door with his cane. "The Royal Navy owns the ship, but it's unlisted. It's a captured French frigate, commandeered for the use of the British Alien Office. I command it, but you won't find my name on the commanders' lists." He grinned. "And all of that was true."

He didn't offer her his name to begin a

search, but he'd answered the question nonetheless. "How did we get on board?"

When he answered, it was with a struggle. "I thought your middle name was Patricia. Persistence would be more appropriate."

"So I've heard." She kept her brows lifted, waiting.

At last he said, "Cal found my rowboat with my men waiting for me. He took us to a midwife, and then in a coach to the ship."

He wasn't telling the whole truth, but she wasn't up to arguing. "The Scot is a resourceful man. Is he here? I would thank him."

"No." He stopped at a corner of the cabin, before a curtained space. "The chamber pot is in there. I'll wait here."

It was stupid to be anxious about his proximity, when his first sight of her had been far more intimate. No doubt he'd been the one to help her to the privy the past few days in any case. He must have held her as she'd . . .

God help her, humiliation was her lot where this man was concerned.

She was behind the curtain with a couple of shuffling steps. Her feet were warm. She lifted a foot. Woolen slippers were on her feet, a thin woolen dress covering her. Realizing where they must have come from, she hoped the midwife had been paid well.

She used the facility as fast as possible, praying no wave would knock her flying while her skirts were up. She'd had quite enough of that.

When she emerged from behind the curtain she was shaking, but she'd fulfilled her needs alone and drew fierce pride from that. She'd gain the strength to fend for herself, or die trying.

As he took her arm again, a knock came at the door. "Enter, West!"

The burly sailor set a simple meal of bread, beef broth, butter, and cold-boiled potatoes on the table. Then he stepped over to her and lifted her in his arms. When she gasped, he said, "Beggin' your pardon, miss, but the commander ain't fit for liftin', an' this is the fastest way to get you comfortable. I've been seein' to your needs for days. I have four daughters, miss. One's just about your age, by my reckonin'. Seirian, her name is — me little shinin' star."

The big man was about fifty and spoke in a Welsh accent. "Thank you," she murmured, exhausted and relieved that the commander hadn't been seeing to her more intimate needs.

The sailor smiled, settled her back in the hammock, and saw to cleaning the privy. When he was done, he brought the tray over to her, saluted his commander, and left.

"You need rest."

Her head was slow-spinning again. Her poor brain was probably exhausted from trying to work out who and what this chameleon of a man was. "What should I call you?"

He turned back to her, brows lifted, his expression unreadable. "I told you before."

Somewhere during the past few days she must have lost her final shreds of propriety. "Which one do you mean? In the week or two since we've met, you've been monsieur and Gaston Borchonne, Duncan, and Commander No Name, and that leaves out the endearments. Which would be your current name of choice?"

To her surprise he laughed, lighting up the shadows in his face. "My duty forces me to wear many hats. Choose whichever name suits your mood."

She forced down a most unladylike desire to punch him. How dare he laugh? "The Scot called you Tidewatcher."

"Best you forget you ever heard that." It seemed he'd sensed her exasperation. "In this game we play, anonymity saves not just my own life, but those of many others. I can either indulge your curiosity or protect some of our best agents — including your family. You should be glad of that. Your knowing so little about me protected you with the Jacobins, I dare say."

He was right. Feeling the heat steal across her face, a hated thief of her dignity, she nodded.

"Enjoy your nuncheon, madame. I apologize for the lack of privacy, but the ship isn't large, and there's only one cabin. I can't ask the crew to set up another space for me."

Despite her indignation, she almost smiled at the word *nuncheon,* as if they were in a London drawing room drinking tea and eating sumptuous petits fours. "Of course" — a brief hesitation — "Commander, I understand." At that moment her stomach growled so loud, he must have heard. She ate before she embarrassed herself further.

Between mouthfuls, the hardest words she'd ever spoken came tumbling out. "I can never go back to Abbeville, can I? I — I must leave my son with him . . ." She used the water to gulp down the ball in her throat, pressed her lips together before she made a fool of herself.

The good humor in his eyes vanished. "I made you a promise, madame. You asked where the Scot went. That's your answer."

Despite the starkness of his words, his return to formality — he seemed as uncomfortable with their newfound intimacy as she was — she believed him. "Thank you, Commander."

"I need no thanks. We made a deal."

Uneasy of where the unseen dance would lead her — because she felt him leading her to what he really wanted from her in exchange for her son — she blurted the first thing that came into her head. "Am I going home now?"

A brief pause, an eye blink, no more. "There's a vital mission here. We can't leave yet."

Again she sensed him leading her to the deal, but she couldn't make herself ask her part in it. "I want to stay in France until Edmond's with me, in any case. Is the Scot really your brother? Is Duncan your real name?"

Another hesitation, but he answered. Perhaps he sensed her withdrawing from him. "Yes, he is and no, it isn't."

Curt now, he didn't like these questions. "When he talked to me, he called you Duncan."

He put a blanket over her. "Did he?"

Within two words he'd gone into shadow, his face lost behind a lock of falling hair and momentary gloom caused by a cloud passing the sun. So he'd lied to her when he'd introduced himself in the tunnel. It made it impossible for her to think of him as Duncan. He wanted her to keep her distance? Then she would. Yet anger flooded her at the thought — and she gave in to her urge to challenge him. "Why did you hesitate when I asked you about my mother?"

He started and lost balance, dropping his cane. "Damn it, could you not startle me? I need to recover as well." His free hand massaged his thigh, and he held himself stiffly, his face pale.

Refusing to apologize or back down since it was what he wanted from her, she waved a hand. "I believe the chairs are nailed down, Commander."

He glared at her. In her experience men hated being put on the back foot. She knew better than to antagonize him when he'd shown a moment of being what she suspected was his real self. When he sat — not putting his back against the wood, giving her an answer for where else he'd been hurt — she asked, "Is my mother well?"

"Your mother was well the last time I saw her. Your father made no mention of any illness in his letters to me."

Looking at him closely, she sensed he wasn't lying; but he *was* holding something back. She was ready to argue the point, to ask when and where he'd seen Mama, but his face closed off. Recognizing the look, she saved her argument for when she was strong enough to continue.

When she'd eaten all she could manage, she handed him the tray. He put it back on the table with the little nailed-on sidepieces of wood that stopped it from sliding off, like a larger tray.

The ship rolled again. "I feel sick," she gasped.

"West!" In seconds the burly Welshman was inside. "Take Miss Sunderland up on deck."

Cradling her like a baby, West took her

outside to the deck. On the port side, four chairs had been rigged with blankets to make two deck lounges. He put her down with tender care, laid a blanket over her, smiled, and left.

The hard wind and driving rain of the waves splashing over the hull revived her like a slap. She dragged in lungfuls of icy air until the queasiness settled. "Why am I known as Miss Sunderland here?"

The commander settled beside her in the other chair. "Most of my team knows Delacorte as our enemy. I don't want anyone suspecting you — or making use of you as a scapegoat. We have a double agent on board," he said in an undertone. His face was pale, but there was clear determination in his eyes.

The time had come. She drew in a breath and asked it, for Edmond's sake. "Tell me what it is you want in exchange for my son's rescue."

The words came out hard and fast. "I need you to infiltrate the house of a certain man, live with him as —"

Panic slapped her like the waves against the ship. "No, I won't. I can't."

He said nothing, but the air swirled with disappointment. And fear, sharp as a honed blade. Answering fright clawed at her like talons in the dark. She couldn't do it —

"What man?" she found herself asking, against her will. Damn it, could she never control her curiosity?

"His name is Robert Fulton," he responded, words prepared in advance. So he'd expected her to ask. "He's an American inventor. His inventions could save Britain."

More questions slipped from her mouth. "What inventions, and save Britain from what?"

"Invasion," he said bluntly.

"Again?" she jeered. "Seventeen ninety-eight wasn't enough humiliation for Napoleon?"

"He'd have succeeded then but for foul weather in the Irish Sea," he replied, with a quelling look. "You have no idea how close he came to being Napoleon I of England."

Chastened, she waved a hand. "Go on."

"I tried to enter Boulogne-sur-Mer just before we met." His voice was measured. "The land and sea levels of security surrounding the town beggar belief. One of my men got in with forged papers, but I haven't heard from him in days. He's been compromised at the least, dead at worst. Bonaparte's arriving in seven weeks, and security levels have doubled." He looked around before he leaned in. "The government refuses to recall the army from Egypt or Ireland, or the navy ships from the Caribbean. A spy of rank must take point, discover what's there in time for Britain to recall our ships and set up defenses. We need time to prepare for war."

The whistling wind snatched some of his words from her; she pieced them together by thinking. "How can the American help?"

The look on his face was a warning to lower her voice. Her gaze flicked to the right and left. When she looked back at him, he nodded and, with difficulty, moved his chairs so they were flush against hers. Even leaning so close to her, she had to strain to hear. "Fulton's been working on submersible boats for almost a decade now. If we could use one of them to pass the ships in the harbor unseen, we'll find what the French want to keep hidden."

Through her shivering, she felt excitement stir. Boats that could sail underwater had existed since the time of da Vinci, and even she'd heard of Robert Fulton, the current world's expert. He'd astonished people for years with underwater travel. How wonderful if she could see one of his boats close up! But if she showed too much excitement, the stranger would take advantage of it. "Why not hire one? Aren't most inventors always short of funds?"

He nodded, with a wry smile. "Good thinking, and he is — but we'd need a navigator as well as someone able to work the contraption. I can navigate above water, but beneath . . ."

"Could Fulton teach you the difference and work the submersible for you?"

He grinned wryly. "Ah, there's the rub. He's a firm believer in republicanism. While he approves of French espionage in Britain, he objects to our spying in France. I've tried many times to bring him to our cause, but despite my best efforts to charm him, he doesn't like me."

Forgetting her pain, she chuckled. "I'd give a monkey to have seen you trying to charm a cranky republican — or anyone for that matter."

"Using cant terms, are we? Most unladylike, Miss Sunderland." There was a lurking grin in those haunted eyes. "But you see the weakness in my plan. Charm isn't my *métier.*"

Still smiling, she shook her head. "I was to woo him to the cause?"

He nodded. "You were to become his housekeeper and assistant, to learn as much as you can about these boats."

"Tell the truth," she said, sharply even though she kept her tone low. "No prevarications or lies, if you please."

A long hesitation. "You may like him . . ." He hesitated again and shrugged. "If you do, anything else would be your choice, Lisbeth."

He'd changed tenses in speaking, as if she'd already agreed. It was the first time he'd used her name since the tunnel: another tactic to soften her. It meant that much to England, then. It certainly wasn't personal. Duty drove this man down a blind alley of damnation. "I told you at the beginning, I won't do pillow talk. That will not change."

He almost mumbled his question. "Even if it saves your country — your family — from the rape and pillage Boney wreaked on Parma and Piedmont? Even if it saves your son from being raised by Delacorte?"

She didn't know if she blushed or whitened. "Is that how you justify asking me to ruin my life?"

"I thought you'd done that already." When she turned her gaze out beyond the ship, her hands curled into fists, he jumped in. "I beg your pardon. I shouldn't have said that."

She stared at the wild world beyond the ship, lead-washed sea and turbulent cloud. Her stomach churned as the ship pitched, but the cold, clean air kept it under control. "Why not? I've been called worse."

"Not by me," he said, voice rough with self-condemnation. "I beg your pardon. The troubles in your life — your decisions — have been partly forced on you by others."

She turned to him, searching his face, but he was staring out to sea. "And?"

"I ask nothing of you that I haven't done myself," he said, voice heavy.

She uncurled her fists. "That's immaterial, and you know it. A man can have a dozen lovers at once and the world admires him for it."

"I judge myself. I've hated myself many times."

Flushing, she floundered into silence. This territory felt far too intimate.

At last he went on. "For me, needs must when duty drives — but I can't force you."

Needs must when duty drives. It was a saying she'd never understood until now — until she heard the personal ghosts in the commander's unseen carriage, driving him down a dead-end alleyway filled with self-loathing. But she felt no desire to mock him. It felt too much like looking in a mirror, seeing her cut and battered face there.

"Is there another woman who can perform this task? One who may have done this before?" She winced as her fingers probed the padding over the scar on her cheek.

He kept his gaze on the sea. "Besides you, there's one woman in France who can play the part with any semblance of truth. I don't know her name or nationality. She could be a princess, an actress, or a brothel madam, or a dozen other professions. She's known from London to St. Petersburg as 'The Incomparable.' Her mission in Paris is as crucial as ours — and from what I hear she's older than you, and too . . . sophisticated. Fulton would see through her. He likes . . ."

"Young women." She shivered and pulled the blanket closer over her body. "I promise nothing. He may not like me."

"He will."

"You sound very confident," she remarked, almost accusing.

He shifted on the deck chairs, as if his back hurt. "I have to be. You're all I have."

A little laugh burst from her. "You really don't know how to charm, do you?"

He grinned as he shrugged. Did her scar show up as much as his did when he smiled? But his scars made him look like a Barbary pirate. Red, swollen, her scars made her look plain ugly.

Yet he believed she could do it. *Do it for Edmond,* her heart whispered.

"I can't go like this." She waved at the rough dress, the woolen slippers.

"We're almost at port. If you give me your specifications, I'll find a dressmaker to ensure you're dressed as a lady."

To port? Where were they? She peered over the deck to land, but in this miserable weather, she couldn't recognize a landmark. She fought a longing to ask if she was looking at England. She'd show no weakness until Edmond was safely with her. "I've lost weight."

"I'll bring a woman on board to measure you — but you must promise not to speak to her, or ask where she's from."

It seemed she must learn to control her natural curiosity in some instances, make the best use of it in others. She fiddled with her fingers again. "What if he finds out who I am?"

"He's a gentleman, madame, never fear. He'll ask you to leave, or if he likes you, he may decide to give us a boat."

Oh, how she hated that she needed the reassurance, and she hated more that he knew she needed it. Of course he knew. From the night they met, he'd led her to this moment. The idea of spying in Le Boeuf had never been more than incidental. She was the center of this mission.

More than anything, she hated that she had no choice but to accept if she wanted her son, and to return to England. "I want to write to my mother."

"Certainly, madame. Give any letters you wish to send to me."

Running out of excuses, she repressed the urge to sigh aloud. "Leave me to think," she said coolly, trying to hide the aching in her heart and throat. She'd thought there wasn't a sacrifice she wouldn't make for Edmond, but this —

"Of course." He pushed himself to his feet and limped away. A silent reminder of the sacrifices he'd made to save her.

When he was gone, she grabbed his blanket, and wrapped herself in it to stop the shivers. Even when she'd been in Abbeville, she hadn't felt so cold or alone.

CHAPTER 20

Rue Laboratoire, Ambleteuse, France (Channel Coast)
September 4, 1802

"I might have known you were behind this particular miracle." Pale and mussed, Robert Fulton glared at Duncan. "My gratitude hasn't changed my principles. I won't enhance the British Navy's already indecent power in warfare with my inventions. To protect itself, France needs a weapon capable of counterbalancing your navy."

In the failing light of late afternoon, Duncan stood outside the dark, crooked house, lost in a tangle of wild-growth brambles above a gorged rivulet leading to the sea. Its roof tiles were clunky and its windows too small, but the attic ran the length of the house, the doors were thick, the locks sturdy, and there were no neighbors for a mile — which was why Duncan had paid a year's rent in advance for the house. When First Lieutenant Flynn told him France wanted to seize his inventions, Fulton had pulled out the inner workings of the badly damaged *Nautilus* and destroyed every schematic for good measure. But if Fulton's turbulent relationship with Boney had sunk to a new low, it didn't change his ideals or lessen his prejudice against Britain. "France doesn't need protection from us, Mr. Fulton."

"Oh, certainly. After invading the Americas, New Holland, and the African continent, Asia, and India, imposing British rule, language, and culture on its hapless inhabitants — at least those you allowed to stay alive — Britain fears the struggling little nation across the water," Fulton retorted in a withering tone.

Acknowledging the hypocrisy in silence, Duncan thought, *How many countries has the struggling little nation invaded, raped, and pillaged since declaring itself a republic?*

But it was obvious Fulton was spoiling for a fight. Duncan felt too amused to give one. The inventor's rhetoric engendered a vision of a mouse attacking an elephant. "It seems your presence and your work are unappreciated in France, Mr. Fulton."

Fulton bristled. "That will change."

"Bonaparte isn't known for his capriciousness." Despite having tried to charm him many times before, Duncan didn't care if Fulton hated him. The trouble and cost of moving the American's paraphernalia to this isolated seaside village was less than nothing, if it gained Britain an underwater boat in good working order. "We'll pay to repair *Nautilus*. Your work with the bombs" — he saw Fulton bristle, and amended, "ah, torpedoes and carcasses, will be easier with a fully equipped workshop and several qualified assistants."

Fulton drew himself up. "This house is acceptable, and the five hundred francs I have . . ." He snapped his mouth shut, cheeks burning with awareness of his hypocrisy. The francs, like the relocation costs, had come from Duncan's pocketbook: more than three hundred pounds sterling and far more than many men earned in a lifetime.

Recognizing futility, Duncan shrugged. "Use it wisely, sir. Bonaparte will never have such faith in you."

"He will when I make the propulsion — you won't trick me into speech!" Fulton snapped.

"I wasn't trying to trick you." Good God, these inventors were brilliant, but as paranoid as a prince's aging light o' love when faced with a young, beautiful replacement mistress.

Fulton gazed over Duncan's shoulder. "I will not allow Britain to turn my inventions into death machines."

He almost laughed aloud at the man's willful blindness. "If we don't, Bonaparte will. It's the nature of men."

"Maybe it's the nature of those *you* associate with." Fulton's look burned with disdain. "I won't work in the British Admiralty with the impertinent and imperious always at my shoulder, awaiting an opportunity to turn *my* inventions to *their* profit. France is finally independent of selfish kings and greedy lords and should thus remain. I wish you a good day, sir."

As the funny door with its diamond-carved insets was about to close in his face, Duncan asked, "Is there anything else you need, Mr. Fulton?"

Fulton's head popped around the half-shut door. "One sheet of glass cut onto four circular shapes for the observation dome, to this specification." He shoved a piece of paper into Duncan's hand. "Twelve iron sheets, and twenty strong rivets. Thirty-eight pounds of steel in strips, as high a quality as you can procure. A pair of bellows, and a portable forge in the stables, mounted on an iron cart and on wheels for ease of movement."

He'd had a list ready. Duncan almost laughed at the audacity. "It will be done as soon as may be."

"Also a horse and cart, reasonable size, and a man you trust to help me with transporting a large item. I need the equipage before first light. I want no one to see what I'm transporting. This item is of great value to me." The defiant look told Duncan Fulton wanted him to ask, so he could go on the offensive again — but why bother? Whoever he sent with the transport tomorrow would give him full information.

"I'll arrange it."

Fulton's frustration boiled over. "Do what you will, you will never buy me." The door closed in his face.

Duncan turned on his heel and walked past tangled gorse shrubs that grew wild above the rock-strewn creek leading to the beach. At the end of the path, he headed northwest across the scrubby grass and sand. Aware of the limp that made him more obvious to any observer, he was glad of the swift night falling. In the dark cloak, he was invisible. Unidentifiable.

At a small cove north of Ambleteuse, he boarded the launch. Twelve sailors rowed him back to the black-painted ship, sitting just inside French waters. Firelight and three lamps lit the commander's quarters when he walked in. He reported to his commanding officer without reserve. Burton and Flynn guarded the doors. "It's useless, sir. He won't change allegiances in our lifetime. He believes democracy will work here, and that Bonaparte's another Washington."

"Certainly," William Windham snapped, "and the French Revolution never collapsed on itself and killed its own people by the thousands." The former British minister at war shook his long, thin head in disgust. "Has he any idea of the economic and military mess Britain's in, thanks to nine years of war forced on us by France's enforced spread of republican ideals across the Continent?"

"I think we can include two failed harvests, the House of Lords always voting to attack Ireland to keep their lands intact, and the Prince of Wales's rabid overspending," Duncan said dryly. "In my opinion, Britain could benefit from some of Boney's financial genius and self-restraint." Indeed, Boney had dragged France from four hundred and seventy million francs of crushing debt to a small surplus in under two years: an amazing feat.

"What are you, a bloody Revolutionist? Are you willing to give up *your* future title and lands to the revolutionary rabble?" Zephyr snapped. "Shall we bring over the guillotine while we're at it? Because we'd all be dead within the year, and then the rabble will turn on one another to lift themselves above the rest!"

He ought to have held his tongue. "I beg your pardon, sir." Huge waves were breaking against the ship. Duncan's thigh ached as he struggled to keep balance. If this was any indication, it was going to be one hell of a winter. "In any case, anything Fulton knows is from Boney's rhetoric against us."

"If he believes that hysteria, he probably

thinks Boney wants peace in Europe instead of becoming the next Alexander. Madame de Staël was right: 'He can live only in agitation, and only breathe freely in a volcanic atmosphere.' " Windham put his hands in his hair, remembered he had a wig on, and blew out a sigh. "Boney *thrives* on war."

If he thrives on it, it's odd that he keeps offering the world peace treaties, and it's us, the Austrians, and Russians that keep declaring war on him. This time, Duncan kept his thought to himself. Zephyr was so thoroughly a man of the upper class he saw declaring war on anyone wanting to change the status quo as an act of defense.

After the long walk to the house and back, Duncan's leg was throbbing like the dickens. Holding on to the edge of the desk, he said, "Fulton has two types of underwater boat bombs that have the potential to revolutionize sea battle: the torpedo, which is a sticky bomb; and the carcass, which is a barrel bomb he's attempting to shoot out of something called a propulsion chamber. If Bonaparte seizes them, he'd give them to the Ministries of Science and the Marine. Within months France could devastate our fleet and invade without fear of retaliation. The army at home is a shambles of drunkards and boys. They'd be helpless against this new *Grande Armée* he's assembled."

"Shall we recall the professional soldiers from Egypt and Ireland, allow those nations to be invaded or run rampant, to relieve your fears?" his superior mocked him. "Show them some proof, and the government might do something."

"It's said he has a hundred thousand trained soldiers besides the twenty thousand around Paris and the ten thousand guarding the Channel Coast," Duncan went on, refusing to be baited. "All he needs is the means to get them across the Channel, and Britain's lost."

Windham snapped, "So much for Boney's wanting peace, then! In any case, why do you think I let you relocate Fulton so close to Boulogne, only three miles outside the first posting of guards? If you find evidence that this *bête noire* of yours exists in truth, Fulton might realize Bonaparte's true intentions and turn his coat."

It was Windham's way to belittle and deride, then act decisively when proven wrong, so Duncan stuck to the point. "We need more ships patrolling the Channel, sir."

"There are none to spare. A hundred ships are chasing privateers across the Atlantic, and a score of them are ship prisons on the Thames, or transporting criminals to Sydney Town. Dissidents are gathering arms in Dublin, so Addington's ordered fifty ships westward. The Admiralty only spared us the half-dozen ships we have because Lord Nelson insisted. You can try to interest the Guernsey privateers with promises of booty, but I doubt they'll move without the king's written permission."

Irritably wishing Windham would ask him to sit, Duncan hung on to the edge of his desk. "We must obtain a submersible boat from Fulton, and a navigator. The house and five hundred francs I gave Fulton won't last long. His inventions are expensive to make and repair."

Zephyr slanted him a look of pure derision. "To give him more until he's given allegiance to Britain is absurd."

Duncan kept his mouth shut about the further promises he'd made Fulton.

Frowning, Zephyr fiddled with a quill and the inkpot glued onto the desk. "Addington will refuse to see the French threat until Ireland's safe. He hangs on to that bloody Amiens Treaty like it's made of diamonds instead of barefaced lies." He shrugged. "Keep your team close. Something's foul in the wind, and these ports are too close to Britain."

Beneath the pithy nature and contempt for the mental acuity of his fellow man, Duncan knew he could rely on Windham to support his operatives. "Fulton doesn't like me, sir."

"So send him someone he will like," Windham snapped sotto voce. "He's lacking assistance. You have a shipwright, don't you, and an engineer?"

"I used Flynn to trick him into leaving Le Havre, sir, and Carlsberg, though an excellent engineer, couldn't convince anyone he's French."

His spymaster thought for a minute. "I've heard he likes pretty young things. The sailors were speaking about a girl on board. If she's pretty, and capable of playing a loyal republican, let him play with her. Maybe she'll wiggle a promise out of him in pillow talk."

Though it echoed his plan, Duncan balked like a horse on a high jump. "Fulton seems a moral kind of man, sir. An idealist."

"It doesn't extend to his bed, trust me. Madame Barlow lived with Fulton for two years while he paid her gudgeon of a husband for the privilege. High ideals." He harrumphed, pacing the cabin. "He likes young, married women with complacent husbands — or better yet, absent." He frowned. "It's Eddie Sunderland's girl on your ship, isn't it — the one you were looking for?" Zephyr stopped at the fire, holding his hands out to warm them. "Hmmm. A pretty girl with charm to spare like her mother, married and with a damaged reputation." He slanted Duncan a questioning glance.

Clasped behind his back, Duncan's hands curled into hard fists. It took all his self-control to speak in a cool, disinterested tone.

"She's only nineteen, sir."

"Don't be a muttonhead. Do you want Fulton's boat or not? I told you he likes pretty young things, and more so if there are no fathers about, or any chance of virginal entrapment."

Duncan felt an odd constriction in his throat, knowing what Eddie, Leo, and Andrew would say to that. It would probably destroy poor Caroline. "Lady Sunderland is ill."

"So let Eddie come for the girl," Zephyr retorted. "He's not tied and gagged in Norfolk."

Since it was an echo of his own belief, Duncan didn't even try to defend Eddie. "She's twice refused the pillow-talk part of the plan."

"Damn it. She's already ruined — so what's her issue?" After a few moments, Zephyr clicked his fingers. "Chit's after redemption, eh? So give her what any girl of our class must want. Get Eddie's promise of forgiveness, or better yet, get her mother to write, praising her courage. That'll give her incentive."

The echoes of his plan rang in his conscience like a bell tolling. From Zephyr's mouth, it felt like a premonition of disaster.

Having taken Duncan's assent for granted, Zephyr had moved on. "Trouble is, Fulton will suspect anyone coming to him now." He clicked his fingers again. "Damage her."

Only strong self-discipline prevented him from sputtering. "No," he said coldly.

Zephyr sighed. "Cut the beef-witted knight act! She's Delacorte's leftovers, and a bloody tavern wench into the bargain. Fulton will give his toys to Boney to play with if we don't win him. Certainly he's both moral and an idealist, but his Achilles heel is pretty young things. I met the girl two years ago. She's pretty enough, but an impertinent chit, and too clever by half. We have to disarm Fulton before he starts suspecting her. We need her to play the pity card — the bird with a broken wing."

"Her left arm is in a sling, and she has bruising and stitches on her face from a shot-out window. She had a slight case of wound fever. Two men beat her and tried to rape her a month ago. Her husband was brutal to her, and currently men terrify her. Will that be enough, or should I do something more drastic?"

Though he'd kept his tone even, Zephyr chuckled. "Sits the wind in that quarter, Tide-watcher? I'd thought you impervious to women."

"The wind sits nowhere. I owe a life debt to Eddie," Duncan said coldly.

Zephyr shrugged. "Very well, her current damage will do. Fulton's blathered on about compassion for the suffering masses. He'll take her in." He turned his hands back to the fire. "He's a closet snob, you know, like most republicans. If he finds out she's a wealthy baronet's daughter, he'll wed her, hoping Eddie will fund his work. Given her ruin in English society, she's probably best off in America." He threw Duncan another sideways glance. "You can't kill Delacorte until we know whose coat he wears. He's the unknown quantity in all this. If we find out whom he's working for, we may get what they're doing and why. Is that clear?"

"We need not arrange the girl's future." Duncan forced an amused look, but he knew when he was being bear-led. "She may have a say in that."

Zephyr shrugged again. "Is she well enough to go within the week?"

"Ship's doctor wants her to rest for another few days, and she needs training before we can throw her into the mission."

"If the girl's unequal to the task, I'll send another woman. But Boney's conscripting men to this new army. Men are pouring by the thousands in for the food and clothing he gives them, and the pay that helps their families. If you're right about your *bête noire,* or the assassination attempt, someone must be in place at Ambleteuse within a fortnight."

Damn it, Zephyr had boxed him right into this corner, leaving him no choice. "I'm fairly sure she'll agree to infiltrate the house, but I won't force her on bedding Fulton."

Having taken his stance for granted, Windham nodded. "Stay in the region with her, and play Lancelot to the girl's Guinevere if it amuses you. Just make certain she fulfills the objective. Pitt and Grenville have given us carte blanche on this matter. Other teams will be coming in as well, including Smith and Wright with some new agents. We must know what's happening in Boulogne, and get Fulton and his toys on English soil before Boney changes his mind."

So carte blanche meant that spending money on Fulton was absurd, but a young woman's ruin was acceptable? Zephyr's hypocrisy over women tolled like a funerary bell in Duncan's head — but this plan with the girl was all he had. He'd been given leeway to protect her. It was all he could hope for. Keeping his voice neutral, he said, "Consider it done, sir."

Another nod. "The tide's turning. If Boney finds out I've been in French waters, we'll be in the basket and no mistake." Windham strode to the door, staggering as another wave hit the hull. "Your leg's injured. Fool, why didn't you sit?" Before Duncan could answer, Zephyr was gone.

The autumn night was shrouded by a thick, cold sea mist. Duncan made his way up to the deck, watching the other black-painted ship disappear. When night fell, it enveloped their ships until they were invisible. Here he felt anonymous, without name, heart, or conscience — a King's Man — and Britain's safety was paramount, even above loyalty to Eddie, who'd been father and mentor for half a lifetime. Here he could betray his mentor's daughter, the woman he'd once hoped to marry, with only a pang of regret.

CHAPTER 21

The Tuileries, Paris
September 6, 1802

It was almost eight. The first consul would make his appearance at the levee any minute.

Georgy's new gown was a lemon-hued watered silk, high necked and in no way tight, but the material had been dampened so the silk clung to every curve. She felt almost naked, and by the behind-the-fans stares and whispers of her compatriots, they thought she looked it. Her heart was pounding, her breathing rapid. She'd visited the Tuileries for months now, but she'd been an innocent, an ingénue, beneath notice. Her appearance had never been as vital as tonight.

You can do this. For Lizzy.

Fortunately, Mama had been an avid admirer of Napoleon since the Red Sea was said to have parted for him in '97 — but how far would that admiration go? Knowing nothing of her daughter's mission, would the Duchess of Gordon create a scene?

"Isn't it rather ridiculous thinking that I, a girl of nineteen, can help you?" she'd asked when The Incomparable had outlined Georgy's expected mission.

"Nonsense, Lady Georgiana; you're perfect for our current needs, and your station puts you above suspicion." She'd had the cheek to grin. "What could be more natural than a well-known, charming girl like you flirting with Napoleon? Your charm is famed throughout the Polite World, my dear. He would be flattered, intrigued. Only smile if whispers circulate about the two of you, but say nothing. Everyone knows his wife is barren, and he's desperate for an heir. And if you hear any indiscreet whispers, as men tend to do when they're infatuated . . ."

She'd frowned. "What if he suspects me? Or expects more than I am willing to give? How would insulting Napoleon with a refusal help my friend?"

"Why should he suspect you? You're being nonsensical. You're a duke's daughter. He won't expect you to become his paramour." She'd sounded reassuring but with a thread of impatience beneath. "You will never be alone with him. You won't know who our people are, but they'll know you. And your friend's mission is in the most dangerous region of France. Things you discover could help her to evacuate at the right time."

Georgy had blinked and frowned. "I see,"

she'd said, hating to think of Lizzy in such danger — but if Lizzy could do it, so could she. "All of Paris knows that the Viscomte de Beauharnais and I are good friends."

"You are concerned he will be hurt?" The Incomparable had asked, her eyes curiously hollow. "It is most commendable of you."

Georgy opened her mouth and closed it before the words could slip out. *Not hurt — disgusted.* "Lady Josephine is his mother," she'd said quietly.

"Who has been less than faithful to Napoleon, just as he has been to her" was the impatient response. "We are in Paris, where people are practical over such matters."

"But —"

"If you cannot do this, Lady Georgiana, please let me know now. Matters are at such a pass between our nations that we need the information as soon as may be — most especially your friend Elizabeth's team. You are the best candidate, but there are others . . ."

"Are things so bad?" Georgy asked, disturbed more than she'd cared to admit by the woman's simple nod. "But — we are at peace . . ."

"An uneasy peace indeed." The Incomparable was just as quiet and serious. "We know there is a plan afoot sometime in the autumn to assassinate the first consul. If he dies, *le bon Dieu* alone knows who will replace him — probably one of the power-hungry generals who make a fortune in war. Or France could return to a Jacobin rule, which will again cause mayhem throughout Europe. Your friend is part of a team in place near Boulogne-sur-Mer, where the assassination is planned, but we need the date confirmed."

"How will my, ah" — she felt herself blush — "charming the first consul help us?"

"He won't confirm when he goes to the Channel Coast, yet the assassins know. We have to play catch-as-catch-can with men whose allegiance to our cause ought to be unquestioned, but they have found funding elsewhere. As such, their true loyalties are now unknown."

Georgy tried to follow the implications, but for the first time in a sophisticated life, she felt like the innocent she really was. How she wished Papa were here! The Duke of Gordon was, as the saying went, awake on every suit; he'd know how to explain all this to her so she understood. "We need Napoleon to stay alive?"

She felt relieved when she got a nod in reply — but the woman's exquisite face was troubled. "The Austrians and Russians want him dead and replaced by a Bourbon monarch. Prussia and Britain, not to mention Belgium and the Netherlands, cannot afford that. For now at least, while he offers treaties, Napoleon is the best chance of achieving peace in Europe. He has brought harmony and prosperity to France and calmed the masses since he's improved the economy and employment for the average Frenchman. Boys are off the streets and in schools. The guillotine has lost more than half its yearly custom."

"I see . . . I think," she said with the frankness that was her greatest charm. "So my task is to get the date for you."

The Incomparable nodded. "Also, if Madame Bonaparte chooses to adopt you . . . let her."

Political waters already churning turned murky, staining the air around her so Georgy couldn't see. Suddenly she felt not nineteen, but nine. "Why?"

That, it appeared, was where confidence ended. To her credit, The Incomparable didn't murmur platitudes, but told her it was best if she didn't know; and that was the end of the matter. She gave her further information on many other matters political, but not regarding Josephine. The Incomparable had left her at that, telling her to prepare herself to meet the first consul.

So here she was in the Tuileries, a downy duckling flying into a thunderstorm. What if Napoleon —

"Lady Georgiana, I know we haven't yet been introduced . . ."

She gritted her teeth, thinking of Camelford's visit, his demands that she find out the same information the British government wanted: the date of Napoleon's supposed journey to Boulogne-sur-Mer. "I swear, if one more person says that to me this week . . ." She turned her head, ready to cold-shoulder whoever now wanted something from her.

And froze, a ship at half mast. Knowing who this man was before he said it. He was younger, more handsome than her dear friend Francis, but with the undeniable Russell face. Dressed in all the male rigmarole expected at the Tuileries, yet managing to look understated and elegant. She sank into an automatic curtsy. "Your Grace, what a surprise to see you in Paris."

"Please call me John." The sixth Duke of Bedford smiled and bowed, then took her outstretched hand in his. "Your mother came to me at the worst time, deep in grief for Francis. But it seemed my brother knew he was ill. A letter came after his death, asking me to . . . look out for you. So here I am, Lady Georgiana, asking your forgiveness for my former rudeness in not meeting you when your mother asked it. I also extend my friendship, if you wish it."

His smile was warm, but Georgy couldn't smile back. She'd never been so aware of her buckteeth, or so humiliated that her dress was close to indecent. With a look, she forgot he was the new Duke of Bedford. She cared what *John* thought of her. One look at him, and she'd tumbled into love.

The trumpets sounded, and the chamber quieted. The doors flung open, and the man she'd met only in passing came up the steps.

Could the timing be worse? And yet — no; for now she had someone else to fight for, to protect with her mission. Lizzy was on the Channel Coast, and John was here. With a half smile of apology she whispered, "Of course . . . John. But now — I beg your pardon, I have something I must do."

"I know," was the duke's surprising answer. A brief kiss on the back of her hand. "Your mother's approaching, and this is not the time for explanations. I merely wanted to tell you there's no need to look so frightened. You're not alone, Georgiana."

He turned and disappeared into the crowd.

"The First Consul," the guard shouted.

Georgy stared after John's retreating back, everything making sense. What other class of people could gather information from France's new royal family, at the royal palace? Who else would be accepted in a place where Napoleon vetted every servant?

"Georgy, what is Bedford doing here, approaching you without an introduction?" Mama hissed the moment she reached her, her fine eyes alight with ambition.

Mama's hopes for her didn't matter. John

was here for *her,* and it gave her strength. She put a finger to her lips and turned back as the leader of the French people came up the stairs.

Why did Napoleon always appear taller than he was? The melancholy face was pale — too pale for a soldier — yet it was still handsome and strong, with gray eyes, chestnut hair, a wide, intelligent brow, and a half smile, showing everything and giving away nothing. He had no affectations of dress as many men of his status did. No medals adorned his breast, though as Europe's greatest soldier since Charlemagne, he had many; his cravat was the finest quality muslin, but tied in a style of simple elegance beneath a cutaway blue coat and black knee breeches. His hat, of which he seemed fond enough to bring in one hand, was a plain black bicorn with a small tricolor pinned to it. He was slim, almost thin, but didn't pad his stockings as so many did, allowing his broad chest and shoulders to proclaim him a man of standing.

He didn't look like any soldier she'd ever met — he'd fit easily into the intellectual crowd. Yet something about him drew the gaze of every lady in the room. Were their pulses pounding, like hers? But theirs would be from excitement. Hers was from sheer terror that a nineteen-year-old girl had to beckon to herself the greatest personage on the Continent — a famous, married man.

You're not alone, Georgiana.

Napoleon has a lovely smile. She turned a copy of it onto him as he moved down the room toward her, a half smile like his, giving away nothing. She let her dark-gold hair, big eyes, and fine figure speak for themselves.

He never passes a pretty blonde, The Incomparable had said — was it from experience? Like some kind of whirling dervish Napoleon was facing her, taking her breath away as he bowed over her hand, kissing the skin of her knuckles. "Lady Georgiana, is it not?" he asked in French only slightly blurred with the Italian, giving it a warm richness.

Ignoring her mother's silent frustration — she'd have to think up a marvelous excuse to Mama for garnering the first consul's attention when the Duchess of Gordon could not — she curtsied deeply. "It is an honor, my lord Consul, that you know me. Yes, I am Georgiana Gordon." She deliberately left out her title. Though it was said Napoleon liked to mingle with members of the *haut ton,* he didn't like being ranked beneath anyone, particularly a woman. So though she introduced him to Mama, she merely said, "My mother, my lord." Born a mere baronet's daughter, Mama liked advertising her elevated rank of duchess a little too much. Neither did she mention that her friends called her Georgy: a familiarity that might give her away to a man as paranoid and fast thinking as Napoleon. Besides, it was said the famous warrior despised anything he could win without a fight.

Taking her other hand in his, he lifted her back up. Peeping at him, she saw the half smile, those gray eyes crinkled at the corners. "You are a friend of my wife's son, *non*?"

She smiled and nodded. "The viscomte is a charming young man."

The smile on his face grew no larger, but she had the oddest feeling it did. "Then it behooves us to know each other, *oui*? Come dine with us, including your charming mother. Then we shall talk, Georgiana Gordon."

Though he'd said nothing untoward, she trembled inside. Whether it was nerves or a physical reaction to a man who was more a force of nature than human, Georgy didn't know. But after a swift look around — John was there, smiling at her — she allowed the first consul to sweep her along the line of admirers to the double-leaved doors that led to the dining hall.

As they moved, she glanced at Napoleon's wife. Though Josephine was on the arm of a handsome young soldier, her gaze touched Georgy in passing. The pity she saw in the older woman's eyes startled her. A tiny shake of the beautifully coifed head — was it sadness or warning? — and then it was gone.

If Madame Bonaparte chooses to adopt you, let her. Why the command disturbed her so, she couldn't say — but she had the feeling she had, indeed, just been adopted in silence.

Napoleon seated her to his right, beside the great English politician and orator Charles James Fox — a singular honor. Her mother he placed two seats down from his wife, beside the Duke of Bedford. Again John smiled at her before turning his full attention to his dinner partners.

Though she bent all her mystery and charm to winning Napoleon's admiration, she felt an invisible presence hovering behind her, as if she trod violent waters in this thin gown.

"Though I am as much of a proponent of human freedoms as you, only think of the upheaval it would cause in established society, my lord!"

Sitting at the head of a former table of kings, his wife on one side, a duke's daughter on the other, and twenty-eight more notables of France and England filling each side, Bonaparte frowned at Charles Fox. "In England, yes, it would; in France, interracial marriages have caused little concern. Upheaval is good when existing systems only work in favor of certain levels of society, leaving the greater population in need. We must do away with all differences between the inhabitants of the two worlds — of blending the black and white and having universal peace!"

Polite calls of *hear, hear* and scattered applause filled the room, causing Bonaparte's mouth to tip up slightly. A longtime politician, Fox knew when to be silent, but he itched to speak. *Is this what you practice in Haiti, my lord? Is this why the people rebel, and you've sent so many troops there? To reinstate this universal peace you speak of and to assure them of their rights? Or will you, as it's been whispered, reinstitute slavery there to keep peace here?*

This was his third dinner at Bonaparte's generous table. Fox knew that every word of this conversation would be recounted in letters home the next day. Normally soft-spoken, Boney was almost yelling. Most at table had abandoned the pretense of polite chat and were listening avidly. Boney liked an audience, as Fox well knew by now. But what was the little bounder leading to?

"In the East Indies a man may have several wives. It should be so in the West Indies, on account of the variety of persons there. Many women inhabit the isles, and a man needs sons."

After a swift glance at Bonaparte's beautiful, charming Creole wife, barren since her fall from a balcony two years ago, all urge to join in on this witty repartee died. The flush

273

touching her cheeks, the distress hiding inside her calm, smiling eyes made Fox wonder if this topic of conversation was introduced solely to upset her.

A whisper came from down the table, where two or three of his generals sat. *"Le petit caporal se retire avec ce discours. Le petit caporal a peur."*

The little corporal retreats with this speech. The little corporal is afraid.

Damn it, Fox had known those bloody troublemaking generals would push Boney to something from the moment he'd seen them here tonight. They needed the prize money war brought, and none of them appreciated cooling their heels in Paris.

Desperate to put it off, Fox attacked his plate with gusto. "Ah, nobody creates a repast like the French! This chicken is divine, my lord. My cook would never think to add crayfish and eggs to chicken as you have with this Chicken Marengo. My compliments to your chef."

It was useless. Boney's face was suffused with heat and his eyes flashed, and Fox knew he was in for heavy weather. The excellent meal curdled in his stomach.

"So tell me, Monsieur Fox, why is it that your government again threatens my life?"

After a collective gasp, the table fell silent. Every ear bent, waiting for his answer.

Fox fought the urge to swear. Dash it, he was no diplomat! What was he supposed to say in front of thirty witnesses? Carefully, he put down his knife and fork. "My dear Lord Bonaparte, there is not the least ground for this imputation —"

"Ah, bah!" A thudded fist on the table sent glasses and cutlery rattling. "All know the two who plot and plan my murder! Your spymaster William Windham's talents are mediocre at best — he is an unprincipled, unfeeling man with no talents, his position gained through birth and inheritance. The Revolution terrifies him because in an equal world, he would have nothing!"

Bluster and truth in the words, confusing him. "Mr. Windham is above reproach —" But the diplomatic lie stuck in his throat. When the Whigs gained government again —

"It is easy for you who only know public debate. But I detest him, along with that Pitt, who have together attempted my life — both in the rue Saint-Nicaise plot and since then."

Fox only stared, waiting for the rest. Boney watched him narrowly. He had an agenda — or was it the generals who'd pushed him into this accusation? — and there was no point saying more until he knew what was really going on here.

"My lord, if you would but speak with Ambassador Lord Cornwallis . . ."

Bonaparte made a noise of disgust. "A man

who has worked against the liberties of others on three continents, for more than thirty years! What do I want with a man like him?"

With a feeling of impending doom, Fox sat silent. If that was how Boney felt about Cornwallis, what was the man's use here in Paris?

"I would have forgiven open enemies in the Cabinet or in the field." Bonaparte slammed his booted feet on the floor. "Attempts to destroy me through the use of agents, or setting afoot the Infernal Machine on the rue Saint-Nicaise, killing innocent children, is intolerable!"

Fox shuddered. The "Infernal Machine" two years ago had killed and injured many, including seven children. It had sparked international outrage and led Boney on a continuing manhunt for the perpetrators. Two Jacobins had been beheaded; another had apparently fled to America — but the British-made shrapnel and gunpowder would always lead to questions of British involvement. Damned clever of the conspirators to think of that.

Pushing back his chair, Fox walked over to Bonaparte, speaking earnestly. "My lord, I assure you both Mr. Pitt and Mr. Windham — any Englishman — shrinks with horror from the idea of secret assassination, especially one of this disgusting caliber. The deaths of children . . ."

The derisive snorts down at the end of the

table were a masterpiece of disbelief.

"You do not know Pitt, it seems," Boney said coldly, growing haughtier by the moment.

"Yes, I do know him," Fox protested, "and well enough to believe him incapable of such an action. I would risk my head in that belief."

Boney's look was compounded of disbelief and odd pity. So none at the table could hear apart from Gordon's daughter, he murmured, "Know thine enemy, Monsieur Fox — is that not an old English saying? You will never gain the ascendancy in Britain until you realize what your enemies are capable of. Or what I am capable of, should they continue to seek my life." His eyes glittering with challenge, he looked down the table. So did Fox. The three generals tried to look humble and appreciative. To Fox's jaundiced eye, they looked triumphant.

"My lord, I do not pretend to understand these matters." The Duke of Gordon's pretty daughter said humbly, looking at her plate. "It is frightening to think anyone seeks your life after everything you've done for France, and your hard work to bring peace to both our nations. I know I am an ignorant girl, but to my mind, you are a hero beyond this one nation, and anyone who wishes to force war upon us for their own profit must face God on the Judgment Day."

That speech was a bloody masterpiece; but how could a girl know what Boney's generals were about? Fox watched the generals subside to low mutters. Madame Bonaparte clapped her hands once and cried, "Well said, Lady Georgiana! She is so right, my love!"

Even the chit's hard-to-please mother looked proud. The new-arrived Duke of Bedford smiled and nodded . . . and Fox began to wonder what the chit was doing in Paris.

With an abrupt movement Bonaparte waved to the servants, who cleared the table with swift precision and brought out dessert. With a smile, the first consul turned his full attention to Gordon's daughter for the rest of the meal. She made him laugh several times. When the time came for the dancing, he led the girl onto the dance floor, leading her in a boulanger.

After Fox led the lady on his other side into the ballroom, he made his excuses and left the Tuileries, heading to his temporary accommodations. Once there he immediately sat at his writing desk. Whig or Tory be damned. He was an Englishman!

The letter he sent Prime Minister Addington was long, filled with detail. The one he sent his friend Lady Bessborough was salacious, dripping with gossip over the girl who'd gained Boney's capricious interest. His wife got a note of loving reassurance that he'd return soon.

His note to Pitt was short and to the point.

My dear Pitt,

Bonaparte publicly denounced you and Windham as taking part in the rue Saint-Nicaise plot. I protested your innocence, but with his generals deriding me, it was an impossible task. Lady Georgiana Gordon is, I assume, one of yours? She diffused the situation with a few well-chosen words.

Boney will not speak to Cornwallis, who is too blunt a soldier for the task of reassurance. He must be recalled. We need a true diplomat at the embassy in Paris, and quickly.

CHAPTER 22

English Channel, French Waters
September 10, 1802

"See how I do it, miss? Nice and steady as she goes, and hammer it to the right thinness."

In the murky half darkness of the hold, they'd set up a makeshift stone forge. Duncan watched the ship's engineer-blacksmith teaching Lisbeth the basics of the smithy. She must know these things if she hoped to prove to Fulton she'd make an acceptable assistant.

She was alternating these lessons with others in the ship's galley, learning how to cook bread, scones, and stews and make passable tea. If she'd never become a professional cook, she was at least hardworking and adept. She'd picked up the basics of the smithy and shipbuilding with ease. Fulton would believe she'd haunted her mythical father's yard as a child.

Gaining further knowledge of housecleaning would have to come in time, apart from things she could do one-handed within an hour. Duncan insisted that she rest and recover in the afternoons. He fed her when she grew tired, helped her dress and undress each day, had even learned to brush and braid her hair. Sleeping beside her in the next hammock, waking with her every day, helping her bathe and dress, seeing her at her most fragile had turned his resentment into a thing of the past. If the intimacy disturbed his hard-won sexual tranquility, her injuries, her constant blush, and her refusal to look at him told him her dismay would be far harder to overcome. The last thing he needed now was for her to shrink from male interest. She had to be ready for Fulton.

He wasn't the only one to feel the temptation and the protectiveness. Half the crew made excuses each day to watch her, or watch over her, especially West, who'd appointed himself her replacement father and general guard dog against randy sailors while Duncan was on duty.

"What creates the sharp edges?" she asked Jonas Carlsberg, her eyes wide and a half smile on her face. The fire lit her hair to stripes of golden honey. Her fascination with the smithy brought the charm of her unusual face to life. "Do the edges need to be smoother to be useful in battle?"

"Well said, miss." Jonas beamed at her, like she was one of his daughters. "This is . . ."

As they watched, Flynn murmured to Duncan, "She's a quick study, and a hard worker."

"Thank God." She was smiling at Jonas, making the new scar crease her face. It must hurt like the dickens, but she never complained. "We have no time to start over with another woman."

"Reports are that Fulton's frustrated by the lack of help." Flynn kept staring at Lisbeth. "His bomb maker was recalled to the navy. His assistant was offered twice as much as Fulton can pay to join the French Ministry of Science."

Duncan felt his brows lift. "Is Bonaparte forcing him to leave France, you think?"

"More like to go and leave everything behind, sir. He'd have had to do that without your donation." Flynn still watched the girl. Duncan didn't blame him. By day she was pretty enough; but here in the half dark of the hold, in the pink dress the *modiste* in Portsmouth made for her, her cheeks flushed in the heat of the fire and the look of fascination in her slanted eyes showing up in light and shadow, she was a thing of grace and beauty. Even the scar on her face didn't detract from the odd appeal she wore like a careless garment.

Being the first young, pretty woman to join the crew, the male attraction was inevitable; but until now, he wouldn't have believed the career-driven Flynn would join the ranks.

This morning as Duncan had plaited her hair, she'd blurted, "Do the sailors watch me because of the scar on my face? Am I — ? If I'm too ugly for the mission . . ."

Even if she had the face of a baboon, her wistful, unconscious charm would lure men without trying. "They come because we've never had a beautiful woman on board before."

She threw him a withering glance. "Please don't lie to me. I'm no beauty. I never was."

He shrugged. "There are many kinds of beauty, madame." He didn't say more. It would only frighten her to know her delicacy, even her scars, made her very close to beautiful now.

Zephyr's right. The damage and her haunting uncertainty will make Fulton play the knight-errant to her lost waif. Her intelligence and curiosity will reel him in, lure to his fish.

Duncan quashed the guilt and wrongness under his heel. Eddie hadn't returned post, which was as good a permission as he'd get. She'd save thousands of lives with this mission. He'd all but demanded permission from Eddie with his stories of the girl's courage and brilliance.

Flynn interrupted his dark musings. "Why doesn't Boney pay Fulton for the boats and bring him in on the project?"

Duncan grinned. "Because he's the un-crowned king of France. Why pay for what he can have by force?"

Flynn didn't laugh. "Bonaparte won't leave Fulton alone for long, sir, not as soon as he knows of Britain's interest."

"He doesn't know where Fulton is yet. We have some time." Sobered, Duncan shook his head. "October twenty-ninth. She'll have seven weeks to win Fulton over."

Flynn stared at the girl, glowing in the fire's golden heat. "Sir . . ."

Duncan heard the hesitant determination in Flynn's voice and sighed. Being with idealistic people made him feel a hundred years old. "I know."

Flynn's jaw hardened. "Sir . . ."

Wheeling away, he saw Lisbeth notice, glancing at him in the half light of the forge. She was as out of place on his ship as Sèvres porcelain in a rowdy pub. Carlsberg, West, Hazeltine, the sailors — even Flynn — had turned protective. Half the sailors waited for her slightest wish, wanting to be the one to give her what she needed. She was disturbing the crew's focus.

He needed to get her to Fulton, and fast. "Get it off your conscience, Flynn."

The words were a burst dam. "She only talks to you, West, Carlsberg, and the cook. She won't look at another man under the age of fifty, no matter how gentle or respectful we are with her. If anyone gives her something, she bolts as if he's going to rape her. How a frightened rabbit like her is supposed to seduce Fulton is beyond me. It's obvious she's . . . well, she's a lady. If Bonaparte gets wind of her . . . you know how he is with well-born girls, especially blondes. She'd have no chance."

The vision filled Duncan's head. Boney had never pretended fidelity to Madame Bonaparte, but young, highborn blondes were his favored bed warmers. No doubt he'd marry her off to some marshal or general when he was done with her, but Eddie would never have her back. And it'd be a miracle if that marshal or general would allow her to have little Edmond with her. Most men didn't care to have reminders of their wife's past indiscretions.

A mulish set to his face, Flynn said, "Even if she's not ruined by association with Fulton or made the first consul's mistress, the more she knows about Fulton's inventions, the more danger she's in. Both sides will see her as a commodity, not a person. Whoever takes her will keep her in the name of national safety and lock her in some admiral's cage."

"Do you think I don't know, Flynn?" It was everything he hated about the mission. In fact he hated it only less than the thousands that would die in a French invasion of Britain. It was useless for the spy to tell himself Lisbeth knew the risks, because his guilt always retorted, no, she didn't. "Inform the men I'll need the launch before first light. She goes to Fulton tomorrow."

Flynn barely saluted before stalking out — then Hazeltine came running in, chest heaving. "Commander, a semaphore message from Boulogne," he murmured.

Duncan snatched at the note, scanned it in moments, and frowned. He read it twice more. Something about the message wasn't right. "Tell Beauchamp to ready himself for a mission."

In the deepest hour of night, the launch struggled through rolling seas. Not even thirty feet away, the ship had already become invisible. With French patrols crisscrossing these waters every sunrise, they had to be gone in a few hours.

Símon Beauchamp, code name Argenteuil after the town of his birth, felt the urgency in the maintained silence until they were off ship. "You have need of me, Commander?"

The commander handed Símon a slip of paper. "Don't read this until you're alone. Tell no one about its contents, and destroy your instructions as soon as possible."

Símon didn't look around at the other sailors. The implications were clear; there must be a traitor on board, but since he'd been entrusted with this mission, it seemed he wasn't a suspect. "I understand."

The relaxation of the commander's harsh

features signaled the approval Símon had long been trying to earn — and he was determined to fulfill his mission to the best of his ability.

CHAPTER 23

Rue Laboratoire, Ambleteuse, France
September 11, 1802

Though it was but September the day was pea-soup thick, half dark in the early afternoon and getting colder by the moment, surrounding the funny-looking house that was the inventor's current home. She'd been given warm stockings and *pantalon* with the dresses made up for her, but still she shivered. The ship's surgeon told her the blood loss she'd suffered could make her feel a bitter cold where none existed, until her body made up for its lack. He'd ordered her to drink beef broth with every meal, but it didn't seem to make much difference.

Lisbeth pounded on the door with its odd diamond-shaped insets, but her undamaged left hand was too weak to have much effect.

At last thudding sounds came down toward her from the top of the house. Standing out of range, the commander nodded and moved into the gorse bushes on the sandy path.

Crouching like that must hurt his leg.

Turning back, she frowned at the Gothic house with its slanting roof tiles, lost in a tangle of gorse and blackberry brambles. Did Fulton really work here? Was the submarine the British were so desperate to have in this house, or was he working on his bombs?

A man with two kinds of bombs, God knew where in his house, who made products of death for a living, and she was only nineteen. What was she *doing* here? She half turned —

The door jerked open to reveal a dark-haired man wearing a dirty smock over crumpled, dust-covered gentleman's clothing. He was younger than she'd expected, thinner and pale, as if he'd locked himself inside the house for weeks on end. But it was a good face, a kind face.

Shaking, she sketched the submissive curtsy of the domestic servant. "*Bonjour,* m'sieur."

He was looking her over in the same manner. Seeing her arm in a sling, the healing cut on her cheek, the suspicion in his gaze softened. "*Bonjour,* mademoiselle. How may I help you?"

With her second glance at Robert Fulton, she knew the commander hadn't lied. Even if his hair and clothing weren't a crumpled mess, his thin build and spectacles askew, the touch of loneliness hidden deep in his eyes told the story. If ever a man needed a carer and confidante, it was Robert Fulton.

"M'sieur, I hear you seek a housekeeper?"

"How do you know, mademoiselle?" he replied like a sheathed sword, the edge still there, making her gulp. There was no trace of accent in his French. Fulton might need a housekeeper, an assistant, a friend, or — God help her — a woman, but he wasn't a man to underestimate.

"M-Martine Latisse in the Wimereux store told me, m'sieur." Indeed, after a look at her, the owner of the only store in the hamlets of Ambleteuse and Wimereux showed Lisbeth the notice board. Word of her injuries would get about; and since she couldn't help paling and shuddering when Madame Latisse asked about her family, she hoped the town would notify her if — *when* Alain came for her.

Let him come. It gives the commander's men a chance to take Edmond. Thinking of her son, how she missed him — the longest fifteen days of her life — gave her the impetus to keep her gaze on Robert Fulton, eyes wide, a young and anxious girl.

Fulton nodded. "Ah, *certainement.* I did put an advertisement on the board." He glanced over her shoulder again, as if he'd seen a shadow or a movement.

Returning to her, he took in the soft amber redingote and dress she wore. Though the look wasn't sexual, she felt like a butterfly in a net. The outfit flattered her figure, and even with the facial scar and the sling, her youth and blond hair almost painted a target on her. *Fulton likes pretty young things.*

In the end, the sling and bruises, or the pitiful sack holding her luggage, commanded his compassion. "You're unwell, mademoiselle?"

This was the critical moment — but instinct told her that to solicit his pity at first meeting would be too much for Fulton to swallow. *Fulton doesn't like me,* the commander had said.

"I am Madame Elise Dupont," she mumbled, going for a half truth. "I can tell you no more about where I'm from, m'sieur, except that I'll never go back."

Fulton released his grip on the door. "My name is Robert . . . Monteaux. Pray, come in, sit down, Madame Dupont." He led the way inside to a small parlor, cold and dark without a fire lit, and waved her to a chair. "Might I say you do not seem old enough to have been married?"

And to have left your husband. The curiosity hovered in the air, unspoken. And though she trembled, she didn't sit.

"Madame?" Fulton prompted in a subdued tone.

Pulled out of her thoughts, she started like a deer ready to bolt, making her head spin. "I . . . I am sorry, m'sieur, I — I thought I could do this, but —"

"Madame, you have nothing to fear here."

With her good hand holding the doorpost,

she looked into eyes that were both sincere and kind. But Alain had been gentle and romantic at the start . . .

Forget Lisbeth Delacorte. You are Elise Dupont. You're here to save Edmond.

Fulton waved a hand. "Please sit down, madame. I assure you, you are safe."

Hand into glove she slipped into the role. *I am Elise Dupont.* Yet she hesitated before every step. Touching the walls for balance, she walked to the chair he indicated. The room was dim and faded and smelled of dust and metalworking.

"You need not answer my question, if it makes you uncomfortable, madame," he said gently, once he'd helped her into a large, padded wing chair, touching only her hand.

"I was a foolish girl," she answered at last, forcing a quiet dismissal into her tone. No matter what the commander advised, her instincts told her to hold on to the mystery.

The room's smell reminded her of the smithy at home, but it seemed to waft down from above. *Surely he's not melting metals in the attic!*

Dust flew up from the cushions as Fulton sat across from her, and she sneezed. "I beg your pardon, m'sieur," she muttered.

"I understand. The place came furnished but was unused for months." Fulton grinned, softening his pleasant, gentlemanlike face.

292

"As you can surely see, I'm in need of someone to look after the house. I may also ask you to help me with things you may deem strange, without question . . . or gossip. And if anyone asks who I am, you know only that I am Monsieur Monteaux, an amateur scientist."

He tossed the last at her like a child's ball, a gentle challenge. Again, thinking of Edmond gave her the strength to hold his gaze. "If you will allow me my secrets, m'sieur, I will respect yours. I will not associate with outsiders. Your need for privacy is precisely what I require."

"I see." His eyes tinged with pity. "Ah, do you have references or relevant experience?"

The way he asked showed his greenness with employing household staff. She fought a smile. Since he believed both sides were chasing his inventions, Fulton would suspect a quick change in her personality. "I worked as a tavern server and cleaner in — my last town. I can cook soup and stews, bake bread, and I can clean. I cannot give you references. I . . . left suddenly." The vision of LeClerc sprawled across the commander's front step, the stair sticky with his blood —

"I left Le Havre rather suddenly myself. The times in France demand, ah, flexibility." Fulton's smile was almost naughty, as if they were fellow conspirators. "Can you start today?"

A lump rose in her throat. A stranger from a foreign country had given her kindness without agenda, or risk to her life or reputation. Why it made her miss her mother with a fierce ache, she couldn't understand. "*Certainement,* m'sieur, but I'll be a slow worker with only one useful arm," she replied calmly, with a tinge of relief: the woman with nowhere else to go. "I cannot lift anything heavy for ten days or more."

"I predict you'll still be more proficient than I at any household tasks, madame." He was laughing at himself.

The commander had known his intended victim well, setting up Lisbeth to play the perfect part. Yet Fulton's self-deprecating wit disarmed her. "If you could assist me with the heavy things for a little time . . . ?"

"I'll feel less of a useless clod, madame. I thank you for the opportunity." With another grin, he sketched a mock bow.

Far earlier than she'd planned, she was smiling. Against her will and her fears, she liked this man; his air of confidence mixed with self-deprecating charm was a neat counterpoint to his brilliance. Yes, she and Fulton would become friends. Then the cut on her cheek stung to the bone, and her smile vanished. *Trust no man. You are here for Edmond, only for Edmond.*

Start disarming him. She mumbled, "Monsieur Monteaux, I — can you please give me a small advance on my wages for — for necessary items?" She felt herself blushing. "I need slippers to wear in the house while cleaning, an apron and cap. I will need oils for cleaning, herbs for my pain and . . . um, feminine needs."

Which of them was blushing more? "Certainly. W-will three francs suffice?"

If she were really a starving waif, it would represent a fortune. Her look held hopeless gratitude and budding admiration. "*Merci, monsieur.*" Ashamed, she looked at her lap. It wouldn't be long until her first task of disarming any suspicion on Fulton's part was complete.

You called him monsieur twice. Stick to the lower-class m'sieur from now on.

She couldn't afford another slip.

It was past midnight, yet candles were still lit on both the second and third floors.

Duncan paced the sandy path a quarter of a mile from the house, where he'd set up a black tent that would be packed up before sunrise. Why was she awake? Couldn't Fulton see she needed rest? He'd thought the man a gentleman . . . if he was forcing her to —

Breathe, man. Fulton isn't the kind of man to force himself on her.

No matter what Duncan told himself, the

image of Lisbeth's cut and battered face returned to haunt him: an eternal reminder of the damage he'd done just by entering her life.

I can't become involved. She's a pawn for king and country. Like me, she is —

But he was already at the house, clinging to the shrubs and shadows.

When his men helped Fulton move in, Duncan had ordered the tiny pantry window to be left unlocked. He'd told Lisbeth to inspect the house tonight and leave the pantry door ajar. He'd never get through it, but he could at least listen.

With painful slowness he pulled the top of the little window toward him. Though he strained his ears, he could only hear creaking of the floorboards. Someone was walking.

A whisper came from behind him. "Monsieur, I'm here to report."

He wheeled around, causing his almost-healed leg to twinge. The boy's whole bearing was taut with nerves. So his first attempt had failed. Without a word, Duncan led Argenteuil to the tent to give him everything he'd need for the next part of his mission.

Inside the house, pacing the floor of her room until she was sure Fulton would be lost in his work, Lisbeth decided it was safe to begin her initial tests. "First step up from the landing squeaks in the middle," she whispered, to help her remember. "Fourth floorboard from the landing window is also loud. Walk against the banister."

Even on the edge of the stairs to the attic where he worked, a stair squeaked. All movement ceased above. Holding her breath, she retreated to her room and snuffed the candle. Soft squeaks followed her all the way down, stopping outside the closed door.

In a panic, she made the muffled sounds of a woman crying into her pillow.

The squeaking steps as he returned to the attic hovered in her ears, echoes of her self-disgust. So this was the life of a King's Woman — deceive and betray, using feminine wiles — and for Edmond's sake, she hadn't even hesitated.

She closed her eyes, but sleep was elusive. How many mistakes had she made today — and how long could she use the part of the bird with the broken wing to cover her errors and he'd still believe her?

CHAPTER 24

Ambleteuse, France
September 13, 1802
Lisbeth found the note in the triangular pantry, right beside the tiny window he'd asked her to leave open.

> Madame, it's been two days. Why have you not come to me? It is imperative that I know what you have learned.

"Are you well, madame? Do you need something?"

Lisbeth froze in place. Fulton had come up behind her, as she was about to make her escape. Every time she turned around he was there.

Even with her back to him she felt his presence, watching — like LeClerc and Tolbert. Like Alain. "Please don't creep up behind me, m'sieur," she whispered.

The silence conveyed his dismay. "My dear girl, I'm sorry. I didn't mean . . ."

I have but six weeks to save Edmond. She

shrank from his reaching hand. "I — I just wish to walk for a little. I still need to purchase, um . . . ?" This time it had the advantage of being true.

"Of course, madame, I beg your pardon. I forgot," he mumbled, his face burning.

The awkwardness of cohabiting strangers hovered in the air: the awkwardness and intimacy she must foster, maintaining his instinct to protect while preventing him from forming any suspicions. "May I go now?" She heard the quiver in her voice, hating the lie by inference.

"It looks set to rain. If you wait —" He stopped when she cringed again. "You're free to come and go as you wish, madame." He sounded mortified.

Crushing a wish to reassure him, she shoved the commander's note into her sling and pinched her aching arm before turning her white, battered face to his. "M'sieur, I need those three francs . . . ? If you can give me a little also for food . . . ?"

"I am a fool in every way." He crossed the room and out, to his library. She heard a drawer open and close again. Within a minute he returned with a handful of coins, his cheeks still flushed, his eyes filled with remorse. "Use what you need, madame. Count no cost."

Knowing his limited pocketbook, she smiled, slow and diffident. She hated manipulating his chivalrous instincts. She slipped the coins into her cape pocket. "Thank you, m'sieur."

"Please return soon, madame, lest my anxiety engulfs me and I begin hunting for you."

Though meant as a joke, she felt the veiled threat. Her smile faded. Wheeling around too fast for her injured body to cooperate, she walked through the door, and closed it behind her.

Trying to keep balance on the uneven path in a hard salty wind, she was halfway along it when she heard a rustle in the blackberry brambles and a hard whisper. "Madame, I'm here."

She started, jerking her arm in its sling. Sudden, savage pain hit her shoulder; her head spun, her legs wobbled and she began to fall.

The commander caught her against his shoulder, making her feel warm and safe for a moment; then he laid her on the cold, damp sand. "Fulton was watching you from the attic. He'll be here any moment." She barely heard him through the whining wind. "Madame, I beg your pardon. I should never have demanded your presence before you were completely recovered."

The echo of Fulton's words annoyed her. "I'm not a child."

"I know that." With a tiny rustle of

brambles, he was gone.

The sound of pounding feet reached her ears. "Elise!" Fulton sounded frantic. "Thank God I was watching you." He lifted her in his arms. She flopped against him like a cloth doll.

In his dirty smock and a coal smudge on his cheek, his pince-nez askew and eyes wild, Fulton was the most unlikely knight she could imagine — but she could only be grateful for his care. Sudden, swirling rain turned sleetlike before they reached the house, wetting them both.

In her room, he laid her on the bed. "You must change out of those damp things. How have you coped until now? I ought to have asked. Madame, may I help you to — to undress?"

Before he'd finished his question, she'd scurried to the other end of the bed, pulled the blankets up to her chin, and snatched up Luc Marron's knife from under her pillow, tears streaming down her face. Instead of Fulton's kind, shocked face, she saw Alain's vivid triumph as he'd left her broken and bleeding a year ago, LeClerc's blazing excitement as he'd jerked her skirts up . . . "Don't touch me. Don't you *dare* touch me!"

Fulton was white around the mouth. "Oh, dear Lord." He took a step back. "I — make a list of what we need at the store; I'll buy it. I'll build you a fire and bring an armchair in.

You can sit and dry your dress in peace. You need to rest and eat. I-I could toast bread over the fire, with butter and cheese. And — tea, yes? Ladies like tea with milk. The farmer delivered milk . . ."

Still in mid-babble, Fulton turned and bolted from the room — and Lisbeth burst into tears, crying as though she'd never stop. It seemed Fulton was already emotionally involved. But she had to learn how to ensnare him sexually, or she'd never get the boat, or save her son.

CHAPTER 25

Ambleteuse, France (Channel Coast)
September 16, 1802

"See this?" Fulton heaved an iron cylinder into his arms. "This is the propulsion chamber for the, um, barrels."

In the small A-shaped attic by the roaring fire, in a wing chair covered in blankets, Lisbeth smiled. He'd stopped saying "corpses" the first time he'd seen her shudder, but he couldn't bring himself to say "bombs." The reality of what he'd created seemed to offend him.

"Releasing a barrel by lighting it, attaching it to a screw outside the submersible, and releasing it by turning the screw gave us too little time to get away. These new barrels are lit once in position in the chamber. They have longer wicks inside the barrel, double dipped in tallow to make them burn slower and remain water resistant. And by using spring propulsion —"

Lisbeth repressed a yawn, but she doubted

Fulton noticed. He did his best work at night. His mind, always spinning like a top, required only a few hours of rest before taking off again with the latest idea. She pushed off one of the blankets and wiggled her feet out from under the blankets to cool them. "I don't understand what spring propulsion is, m'sieur."

She'd learned not to ask veiled questions. Fulton's mind was literal. If she didn't tell him she was confused, he'd assume she understood, and move on with his explanation.

Something had changed since that moment in the rain . . . or since the episode in her room. The commander had been right. Compassion was the key to Fulton's trust — or maybe they'd underestimated his loneliness.

He'd come into her room the next morning after knocking. "You've been sleeping in that dress, madame, and cannot yet fix your hair. I assure you, I can do this. For a time my mother was very ill, and I stayed home to care for her. I shall be to you as I was to her."

Why his blank eyes and wooden demeanor reassured her, she didn't know. Perhaps it was because he looked so — so like a servant. Or was it the reference to his mother?

This was a golden opportunity. "I am sorry if I look disheveled, m'sieur. I cannot use my left arm to reach the buttons at the back, nor can I lift it yet to braid my hair." And she

304

wondered if the commander had bought all her dresses with back buttons for this purpose. *Rouse his pity.*

But the necessity of involving Fulton's emotions left Lisbeth not liking herself very much. His kindness made it hard for her to maintain distance, but her conscience dimmed as the weight of missing her baby grew. Day and night, she ached for Edmond, prayed for him, cried for his loss, and imagined him with the greed of unending grief. He was four months old now. Did he have his first tooth yet? Had she missed that first smile with a little tooth peeping like gleaming ivory?

"I will show you the same respect I have for my mother, madame," he'd vowed — and Lisbeth shoved aside the tearing sorrow and accepted his help. Edmond needed his mother, and Fulton was a man grown. If he was hurt, she'd be sorry, but it was his lookout.

From that morning Fulton helped her dress and undress, brought hot water for her morning wash, lifted anything, and made their meals. She taught him to braid her hair, as she'd taught the commander. But there were still too many hours in the day to worry about her. So the lonely master took on a pupil. It didn't matter if she understood or not; he had an audience, and he didn't have to worry that she'd hurt herself. That seemed to be enough.

He showed her one end of the chamber. "See the coiled steel?"

Tilting her head, she nodded. He didn't like unnecessary interjections like *yes* and *I see.*

"That's a spring," he told her. Squelching an urge to smile, she nodded again. She knew that, thanks to her childhood pestering of the local blacksmith. On board ship, Carlsberg had taught her the history of spring coils: first known use on the wheels of a pharaoh's chariot thousands of years ago, and still in use for anything from carriages to spring-lock rifles.

Lisbeth didn't know whether she'd gained Fulton's trust or had become his captive audience. He wouldn't let her leave the attic except for intimate necessity, or to sleep. He brought her up here as soon as she left her room in the morning, put heavy woolen socks on her feet, and covered her with blankets. He fed her through the day with cheese sandwiches toasted over the fire on forks, and the pots of strong tea he made for her. And he'd talk, and talk.

"A spring?" she encouraged, when it seemed he'd become lost in checking its tension.

"Oh." He started in comical guilt. "I'm experimenting with high-tensile steel. Iron rusts far too quickly and loses recoil. It also needs constant oiling, especially if it gets wet."

She kept her tongue between her teeth. He wasn't ready for intelligent questions, didn't want to know her cover story, or about her tomboy years in the smithy and stables. He'd painted his own portrait of her as a delicate lady who'd roused his chivalry, who needed her mind instructed as she healed. She wouldn't shatter his illusions. The less he thought she understood, the more he told her.

"We put the barrel in the chamber, light it and seal the cork with tallow, hold it for a few moments to increase the power through tension, then let go. So far the farthest it has gone is twenty-seven feet. I'm hoping this better steel that the — that I procured will go farther . . ."

So Fulton isn't above little fibs. She quashed a smile, knowing well who'd procured the high-quality German steel with so few impurities.

"One day I believe a better method will come through steam-engine propulsion. If I can find the correctly shaped chamber and modify the barrels so they can travel through the water for at least sixty feet —"

"Through steam what, m'sieur?" She knew about steam engines, but how it could propel a bomb through a chamber and shoot it through sixty feet of water was a mystery.

Fulton's face blazed like the fire he'd built to bend the thin lengths of steel he'd smelted on his small forge. "Steam-engine propulsion is the way of the future, both for propelling ships in a dead calm, and for any machine . . ."

At last she'd stumbled on the right question to unlock the eloquence she most needed to learn about. She bit into her tenth cheese sandwich in two days, sipped the tea he kept hot in a cast-iron pot by the fire, pinned a bright smile of interest on her face, and prepared to settle in for the lecture. The more she learned, the more went into her journal that night, complete with detailed sketches, as close to the correct proportions as she could do.

When she could leave the house, she'd throw out the musty cheese and procure chocolate, apples, potatoes, carrots, onions, cabbage, and meat at the store. But the secrets she'd learned during the past few days had made her stomach's sacrifice worthwhile.

The Coastal Road to Boulogne-sur-Mer
September 16, 1802
Símon arrived at the latest road dressed as a farmer's lad, hair and brows dyed reddish brown, a ruin of a hat crammed on his head. "Your business?" a soldier barked.

He waved at the donkey and cart he'd hired

this morning. "Carrots and beans for the Friday farmers' market, m'sieur."

The soldier frowned. "Surely you've heard that only those on military business are now permitted to pass?"

Símon held in the frown. Had they been warned about him? Was his costume not good enough? "M'sieur, how are we to survive? Never mind," he blurted as the man lifted his musket. "I'll go house to house, for my father will beat me if I return with a full cart."

He turned his donkey around and walked away with slumped shoulders. It seemed the commander must procure a military uniform from somewhere. In the meantime, he'd have to report his latest failure.

The commander's orders were clear. Símon must find a way inside Boulogne, to find out if the first man the commander had sent inside, Peebles, was alive or dead. Either way, as a bona fide Frenchman, Símon was to take his place. If Peebles had sold out, he had to die.

"You are Argenteuil, and one sacrifice can save thousands," he whispered to himself, wishing he could feel a sense of higher purpose, instead of feeling so young, so vulnerable — or so sick.

CHAPTER 26

Ambleteuse
September 21, 1802

Even at midday the world was enfolded in white twilight. The sea mist shrouded the shore, in a rare day without wind. Huddled in a gray cloak and dress, mist enveloped Lisbeth until she was lost in it. With every step, her feet either sunk into the squelching wetness of sandy soil or she almost turned her ankle over on the stones littering the beach. Rain fell like tiny darts, its icy sharpness proclaiming an early winter. She was a fool to be out, but every time Fulton dressed her or touched her hair, she felt smothered by his tender domination. After enduring day after day of his excuses to keep her at home and with him, today she'd slipped out the door when he used the water closet.

A red rag was caught in a gorse bush just out of sight of the house. She undid it and rushed on in case Fulton came to find her.

The note was damp, more than a few days

old by the deep creases.

Meet me at the river bend past the fort.

He had included a rough map of the area.

How many days had he been waiting at the river bend for her?

Fifteen minutes later she passed the looming shadow of Fort Vauban, a dark phantom in the curling mist as she headed toward the river mouth. Waves broke at the base of Henry VIII's fortress, slapping against heavy stone. Soft whooshing sounds followed as loose beach stones skimmed over each other. She felt a hidden presence on the parapet, watching her.

"*Bonjour,* madame."

Startled, she realized she'd reached the river bend already, three hundred feet past the fort. The commander sat on the sandy hillock above the rock-edged river, wearing a gray cloak. In the thick curls of mist, all he need do was turn into the tussocks and he'd disappear. His face, dark and strong in its rawboned fashion, was just as obscure.

How did he seem a thousand miles away even though he was right here with her? She hated that he controlled this game, that he knew her secrets, had seen her body, and she didn't know anything about him.

"May I assist you, m'sieur?" During her training on the ship he'd made it clear she must never slip out of character, but it was easier than she'd expected to speak in her haughtiest voice.

She'd picked up a handful of stones on the way. She dropped them in the direction she'd just come, using a simple code they'd worked out on the ship. *Someone is watching.*

"I beg your pardon." He stood, bowed, and vanished. He would find her.

Gathering her skirts and cloak, she forded the river at its shallowest point and headed toward a small promontory around the bend, where the cliff and rocky beach beneath it were lost in the mist. Soon, so was she. Fulton had told her the rocky part of the shore was favored by local mussel collectors, but only at sunrise or sunset. It should be deserted now, but she wasn't sure.

She fought the urge to look up the cliff. She didn't know if the specter of someone watching was real, or a well-founded paranoia after the past few weeks. Could it be Alain?

A crunch of pebbles heralded the commander's arrival. The sight of his gray cloak reassured her now. "Who was it?"

"There are soldiers stationed at Fort Vauban, I think. I didn't see anyone else, apart from a farmer with a cart."

"I've seen the soldiers too — too many. It was supposed to be only minimal manning there under the terms of the treaty." He sat at a careful distance from her. "Thank you for coming, madame. How are you feeling?"

"I didn't escape Fulton's constant concern only to run the gauntlet of your anxiety," she snapped. "I'm fine."

He didn't answer. An apology for asking after her health would be absurd and would only vex her more. But the intimacy of the things he'd done for her from the first night had created some kind of abyss inside her.

Annoyed for taking her confusion out on him, and more upset that he allowed her to do it, she watched foamy waves racing over the rocks, mussel shells clinging to them. Crabs scuttled in and out of the foam as she struggled to gain control. "The bruises are gone. Fulton says my arm can come out of the sling in another day or two. I've been taking it off to perform light tasks, such as cooking something besides his one cooking talent, toasted cheese sandwiches."

As she'd hoped, he chuckled. "So Fulton is concerned for your health?"

She nodded, stiffening in anticipation.

"He's good to you?"

"I'm not sharing his bed." Sharper words than she'd intended.

"Of course not, madame." He glanced at her sling, the slow-healing scar on her face. "He's a gentleman."

The ill-hidden pity felt like a whip lashing at her. "Fulton's brilliance and his vocation make him lonely. Few people can understand him. He needs an audience, a sounding board for his new ideas. My injuries gave him the excuse he needed to let me into his world." He made a small movement, but she went on as if she hadn't seen it. "I'm learning about spring propulsion and the shape of the bombs. I'm asking ingénue questions and making notes when I retire." She handed him a small oilskin pouch. "I pretended not to understand spring propulsion after a few lectures, so he gave me a practical demonstration of it, taking me to see *Nautilus.* The shell's still damaged, but he's repaired most of the inner workings. He was delighted in my interest and allowed me to sit inside and test things. I've made drawings of it all, as you see."

He opened the packet and scanned the notes. "This is excellent, madame, precisely what we need from you. Has he shown you the craft tethered in Audresselles harbor?"

She shook her head, the feeling of failure returning. "Has Bonaparte arrived yet?"

"He's not due for five weeks," he replied, voice hard. "But they can't hide the increased security, both on land and at sea."

She had five weeks to charm Fulton into giving her the boat hiding off Audresselles Beach. Splashback from a wave hitting another rock half drenched her. She sighed; more tussling with the hated washboard tomorrow. "Here is a letter for my mother."

He pocketed it without comment.

She began to wonder why she'd come. "Are we . . . um, are we still being sought over LeClerc's murder?"

"I've heard nothing about you, which probably means Delacorte's still laid up, or on another mission."

She relaxed for a moment, then realized what he hadn't said. "What of you?"

He shrugged. "When we were still on the ship, I learned the French want to question Gaston Borchonne regarding LeClerc's murder, and the murder of several gendarmes."

The curtness in his tone sounded almost like shame. "Did you kill them?"

A tight glance. "I would have if it hadn't been done by Delacorte first."

She didn't know why he sounded reproachful. "Should you be here? What about your brother?"

He shrugged. "Don't fear for Cal. He was in Abbeville for months before I arrived, infiltrating the Jacobins. He knows how to hide."

There's something else he's not saying. Again. She repressed a sigh.

"I suppose Cal's as good a target for Alain as any, seeing as I escaped with a man who resembles him," she remarked, to see if it would rile him.

He nodded, tension running deep, and she felt small and mean. "Take care, monsieur.

315

Would Bonaparte's spies ask for your name before killing you?"

His eyes glinted. "I'm safe enough, but the hunt for Borchonne means I'm limited in what I can do in public. So I send my men on the dangerous missions and remain in hiding here."

The slight smile was different from any he'd shown her before. His eyes were warm as they rested on her — but it made her want to run. "I . . . I see. I will let you know when I have more to tell." With difficulty, she rose to her feet, but she swayed.

He took her hands in his, drawing her against him. "You're still unwell."

"Stop it," she tried to snap, but she sounded weak, feminine. "You're injured, but you're here. If I was a man, you wouldn't say it."

He hesitated, then nodded. "You're right." After a moment, he said, "If the situation with Fulton becomes uncomfortable, I'll see that you return to your family with full honors."

Suddenly he felt too close. She liked to breathe without feeling as if she'd just run a race. "I'm not a soldier." Still too sharp. She struggled against another apology.

"No, you're something far more difficult," he said with respect in his voice she couldn't doubt. "War is ugly, but soldiers see their battlefield and their enemy. They receive public honor and often a fair fight. In this game we play to prevent war, and women endure the same dangers as men, and many others harder to bear."

She turned her head, her frowning gaze staring out to sea. "Wars have never been fair on women." Last night, she'd come to a realization. No matter what happened now, she'd lived with Fulton. In the eyes of the world, she was ruined by inference. She could save Edmond, but he couldn't live with her if she wanted him to be a gentleman.

He lifted her hands and pressed them to his lips, shocking her. "My men await the right opportunity to take your son without risk either to him or his grandmother." He too looked out to sea. "Your mission is harsh and murky with blurred lines, yet you fulfill your duty with more honor and less complaint than any woman I've ever known."

The earnestness in his voice shook her; his touch, meant as reassurance, left her unsettled, almost fearful. She jerked her hands from his. "I must go. The mist is thinning." She turned to head back toward the estuary, knowing he was waiting to catch her should she fall again; but she refused to look back as she started off. She'd never allow a man to carry her again, if she could help it —

Then she slipped on a bit of moss and began wobbling, falling back — and then she was cradled against his chest, his arms holding her with tender care. "You foolish girl," he chided, in a tone she'd never heard from him. "Why did you come when you're still not well enough?"

It was foolish to struggle. "Why do you wait for me every day in the cold and wet, when your leg must still be in pain?" She felt the give in his leg with each step he took. "Why do you carry me when your wounds might reopen? I'm no lightweight."

He chuckled. "I doubt you've looked in the mirror lately. You're a bundle of feathers."

Typical of the man that he didn't answer anything about himself. "Ten days of cheese sandwiches and stewed tea. I must visit the store soon. The cheese has become musty, but Fulton doesn't even notice. If I eat another cheese sandwich in my lifetime, it'll be too soon."

He laughed again. He didn't speak until they were around the point and on sandy ground. "We're a pair, unwell and carrying on, denying what's obvious to everyone else."

This gentle banter was just what she needed to recover from feeling so off-kilter. She didn't stop to wonder why her serious stranger could make her smile even in the worst situations, or why she felt so safe whenever she was with him. "You can put me down. I can walk now."

He shook his head. "You're too pale."

"I'm tired of men carrying me hither and yon. I'm not a weakling," she complained, but without real rancor. She felt *secure,* even knowing the world around her was disintegrating.

"You wouldn't know how to be weak," he murmured in a fierce undertone, heading up the river path back to the house. "If I've carried you before, if I carry you now, I'm attempting to make up for other men's failures to *be* men."

Lisbeth shivered, but didn't answer. Wrong, it was wrong to feel safe with him. Wrong to trust him, but she couldn't stop it.

At the final bend before the house, while they were still out of sight, he let her down. "If you come out again before you're truly ready, I'll do something dire next time."

She shrugged. "I'm sure most other underlings obey your commands without question when you threaten them with these unknown dire consequences."

"Yes — but you have no intention of following their excellent example, have you? You've gone your own way from the night we met." He mock-sighed. "I suppose I'll have to think of something drastic enough to enforce your instant obedience from now on."

The gentle teasing made the quick laughter wither on her tongue unborn. She stared at him, her breathing uneven, feeling as if she'd just woken from a deep sleep. They stood in a gray mist curling around them like a cat, an illusion of privacy.

"Go in now," he said in a cool tone, turning aside. "Take care in this mist, you might slip. When I saw you leave the house, I left a bag of fresh food and a jug of milk at the kitchen door as your alibi. No cheese in sight, I promise you."

Crushed, she turned away, slow and careful in case she began to feel weak again.

"Elise? Is that you?" Fulton's anxious voice came as soon as she entered the house.

"Yes, m'sieur. I have supplies. I'll be up soon with fresh tea," she called.

But even when she was installed on her chair in the attic, drinking tea with Fulton, and eating the seedcake that tasted like ambrosia, her breaths still came in fits, like a wind changing direction. Her body was warm, and her fingers trembled.

Must she always go by reverses? Her husband couldn't arouse her, and the man she was supposed to seduce felt like her best friend; but Duncan, a man she still didn't know, had stolen something precious from her with a touch. But she doubted he even realized he had it, and probably wouldn't want it if he knew.

CHAPTER 27

Ambleteuse
September 24, 1802

"Hold it high and steady, Elise. How can I slot the spring in if you wobble the chamber?"

For almost half an hour Lisbeth had been squatting beside the rough working table that wasn't long enough to hold the propulsion chamber steady. Her arms had been raised for ten minutes. "M'sieur, are you aware how much this chamber weighs?"

"Of course, I couldn't make the calculations if I — you're wobbling the chamber again —" He pulled at the other end of the chamber, and off balance, she wobbled on her bent legs. Smothering a cry, she grabbed at the table.

"The propulsion chamber is one of a kind! We cannot afford to damage it . . ." He finally looked at her, an expression of comical guilt crossing his mobile features. "My dear, I beg your pardon. When I'm working, I forget you're injured. Is your shoulder hurting very much?"

Though the swelling had disappeared a week ago, her shoulder ached beneath the weight of the propulsion chamber she held aloft for him while he inspected its cavity. "A little," she admitted, holding the laughter in. Brilliant and distracted, a complete gentleman yet so demanding in his work, Fulton could make her laugh when he wasn't trying — and though the work was exacting on her injured body, it was so stimulating she often forgot the time herself. After a lifetime of running away from her life, she felt as if she'd become a true part of something important, her intellect valued, her assistance needed.

He grinned with a sheepish air. "You're so useful to me, you see. At these times I forget your arm only came out of the sling last week."

And that it's after 3 A.M. also? She tried to smile, but her facial muscles refused to cooperate; her eyes watered and she yawned again. "M'sieur, my leg has a cramp."

Fulton checked his fob and clicked his tongue. "I'm used to working at night with men who are as strong as I am and used to little sleep." He gently took the propulsion chamber from her and laid it on the floor before he helped her to her feet.

Reveling in being upright again, she stretched her legs, arms, and back, which were all aching. She pressed her hands into the small of her back and twisted, with a luxuriant sigh.

"Go and find your bed," he said in a muffled tone. "We can continue after breakfast."

"Yes . . . um." She yawned again. "Thank you, m'sieur." Tripping over twine he'd left on the floor, she avoided his helping hands, ready to save her.

"Elise . . . I . . ."

He'd slipped into calling her by her French name. Usually he said the name with gentle concern, or with absorbed abstraction. But now he sounded husky, with intent —

She closed her eyes. Had she roused him just by stretching? Or had he felt it all along while dressing or undressing her and had hidden it until she was close to complete recovery?

Think of the mission. Think of Edmond. She kept the shudder inside and forced herself to turn back. *Smile at him. Encourage him. Do it for Edmond.*

Unfortunately, even her love for her child couldn't force the lie from her. She looked out the window, watching the swirling snowflakes landing on the glass. "*Oui,* m'sieur, may I assist you?" She cringed on hearing the cold submissiveness in her tone.

Forgive me, Edmond, her heart whispered.

"How . . . how o-old are you?" Yes, by his stammer, she'd put him off.

323

She frowned. How *old* was she? She blinked, but no amount of reasoning could make her see why he'd asked. *Tell the truth whenever you can,* the commander had said. "I'm nineteen."

She saw the dawning horror in his eyes. She could almost see his thought, *I am twice her age.* "Almost twenty?" he asked, sounding chastened yet hopeful.

Edmond's safety relies on this mission. Fulton's a good man, attractive and kind. But unfortunately for all her self-talk, even the image of Edmond's face in her mind didn't help. She liked Fulton very much, respected him, adored working with him — but she didn't know how to feel anything but horror at the prospect of sharing a bed with him. "I turned nineteen in August."

"I . . ." He pulled his hands through his hair, leaving it in spikes. With his spectacles off-kilter at the end of his nose, he looked almost demented. How could she want to giggle at this awful time? "And you really have been married?"

Still holding laughter in, she shrugged, her big toe shuffling the rug's edge. "I still am married, m'sieur."

Another hesitation. "Where are you from — originally, I mean?"

"Why would you wish to know, m'sieur? Am I not giving satisfaction? Do you want to inform my — my husband . . ." She let her voice break and she wheeled away, back to the window and the night. "I will be gone by sunrise. Just please don't find him, or tell him about me."

"My dear girl . . ." He strode forward, but she stepped back until she was against the door, the trembling visible. "It was he that hurt you, wasn't it?"

Slowly she nodded. "More than once."

"I'd never try to reunite you with him," he faltered, but with sincerity. "I abhor a man who hurts the woman he's promised to love and protect, or his defenseless children."

She jerked as if he'd slapped her.

"Elise!"

She blinked, looked at Fulton. His eyes were wide, face pale. "What did I say? Elise, my dear, I promise you are safe here . . . please don't cry."

She hadn't realized hot tears were streaking down her cheeks. "*Mon pardon,* m'sieur." What was wrong with her? She'd become a regular wet goose since her injury.

"I'll get some water." Fulton ran for the door.

She shook her head. "I'm going for a walk." Both sentences were punctuated with hiccups but said with determination.

Turning, he blocked her way out. He looked uncertain, almost afraid. "Elise, it's so late . . . the weather — your health — I cannot countenance . . ."

"*You* countenance nothing." Still hiccupping, she glared at him. "Outside of the work for which you pay me, my life and choices are my own."

After a brief hesitation, he lowered his gaze. "Again, I beg your pardon." When she moved, he stepped aside to let her pass.

She snatched up her cloak on the way out of the house; but, still encased in slippers, her feet soon became wet with the falling sleet that at this time of year came at night. Soon they were numb with cold. She reached the bush at the end of the path where the commander set the red rag, pulled it out, and wrote with the pencil she kept in her cloak.

Fulton made advances tonight. I refuse to ruin myself based on empty promises. Tell me how the rescue of my son is progressing, or I will return to Abbeville. I will not leave my son there, no matter what the consequences. I trust I am making myself clear.

Duncan watched her hood fall back as she walked away. A slanted touch of moonlight through the heavy cloud illuminated her half-loose braid. Even in falling sleet, shrouded by her cloak and the clouded moon, she glowed like the embers of a blacksmith's forge, soft and golden.

By day she remained in hiding behind a

wall no man could penetrate. But when night fell and she was alone, her inhibitions sloughed off like an unwanted skin, and she became the woman he'd seen only in snatches.

If she knew he was watching her, she'd revert to the marionette of the tavern.

Or would she? his mind whispered, remembering the way she'd looked at him three days ago.

He shut the thought down as if it was the lid on Pandora's box. *She's not a woman, she's a valued team member. Think like the King's Man you are.*

He grabbed the note and read it, nodding. Fulton saw her by day, worked with her by night. No wonder he was already ensnared. Would the bird with the broken wing by day and the unconscious siren by night fascinate the American enough to offer marriage?

Fulton's no fool. She gives herself away with every word and movement. He must already know she's a lady. He'd marry her if he knew of her family. Eddie would fund his work for life. The property near Bath her grandmother left her would make an ideal place for his work —

If he didn't sell it for funding, that is. On marriage, her property becomes his.

No, he wouldn't tell Fulton a thing about her. She deserved a chance to find a man who wanted more than work, sex, and her money.

If Fulton only wanted her as a mistress — and he'd shown that by his lack of respect in his half offer — it was obvious he didn't know who she was.

If she returned to England unmarried, she'd be the one to pay the price for being a young girl deceived. In their world, women suffered the consequences for their bad choices, but rarely men — and that wasn't about to change while even so few men had the vote.

He pushed the note into his pocket. She'd made herself very clear: she wouldn't take Fulton to bed without her son's safety assured. Rescue efforts had to be redoubled.

Unconscious of his observation, Lisbeth slipped into the house. Candlelight wavered in her room, soon snuffed. Either she'd avoided Fulton or refused him her bed. Duncan wasn't surprised. Since he'd met her, he'd only seen her holding to the morals her mother raised her by. She'd been born a lady, and a lady she'd remained, no matter what Delacorte put her through. She wouldn't take Fulton to her bed for gain, or duty. Perhaps not even for her child.

He wrote on the back of the note:

At last report, Delacorte has half a dozen hired men surrounding the house. Cal and his men have had no chance to take the boy, but Cal managed to speak to his wet nurse. She is willing to come with the child. Cal has four men, and given Delacorte's recent reverses, I doubt he can afford to keep six men there for long.

He gritted his teeth and forced himself to write the next words.

My brother has sworn to save your son. If you do not trust me, madame, trust him.

CHAPTER 28

Rue de Miromesnil, Faubourg Saint-Honoré,
   France
September 24, 1802

Georgy flung herself into her dressing-table chair and unpinned her hair. It had been another long night at the Tuileries. She longed for John to come to her, to hold her and say he was going to end this madness. But it was night; he wouldn't risk her reputation that way, or give Napoleon any reason to suspect her.

At least Mama's blatant matchmaking attempts to men of the highest estate worked in Georgy's favor. John, a duke, had entry to the house at any decent time, but Camelford, a mere baron, couldn't get time alone with Georgy. Not that he was courting her. No, he'd made it very clear all he wanted was to discover what she'd learned.

So while Camelford kicked his heels, getting madder than a hornet by the day, she and John spent hours talking, laughing, playing games, and exchanging information.

"I'm no agent for the British government, just someone who may enter the Tuileries any night I choose. Because of my unique position as Francis's brother, I have a perceived right to watch over you," he'd told her on his first visit. "Even Napoleon accepts it. That's how it was put to me, and why I made a sudden decision to come to Paris."

Though the admission hurt a little, Georgy felt the warmth fill her cheeks. "I'm glad you came, for whatever reason," she'd murmured, unable to look at him.

"I, too," he'd said softly, and the words felt more intimate than a touch. "I wish to always be honest with you. But for now it must be this way, Georgiana. You will be the new interest of the first consul, and I your brother-protector and hopeless lover."

The word *lover* made her blush harder. "You know . . . Francis and I . . ."

"I know. Francis told me." He took her hand and patted it, smiling. "It's quite all right."

Night after night they played the charade at the Tuileries. Napoleon was too busy to see her through the day, and she assured him she didn't expect it, though he sent her several exquisite gifts. Friendly from the first evening, Madame Bonaparte invited her to several gatherings. When there, Josephine asked the oddest questions, which Georgy always tried to answer with truth. John attended these functions also, though he rarely approached her, and never for private conversation.

By night she was Napoleon's, seated beside him at dinner, dancing with him as much as French society dictated was proper. Eugene de Beauharnais had faded into the background, finding another rich young lady to pursue. And the whispers had spread across the Channel to the London gossip rags, which all raved about a certain, half-naked Lady G— G— (*ooh, delicious, my dear! Could the G be Godiva?*) becoming the next Madame Bonaparte.

And all to no purpose: Napoleon told her nothing worth repeating.

But tonight she finally had something to tell. She ached for John with a fierce longing. If only he could sense it —

A tap at her window filled her with unexpected joy. Could it be — surely it must — ? She ran over, threw up the sash — then her heart tumbled to her slippered feet, seeing the harsh-featured face glaring up at her. "I hear you have something to tell me, Lady Georgiana. I suggest you come down, or I'll come up to you."

He didn't need to say more. To get what he wanted, he'd ruin her reputation without a second thought. She nodded and slipped out of her room. The footman she'd suspected of being in Camelford's pay opened the front door for her, handing her a cloak.

She threw it on and pulled the hood over her loosened hair — but even if she were discovered with him *en déshabillé,* she'd accept ruin rather than be forced to wed a boor like Camelford.

He met her within three steps of leaving the house, and grabbing her arm, pulled her out into the middle of the street. Looking down his nose at her in the light of the street-lamps, he looked terrifying. "Well?"

She lifted her brows. "What makes you think I have anything to tell?"

Camelford sighed harshly. "Don't try my patience, Lady Georgiana. I'm not telling you how I know, only that I do. Do you have a date?"

She shook her head.

His face grew darker. "Then I'll get word to the first consul that you've been meeting the Duke of Bedford by day, and you're a suspected agent of the British Alien Office."

The threat wasn't empty. Camelford didn't care about her, or John, or the British Alien Office; he cared only about his agenda. "Why should he listen to you? Why should he believe you, after Apr—" She faltered there, for in his face was a promise of violence. And in his fists.

"I don't care either way. He'll get rid of you just in case, and will probably toss out every English visitor to France on the strength of it. How will my cousin feel about that?" When she hesitated, torn, he snapped, "The famous Madame Jeanne Recamier is the British spy known as The Incomparable. I'd wager Boney doesn't know her identity here either — but by Jupiter, he will. I'll take out a half page in all the Paris newssheets if I must."

Her resistance collapsed. She was no agent or *femme fatale,* just a girl alone and out of her depth. Quivering, hating him more than she'd ever hated anyone, she turned and hurried inside the house, feeling soiled . . . and a failure to her country.

"Damn it!" Camelford muttered, seeing his best chance at discovery fleeing into her house — and guts to garters, the stupid chit would take care never to be alone again.

Women were a waste of air in the world, apart from breeding the next generation. They ought to be confined to the house until and after they married, not interfering in matters beyond their comprehension.

"Lord Camelford," came a low voice from behind. Camelford whirled, pulling out his stick sword from his cane —

How it came to be lying on the ground three feet behind him, he didn't know, but he looked at the skinny rat who had approached him with more wary respect. "What is it you want?" he snapped, rubbing his throbbing wrist.

"My master would like a few words with you," the rat said softly, his eyes peering up and down the road.

About to consign the rat master to hell, Camelford forced himself to swallow the words, and ask, "Who is your master?"

The rat smiled. "He said to tell you he has the date and time you seek. Come." And he led the unresisting Camelford onto a nondescript coach, heading to the north of the Île de la Cité.

CHAPTER 29

Wimereux (Channel Coast)
September 24, 1802
Boom-bang — the deep resounding through the scrubby forest told a tale Duncan, waiting at the cross paths just inside Wimereux for Argenteuil to return, didn't want to hear.

A second boom came from a different weapon. The echoes of both returned to him in waves, pulsing like changing tides; then there was nothing but the howling of air currents moving in from the Channel. The boy must be dead, and he must let the body rot on a forest path in France, as if he didn't matter to anyone. It was time to run.

The dead are unimportant; deal with the living: this was the inflexible rule in his world. Disobeying orders could bring death to hundreds, even thousands. He'd left dozens of bodies to rot or sink beneath the waves, with a silent prayer to God to take care of them.

This time his prayer felt blocked by the

voice of his conscience.

Damn the girl for changing him. Ever since he'd seen her lying in her own blood, she'd stopped being a faceless sacrifice for her country. Her near death made him sick to his stomach. Pushing her at Fulton when she was so delicate robbed him of sleep. The scar on her face made him second-guess every risk he'd asked her to take.

She wasn't just "the girl," or Eddie's daughter making the acceptable sacrifice. Fragile and brittle, terrified and still trying to fulfill a mission that went against every principle she'd been raised by — willing to destroy herself to save her baby — she'd become Lisbeth: a damned little heroine in his eyes.

Now Argenteuil had become Símon, and he was young, so brave and young.

Damn it. He ran down the path toward where the fading explosion still echoed.

"Hold, lad. The Frogs'll be on us in a minute."

Without thinking, Duncan pulled his pistols, loaded and cocked . . . then the accent penetrated. The man came into view, a great hulking brute in a black cloak, carrying the boy.

Duncan scowled. By the scar near his ear, it was definitely Alec Stewart this time. He ought to have known the man would keep interfering.

Stewart slipped into a barely noticeable side

path off the major one, heading northeast. "This way, lad, or they'll know the boy's not alone."

Gritting his teeth, Duncan moved onto the side path. When Stewart crouched down behind scrubby growth, he followed suit. "You were supposed to stay in England," he whispered.

Stewart grinned. "Zephyr sent me as backup, lad; you knew he would. Now come on."

He barely heard. "Why you and Cal both keep involving yourselves with me —"

Stewart turned on him, frowning. "You've met Cal? Where is he?"

Duncan frowned, wondering why Stewart didn't know where his own twin was. "He was in Abbeville until a month ago, infiltrating the Jacobins."

"Ready to protect you at a moment's notice, you mean," Stewart muttered. "It's why we joined the cause in the first place."

Duncan sighed in frustration. Bloody Zephyr with his plots and plans, using all three brothers as each other's alibi. The spymaster would use, destroy, and toss away all of them if it meant peace for Britain. "I didn't force either of you to become my alibi, nor to become the Destroyer Twins — *Apollyon,*" he murmured, mocking their code names: Apollyon and Abaddon.

Following his usual manner of ignoring

Duncan's hostility, Stewart only shrugged. "So where is Cal?"

"He's in Eaucourt, trying to rescue —"

"Your lass's son," Stewart filled in when he hesitated, sounding exasperated. "Bloody idiot thinks he's Jason and all the Argonauts together. Has he got backup at least?"

Duncan nodded, refusing to discuss Lisbeth. "Three of my men."

Stewart peered around the bushes onto the path. "Whoever shot the boy must have gone for reinforcements first."

"Give me the boy," Duncan whispered fiercely.

With Argenteuil cradled in his arms, Stewart grinned. "And have you run off when I have the pleasure of your company?" Alec pulled some rags from his cloak and began wadding the boy's injury, high on his chest.

Duncan ground his teeth. "Do you wear that cloak to make fun of me?"

"No, lad, I do it to protect you," he retorted in a gentle scold, just like a brother. Like Leo treated Andrew.

Duncan kept his aching jaw clamped until he could control it. "There's a rumor that one of the Destroyer Twins is being implicated in the rue Saint-Nicaise killings of 1800. I know it wasn't me. So was it you or Cal?"

Argenteuil's wound was strapped down tight. Stewart's head tilted. "So my brother's

Cal, but I'm not Alec?"

"Answer the question, damn you."

Stewart shrugged. "It was me."

The three words carried a world of unspoken ghosts: a silent symphony of requiems, each one with his or her face. It seemed Duncan had more in common with this unwanted half brother than he'd have believed only minutes ago. He opened his mouth, but closed it. What was there to say? This Destroyer Twin carried more pain than his laughing mask showed, and he of all people ought to have known that.

"Hush now," Stewart whispered, cocking his head down the path. The thuds of booted feet came and slowly faded. Both men stayed still for several minutes in case they returned.

Stewart looked down at Símon's wound. "The boy needs more help than I can give."

"Give him to me." Duncan held his arms out.

Stewart shook his head. "Are you aware there's talk about incarceration of all foreigners — especially those on the Channel Coast? A British spy was shot in Boulogne-sur-Mer the other day. Boney's visit must be close, and Fulton's getting a name here. They don't know your lass is English yet, but it will soon be dangerous for her."

"A British spy was shot in Boulogne?" Duncan asked sharply, stomach sinking.

"A dark-haired man, midtwenties. He was

340

yours?" With a heavy heart, Duncan nodded. Stewart said quietly, "I'm sorry, lad. They threw his body in the river outside the city walls with a chain around his neck, calling him a British spy seeking Boney's life."

Poor Peebles. Duncan struggled to think. Who'd found Peebles, and more important, what had he given away? Who'd given him over? Was it the rat in his team who'd given Peebles's name to the French?

"I intercepted a semaphore from Boulogne two days ago," Stewart whispered. "Did you receive notice of it?"

Duncan shook his head wearily. Confirmation received of that damned double agent on his ship, but at least he had a definite lead now: he could check which of his signalers was on duty at the time. "What did it say? What time was it?"

"It's all written here." With a short struggle, Stewart managed to pull out a wad of paper wrapped in oilskin. "All the details are there. Only you could tell if it's from your man or not."

Duncan pocketed it with brief thanks. "We have to get Símon to help first."

Lisbeth. Símon. Peebles. Had Camelford made it inside Boulogne? Would the next body be that of a cheeky, red-haired Cockney cabin boy with an uncanny eye for trouble?

All raw recruits under twenty-five, all sacrificed in the name of king and country.

Would the king ever know their names? Would their names be on lists of national heroes?

Wishing his team was anywhere but here, Duncan muttered, "Did Zephyr send you?"

"He asked me to keep an eye on the situation. Somebody has to scuttle the assassination if Fulton and your lass are to stay safe."

It sounded odd the way his fluent French was interrupted by the totally Scottish *lass*. "I thought you weren't Zephyr's — quote — 'puppet' any longer, Stewart. And don't use the words of your nation, it gives us away," he said coldly.

The smile was evident in the other's voice. "We go this way, lad." With that, Stewart led the way through the eastern side of the scrub, off the main path onto a small creek bed. They trudged in silence, avoiding slippery rocks and pools of water. Then Stewart looked at him, eyes somber. "This has rattled you, hasn't it — the boy's injury? You're blaming yourself for it?"

"Who else is there to blame?" Duncan whispered fiercely. "I sent him."

They stopped off to one side of the creek. Stewart sat down, cradling the boy in his arms. "He chose his path," Stewart said, voice gentle.

"He had no idea. He's twenty-two." Duncan looked down at the boy, with the pale stillness that comes before death. Lisbeth had survived it by the miracle of Clare's knowledge, but Clare wasn't here. "Peebles was twenty-five. I sent him into Boulogne, and now he's dead. Símon had only five months' training, and he's been shot. I should have gone — I'm the experienced agent."

"How old were you on your first mission — seventeen?" Stewart shot him an intense look. "How old is the girl you sent to Fulton? How much training did *she* receive, a week, two? I note you don't suffer the same pangs of conscience over her, yet she's younger, and nearly died only a few weeks ago. Do you not worry about her because you expect her to work on her back?"

Duncan's hands curled into quick fists —

One of Stewart's arms came out from holding the boy and flashed across his chest, blocking the attack. "No, damn you, answer me! Why the hell are you making a whore of that poor girl? Hasn't she suffered enough?"

He snarled back, "Like the fifty victims of the rue Saint-Nicaise? How old was the youngest child that died — seven? How do you justify *your* duty that day?"

Stewart whitened. "I don't." Two words slamming a door on a house full of ghosts.

He hadn't expected to feel so shamed. Duncan lowered his gaze. "I'm sorry."

"I am too. You'll never know how much." Looking into Duncan's face, Alec didn't bother to hide the suffering. The damage.

So that's why he resigned from the Alien Office. Duncan hated the insight. He didn't want to like Alec Stewart, and he didn't want to empathize with him.

"There was no one else to send," Duncan murmured, wondering when he'd sat beside Stewart. "Eddie sent me to find her, to see if she was well and happy, and bring her home if she wasn't. The situation was thrown into my lap the night I found her. She was working at the tavern where political dissidents meet. While I was trying to recruit her — just to listen in at the tavern — Delacorte set us up for murder and tried to have her killed. I got her out."

"I understand the need, but why not send her home when she was so injured and ask Zephyr to send a more experienced woman?"

Duncan hunched up one shoulder. "Didn't you hear me? There was no *time.* Fulton's no fool. He'd have seen through an experienced woman, but he has a weakness for young girls. And she's not working on her back," he growled. "Fulton's a gentleman, and she's still fragile."

"Too bloody fragile to be here." Alec shot Duncan a look, and his face softened. "That's why you're camped by the house. Why you're handing over assignments to your men. If Fulton crosses the line, you'll take her away."

He caught himself just before he nodded. He didn't want to bond with Stewart, the perfect mirror of all he could never be: a family man, a brother — and legitimate. Now he'd become the mirror of his conscience, seeing Lisbeth as he saw her — so young and vulnerable. Now Stewart was saying everything Duncan had been trying to deny these past weeks. His duty, even saving a nation, was no justification for destroying her. There was no such thing as acceptable sacrifices of innocent girls. That was something monsters like Fouché and Delacorte did.

He jerked to his feet. "I should go."

"One day you'll trust me," came the quiet voice from behind him.

Duncan swung back. "I told you: I want none of you, or your family."

"Yet you turned to me in need. They're *our* family, Duncan." Stewart wasn't the slightest bit out of breath from carrying the unconscious Argenteuil, even when they climbed up the other side of the creek bed to a small road. "Your mother, Meggie, was younger than your lass when she had you. She was an orphan, alone and scared after our father died, which was why she took Annersley's deal. She died of an inflammation of the lungs many years ago. We're all you have."

"I have no one." Early life had proven it to Duncan beyond doubt. He wasn't Annersley, with all the inbred disdain for and abuse of those in a lower position. He'd never quite be a Sunderland. But he'd *never* become a

Stewart. Why did Alec keep bothering with him?

He had a life of duty to king and country. It was his pride, his purpose.

"You do have us," Stewart said gently. "Our grandmother's in her eighties and frail. Granddad's ninety-two and hale enough, but he can't last much longer. They pray every day for you to join the family before they die. It means everything to them."

That was beyond his comprehension. How could the Baron and Lady Stewart want to know the bastard-born child, the son of a chambermaid — and the cause of their son's death? "We need to get the boy to someone who can give him medical help." Conversation closed.

"You can't take him to your lass. It puts her in greater danger."

The calm assumption of authority irked Duncan, as did the continual references to his *lass*. "Doesn't your being here put me in danger, since our resemblance is so strong? Isn't that why Zephyr recruited you and Cal in the first place?"

"Odd the way you'll name Cal, and not me. Must be something I've done," Stewart stated with a return to that infuriating cheerfulness. "Right now it seems we're all needed where we are, or Zephyr wouldn't have sent us. But, aye, Cal and I have acted as your alibi on many occasions, as you've done for us. In fact you've saved my life more than once just by being somewhere else, including when you were in London while I — during the rue Saint-Nicaise debacle."

Sensing the anguish beneath the flippant attitude, Duncan closed his mouth.

"That's it, lad. You're wasting perfectly good sarcasm on me." Stewart was laughing again. They turned a corner, and there was a tiny farmhouse, tumbling into ruin.

Stewart led them into the stable. A cart waited with a donkey in its stall. Stewart laid the boy on the hay and covered him with a rough horse blanket. Duncan hitched the donkey to the cart. Stewart pulled off his cloak and threw it over the boy. Beneath that cloak, he wore a mud-splattered farmer's outfit that wouldn't cause comment. "There's a retired doctor ten miles east."

Duncan had had a plan ready to go, but muttered, "Well done."

"Aye, I know you resent it, lad, but we're both trained to have that kind of forethought." Stewart grinned at him, so absurdly like him, angular, dark with slashing eyebrows and a hawklike nose. "Don't scowl at me, Duncan. It isn't my fault we all take after our father."

My father, he's always throwing my damned traitor Jacobite father in my face!

He didn't even remember making a fist, but his knuckles hurt, and a gush of blood erupted from Stewart's nose, joining the blood from Símon's wound. Stewart staggered back with the blow dealt him, but he kept grinning.

Horrified by what he'd done, Duncan muttered, "Put your head back."

Stewart shook his head, leaving it hanging forward. "It's best to let the blood flow, Granddad says. He ought to know, the amount of fights he's been in. Aye, you're a Black Stewart and no mistake. We're all firebrands."

"I never lose my temper," Duncan growled.

Stewart's brows lifted in that ghastly, bloodied face. "That's because you've not yet been to a family dinner. There's always a punch-up going on somewhere. There're real shenanigans. You must come sometime, let a bit of that hot blood out. You'll have the time of your life."

Fighting an insane urge to laugh, Duncan pulled his cloak tight around himself. "You're wasting your attempts at humor on me. Take the boy and get out of here."

Stewart glanced at Símon and stilled. "All I can do now is to bury him. I'm sorry, lad."

Duncan saw the boy's face and bowed his head. "Do you have a sheet? He deserves to be buried at sea with full honors. It's what he would want."

Stewart nodded. "He'll be ready for you by full dark."

"Thank you." Unable to bear looking at the boy, Duncan headed for the lane that locals had begun to call rue Laboratoire and the tent he erected every night, where he could see her moving about and know she was safe.

Safe for how long? She's nineteen . . . nineteen.

The sun had long since set by the time Duncan was inside his tent. After lighting the tiny lantern, just enough to read by, he pulled out the message from Boulogne that Alec had intercepted. The moment he read the first three code words, he knew who'd sent it. "Good God," he groaned. This had all the makings of a disaster, with no way for him to stop it — just as he couldn't change Lisbeth's mission. With only weeks until Boney's arrival, he couldn't install another woman without Fulton knowing she was a plant.

If only she knew the game better! If she was worldly wise like other female agents, or at least more experienced; if those damned scars didn't make her so delicate, so haunting. If only she didn't treat him as a gentleman, when he was a bastard guttersnipe who was only ever going to betray her. Then he could bear it all better.

Sitting cross-legged on the camp blanket, by the uncertain light of a turned-down lantern, he scribbled another message to Eddie. This one was even less formal than the last.

For God's sake, your daughter will become Fulton's mistress any time now. One word from you, and I'll send her home. The choice is yours.

But he already knew the outcome. Eddie would only throw the burden back upon Duncan by his silence, and blame him for the consequences. The dilemma, and Lisbeth's ruin, or even her death, would be his to bear.

Lisbeth. Símon. Peebles. Mark. How many of his people would die or be ruined for life before this was over?

Duncan buried his face in his hands.

CHAPTER 30

Ambleteuse, France
September 27, 1802

Lisbeth and Fulton ate a simple supper of stew and bread in the kitchen, by the fire.

"I hope the meal is acceptable, m'sieur?"

"Your meals are always delicious, Elise."

He was watching her again. For three evenings now, he combed his hair before coming down to supper, put a clean shirt on, and laid aside his spectacles. He looked younger, more eager, more focused on her. Handsome, if one liked the serious, studious type of man.

"I am glad you like it, m'sieur." She squirmed at her tone, so stilted and formal. For three days she hadn't dared to smile or wear her prettier dresses, and she couldn't make the slightest feminine movement lest he take it as provocation.

What could she say, when every normal word seemed fraught with danger?

It was as if he heard her thoughts. "Won't

you call me Robert?" he asked plaintively yet again, always watching her, avid for any hint of change. He sighed when she dabbed at the stew with the ends of her bread as if she was starving, her gaze fixed on her plate.

He helped her clear the dishes after. "I was thinking of a new additive to the steel for the coil. Perhaps tonight we could work on the —"

She bit her lip. "M'sieur, I've been awake since before sunrise, and my shoulder's aching. Would you mind if I . . ." Not knowing how to put it, she floundered into silence.

The hope blazing on his face turned to anxious regret. "Oh, certainly, my dear girl. I've worked you like a galley slave these past weeks. Go to . . . um. I can . . . work alone . . ."

Her head drooped. She watched her twiddling fingers as if they held the secrets of life. Their unfinished sentences felt like a jagged symphony in her head. So much she couldn't say. So much he wanted from her. So much she needed from him. So much she wanted to run from.

"Elise . . . perhaps it's best if I terminate your employment. I'm far too tempted by you."

As if flung from an evil dream, there were the words she'd feared. She squeezed her eyes shut, seeing a little rosebud face, blond half curls, and innocent eyes. There wasn't a pore or cell of her that didn't ache for her baby. Not a thought that wasn't terrified of Edmond becoming like his father. She couldn't think, could barely breathe, but forced words out. "Please . . . Robert, if — you like . . . you may visit my room tonight." She couldn't look up. Ridiculous temptress couldn't make the offer without becoming greensick, shaking with fear —

"Ah, Elise, my dear girl, you've made me so happy." She was in his arms. He held her in complete tenderness, and again she fought the tears. He was a good person, kind and brilliant — but when it came to sex, he was no different from any other man.

Or was he? When she didn't speak, gentle fingers tipped up her face. His body grew tense against hers. Unspoken questions filled those kind eyes.

It was always going to come to this. Smile at him. It's not his fault that I despise myself.

Her smile was a stillborn thing, vanishing with its dawn; but he relaxed and leaned forward until his forehead touched hers. "You're nervous. That's understandable, my dear. I'll wash the dishes. You go upstairs and — and prepare yourself . . ."

Forcing herself not to bolt, Lisbeth nodded, tried another smile. Its ghost vanished, walking in the dark with her morals and regrets and her self-respect — all the things she missed when she looked into the mirror and saw a stranger with her features. Like grist in the mill, she'd ground down one principle at a time. Only a vision of a sweet baby face led her on, bull to the slaughter.

"Thank you," she whispered, and fled the kitchen.

As she climbed the stairs, she refused to listen to her conscience. If she ruined herself, if she must give him to her parents, or one of her brothers, she could at least be glad she'd played her part in saving Edmond from becoming his father's son.

Or, it seemed, his mother's.

Twenty minutes later Lisbeth sat at the edge of her bed, waiting for Fulton to enter.

He'd laid the fire for her hours ago. She'd lit it, warming her bare toes and fingers. Yet still she shivered in the pretty, filmy night rail the commander had bought for this purpose.

She'd never worn something so revealing before. Was that why her feet kept twitching?

Her hair was still braided. She couldn't bring herself to loosen it as she'd heard men liked. Surely it was what a whore — a *mistress* — would do?

She looked around. Though this had been her room for more than two weeks, there was no sense of belonging, no sense of home. Was this how all mistresses felt — empty, terrified, wondering if anything their lovers gave was truly theirs, or only on loan until they grew tired of them?

Scratching on the door heralded Fulton's presence. This was it, the moment she came undone; but Edmond had no one else to save him. "Come in." Her voice sounded brittle.

Fulton entered and closed the door behind him. He was arrayed in a red banyan, tied at the waist with a silken cord. Though his smile was tender, his gaze swept her body in the negligee, and her heart pounded so much she couldn't breathe. She lowered her gaze, but even his feet were naked. Anything unclothed was a threat. She stared at the floor, wishing he'd hurry, get this over with.

The silence grew dark, like the shadows of the fire dancing in the colder corners of the room, broken only by the soft popping of burning logs. Why didn't he *do* something? Was she supposed to start it? Who started what or took their clothes off?

"You've never done this before, have you?" he asked at last.

She heard the scornful laugh and wondered who else was in the room. It couldn't be her, the woman sent here for this purpose, to seduce him into giving her a boat so she could save her son. She was a woman on the verge of her great success as a spy. "I'm nineteen, monsieur. Until I married fifteen months ago I was at home with my mother."

She felt him stiffen. "I believe you worked in a tavern?"

"My husband left me to starve." Her teeth snapped together. She spoke through them. "I served food and drink and cleaned up after closing, monsieur. I worked to pay for my room and to eat. I *never* took a paying customer upstairs."

"But now I am making you feel like a whore."

The sad insight shouldn't have startled her, since she'd pushed it in his face. But a flurry of panic flew around inside her like a pack of moths. "I-I'm sorry . . . I . . ."

"Why did you make me this offer?" he asked. "Look at me, Elise, and tell me."

Her gaze fluttered up. At the sight of him so close to naked, all the warmth drained from her face. She must look like the snow outside, just as white, just as cold. All the words she'd rehearsed the past half hour fled and she floundered, a landed fish waiting to be gutted.

Her fingers twisted around each other until they ached; she could barely breathe. "He-he has my son."

"You have a *child*?"

The horror in his voice barely touched her. Without warning she'd become wrapped in the past, flung back to that night in The White Goose where Edmond was conceived. "He took Edmond away the night he was born," she said, struggling to remain on mission.

"Why did that propel you into asking me to

your bed tonight, Elise?"

Not even knowing she did it, she shuddered. "He hid what he was until we returned from . . . from . . ." — *don't say Scotland, fool* — "nine days later. We needed my family's blessing, he said. My father wouldn't let us in the door. I thought it was for marrying against his will, but now I think he knew the truth, knew about the things he does. I can't let my son grow up to be like his father, hurting people and enjoying it." Without conscious thought, she touched the scar on her face. "I have to save my baby."

Fulton sounded subdued. "I'm so sorry for what you've been through, but what does this have to do with me?"

She gave a little shrug. "My father won't forgive me if I enter into this liaison with you. I don't expect it of a man of his pride. But he'll take his grandson — or if he refuses, Mama will. She has such compassion for those suffering in our village, you see. If I can get Edmond to" — oh, *stupid,* she'd all but said *to England* — "to my parents, they'll raise him as he ought to be."

"As a gentleman, you mean?"

Wrapped in her dilemma, she sighed and nodded. "I'll be ruined after this. It's the best I can do for him."

Another soft pop sounded as wood crackled and splintered in the fire. And then Fulton spoke. "You need my help? Is that why you agreed to this?"

"Oh, no, monsieur, I don't expect you to become involved. But if I . . ." She trailed off in horror, realizing what she'd almost said this time. *If I fulfill my mission.* Then she realized what she'd already done — said *monsieur* three times, instead of the servile *m'sieur.* She scrambled to finish the sentence. "If I lose my position, I have no money, no way to get my baby home." She looked at her toes scuffing on the rug. "What happens to me is nothing. Only Edmond matters."

Fulton muttered something she couldn't hear. "How do you plan to recover your son?"

Shaking and cold in the fire's warmth, she stuttered, "If-if I save enough, I can return, take my son when my husband least expects . . . he leaves home often. Edmond stays with his grandmother, who — is not well . . ." Oh, how stupid! It had sounded so much better in her mind. But if she couldn't stop Alain from hurting her, how could she expect to take her son from him without help?

"Is your *belle-mère* a lady also?"

Lisbeth frowned, unable to see the point of his question. "My husband's father was a *châtelain,* a hereditary knight. But Marceline, my *belle-mère* — has suffered . . ."

"I understand," he said. He probably did, having lived here for the better part of a decade.

He seemed to be waiting for her to speak,

but she didn't know what he wanted her to say. At last she whispered, "Shall-shall we begin? Will I take off my night rail now?"

"Dear Lord, what a mess," he muttered. "No, Elise, you will continue as you have done since your employment began. I beg your pardon for any distress I have caused you." With a new tenderness in his eyes, he picked up her hand and kissed the back of it, bowed, and left the room as quietly as he'd entered.

A soft rustle outside his tent didn't alert Duncan at first; it was the season for late-night winds, he was pitched amid brambles, and lost in his thoughts. But then a male voice calling softly, "Hie there," had him scrambling up and to the tent flap.

"Fulton." He greeted the other in an under-tone, resigned to whatever the American was about to say. He'd known this time would come; the man was a genius, after all. "Come in, make yourself comfortable," he added, sweeping a hand to his roll-up blanket with a fine irony.

With lifted brows, Fulton squatted down on the makeshift seat. "She couldn't go through with it. You ought to have known that about her."

There was no point in deception. "I knew she wouldn't, unless . . ." He left it there.

Fulton's mouth twisted in an ironic smile.

"Precisely so. I am here now to tell you that I will *not* go to England. Neither will I give your Admiralty one of my boats, or a specification on how to make one. That will not change."

Intrigued by the odd tone, the thinly veiled hint, he waited.

In an even thinner voice, edgy, Fulton said, "I will, however, teach her what I assume she was sent for . . . how to use a submersible. Why do you need it?"

The other's gaze held his, demanding truth. But though he must give in, Duncan wasn't about to give the whole game away to a brilliant, stubborn republican. "Something dangerous is happening at Boulogne-sur-Mer. My man was killed there last week. There's a plot to kill the first consul, who will visit the region in a few weeks. We need to know why Bonaparte has blockaded the town by land and sea."

"Ah, I see — a sneaking entrance, using my submersible. You suspect invasion, then." Fulton nodded. "I will teach Elise — is that her real name?"

"It's not my secret to tell." What a day this had been.

Fulton's smile was secretive, accepting the challenge. "I will teach her how to use my smaller submersible and allow you to borrow it one time, to — ah — visit Boulogne on one condition. You are to leave Elise strictly alone for the next few weeks."

"Why?"

"I believe she's been through enough, without your demands being added to them."

About to repeat his question, Duncan saw the truth when Fulton's gaze met his again. The American had divined what had always been there to see: Lisbeth was a lady, and not just born. She was a woman worthy of respect — and worth marriage.

"You have enough to do, in attempting to save the first consul, and Elise's son," Fulton said quietly, surprising Duncan with the knowledge. Why had Lisbeth told him about Edmond? "She will have more than enough to do, learning how to work the submersible. She still hasn't completely recovered from her injuries."

Guilt again, always the damned guilt where she was concerned. There was nothing to say.

"You need not concern yourself with her welfare. I will take good care of her — and there will be no further importunities."

Duncan felt gritty sands of anger he couldn't wash off. He was too bloody *tired* for these undercurrents. "If you force her into anything she doesn't want, I'll —"

"No need for threats, Commander," Fulton interrupted, sober. "Elise is a lady. I will treat her as such at all times."

Duncan stilled. "I understand."

And, damn it, he did.

Fulton nodded once and left the tent without a farewell. Detente declared, each getting something he wanted. Neither trusting the other an inch. Lisbeth both their neutral ground and their battleground.

Left alone, Duncan didn't unroll his blanket; sleep was more impossible than ever now. Assassination, invasion, and war crept closer with each sunrise, a few men and one brave girl attempting to hold back the tide with a small underwater boat.

CHAPTER 31

Neufchâtel-Hardelot, Channel Coast, France
September 27, 1802

"Your papers and permission to enter Boulogne-sur-Mer, *s'il vous plaît,* monsieur." The soldier held his hand out.

Now neatly bearded with foppish curls and wearing the latest in clothing for the rising businessman in France, Camelford kept his face in the shadows. Much as he hated taking the advice of an impertinent Cockney boy, he had little choice. "Marcus."

The cabin boy hopped down from the box, his face inquiring. Aching to yell at someone, or to scratch this beard that disguised his features, Camelford made himself wave a languid hand.

Mark spoke in rapid French. In seconds, the soldiers' suspicions softened. Aylsham's Cockney boy had been right — again — and Camelford gnashed his teeth.

He didn't object to low-class boys cleaning chimneys or sweeping streets. He didn't mind

Frogs if they lived in France. But his blood boiled when he remembered he couldn't find out where to kill Boney without that bloody ugly French nobody Fouché, who had the nerve to call himself a spymaster. Camelford burned alive every time little Frog soldiers blocked his path here, demanding his papers as if they were somebody. And the mere thought of strutting little Corsican soldiers taking over the French army, and then walking into the rightful position of kings . . .

But by far the worst indignity was being forced to leave this ill-bred, rude-spoken Cockney cabin boy to deal with the soldiers every few miles.

None would *dare* question him this way in England; a mention of his name and title and he passed almost anywhere. Entry to most other places could be bought — apart from insipid, death-by-marriage places he'd never attend, like Almack's Assembly Rooms. He'd marry one day, but not to some frightened little debutante in a white dress and pearls. His cousin Hester Stanhope was intrepid, deeply interested in the politics of the day — and half a Pitt. She'd already rebelled against her stupid revolutionary father, Earl Stanhope. She was perfect. She'd broken it off with him once, but he hadn't given up hope yet.

But he couldn't get home until he'd killed Boney — that jumped-up Corsican usurper calling himself the first consul. But how the hell was he supposed to kill the strutting little martinet if he couldn't get into Boulogne? He hated needing Mark. It *infuriated* him.

"Your papers and permission, Monsieur Jaulin?" the soldier asked, with more respect than he'd shown before the cabin boy's interference. Damn the boy . . . Camelford pulled out the set of stolen papers from Aylsham's ship and passed them over.

"Is everything in order?" he asked after a minute. "I have important business to conduct in Boulogne for the first consul."

The young man flushed and returned his papers. "*Oui,* monsieur, all is well. You are related to the Jaulin shipping family in Boulogne?"

"Would I be here if I was not?" The impudent bastard frowned at his tone, and Mark frowned from behind him and mouthed, *Apologize.* Damned if he would! "My brick is cold and I am tired. I have important business, and this is the third barrier I've encountered today."

"*Oui,* Monsieur Jaulin." The young soldier sounded chastened.

Camelford turned his gaze ahead, refusing to acknowledge the soldier's farewell wave. He was too busy stifling the urge to kill them all . . . especially Mark. But he'd got inside Boulogne-sur-Mer, and that was all that counted. From now on, he'd take control of matters.

Tethered to land by four ells of long rope tied to iron stakes was the tiny submersible Fulton had pulled from beneath the water and into the small, deep cave beneath a short cliff. "This is *Papillon,*" he said with unmistakable pride, lifting the lantern. "I made her myself by hand, after the model created by David Bushnell. Mine is a little wider and taller, so it can accommodate two."

Mouth parted in amazement, Lisbeth walked around the little submersible boat, hardly caring that her dress and boots were wet from the incoming tide. Almost onion shaped, the little craft looked like a fat wine barrel, with tight-packed dark beams and brass coopering around her top, bottom, and middle. He'd opened the entrance hatch directly on top of the craft, with horseshoe-like stairs made of beaten iron leading to it. A rudder was a third of the way down on one side, two propellers nearby, one above it, one below. An odd-looking contraption, a twisted piece of metal Fulton called the torpedo-attaching screw, sat sticking out beside the hatch. The air tube was like the end of a trumpet emerging from inside the observation dome, a foot above the hatch, but Fulton had modified it so it could be pushed higher from inside. Two small rounded windows curved around the brass at the top of the observation dome.

"The windows make it possible to view the outside world when we are at the surface," he explained when he saw her staring at them. "I am trying to make some form of movable telescope so I can see from beneath the waves. Come, my dear, and I'll take you on a voyage such as you've never known before." Taking her by the hand, he led her around the craft to the horseshoe steps. "Take your time and do not fear, I am right behind you."

She was wet to the knees by the time she worked up the courage to set a foot on the bottom rung — and she understood why Fulton had insisted on her wearing her oldest dress and highest boots for this journey.

"I will help you." With his supporting hand at the small of her back, her confidence grew, and she took the next step. The next she took alone.

Soon she was looking down into the craft that would take her beneath the ocean.

"Courage, Elise," Fulton said softly. "I know you have enough to spare. Swing your feet in, and drop down onto the bench. There's a pole inside for you to hold on to for balance."

Drawing a slower breath, she put one foot inside the hole, and the other. Sitting at the hatch's opening, she breathed again, and dropped down.

Holding the pole, she sat, looking around in wonder. There were levers and cranks and other contraptions, making space limited. She wouldn't be able to stand up straight once the hatch was closed, especially with the little wheel beneath to lock it from inside.

Fulton soon dropped down beside her, proud as a new father. "Isn't she wonderful?"

Awed, she nodded. "How did you manage to get this all the way out here?"

He didn't look at her as he released the quadruple-plaited ropes and unfurled the black sail. Then the tide did its work; like a little sailboat, *Papillon* flew ahead with the wind. "I . . . had it moved when I first came to Ambleteuse."

Fulton really dislikes the commander. There was a downward slant to his mouth and displeasure in his eyes just thinking of how the submersible had been moved. To soothe him, she asked, "But how does this boat sink?"

"I'll show you, once we're in deep waters."

This is my mission. She nodded and waited, but her stomach quivered with nerves.

Once they'd reached open waters, he packed up the sail and closed the hatch. "Now I'll show you the pump."

Without fresh air, Lisbeth held her stomach with both hands, fighting the roiling.

"Here, my dear." From his pocket Fulton fished out a small sack and held out a thin white stick. "It's a confectioner's treat, made to my special order. It's flavored with chamomile, peppermint, and wintergreen. You suck on it to relieve *mal de mer.* The first few times inside a submersible boat can be a nightmare for the uninitiated. If these don't work, I have others made with ginger and chamomile."

With a smile of real gratitude, she took the sticks — and to her surprise, they did help the nausea to subside.

"To submerge *Papillon,* you use the pump to bring seawater into storage tanks set in the keel. It's hollow beneath our feet." Fulton worked the little, fat pump, and the submersible sank smoothly downward. "The weight of the water makes us drop farther below the waves."

A single lantern lit the entire cavern. She was inside a fat little barrel dropping beneath the ocean. The tight-packed wooden beams lined the copper-riveted outer shell, held in place on the inside by bent ribs of dark wood and more copper, the coopering holding everything together.

Fulton moved two of the levers and cogs, explaining which was a propeller and a rudder.

The windows of the observation dome were half the size of portholes in a ship, and useless to see anything underwater. The little chamber was heating up fast, though the night was cold and the waters almost frozen. Lisbeth's wet legs were warming so fast she tossed off her cape.

There were ropes coming out from each end of the pipe. A single hook hung from the pipe, holding the lantern in the exact center of the chamber, to throw light in every direction and keep the lantern away from anything that could burn.

"How do we go back up?" Knowing this felt vital to keeping from panic.

"To resurface," Fulton corrected as he worked the pump lever up and down, "I let the water out again by moving the lever in the opposite direction."

She shook her head. "You're truly ingenious, m'sieur." She was *beneath the sea.* It was unnatural and terrifying — yet there was an element of vivid *life* in this courting of death.

Fulton worked levers to make the boat move. "The original genius doesn't belong to me. David Bushnell's was the first working 'turtle.' During the American Revolution, he attempted to use barrel bombs to sink British ships — but he didn't invent the idea of filling the keel. Leonardo da Vinci worked on submersible boats, but a sixteenth-century English innkeeper named Bourne thought of bringing water into the keel to make the capsule submerge."

It was time to do more than passively learn what she could. "How can I help?"

"We need balance. Stay there for now." Fulton grinned at her. "It's exciting, isn't it?"

"Amazing." She stared wide-eyed at everything. "Terrifying. Wonderful."

"I've lost that awed feeling." He sounded wistful. "The first few times, it was like I engaged in hand-to-hand combat against the sea. I felt so alive."

That was *it*. She'd never felt so alive as this moment.

"But I needed to change perspective. Twice the windows of *Nautilus* broke after the barrel exploded too close. *Nautilus* is heavy and sinks quickly. We had to escape and swim to the surface or drown. *Papillon,* being lighter, will take longer to sink." He chuckled, as though risking their lives was a joke.

"See the propeller cranks behind you? Turn only the lower one." He prompted her gently, "Elise, turn the crank. We need to be moving before I consult the compass."

Lisbeth snapped her mouth shut, found the crank, and turned it without knowing what she did, for only three words pounded in her brain. *I can't swim.*

If there were another accident today, her heavy skirts would pull her down. This frigid black water would be her grave. An anonymous death, soon forgotten.

Two years ago the girl she'd been had

despised the conventional things in life. She'd wanted to save the world, or at least *see* it as the men in her family had. But now, locked inside a floating tomb, the last shreds of her wanderlust dissolved; the child Lisbeth waved her final farewell. All she wanted was an ordinary life with her baby.

But what if war came and the commander needed her for other missions? His promises might never come to fruition. She could be stuck in France for years, with no papers, no way to save Edmond, no friends apart from Fulton, and no way home.

Home. She wanted a home of her own — her baby, and a husband who valued her — but that was for a distant future. If she didn't concentrate, she could die tonight without seeing Edmond or holding him again. Mama might never hold her grandson.

"Elise, the mechanism is delicate. Your movements must be smooth and constant."

Fulton's admonition pierced her consciousness like a honed knife. She jerked to a stop as cold crept through her veins like the cobwebs of a spider in the snow. She panted as if she'd run a race.

"Smooth and constant," Fulton repeated very gently.

Refocusing again, she said, "I beg your pardon, m'sieur. I-I was thinking . . ."

"It's natural to think of life when you understand how easily you could lose it. Even to think of painful memories reminds you you're still alive."

"Yes." The word grated from her throat.

As if emphasizing Fulton's words, *Papillon* bucked. Gasping, they both grabbed the pole, even though the ropes around their waists anchored them to their seats. "I warned you that would happen." Though he was even kinder now than before, Fulton didn't look at her — and she wondered whether it was sexual disappointment, or if he really cared for her.

Chapter 32

"No, me lord, I keep *tellin'* yer, you can't go out into the town no-how. Someb'dy killed me poor mate Peebles t'other week. There's bully boys runnin' round in Frog getups, demandin' papers off everybody and lookin' for foreigners." He pronounced it *furriners*. "You'd blow yer chimney piece and lob off some bleeder's head for sure. I'm just a little fella. Nobody's lookin' at me. I can get just about anywhere you need."

Interned at an inn in the old town high above the harbor, Camelford glared at Mark. This had been going on for weeks now. Stuck inside this second-rate inn, eating in his rooms, pretending to be sick, while the boy came and went at will. The impertinent brat loved to bring him information, proving his worth, believing he'd become indispensable — that he'd become one of Camelford's permanent staff when he returned to London.

There was no chance of that. All those in his employ were respectful of their lord, very well aware of their station in life, and grateful for everything given them.

This cheeky horror of a Cockney child would never fit in.

"So what's your information on movements of troops, or any visits of state?"

Mark scratched his head. Camelford shivered, imagining the creatures crawling through the boy's hair. "Well, I ain't quite sure what you mean, but there's loads o' blighters on the hill over that way. All those blokes what're in uniform." Mark pointed toward the hills. "They're changin' the guard mighty regular on the roads north, I hear. Makin' sure the fellas is fresh. And load of 'em is talkin' 'bout bein' sent to some place tomorrow." *Termorrer,* Camelford heard and shuddered. "Place is called port brick."

It's Pont-de-Briques, you ignoramus — Boney's stolen villa. "For what purpose?"

But he already knew . . . and with the information he'd been waiting for the past few weeks now in his hands, young Mark had run out of usefulness.

Open Waters, Audresselles, France (Channel Coast)
October 27, 1802
"How far, Elise?"

Lisbeth peered through the window. Spend-

375

ing the night in the semidark, her muscles stiff and aching, eyes itchy with no sleep, even the uncertain light of early morning half blinded her. It took a few moments to make out the shape of the faux bomb floating in the choppy waters, with white dots painted on it to see in the gloom. "Twenty to thirty feet, I think."

Fulton sighed. "Three weeks, and we're still at an unsafe distance."

At last she asked the question that had been on her mind for weeks. "Why are you teaching me to use *Papillon*? Surely if you repair *Nautilus* . . . the spring propulsion . . ."

He slanted her a steady look, and she caught her breath. What was he not saying?

The warm air felt stifling in her throat. Just looking at the fresh air through the window made her long to drink in cold, clean air. Fulton opened the hatch whenever he needed to reattach the barrel, but the air heated again in minutes. Exhausted and stinking of sweat, eyes stinging and aching, for the past three weeks now she'd been telling herself to put her mission first — more so than ever now, since the commander had left her with only a note.

I need to concentrate on the other part of my mission for now. I trust you to fulfill

your part without my constant atten-
dance.

T

Of course the commander needed to concentrate on the upcoming assassination attempt on Napoleon; but that he trusted her
to fulfill her mission without his constant at-
tendance filled her with pride. She'd not let
him down. "Perhaps if we made one more attempt — ?"

Fulton shook his head. "The patrols will be
coming soon, and we've been up the night
through. Tired people do not make the best
decisions or aim well. Help me bring the barrel back, please, my dear."

Hiding her relief, Lisbeth held the rudder
tight while he lifted the hatch of the observation dome to throw the hook-ended rope
through a metal ring at the end of the faux
bomb.

After six tries they at last got the carefully-
weighted barrel in. No point in wasting good
wood, and it meant they wouldn't be caught
with real bombs if the French found them.
The worst they could charge Fulton with was
remaining in France without official permission.

Fulton turned to the pump to submerge
Papillon. Though he showed little emotion,
she sensed his frustration, and shared it. "I'm
sorry, m'sieur. I was so hoping to . . ."

He weary smile had little to do with physical tiredness, but he said nothing.

On the way back to Ambleteuse in the pony trap, he said, "Yesterday I received a letter from my friend Thomas Paine, who recently took a ship to America. May I share it with you?"

Fulton had spoken of his friend Paine on several occasions in the past few weeks. A radical English pamphleteer who'd escaped death during the Terror because the guards mistakenly marked his door on the wrong side, he'd never learned the lesson of caution. Fulton often entertained her with tales of Paine's more outrageous exploits. "Certainly, m'sieur."

With a little smile he said, "Some of it I will not bother you with, since it concerns friends of mine he's met — republicans, and nobody you know. But this, I think you will like. He fancies himself an engineer. Please bear with me while I translate into French.

"I hear of your sea trials with Nautilus. *Though naturally I am sorry to hear of your tribulations in finding success, I must say, what are you about, my friend? I urge you to try the gunpowder I mentioned on more than one occasion. Used in the correct manner, it would propel the corpses to their destination while your craft remains at a safe distance —"*

Lisbeth's burst of laughter had him chuckling. "Use gunpowder to propel an explosive device inside a wooden submersible? Is he mad, m'sieur? Does he have any idea of how careful we must be with a simple lantern, or in lighting any fuses so we don't sink at sea?"

"Paine does love to make things go bang." Fulton grinned at her, making her feel warm and happy. The memory of their painful encounter faded more with each hour and day he treated her with such respect.

"I would prefer I wasn't one of those things, thank you," she said, and laughed again.

He read more of the letter to her, about Paine's inventions and how they fared. "It seems he's building iron suspension bridges now. I hear there's even one in my home state of Pennsylvania. I'd love to see it," he said, with a wistful sigh.

"Do you think he'll ever sell one of his own ideas?"

His expressive face fell into gloom. "I wouldn't presume to judge, considering I've only sold my art vista of Paris soon after I moved to France, and nothing since, not one invention. Though I still receive royalties from the art vista, it cannot sustain my work, only my life."

She nodded sympathetically. He'd first come to Britain, then France, on an art scholarship. He was a very talented painter, but it was his inventions that held his heart.

Without the commander's patronage he wouldn't be here. It was a source of frustration for him to accept the help from a man he didn't like. He never once displayed gratitude for the money and help given. It was most unlike him.

Fulton went on, clouds still covering his expression. "Sometimes I think I'll never sell a real invention. The only one that's had any real interest —" He sighed and shook his head. "I couldn't bear to go down in history as the maker of inventions that promote war and create widows and orphans."

"You won't," she said almost dreamily, cuddling into her blanket. "Your brilliance can't be overlooked forever. Your submersible work, your work with steam engines for ships, is incredible. One day the world will know your name, and your inventions will be used around the world."

"Do you think so?" he asked, his eyes alight with eagerness.

She smiled. "I know it. I can't explain it, except that I believe in you and your work."

He patted her hand. "Thank you for your belief in me. I only hope I win the race. There are many others with similar aims to mine, especially in regard to steam engines for ships. Some have even made their engines work, if only briefly."

She smiled at him. "I know you'll make it further and faster than anyone else."

They were almost home.

Strange how it no longer felt alien to call the crooked house *home.* In the past few weeks, Fulton had made no overtures of any kind, nor given her those eager looks or asked her to call him Robert. He treated her as a working partner — and that allowed her to relax in the house and learn to appreciate its quirks.

He'd wrapped her in a blanket, covering her damp, cold legs. Though the morning was chill with coming snow, Lisbeth felt comfortable, almost happy. She would be so much happier if she didn't have to make reports on her work or betray her dear friend to save her baby. If Edmond were here, they would almost feel like a family.

"Here we are," Fulton announced, shaking her from her reverie. He stopped the cart, removed the blanket from her legs, and helped her down. "I'll be inside soon."

"I made bread last night, and porridge. Breakfast won't be long."

"With pots of chocolate?" he asked in blatant hope.

She laughed and nodded.

Over breakfast at the small table by the cavernous fire, he said suddenly, "You asked why we are now working on *Papillon.* I thought if you knew how to work her, then you can help me work with *Nautilus* when it's repaired. You may even help me repair it —

that is, if you would like to. In return for your time and lack of sleep, I would help you around the house."

Excited, she looked up from her toast, with a wide smile. "Would you really trust me so far? Oh, how I would love to help you repair *Nautilus* —"

He smiled at her, but again, it held no sexual intent: it was a gentle thing, almost reverent. "You really are enthusiastic about my work, aren't you, Elise?"

She nodded, too exhausted to think about his expression, too thrilled that he respected her enough to make her a partner in his beloved work. "How could I not be so? The things I've learned . . . going under the sea — perhaps the first woman ever to do so . . ."

"I should think you are," he said, still smiling. Then he added, with clear hesitation, "So if I needed to leave France, would you agree to come with me?"

Like a runaway team pulled up hard, she skidded to a halt. She felt her eyes growing big with apprehension. *Entrap him. Do it for Edmond.* But she couldn't make the lie form. She liked, respected him too much: the first true friend she'd had since Georgy. "I . . . m'sieur, I thought you understood. I am not . . ."

"I won't distress you again by asking you to be my mistress, Elise." He didn't touch her or threaten her with any kind of intimate glance. He sipped at his chocolate, and she drew a sigh of relief. Then he added, "What I am asking, in my clumsy fashion, is whether you would become my partner in work — and in life." He took her hands in his, looking into her eyes, and she saw the true affection there, the yearning. "Elise Dupont, will you do me the immense honor of divorcing your husband, and becoming my wife?"

CHAPTER 33

Boulogne-sur-Mer, Channel Coast
October 28, 1802 (Afternoon)

The *sous-préfet* of Boulogne-sur-Mer looked up when a quick hard knock came at his office door, rather than the usual polite scratching. "Enter," he said curtly.

His brows lifted when his secretary came in carrying a skinny, red-haired urchin in dirty clothing, his chest covered in blood. "*Citoyen* Masclet, this boy collapsed outside the building a few minutes ago. He insists on speaking to you before seeing the doctor."

With distaste, Masclet noticed the lower-class clothing — a coach or boot boy — and the blood dripping onto his new carpet, but he waved his hand. "Speak, child."

The boy opened eyes bright with suffering. "I was coach boy for Monsieur Jaulin," he gasped, confirming Masclet's belief. "He's gone to kill the first consul."

"Why?" Masclet didn't waste words. It didn't look like the boy had many left.

"Jaulin's papers are faked. He's Camelford. I saw his papers. That's why he stabbed me."

"Where has he gone?" Masclet asked urgently. The name alone was enough to know this was the assassination attempt he'd been warned of. That mad Baron Camelford —

But the boy's head lolled on the secretary's shoulder, pale unto death.

He'd get no more from him in time. "Call a doctor for the child, and return. Make certain he has a room made up for him filled with every comfort until he recovers or dies." He crossed to the desk to write an urgent message to be taken to the Camps de Boulogne.

The Road from Dieppe to Boulogne-sur-Mer, France
October 28, 1802 (Sunset)

The old coach bypassing Boulogne-Sur-Mer on the Dieppe-Calais road was plain, with two horses pulling it. The suspension on the wheels was poor, the squabs shabby. The man riding inside the coach smiled. He'd roughed it on too many campaigns to care, and no locals or travelers that passed the coach on the road gave it a second glance.

Napoleon had left Dieppe in his opulent coach — former consul Sieyes's favorite — pulled by matching chestnuts. He'd refused a new coach and horses on becoming France's sole leader. To waste funds on vanities when

France was in such financial hardship was political suicide.

Two miles past the second checkpoint, he'd sent the coach back to Saint-Cloud, including his military trumpeters, his Swiss Guard, and armed outriders. One of his guards was of similar height and build. He wore his lord's clothing now and sat in the beautiful coach heading for Paris, while Napoleon climbed into the badly sprung coach awaiting him. His two favored drivers changed into the attire of ordinary coachmen and jumped up into the box. They'd picked up two new passengers another five miles up the road. Those two looked out each window while Bonaparte kept his well-known face out of sight.

So far as anyone knew, the first consul was returning to Paris. The spies who dogged his every step had been interrogated at the checkpoint behind Napoleon. Not having seen the exchange, they would catch up with and follow his splendid coach when it turned off onto the Amiens-Paris road. They'd only know the deception when it was too late. They'd only know the significance of Boulogne-sur-Mer when it was far too late.

"Pont-de-Briques ahead, my lord," Mynatt announced, and with a sigh, Napoleon saw his favorite villa come into view. He wondered where his new assassins were at this moment. It looked like snow was coming.

Bivouacked in a gully amid the sand hills to the west of the Calais-Boulogne road in the deep night, Duncan was woken by a movement. He rolled out of the blankets and got into a crouching position, knife in his hand. Someone was pulling at the laces tying the tent flaps together. "Who's there?"

"It's me, lad." A lantern lifted, and he saw Alec Stewart's face. "I'm glad you're already here near the road."

Something in his voice alerted Duncan. Stewart would never compromise a mission by coming here without strong need. "What's wrong? Have you heard from Cal? Is it the child?"

Stewart smiled. "I did hear from Cal, as a matter of fact. Cal."

Cal's face appeared behind Alec's. "The child's still safe, never fear," he whispered, "but I met with my former friends the Jacobins two days ago. Furious at Delacorte, and without direction from Fouché, they told me about the plot here. I thought you might need my help."

"And thank God for that," Alec said. "Four of my men disappeared from their stations. They've been following the Gaillards, O'Keefe, and the other three conspirators the past few weeks, but now they've all disappeared. Boney's people raided Raoul Gaillard's cottage in Lille and found a cache of weapons, but nothing else. My men have had to leave the region — they were seen and described."

Cal said, "It seems Camelford's here somewhere. They put up a five-hundred-franc reward just today for the capture of a man matching his description."

Duncan was up and pulling on his boots. "We have to stop him, and anyone else who shows up. Unfortunately, there's also a problem with calling in my men."

No experienced spy needed an explanation. Cal swore. "Then we're in the basket. D'ye suspect a double agent or a Frog?"

"I wish I knew. Alec's intercepted semaphore gave me some direction, but he's hiding himself well."

"Things must be improving if you're calling me by my name at last." Alec winked.

Duncan rolled his eyes, shook his head. "I've put my longest-serving men on the task of working out who was on duty during the exact time you intercepted the semaphore. I have seven on that semaphore duty on rotation. Since I began suspecting my men I've had two men on at once, one to code and one to be sure nothing is added or left out. But during the shift in question, there were four men on forecastle duty, all with conflicting stories as to why they switched places before the bell tolled. I have seven men I trust, but three are already on assignment."

Cal swore again. "We'll have to take our chances with the ones you trust and hope to God we don't discover our rat on the road. Boney stayed in Dieppe last night, and several plain coaches also entered Dieppe overnight. I believe he'll switch out coaches and come here today."

Duncan nodded. "I'll call my most trusted men in. Help me pack up the tent."

Ambleteuse-Wimille Road
October 29, 1802 (Afternoon)
The coach swerved around the corner, avoiding another rut in the back road. Napoleon barely noticed. He was a soldier who'd slept on the ground on bivouac with his men, led them into the hardest of sorties. A bad coach was nothing.

Just then the heavens let loose with a sudden, hard snowfall.

If I were going to assassinate me, it would be now, he thought calmly.

Two minutes later a thud came on the ceiling. "My lord, there's blood staining the snow beside the road. I think it's a man," his coachman — both drivers were fully trained soldiers — reported by hanging sideways off the box until his snow-flaked face was near the window.

"*Bien. Merci,* Mynatt." He turned to the trained sharpshooters inside the coach with

389

him. "Take him if he's alive."

One of the men jumped from the coach. After a brief inspection, he kicked the body in the male parts. "He's dead, my lord, but not for long." The man climbed back in, shivering. "The blood was cool, not frozen. The snow's covered the tracks."

"Bien." Were the conspirators falling out? Or had someone else entered the game? Camelford was the kind of arrogant inbred who'd kill a man for getting in the way of his plans, and he was stupid enough to be caught. "Keep on the lookout for any traces."

The sharpshooters reconnoitered the area. "Sorry, my lord, but it's impossible to know without a thorough search, and this terrain would take hours now it's snowing."

Yes . . . the terrain was bad for him, but *bonne chance* for his enemies. Yet the mounting odds only made Bonaparte think better, react faster. He tapped on the coach to move forward. "Be prepared for attack."

Rue Laboratoire, Ambleteuse, France
October 29, 1802 (Early Afternoon)
In the middle of a sudden snowstorm so intense that Fulton had spent the afternoon in the stable repairing *Nautilus,* a knock came at the kitchen door.

The white afternoon was softening to the indeterminate gray of pretwilight as Lisbeth scrubbed the kitchen table and butcher's block. Who could it be? In almost two months nobody had ever come here, and it wasn't likely to be the commander at the back door, not this day of all days. He had to be off somewhere foiling the assassination attempt . . . if there really was one.

Well, whoever it was, she felt some relief that she wouldn't have to *think* about Fulton's proposal for a little while — then her heart began pounding. What if it was — ?

Don't be stupid. Alain wouldn't knock at the door.

Still, she slipped a cutting knife into her apron before she went to open the door.

A rail-thin stranger stood in the doorway facing her. His cheeks were rough and red from walking through the snow. He wore a uniform of the French Army, but it was dirty and ragged, like his cloak. He had an uncertain smile and an empty sleeve where his arm had been. Covered in snow, he shifted from one foot to the other. "Mamselle, I-I have not eaten in some time . . . if you have anything, bread and cheese, or milk . . . ?"

The stranger couldn't look at her, but swayed on his feet.

"Oh, come in, m'sieur." Taking his only arm, she led him to a chair by the fire and dragged the small table over so he could lean on it. "I made soup. There is plenty left."

She laid an extra log on the fire, set the soup back to heat, and added the teakettle to the wide fire hook. Then she cut bread and took the butter from the pantry.

"Thank you so much for your kindness, mamselle. I-I do not like . . ."

She turned her head to smile at him. "I understand, m'sieur. If we cannot share what we have with a fellow man in need in these dangerous times, what sort of persons have we become?"

His return smile was no more than a humiliated stretching of lips. "I am Serge Mareschal, late of the Armée Française." He waved his hand at his empty sleeve. "Now, I am nothing."

Knowing how she hated pity, she forced it from her tone. "Don't say that, M. Mareschal. We are not defined by what we do or how we appear." Knowing it for a lie — every society had hypocritical standards — she stumbled on, "All of us have value to our families, to our country, and to God."

Mareschal shook his head, but didn't speak.

"I am Elise Dupont." She sketched a dipping curtsy and made the tea. As she served him she asked, "Do you have a family, m'sieur?"

"My son is three and my daughter is five, and a third on the way," he replied, in a tone of shame, wolfing down the food. Then he looked up, flushing dark red. "If-if you have some more soup to spare . . ."

"I will give you what I can." Stifling a yawn

— it had been weeks since she'd slept the night through, and now Fulton's proposal filled her mind in quiet hours — she waved off his humiliated gratitude. "I have bread, cheese, meat, and milk as well as soup." Another yawn; she felt slow and stupid. "All I ask is that you return the basket and stone jars. These are not my things to give. I'm merely the housekeeper here."

After he'd eaten, Mareschal said, "I'll impose no further on your hospitality, mamselle." Then he mumbled, "I am truly sorry, but I was given no choice . . ."

He stamped his feet, and two men rushed in from the back door. As Lisbeth screamed and tried to pull out the knife, they hit her on the side of her head. Her legs lost their power, and she sagged. Powerful arms took hold of her and dragged her from the house as everything went dark.

CHAPTER 34

Fort Vauban, Ambleteuse Beach
October 29, 1802 (Afternoon)

Sweat beaded Lisbeth's brow despite the intense cold of the room. It was ridiculous; she certainly didn't feel hot after being carried through a heavy dumping of snow without even being covered with her cloak. The soldiers who invaded the house had brought her to this old fort on the beach she'd passed so many times on her walks and left her in this half-frozen room in a chair far from the fire. Her hair was damp, her dress wet, and she couldn't get warm. The room was late medieval with its high, uneven whitewashed walls and thick, heavy beams. Wind whistled in from poorly fit windows and cracks in the walls.

"Madame, I asked you three questions. I expect answers."

Lisbeth met the colonel's eyes, and for the third time, gave the same answer. "My name is Elise Dupont. I moved here recently from

Abbeville."

For a long minute Colonel Lebrun, a graying, portly man, just watched her. He was seated at a lopsided desk, his back close to the fire. "And the rest?"

She held in the urge to sigh. If this was Bonaparte's idea of a military interrogation, he needed to train his people better. "I don't know any Monsieur Borchonne. I am just a housekeeper, m'sieur."

Lebrun seemed unmoved by her deliberate stupidity. "When the sun rises, you'll be escorted to Boulogne for more formal questioning. Best if you speak to me now, you know. It gives you a chance," he said, his would-be encouragement touched with a calculating expression. "Because you see, if you're found to be in collusion with Jacobin or British spies, madame, you can expect the guillotine."

Ambleteuse-Wimille Road

Lying amid the sand grass less than two miles north of the Camps de Boulogne, Camelford saw the coach heading his way. Right on time, exactly when and where Fouché had told him to be. Now all he had to do was lie still and wait.

He'd always found simple plans were the best. Such as killing a loudmouthed, red-haired thorn in his side to leave no traces behind of his weeks in Boulogne, or paying a struggling merchant today to take him out of Boulogne, smuggled in his carriage. Simple, effective, and the merchant's family would get a thousand francs in lieu of his safe return. He'd been a pig of a man in any case, chewing food with his mouth open, and spraying chunks of it on Camelford as he spoke. Such mannerless apes deserved death. No doubt his family would be grateful to him.

It was time; the coach was close enough. Squinting through the thickest grass he'd found in the field, he lifted one of four rifles he had with him and shot the front horse.

Fort Vauban

"We found no record of your life in Abbeville, Madame Dupont. Tell us why that is."

Lisbeth tried to make her mind work, but she felt as if she'd run for miles. Her heart was fluttering like a bird in a cage it couldn't break. "I don't come from there." She heard the quiver in her voice. "I come from Bergerac, in the Dordogne."

"If you're from the Dordogne, why do you have a northern accent?"

"I . . . cultivated it." She switched accents, speaking in pure Aquitaine French. Once more she blessed Grand-mère's "French accent" games. "My husband is violent" — she touched her scarred cheek — "and gives his mistress children. I am not barren, m'sieur, merely neglected. I can't go back to a man who despises me and refuses to give me a child."

She'd selected her reason carefully during her sleepless nights. Violence was no reason to leave a husband in the eyes of the law, but Catholic traditions prevailed despite the Revolution. For a man to refuse to give even a hated wife a child went against the laws of God.

Yes, she'd chosen well. The uncertainty was clear in Lebrun's eyes.

"May I ask why you felt it necessary to check my background, m'sieur?" The fear in her voice wasn't feigned. "Is my husband trying to find me?"

"Madame, you are safe," the colonel said in a crisp tone. "The first consul has asked us to interrogate every person recently come to the region." At that moment a man ran into the room with a note. The colonel read it and looked up. She shivered at his expression.

"I require knowledge about your employer." His voice was gentle; the look in his eyes, inflexible. "What is he working on in his stables with his odd-smelling smoke and his portable forge? We have already ascertained that his name is not Monteaux. I believe the American inventor Robert Fulton is reclusive and speaks fluent French."

She shivered, as if he'd thrown cold water over her. Her head still pounded from the blow she'd taken in the kitchen, making her slow and stupid.

The colonel smiled: a chilling thing. It seemed Napoleon had trained his men well, after all. "What do you know about the death of Jean LeClerc, Madame Dupont? Or should I say, Madame Delacorte — formerly Elizabeth Sunderland, known as the British whore of Abbeville?"

Then he crossed the room and leaned over her, still with that smile that promised a more frightening future than a mere physical attack. "Now, *Elizabeth,* you'll start telling the truth."

The Wimereux-Wimille Road (North of Boulogne)

A shot took out a lead horse. As it fell the others neighed and reared.

The coach tipped to the right. The sharpshooters fell to the floor of the coach, dropping their rifles. Bonaparte threw his weight onto the left side of the coach, dragging one of the shooters with him. The weight was enough to make the coach fall to wavering balance —

Boom! Another shot sounded. Mynatt cried out and fell off the box.

Men fell in war; it was a soldier's reality. But Bonaparte prayed for *le bon Dieu* to keep his friend Mynatt alive. "Keep going, Beaumont," he yelled to the other driver.

Beaumont yelled, "I can't, my lord, the lead

horse is dead."

A shot whizzed by his ear. If he hadn't had the glass removed yesterday, he could have been dead, injured, or panicking.

A good plan, this. Simple and effective. They were prepared for me to fight.

Keeping in the shadows, the first consul — still a soldier first and foremost — snatched up a rifle, took aim, and shot. Having practiced since his teen years, he could shoot straight even in gathering darkness and under unsteady conditions. The man rolled in time and grabbed a second rifle. Recognizing the face, Napoleon snatched up another rifle, took aim, and fired. His attacker cried out and dropped the rifle, his shooting arm made useless.

Bonaparte kicked his sharpshooters. "Take that man alive."

Frog-marched to the coach by the sharpshooters that had rendered his arm useless with a single shot through the muscle — if he knew which one had shot him, he'd *kill* him — Camelford faced the man he loathed above all others. Before he could look down his nose at the Corsican piece of gutter trash, the two soldiers pushed him — *Camelford* — onto his knees.

Boney smiled down at him. "We meet again, Lord Camelford. Your cousin Mr. Pitt will be glad to know you've been recovered safely. You will be returned home . . . at a price." The smile grew. "Last time there was no public consequence. Now, I will not be so forgiving. You will become famous throughout France and England as the man who couldn't kill Napoleon Bonaparte *twice.* The name Pitt will be synonymous with failure throughout England."

Twitching, Camelford's gaze shifted. Bonaparte had had expert marksmen in the coach with him. Such a departure from his usual method of aping Caesar or William the Conqueror, always needing to take the lead himself, showed a brilliance Camelford never thought he'd have to prepare for. A man so lowborn and lacking in gentility could be an excellent soldier, but when had he become such a brilliant tactician?

And a gutter-trash cabin boy had warned him that Boney would do something like this, damn his eyes! It was against the will of God that the lower orders outthink their betters. It was *intolerable.* Either the devil was with him, or Boney had a highborn Englishman in his pay . . . it was the only logical explanation, and he'd find out who, as soon as he returned to England.

CHAPTER 35

Fort Vauban

"Tell me about the man masquerading as Gaston Borchonne, where he is, what Fulton's inventing, and what he means to do with it."

The colonel was no fool trying to dominate her with beatings or sex. Lisbeth couldn't see how to undermine this patient, smiling interrogation. There was no violence, no yelling. He smiled when she lied, as if he knew the truth and expected her not to speak it. She'd tried weeping to convince him she was a weak woman being dominated by the big strong man, but he'd advised her not to waste his time. Layer by layer he'd stripped her games, and she became a little more frightened.

It was as if he knew her, was certain what she'd say or try next.

"Again — tell me about the man calling himself Gaston Borchonne, what Monsieur Fulton's inventing, and what he means to do with it."

Lisbeth stared at him, eyes big and sad. "I told you, Colonel. I don't know."

"I think you do." Colonel Lebrun leaned closer. Strange, his breath was pleasant coffee, but all she smelled was death. "You're a British spy. Why else would a married English lady be living with an American who invents subversive machines with exploding weapons?"

She sighed. "I found somewhere to live and work after my husband gave me no home or choice of living, then tried to kill me."

His expression was akin to pity. "If you don't tell me, you'll face a harder inquisition tomorrow, madame. Or do you not know Lord Bonaparte is here and blaming the British for the latest attempt on his life? You're very conveniently placed to help with the attempt . . . or to take the blame, as it seems your friends have deserted you."

She opened her mouth, then closed it and shivered. A bucket of ice water tossed over her soul. The commander had been gone for weeks.

No, he wouldn't desert me. He swore he'd save me.

And you believed him, but didn't you always know you were buying a pig in a poke? If it comes to you or the mission, you knew what he'd choose.

The little smile playing around his mouth

told her the colonel knew she was panicking. The first lesson in how to make a woman betray herself and others: cut her off at her emotions. Hell hath no fury . . . especially if he knew she'd remained strong during other interrogations.

And he *did* seem to know it. But how?

That ice bucket became her soul. She doubted Luc knew enough to betray her — and the Jacobins hated Napoleon. That left only one person.

She no longer had to put on a show of terror. If Alain were here, there was only one way to cut *him* off at the knees. The colonel wanted the truth, so she'd give it to him.

"Colonel, in the sixteen months since I arrived in France I've been beaten, cut, shot at, and raped, my child stolen, and that was only my husband's treatment of me. You know my name. I presume you've been told that my father, who is a King's Man, trained me. But my father is a traditional man who disowned me for eloping with an enemy spy. Can you see a loyalist who left me to my fate training me to this work, when it is a shame and disgrace for a lady to do anything but marry well and bear children?"

"Would that not be the perfect cover for a spy?" he asked, still smiling in the way that chilled her, but something had crept into his expression, some kind of doubt.

"I see your point — but as the daughter of

a mere baronet, my actions are scrutinized far more closely than, say, the daughter of an earl or a duke. You are old enough to remember this about French society." Encouraged by the growing uncertainty in his eyes, she went on, "You must have some record about me. You must know that, until just over a year ago, I was raised in the country with my mother. I only left home to visit my grandmother, and once for the London Season. I am only nineteen now. How could I be a trained spy when my father only came home four weeks of the year? When did I have time to spy for Britain when I was with child nine months of the time I've been here and working ten to twelve hours a day since two weeks after the birth of my son?" Her cheeks burned as she added, "None of those hours at work were spent, ah, entertaining the patrons in a room upstairs. This fact upset Monsieur Marron, the owner of Tavern Le Boeuf greatly, as I'm certain he'd tell you. So again, I had no chance to gather information for anyone."

Good, she could see more seeds of doubt sown by facts the colonel could check. Throwing pointy little rocks at Alain's castle of glass — and by the look in the other's eyes, she'd hit the target with accuracy.

She allowed pleading to enter her expression. "You see the scars on my face. Do you think I can withstand this kind of treatment for long? I'm tired, and my head hurts from where your men hit me. I just want to go home. Don't you think I'd tell you if I knew anything?"

"That would depend on what you were promised," Lebrun said, the strain showing in his conversational tone. "Such as the return of your child to you."

Before she could catch herself she'd gasped . . . and Lebrun slowly smiled.

Rue Laboratoire, Ambleteuse

It was barely six, but early night swamped the thinning snow until it fell, defeated, in the darkness and cold. The crooked house had also given into the weather's domination, dark and silent, with none of the warm laughter Duncan had heard in recent weeks when he'd come to check on Lisbeth's well-being. There was a low light in the kitchen, but none elsewhere.

The only sign of life was in Fulton's stable. A crack of light showed through makeshift curtains, and cheerful whistling from behind the big wooden doors. "M. Fulton." Duncan banged on the doors barred from the inside. "M. Fulton, we must talk."

The whistling halted. "Go away, Englishman. I won't give you anything!"

"You're in danger, as is Madame Dupont."

After a silence, Fulton called, "Prove it."

He leaned into the doors, calling as softly as he could through the crack between them.

"There was an attempted assassination of the first consul near Boulogne two hours ago. By now he'll have ordered the capture of all foreigners in the region. Your inventions will be forfeit, and Madame Dupont's husband will find her and kill her."

Banging sounds came, and the stable door jerked open. Fulton was his usual disheveled self, wearing the stained smock, his hair a mess, spectacles askew. "Why don't we call Elise by her real, English name?"

He'd expected this since Fulton's invasion of his tent. "She's Elizabeth Sunderland, daughter of Sir Edward Sunderland of Barton Lynch in Norfolk. If you don't want to come, I won't force you, but I assure you Miss Sunderland will come with me, no questions asked."

Fulton frowned. "Miss *Sunderland*? Is she not married? Hold —" His eyes widened. "Is she really Sir Edward Sunderland's daughter?"

"Yes, she is." There, he'd handed Fulton the key to saving her from ruin. "I will explain it all later. Right now you're both in danger. Will you come or not?"

Fulton hesitated, still frowning. "She truly is in danger?"

Duncan nodded. "Her son's father is Fouché's man and possesses the same proclivity for giving pain. He doesn't know she's working for us yet, but when he does . . ." Deliberately, he trailed off, leaving the rest to Fulton's imagination.

Fulton paled. "Fouché . . . ah, I see."

"If he discovers she's working for us here, close to Boulogne, seizure of your work would become a priority. Fouché would send Miss Sunderland to a brothel. He does that to women he has no use for." Duncan looked at his timepiece. "My ship is at your disposal. You can go wherever you wish, no fear of seizure. Your work will remain your own, if you'll accept my word."

After a moment, Fulton said, "Whatever our differences in ideology, you are a gentleman. And . . ." He lifted a brow. "I've worked on *Nautilus* for weeks, but she isn't ready. However, I'm sure you know about *Papillon,* my smaller, lighter submersible. It is roped underwater in a cave north of Audresselles Beach. It can easily be towed to your ship by a six-man rowboat. I've been coaching Elise — ah, Elizabeth, in its use for the past four weeks. She's become quite proficient."

Duncan sagged in relief. "Thank you."

The American said, "Let me be clear. If I do this, it's on the condition that Elizabeth is sent home, her child returned to her."

Duncan's eyes narrowed. "Her son's rescue is not contingent on her success."

"I take leave to doubt that — as, I believe, does she," Fulton said, smiling in a way Duncan didn't like. "Elizabeth will receive *Papil-*

lon as a deeded gift from me, to do with as she wishes, on the written promise that her son will be returned to her safe and whole."

The commander burned to ask, *Why not just offer both to her as her betrothal gift?* Instead he simply bowed.

"Is she married? She believes she is," Fulton pressed.

"Did you hear me? She's in danger. I don't have time to forward your courtship," he snapped, but he saw the writing on the wall. In moments Lisbeth had gone from potential mistress to prospective bride, thanks to three words: *Sir Edward Sunderland.*

Zephyr had taken Fulton's measure on accurate scales. Fulton was either a closet snob or just a pragmatist. The world turned on money and influence. If he hoped Eddie would welcome him to the family and fund his work in exchange for Lisbeth's redemption, he'd be right.

Duncan turned away. "Horses and carts are coming for the heavy lifting."

"*Nautilus* is heavy. Even roped down, it will need two men to hold it in place."

"My brother will see to it. He'll be here soon. I'll go to Lisbeth." Duncan's use of the name implied an intimacy she hadn't given and he hadn't earned. It wasn't fair, but he wasn't in the mood for fairness.

"Perhaps it's best if I go to her." Fulton flushed and mumbled, "She's probably having an afternoon nap. I've worn her out with work by day and teaching her how to work *Papillon* by night. She's so tired, with, ah, a great deal on her mind." His cheeks grew even brighter, if it was possible; so red, Duncan wondered if he'd broken his word to stop importuning her.

"Never mind. I know where her room is." Duncan ran for the house, meeting Alec on the way. "Help Fulton. I have to go to Lisbeth."

Alec's brows lifted, but he nodded. "Cal's here, too. I left your orders with Flynn."

"Good." Duncan strode in, up the stairs and to her room, hoping he didn't frighten her with the rude awakening —

She wasn't there.

He checked the attic, in case she'd taken the chance to search without Fulton's knowing; it was cold and dark, and fear as remorseless as the day he'd just endured cut him with a pointed tip. He searched every room in the house, but each was empty. He paused a moment at the kitchen before running back to the stable. This time he noticed the fort on the beach was blazing with light. At the door he snapped, "Lisbeth's been taken."

Fulton gasped, and Alec dropped his end of a long steel contraption. Cal looked up sharply from unwinding rope. "What the hell — ?"

Duncan cocked his head at his brothers,

409

and they crossed the stable to him. "It has to be Delacorte. I believe he was the one who killed my man Peebles in Boulogne. He must have forced some information about our mission from Peebles. Then he came here, set himself up at the fort, took your men hostage last night to keep us busy with the Boney assassination, and came for her."

"Bloody clever," Alec muttered. "But he hasn't reckoned with us, lad. We'll get her."

Fulton stammered, "But how . . . I was right here! Why didn't they take me?"

"There are several boot marks by the back door and across to the path, going in and out again." Duncan stared hard at Fulton. "They didn't want you — yet. They passed right by you."

The inventor's cheeks were chalky. "W-when I'm working I tend to block out everything else. My family says a battle could erupt around me and I wouldn't notice . . . ."

Turning his back on Fulton, Duncan looked at his brothers. "Taking only Lisbeth proves that Delacorte's behind this. He's probably hoping to frighten her into giving us up, and leading them to Fulton's inventions."

Cal said quietly, "There are other reasons why he'd feel it was imperative to take her, lad. He probably wants her dead before certain truths about his personal life come out."

"She doesn't know those truths yet," Duncan growled, knowing exactly what he meant.

"Aye, but Delacorte doesn't know that, and he can't ask her without incriminating himself."

Abandoning the topic that would only cloud his mind with anger, Duncan pointed down the hill to the beach. "Fort Vauban's lit up. She's still here."

"Aye, for now, but not long," Alec said. "He'll want to take her to Boney at Villa Pont-de-Briques. Boney would love to blame British spies for the assassination attempt, and Delacorte must know the man rarely sleeps. He'd want to take her by night, to hide his part in all this."

"He'd want her unable to talk." Urgency grabbed him. "We need lots of ammunition. I have rifles and pistols stored behind the stable, but we'll need explosive devices."

"I have only pistols here. Other weapons are at the farmhouse." Alec made as if to run.

"No, wait. I have barrel bombs here, and something better." Fulton raced to the other side of the stable, to a covered mound in the corner. He pulled out something shaped like a porpoise but with porcupine spikes. "These are torpedoes — sticky bombs with a timing device. Push the spikes into any wood, and use the timer button to make them explode. There are six. Take them all. Just save Elizabeth. If she . . . I'll never forgive myself if they hurt her."

"We'll get her back," Duncan vowed, just as quietly. She wouldn't be another Simon, another Peebles. "Take only what can't be replaced — and keep on the watch. They'll come for you, Fulton. If you see them coming, leave everything and go."

The protest on Fulton's face vanished. "Just save Elizabeth. Nothing else matters."

"We will," Alec and Cal said together, both looking at Duncan, the knowledge and the determination there. Damn it, they were doing it for *him.* Playing at big brothers. Trying to force him into the family — but he had no time to think about it.

"When my men come, use only those you absolutely need. Send the others to the fort with all possible firearms."

Fulton nodded. "Go."

As one, Duncan, Alec, and Cal turned and ran.

Chapter 36

Fort Vauban

Colonel Lebrun leaned back in his chair, looking warm and comfortable by the fire. "It's said LeClerc followed you home, expecting certain favors you gave him on regular occasions."

No longer knowing if she could trust the commander's lessons, Lisbeth shivered. But cold, vulnerable, and tired, a young girl was more likely to blurt out stupid things: Leo had taught her that the day Papa dragged her from his carp pond and left her wet and miserable until Leo whispered, *Just admit your fault* — and when Papa sent her to bed without supper, Leo smuggled bread, butter, and milk upstairs for her. *Fooling the captors is what Papa calls the first lesson of capture, but it works just as well at home. Admit to the lesser sin of fishing, making sure you look sad and wretched, and Papa won't think to blame you for riding his stallion.*

Thinking of that long-ago day she said,

trembling, "He followed me on several occasions, but on the night in question . . ."

"We have a witness who states that the man who called himself Gaston Borchonne shot LeClerc," the colonel interrupted smoothly.

She almost gaped. She'd forgotten Tolbert . . . silly, forgettable Tolbert, LeClerc's acolyte. "Yes, he did, in the foot. From that time M. Borchonne was constantly in my sight. He had no time to return and shoot M. LeClerc —"

"So now you admit to knowing Borchonne. Why should I believe anything you say?"

Think, just keep thinking. The violent headache and shivering were the only things keeping her from falling into exhausted slumber. She felt as if she'd been running from the day she'd arrived in France, unable to take a breath without Alain's control. He was the demon she couldn't exorcise.

"Madame, why should you lie, if you've done nothing wrong?"

She held his gaze. "I was taken in my kitchen by a ruse, hit on the head, and brought here without a cloak, sitting far from the fire. I'm cold and I'm scared. I-I thought my husband might have come for me . . ."

"I assure you he is not here, madame."

From her time with Alain, she knew how this worked. The colonel had reassured her; now she must give something back. "Not everything I said was a lie. I am nineteen. I was raised in the country, and my father would die before training me in espionage. My husband uses violence on me, and he stole my baby. The last time he was near me, he gave me this." She pointed at the scar on her face. Looking in Lebrun's eyes, she said, "The owners of Le Boeuf tavern, Messieurs Mathieu and Luc Marron, will confirm that in the year I worked there I never went upstairs with any man, never allowed M. LeClerc any intimacy. M. Luc Marron even gave me a knife to defend myself."

There was a look in the back of the colonel's eyes, some trace of doubt or pity. "So LeClerc tried to rape you, and you fought him off?"

"Not that last night, though I assume it was what he wanted." She looked in his eyes. "I met the man I knew as Gaston Borchonne a week before. If your witness was M. Jacques Tolbert, he was the one holding me down as LeClerc tried to rape me. M. Borchonne arrived and threatened to shoot them, but let them run away. Why would he do that, only to kill him a week later? Would he shoot him in the foot and warn him off, and then kill him?"

"Madame, how can I believe you?"

Her hands twisted around each other in her lap. "Would you want your sister to lie to strangers if she thought her violent husband was after her again?" To add emphasis, she touched her scar. "Ask Luc Marron. I am no whore. My husband made it up to set the town against me. I don't know why. I can only assume it's to gain public sympathy over his abduction of my son."

"Luc Marron is dead," the colonel said, still in that conversational tone. "He died the night you escaped from Abbeville."

She gasped, couldn't catch her breath, and hiccuped. The colonel handed her a glass of water and, after a few moments, a clean handkerchief: another kindness for which, by the invisible rules of interrogation, she'd have to give something in return.

After she'd composed herself, she said, with tears in her eyes, "Pardon, Colonel. Luc was my friend. You can see this scar is new. My husband shot the window next to where I was sitting, breaking glass all over me. I believe he tried to kill me when his plot to have me guillotined for LeClerc's murder failed. I don't know why he hates me so much. I never understood it."

Lebrun frowned. "Can you prove any of these accusations?"

The quiet, unmoved tone left her with no choice but to take the offensive against Alain. "The man who gave you the information on me — was he in his early thirties with blond curly hair, bright blue eyes, and a large mole on his right hand? Did he dress with the air of a gentleman and speak with the accent of the *ancien régime*?"

At the colonel's startled look, she drew a hard breath and began muttering to herself. "He's allowing you to conduct this investigation, but he's in the next room, listening and sending notes, telling you what will hurt, upset, or weaken me. He wants to force me to admit to being part of the assassination attempt today. That's why he didn't take Monsieur Monteaux. He can't afford to have any reputable witnesses to prove my innocence in the assassination. He can't be involved because I'm a nobleman's daughter, and Napoleon can't afford yet to have the European Tribunal investigate my death. He wants me dead, but he wants you to do it for him."

The colonel opened his mouth, and it hung open. "Who is he?" It came out a whisper.

Lisbeth threw him a bleak smile. "My husband."

Breathing too fast, feeling sick, all she knew was that she was trapped in this locked fortress, and Alain would walk in at any moment.

Ambleteuse Beach
"There are only two men on the ramparts, probably only two by the gate. That means there are probably no more than a dozen men in the fort in total." Alec shook his head. "This is a sloppy operation."

"The lass can take advantage of it. She

seems a clever girl," Cal said.

"Nothing Boney or Fouché does is this disorganized." Duncan nodded. "This whole plot has echoes of Abbeville. This is Delacorte's work on limited funds. He's running on fury."

"Unless it affects Lisbeth's rescue, lad, let's stop talking and start doing."

Duncan snapped, "You've been out of the game too long if you think it doesn't affect it."

Alec grinned. "That I have. You're in charge, lad."

At last it stopped snowing. Duncan drew in a breath and expelled it, seeing its thin white fog in the dark. "Lisbeth will be helping us already, if she's able to think beyond her fear."

"She has no reason to trust anyone," Cal agreed.

"Apart from you . . . and Fulton, it seems," Alec added.

Duncan growled, "Let's get on with it."

"Aye, right." Cal pulled a sticky bomb from the sack.

When Cal was going to put the sack down, Duncan grabbed it from him. "We need to use two bombs."

There was a brief silence. "These soldiers didn't do it to her, Duncan."

Duncan sighed. "Look at the gates, Cal. They're old and thick. We need to make sure the gates blow apart the first time and disable the guards."

Nodding, Alec reached in and handed Duncan a second bomb.

Using their cloaks as covers, the three men moved over the wet pebbles of Ambleteuse Beach toward the fort. Three feet from the gate, Alec fanned his cloak wide as a cover while Duncan pushed the spikes into each gate at its base, near the inner edge. Then he lit the fuses and set the timer, and they bolted back down the ramp and across the beach, leaping into the scrub at the top of the old seawall.

Fort Vauban

"You say the blond man has an interest in seeing you dead?" the colonel rapped out.

At last they were getting somewhere. Lisbeth's gaze flittered around the room as if it held monsters. "My husband will kill me to keep my mouth closed about his murdering LeClerc. I —"

Her open mouth froze when Alain stepped into the room. He leaned heavily on a cane; beneath his curly hair his face was as scarred as hers. He had the same damaged warrior look as the commander now, except his beautiful eyes glittered with hate. "*Ma chère,* how loyal you are to a man you claim to be a stranger, yet so disloyal to me, the man you vowed to be loyal and obedient to for life . . . until death us do part. Perhaps that time has arrived, before you feed the poor colonel any more lies —"

BOOM! A massive explosion shook the fort; a halo of fire and wood splinters filled the window on the side of the fort facing the town. Startled shouts came over the sound. Thin lines of smoke drifted in through the cracks in the walls.

Alain's face whitened. "What have you done, you stupid bitch?" he snarled in English.

Before she could begin to think of an answer, a second boom made the windows rattle. Another series of shouts came, and masculine screams filled with pain.

The colonel ran from the room. Lisbeth faced Alain alone.

CHAPTER 37

Screams filled the night, howls of pain and terror.

Flames leaped above the smoke, and Fort Vauban's gate blasted in the center. Duncan ran up the ramp to the fort, pulled out two loaded pistols, aiming at the gates. Alec and Cal were beside him in moments, weapons primed. "Let's give the fire something to chew."

The ball shot exploded in the wood, weakening it. Gunpowder sent the flames higher. Fire filled the gate, and pieces of it flew in all directions, but not enough to get through.

The three men threw down the spent pistols, and as one picked up the loaded Brown Bess rifles. With a quick double boom, the ball shots hit the burning wood; the gunpowder exploded. With a massive creak and a thud, the center of the burning gates burst open in a hole big enough to run through.

They threw off their cloaks in case they

caught fire and raced through the gates past a small crowd of panicking men scrambling over the living and dead littering the small courtyard.

The vision would haunt Duncan's dreams later. For now, he had to find Lisbeth.

Alec pointed. "Stairs past the inner courtyard." Pulling their pistols, they ran into the fortress and up the narrow stone stairs, worn and slippery with age. As they reached the second story Duncan felt a presence and snarled, "If you want to live, come out now."

From a recess a one-armed man stepped out, a man barely Duncan's age, looking sad and resigned. "You've come for the girl?"

Narrow-eyed, Duncan nodded.

"I'll take you to her. Please don't kill what remains of the men. I am — was — the lieutenant here before we were taken over. The men will listen to me when I misdirect them."

Outnumbered and almost out of weapons, Duncan didn't dare ignore this particular miracle. "Why would you help us?"

The man stared at each of them in turn, seeming bemused.

"The girl," Duncan growled. "Where is she?"

The man shook himself. "Bonaparte's man has my wife and children. He forced me to take part in a plot to bring her here, but she . . . was kind." He led the way up worn stone stairs to the top story. "Be gone from France before sunrise." It seemed he couldn't stop staring at them, one face to the other. "She has — you, also, or one of you — has been accused of murder."

Duncan snarled, "What did he do to her?"

The man hesitated. "The colonel questioned her for hours. She's due to be transferred to the first consul at Villa Pont-de-Briques before sunrise. When the gates exploded, the colonel ran out, but the other man —"

"The man that took over the fort — is he Bonaparte's man?" Duncan asked sharply. The man nodded. "Describe him."

"He has blond hair and dresses well, but his face has recent scarring, and he walks with a cane. He'd just entered the room to question the lady when the explosions happened."

"It's Delacorte," Cal muttered. "I shot him two months ago."

With a small cry Lisbeth stumbled down the stairs. Alain Delacorte was right behind her, holding a pistol to her head.

As Lisbeth stopped, she saw the commander rock back on his heels and take in the situation. She also saw the two men behind him. One of them subtly tipped his head at the one-armed man, but the one-armed man looked to Alain with a servile expression.

"Monsieur, what shall I do?"

"Get half a dozen men and bring them here. These people are English spies, to be taken to Lord Bonaparte at Pont-de-Briques before sunrise."

"*Oui,* monsieur, it shall be done." The one-armed man turned and vanished.

"So which of you recently played the part of Gaston Borchonne in Abbeville, and which of you played the Jacobin and shot me?" Alain purred. When none of the men answered, the smile in his voice only grew. "I saw two of you in the rowboat. Information about two look-alike British spies has gone to all the relevant places. Now it will be three. Come, you might as well speak, gentlemen — you are surrounded, you know. It was a brave but misguided attempt to rescue my beloved wife. You ought to have left her, really. Now you'll all be tried for the murder of several gendarmes. The murder of police is a very serious matter."

"So is forgery, the poisoning of a clergyman, and the abduction of a baronet's daughter." The commander's face was hard. "These are international crimes the king would interest himself in. M. Fouché would likely disavow knowledge of you, and the first consul would frown upon your acts in these delicate times. Do you dare to risk taking us to him?"

"Perhaps not alive," Alain replied, still smiling.

"I left proof of your misadventures with Lord Grenville a few weeks ago. The papers are to be sent to M. Fouché and the first consul should any of us be taken or killed, even by seeming accident," the commander's other brother added. He had old scars, which proved he wasn't the brother she'd met before. "I have the receipt of the standing order, if you're interested in taking a glance. It includes the lass there." From his pocket, he brought out an oilskin packet.

Alain didn't reach for the packet. "Go," he snarled, and all but threw Lisbeth at them. As the commander leaped forward to catch her, she heard the banging of Alain's cane heading back up the stairs.

The commander's hood fell back with the force of catching her. His hair was matted, his face unshaven, eyes hollow. "Did he hurt you?"

Overwhelmed, Lisbeth shook her head. She could hardly believe he was here. "I am well."

He frowned, peering at her. "They hit you. There's blood there." His finger trailed over the lump at the side of her head with a tenderness she'd never known.

"It will heal," she whispered. She saw the one-armed man stride out from a side door on the landing, and she froze.

"The path is clear. The blond man has left the fort. I thank the Lord I did not have to hit him," he whispered. "Go, and fast. He sent information to Lord Bonaparte about the lady's capture some time ago. Soldiers are coming to take her to Pont-de-Briques. I cannot stop that."

The commander put her down. "Can you run?" He didn't wait for her answer but led her downstairs, holding her hand. They reached the base of the fort, and she turned her gaze from the dead and dying. Still wondering how the commander knew M. Mareschal. And for how long.

They ran out and up the beach, over the hill and around the curve to the wilder places. Every moment she expected to hear the explosion of pistols or rifles. The thought of ball shot in her back, or Alain capturing her, gave her the impetus to run harder.

"How long will it take you to pack your things?" the commander panted, running beside her. "We have to be gone by dawn."

"I knew my mission would end soon. I packed days ago." Lisbeth felt unexpected sadness at the thought of leaving her life of the past seven weeks, being treated as an intelligent equal; Fulton quietly changing the world on the fringe of war, and because he valued her as a team member, helping with the mundane chores.

Then she remembered his proposal; she'd promised to answer him within the week. "Where's Fulton? They knew who he was. I think they want his inventions."

"He's well, and packing. We all leave France tonight, inventions included."

She stopped so suddenly the commander, still holding her hand, stumbled. The others paused. "I won't leave France without my son."

The brother she'd met in the coach weeks ago spoke. "When I commit to a mission, lass, I don't give up. When I see you safe, I'll return to Eaucourt. Delacorte has the house surrounded — I think the ship's mole informed him of my presence — but I have a plan."

The scarred brother she hadn't met said, "I swear we will bring your son to you."

Half a dozen men came down the hill. "Sir, is Miss Sunderland well?" Lieutenant Flynn sounded anxious.

"She is. Return to the house," he called back. "Go with them, Alec. Fulton will need help." The scarred brother nodded and ran with his men for the house. It was only when they were gone that the commander spoke again, far quieter. "Cal, you need to return to Eaucourt. We'll take you by sea. It's too dangerous by land, with the posters. I'll need you to send semaphores on what we discussed tonight."

"Aye, lad, consider it done. And, lass, your son will be with you soon." Cal turned and ran past the house to the stable.

Holding her by the arm, the commander

moved in his brothers' wake.

Stumbling along beside him, she said, "I will not leave my son."

"You can't stay in France any longer," he said, through heaving breaths.

She glared at him. "I will *not* leave my son."

"If you stay here, Edmond will be motherless. Delacorte will see you beheaded."

Lisbeth stepped back and stumbled on a tussock. "Put me down," she protested as he picked her up. "The colonel threatened Edmond with death if I didn't betray you all!"

He turned on her. "Did you betray us?" he asked fiercely.

"Did you betray me?" she snapped back. "Will you sacrifice my son to save England?"

"No."

Strange, how she believed the brief, furious answer. Weak or stupid to always want to believe him — but then, who else did she have? Lisbeth frowned. "Don't you see? If I leave France, Alain can say I deserted Edmond. No court in the land would give him to me!"

"None will anyway with your reputation," he snarled, running uphill so hard she bounced in his arms. She pummeled his chest to get him to put her down. "Think like the operative I've trained you to be! Delacorte would have done that the day we left Abbeville. The only way to rescue Edmond now is to steal him — and everyone in the town knows you. Why do you think Delacorte ruined you and came after you now? If he can't kill you, it's obvious we have to make him think he's chased you out of France for good before his vigilance will relax. Then Cal can put his plan into action."

Startled, she stopped punching him. "That's sensible," she conceded. "But —"

"I understand," he said through gasps. "He's your son. It feels as if you're deserting him."

She nodded, closer to real tears now than she'd been through any part of the colonel's inquisition. "What if it's the only way to save Edmond, as well as saving your life?" He looked behind for a moment before running even faster, but one leg dragged a little.

He must be in pain again. She couldn't answer him; but how could she doubt him after all he'd done tonight? "All right," she said slowly. "I will trust you with my baby's life."

"Delicately put," he returned with some wryness, and she flushed. "I'm not offended, Lisbeth. But you have to leave France tonight. Trust Cal and Alec to save the boy — they've saved us both, more than once."

He was telling the truth; she knew it, but she couldn't relent. "I want to know what you meant by what you said to Alain before, about the forgeries and other things."

"I'll tell you when we're safe on board ship.

And you'll tell me everything you said in interrogation." He was limping now, but ran harder, outrunning her inquisition more than the soldiers chasing them.

By the time they arrived at the house, carts and sailors were everywhere, having come from Duncan's ship with half a dozen of the biggest lifeboats it had. The half-repaired *Nautilus* was heading to Audresselles with a dozen men to row it to sea on a boat they called a launch. *Papillon* had already been taken from its mooring north of Audresselles Beach to the ship on the second-largest boat. Alec and Cal hopped on the attic cart, joining Fulton and another man.

It seemed Duncan was from a family of Scots. It felt surreal. He was so quintessentially English. So alone.

"My dear." Fulton grasped Lisbeth's hands in his, eyes worried. "They hurt you! I am so sorry my inattention led to this. I thought we were safe here."

"No time," the commander said briefly, forcing their hands apart. "Go, make certain my men left nothing behind you need."

She ran inside and up the stairs.

Within ten minutes, Lisbeth's bags had gone, holding her clothes and intimate necessities. She stepped over the back threshold and climbed on the last wagon. No point in locking the door when they'd only break it down.

Duncan — it seemed it *was* his name, his brothers used it freely — clucked his tongue. The horses began pulling the cart, but before they'd gone a mile, lights flared in the distance. Bobbing torches were coming up the hill from Ambleteuse. "Grab a sack and mount a horse."

Leaving the load behind, she grabbed a sack and ran to the horse. Duncan was already unhitching them from the wagon. He passed her a knife. "Cut line."

She sawed through the rope, pocketed the knife, and mounted as fast as she could.

"Gallop," he said tersely.

They turned off onto the uninhabitable land, cutting straight across the scrubby sand hills heading northwest. Her beast was a carthorse; a slow clop was its normal pace — but she saw light touching the eastern hills, panicked, and smacked the horse's rump to force it into a gallop.

Gradually — too slow, the lights and sounds were gaining — the broken sand cliffs of Audresselles came into view, the terrain hardening to ancient flat rock and sand. The whining horses' breaths steamed, streaming back in the Channel wind. Daylight stood defiant on the eastern hills, on the edge of the clouds, surly iron gray. The wind whipped her hair around her face and into her eyes, dragging icy tears down her cheeks. Even her gloved fingers were numb. Her nose felt likely to fall off.

The last rowboat was a deeper shadow on the churning water, moving northwest to sea. Duncan halted the trembling horse and gave two short, piercing whistles.

The boat came about, heading for shore.

The deep boom of musket shots split the air; ball shot screamed past them, and the sweating horses whinnied and reared. Duncan snatched Lisbeth's reins, grabbed her by the waist, and swung her off. "Run!"

She stumbled down the rocky path, across the sand, and into near-freezing water. She gasped as the cold hit her thighs, but then another shot hit the water beside her and she waded faster. The moment she reached the rowboat two sailors hauled her up by her arms. "We've got you, miss."

Another boom came, and water splashed up. "Turn tail!" Duncan yelled as he threw himself up and over. Shots came thicker as the men jumped around. Duncan took another oar and passed one to Lisbeth. Against the incoming tide, they all rowed for their lives.

CHAPTER 38

English Channel (English Waters)
October 30, 1802

"This is not negotiable. The moment I put foot on English soil your admirals will confiscate my work and force me to work for them. I refuse to leave this ship!"

Sitting at his nailed-down desk in the commander's quarters of the ship, Duncan fiddled with a quill. Fulton wasn't backing down — and unfortunately for all Duncan's arguments, he knew the American was right. One of the Admiralty would seize Fulton's work in the name of peace, and he'd never give it back. If some clever Johnny replicated the inventions, it would be the admiral sitting pretty on the profits, cheerfully ignoring its inventor's rights.

"Fulton has the right of it, Duncan," Alec said, with a meaningful look.

"Well, you choose a safe port! Boney controls all of 'em in northern Europe, and he'd steal everything just as fast, and take the profits," Duncan snapped.

Fulton snarled, "I'd prefer my work to be in the hands of a republican than a royalist!"

Good humor restored with the naive remark, Duncan smiled politely. If Boney had been the best thing to happen to France in decades, his overweening ambition would see him crowning himself sooner or later. If Fulton couldn't see it, Duncan wasn't about to burst his bubble. "I fear he'd take more than your inventions. Once they were with the Ministry of Science, I doubt he'd leave you alive. Are you willing to give your life for the glorious Republic of France?"

Fury and dislike burned in Fulton's eyes. "How do I know the whole scenario yesterday wasn't a setup by you to seize my inventions? I didn't see any danger."

In the stunned silence, Lisbeth said from her seat by the fire, "I was hit on the head, dragged to the fort, and interrogated for hours. My husband held a pistol to my head. Do you think I'd willingly go through all that, just to gain a boat . . . or do you think I'm lying?"

Fulton, Duncan, Cal, and Alec all swung around to Lisbeth, sitting in a wing chair by the fire. She kept the scarred side of her face in the shadows, but that only highlighted the lump on the other side of her head, the delicacy of her pale face. As she sat quietly in a corner, they'd forgotten she was there.

Voice and hands shaking, gaze on her lap — the trauma was clear. A flash of remorse came and went, lost in admiration. Almost any other woman would be in nervous prostration with all she'd been through, but she was here, doing her duty.

His mobile face filling with guilt and shame, Fulton crossed the length of the commander's cabin to her. "My dear, of course I don't. You are the one honest person in all this."

In a low voice, shaking, Lisbeth murmured, "For a while, I thought the same as you. I thought he'd deserted me. I wondered if the whole thing was set up. But they saved my life. They bombed the fort. They stopped him from killing me. It was real, Mr. Fulton."

He patted her hand, but she withdrew it. His hand hovered awkwardly above her lap before he stood. "Why did yesterday occur? Where were all of you when Lisbeth was taken?"

It was a good question. Lisbeth looked up, met Duncan's look, hers uncertain, her trust a rope frayed with overuse. She deserved to know where he'd been.

Mentioning his promise to Fulton weeks ago would only leave her feeling more betrayed. Duncan chose his words with care. "You know why we came to Ambleteuse in the first place."

"October twenty-ninth," she said, slowly, frowning. "The colonel at the fort said there had been an attempt on Napoleon's life yesterday."

A stifled sound came from Fulton, still standing beside Lisbeth, giving himself rights Duncan doubted Lisbeth had offered. The battleground still existed weeks after his withdrawal. "Did he survive?"

"Aye," Cal said when Duncan didn't answer. "The conspirators disappeared a few days ago. Only one remained to make the attempt, which is why it failed."

The shadowy figure who'd been silent since entering the room finally spoke. "I was sent to scarper the attempt without giving away my loyalties."

Fulton frowned at the man who refused to come into the light. "Who are you?"

"Deville," the man said curtly, "though you can also call me O'Keefe. I joined the ship yesterday." The air pulsed with the explanation he refused to give — to Fulton at least.

"Are you French or Irish?" Fulton demanded, and Duncan hid a smile.

"Both," the agent code named Tamerlan snapped, "and a British agent since the betrayal of the principles of the Republic when the Terror started. It sickened me to my stomach, seeing women and children guillotined, raped, or left for dead in the name of freedom."

Fulton flushed heavily, as he opened his mouth and closed it.

To mend fences, Duncan said, "Twelve men were sent to the Ambleteuse region to kill the first consul and replace him with a Bourbon prince. Deville worked on them all, and they left France before Bonaparte arrived. Most of them have ties to the British government, and we can't afford to break the peace."

Fulton frowned. "Then who tried to kill the first consul?"

"I'm assuming an English lord named Camelford," Alec put in when Duncan didn't want to answer. "He's madder than Bedlam. He ought to have been locked away years ago, but he's first cousin to William Pitt."

"Ah." Fulton's voice was rich with irony. "The English aristocracy will protect their own, no matter what the damage to others."

"Not my family," Lisbeth murmured. Suspicion shattered, a wineglass with blood-red wine seeping on Fulton's boots. He turned to her, face alive with emotion, but stopped when she looked away to the fire. The lady was fair and cold.

Damage. And Duncan knew he'd done it to her by his inattention to all but the mission. By trusting Fulton to keep her safe . . . and all to get a damned stupid boat.

"That's where we were yesterday, Lisbeth," he said, willing her to hear. "If I'd known Delacorte was here, I'd never have left you. I'm sorry."

She neither moved nor spoke. Her eyes had

the blind distance of the night he'd met her.

"Call the right spade, lad." Alec crossed the room to Lisbeth, but stopped at a safe distance, looking down at her with an odd affection, seeing that he'd only met her yesterday. "Lass, Duncan was near you the whole time until yesterday. I'm sorry, lass. I believe Delacorte took my men so we'd do exactly as we did, and you'd be left exposed."

No response. Her only movement was breathing, and her fingers, twisting on her lap.

This was *his* fault. He'd relied so heavily on her strength, he'd forgotten she was barely a woman, and one who'd seen more than enough pain. "We came for you the moment we knew." Duncan halted before naming her again. He had no right. Shoving down the odd ache inside him, he turned to Fulton. "I swore there would be no confiscation of your inventions, and if that means staying aboard ship until we find a safe port for you, so be it. What's important now is getting *into* Boulogne harbor and discovering what Boney's hiding."

When Fulton didn't answer, Alec shrugged. "By the murder of your younger agents, it's obvious he's got something vital there. His obsession with becoming the next William the Conqueror or Caesar makes it obvious it must be an invasion fleet, or he's preparing for war." When Fulton made a scoffing

438

sound, Alec grinned instead of taking offense. "Do you deny Boney's attempt in 1798 via Ireland, sir?"

Fulton made a dismissive gesture. "You were at war then."

"And that excuses invasion, when our army was on the Continent and in Egypt?"

The American shrugged. "It would have ended the war, wouldn't it?"

Duncan snapped, "So it's fine with you that thousands of innocent people die if they're ruled by a king, but not if they are part of a republic? Their lives are worth more to you?"

"He would have *freed* Ireland, Scotland, and Wales from domination!"

"As he freed Piedmont, Parma, Venice, and Switzerland?" Duncan retorted without a trace of mockery evident in his voice. "I'm sure the women of those nations thank Boney daily for the invasion that freed them of their homes, men, possessions, and virtue."

Fulton flushed and muttered something beneath his breath. "He stopped them as best he could, and you know it — unlike your generals in our war for independence."

"Bonaparte's preparing for war again. I'm certain of it," Duncan said quietly, holding Fulton's gaze; but the inventor turned from him, breathing harshly. God help them all, he was going to withdraw his support —

"Your agents were murdered?"

Duncan breathed again in relief. This odd,

brilliant girl was saying the right thing at the right time, even through her suffering. "Two of them, both under twenty-five," he answered, feeling the dull ache grow. "A boy of fourteen is somewhere with that mad lord who likes to kill people he considers beneath them."

Her face turned, no more than a moment. Eyes still lost, haunted. Looking beyond him to something only she could see. "You used a boy of fourteen."

He was the one flushing now. "He's my cabin boy. He escaped with Camelford while I was in Abbeville. I didn't know Camelford was on my ship. He posed as a fourth lieutenant."

A mere shake of her head, and she contemplated the fire again. "Rather than fight over where we can't go with Mr. Fulton's inventions, can't we go to Jersey?"

They all stared at Lisbeth.

"Jersey's an English port, Lisbeth," Fulton said gently, his eyes softening.

Duncan saw the effort she made to hold her temper in her tightened mouth, her half-curled fists. "Yes, but until we decide on a safe port, or if we do need to work on *Papillon* or *Nautilus,* it's a compromise. The island is close to France, and they're a fiercely independent people. Neither side needs to know we're there. And perhaps it has a shipbuilding port that's no part of the British navy — a private one?"

Though she didn't look at him, Duncan was the one who answered. "Yes, it does."

She stammered, "Also, would there be a blacksmith willing to take payment to share his forge? If we paid enough, might he give us private space to work without spreading gossip?"

Oh, the clever girl. In a feminine, self-deprecating manner she was wresting control from Fulton and leading the horse to British waters. Hiding a smile, he waited for Fulton to answer.

Fulton conceded, "It's a good compromise for now. Thank you, Lisbeth."

For the first time since her rescue Lisbeth smiled, humble and shy, her face still half in the shadows. Fulton lit up with warmth. His return smile was tender.

Duncan had no right to know if her feelings for Fulton were pretense for the mission, if the temptation to become respectable was pulling at her, or if she really cared for the man. It was her choice to make, and not her fault that either option made him bloody irritable.

"It's best if I start teaching the two men you choose to take the voyage in *Papillon* now," Fulton said.

Duncan nodded. "I was thinking of Lieutenant Flynn, and myself, of course. Flynn's a shipbuilder's son and would have some expertise."

Fulton frowned. "He's almost as tall as you are. Two men of your size could never fit. There'd be no room to operate *Papillon.* If you go, Commander, the second man must be much smaller. Though it would be an advantage if he has the knowledge you mention."

Duncan sighed. "It's unfortunate that Carlsberg is, ah . . ."

With hidden smiles, the men thought of the plump ship's engineer.

Nobody bothered to ask Fulton to go on the mission. He'd given Lisbeth the boat to fulfill his own purposes, but made it clear he'd rather die before he helped the empire he despised.

"That lets us out. It's a hard life," Alec muttered to Cal, mock morose.

Fulton went on, the humor wasted on him. "Don't forget the man you choose must be comfortable in enclosed spaces. It gets very warm inside, and the air tube only lets in a trickle at a time. It's enough to keep two men alive, but if one of you should succumb to panic —"

"I won't panic," Duncan said curtly.

Alec and Cal stopped sniggering, and he realized — again — the Black Stewarts knew more about his past than he was comfortable with.

"I think you gentlemen are overlooking two

— no, three salient points." When the men turned to Lisbeth, she said in an even tone, "One: I'm small enough to fit. Two: after many weeks of instruction, I have the required knowledge. And three: as *Papillon*'s legal owner, *I* am the one with the right to choose my crew."

Indeed, Fulton had given her a deed to the underwater boat that morning in a private ceremony; but whatever he'd hoped to gain from the gift hadn't materialized. Though touched and grateful, she'd seemed to size Fulton up anew. The girl was nobody's fool — and if Duncan hadn't had prior experience with her unpredictable brilliance and stubborn courage, he thought his jaw would be dropped as low as Fulton's was right now. He felt unwilling awe at her spirit, and an absurd urge to protect her. Absurd because though she'd been through more than enough, he knew she'd still fight him all the way for the right to go on *Papillon.*

Before Duncan could speak, Alec burst into delighted laughter. "Aye, you tell us, lass! It'll teach us to think before dismissing a woman's strength, not to mention property rights."

Lisbeth grinned at him.

Duncan interjected before Fulton could protest. "Miss Sunderland, while I agree with the owner's right to choose the crew, you also have overlooked a salient point or two."

Smile fading, she turned to him, brow

lifted. "Yes, Commander?"

He didn't react to the subtle taunt in her tone. Every time he called her Miss Sunderland, he knew she remembered anew that he still hadn't told her the meaning of his threats to Delacorte at the fort. He'd tell her, but right now he had more important things on his plate.

Fighting the anger that he felt put in the wrong by her again, Duncan spoke flatly. "You're barely past serious injury. This mission will take days, not hours. We must go before sundown tomorrow. In your state, I'm not certain you'd be able to complete such a mission."

"Perhaps, but you have more reason to take me than leave me behind. I'm the only one besides Mr. Fulton with enough knowledge of *Papillon* to undertake this mission, and teach my partner as we go." He couldn't refute it, and she had the grace to keep her triumph to herself. "You said there were two points?"

"The tunnel," he said. "When it ran out of air, you panicked."

Resting on the chair, she pulled herself up. "The panic lasted seconds only. While not sleeping in over a day, seeing a dead body, and being set up for murder might be everyday fare for *you,* it was a first for me. I was overwhelmed."

"You're in much the same state as then."

He didn't dare acknowledge that he'd vomited the first time he'd seen a dead body; but he'd been only fifteen. "It may take a full day to reach our destination. The air gets so warm you can't breathe . . ."

"I know that. I've spent entire nights in *Papillon* for the past four weeks, and as Mr. Fulton will tell you, I never panicked once. How many submersible boats have *you* been in for hours on end, to know whether or not you'll panic?"

Alec sniggered again, and even Cal chuckled.

Duncan turned on them. "Stubble it, *lads*. Behave like grown men or leave my quarters."

The Scots smirked before quieting down.

"I've had experience of a different kind — and in my opinion, experienced sailors are the most logical choice."

"But the choosing is not yours. *Papillon* is mine —"

Duncan sat straighter in his commander's chair. "I am the commander here." Realizing his mistake when her mouth turned down and her nostrils flared, he softened his tone. "You've done a fine job, Miss Sunderland, done what none of us could have —"

"Don't patronize me." Her tone was frozen. "I fulfilled my mission to the letter, while keeping my principles. How many of *you* can say that about your first mission?"

"Not me, lass," Alec admitted cheerfully. "I

445

was acting as the lad here's alibi, but after a night on the tiles, I met the sauciest little barque of frailty —"

"Stop right there, Stewart!" Duncan snapped. "A lady is present!"

"What's a barque of frailty?" Lisbeth sounded bewildered. "Isn't a barque a ship — ?"

"That tale, or its explanation, is not for Miss Sunderland's ears," Fulton put in hastily.

Lisbeth sat up straight. "Who made either of you my legal guardian?" Light from the fire fell on her face, the bruises and scars making her seem even more fragile, but it didn't show in her voice. "What renders you fit to judge what I can and cannot hear?"

"I'm treating you as the lady you are," Fulton said, bewildered.

"It's a little late in the day for that, sir! If we're applying society's hypocritical standards, you should turn your back on me, or make the same offer you did weeks ago."

His color high, Fulton muttered, "How long must you make me pay for one lapse in judgment, my dear? Haven't I since made up for that, even before I knew —"

"Before you knew who my father was?" she shot back.

Fulton had the grace to blush still more. "I thought I had changed the discomfort between us weeks before then," he mumbled,

446

shooting a glance at the other men.

Duncan felt Alec glance at him and shifted in his seat.

"You did, Mr. Fulton, but —" She hesitated, and Duncan saw the hurt in her eyes as she glanced at him. She went on in a different tone. "But . . ." She shrugged, an imperfect attempt to hide the wounds she carried inside.

Fulton crossed the room, crouched before her, and said, low, "Lisbeth, you earned my respect, and more. You surely know this. Please tell me you've forgiven me."

Her gaze flicked to the others in the room, and she frowned and nodded. "Certainly, sir." She tugged her hands from his, her color rosy.

Fulton could go on bended knee any other time he chose. Duncan was trying to stop an invasion. "Resume your seat, Fulton. We have to discuss which other man —"

He could have bitten his tongue when Lisbeth's fury turned on him. "Oh, of course it must be a man that goes, mustn't it? Despite all I know of *Papillon,* and that *I* own it, you won't even contemplate my presence on the mission. Are you afraid I'll faint, or get my courses and cry on you?"

With an enormous grin, Alec said, "That's it, lass, discomfit us — we deserve it. Mad hypocrites we are, all of us men, and our rules."

Lisbeth mock-glared at Alec, struggling to

choke back a giggle. Alec winked at her while Duncan fumed in silence. Cal neither moved nor spoke, but the slightest smile was in his eyes. And Fulton looked proud of her defiance, damn him —

"Out!" Duncan roared. "All of you but Miss Sunderland."

If he were in a better mood, it would be comical to see how the others turned to him, brows lifted as if they were at a raree-show seeing a freak. But whatever they saw must have convinced them to file out . . . even Fulton.

Lisbeth stood, her chin lifted. "If you only wish to yell at me, I think I'll leave."

With difficulty, Duncan reined in his temper. "I apologize for my lack of manners, Miss Sunderland. Will you please listen to what I have to say?"

Though the wary look remained in her eyes, she sat again. "I will listen, sir, but I make no promises." She kept her gaze on him when he didn't speak. "Oh, I see. You were going to make me rest while you went on the mission — or perhaps send me ahead to Jersey? What good would that do now, sir? You have your boat."

In the half shadows of the fire, first the lump on her head came to light, and then the scar. And then those slanted eyes, sore from what she must see as his treachery. "It's not that . . ." True, nobody had her qualifications

— but in truth, he was damned scared to take her on *Papillon.* What the devil could he say to convince her? He knew she wouldn't make it there and back, just by looking at her. The strain of the past few months had left the girl like blown glass, ready to shatter if the slightest pressure was put on her.

To buy time, Duncan crossed the room and sat opposite her. This wasn't a conversation to shout across a room with sailors passing the door, or to be overheard by the double agent he hadn't yet discovered. Alec and Cal, as trustworthy and capable signalers, had taken over the task in shifts until they reached Abbeville. At least he could breathe easy, knowing Boney couldn't have the information on *Papillon* in time to thwart the mission. But Cal had to return to Abbeville to rescue Edmond, or he'd lose her. That gave Duncan perhaps three days to find the mole, because Alec couldn't signal alone all day, every day. The commander trusted Flynn and Burton, but then he'd trusted all his men until he'd realized he had a double agent. Right now he couldn't trust his own instincts.

He felt control of the mission crumbling in his fingers like old bread. In truth, he was damned scared because there was no one else he *could* take with him; but he couldn't look at her without wishing to God he'd sent her home weeks ago. She'd fight like the devil to prove she was strong enough to complete the mission, and that would weaken her still further.

When he didn't speak, Lisbeth lifted her chin, eyes flashing, like a kitten ready to spit. "You refuse me because I'm a woman? When I've never failed in anything you've asked of me? In fact, I remember saving *you* once."

He might have known not to underestimate her. "You haven't let me down, Miss Sunderland. I'm grateful for your assistance —"

"But my usefulness is limited to the kitchen and bedchamber, is that it?"

He felt his cheeks heating. "I've never said that."

"What did I learn on your ship? How to cook and clean! You gave me pretty dresses and shoes, and nightwear that made me blush when I put it on at night. Would you have given such instruction or clothing to a man you'd sent to Fulton?"

"It wouldn't have got me far if I did," he retorted, and almost hit himself. She'd baited her trap to perfection.

Her mouth turned down. "I believed you had greater discernment than the average male. It seems I was wrong."

His ire boiled up, but he threw water on his temper. What she'd revealed was far too important. *Nightgowns that made me blush when I put them on* — and he understood the wounded look in her eyes. If Fulton had fallen into the usual male trap of judging a woman by a man's needs, so had he. "I beg your pardon." He leaned forward, taking her hand in his. "You've more than proven your worth. This mission would have failed without you — and, as you say, you accomplished it without losing your principles."

She pulled her hand away. "Don't pat me on the head, Commander. You wouldn't have spoken so to any other team member."

He found himself chuckling, even as he shook his head. "Forgive me once more, Miss Sunderland. My only excuse is that no other gently reared girl — or man — your age could have endured your life the past year. I hardly know how to treat you."

"Woman," she said quietly.

She was right; she was no longer a girl, had none of a girl's tricks or traits, and she knew her mind. "Yes," he conceded, "but to return to the point, you can't deny you don't have the equivalent of my physical strength, and what physical strength you have is depleted."

"True, sir, but *you* don't have my knowledge of submersibles. None of your crew could learn everything I have in a day or two — and as you've said, it's best to go now. Given our time frame, I am not merely the logical choice. I am the only choice."

She had him there. "If you're called the weaker sex in the Bible, it's certainly not in the ability to argue," he muttered, feeling outgunned on every score.

Her eyes twinkled. "I believe St. Paul was also, as St. Peter put it, just a man," she said, with a soft gurgle of laughter. "One with no knowledge of the strength a woman faces monthly, and in enduring the travails of childbirth. But be assured I will never take off my hat in church."

She'd deliberately repeated her assertion about monthly cycles to discompose him. The girl's impish sense of humor caught him out every time. He grinned. "I now understand what your father said about needing to take to you with a birch switch."

She laughed. "He couldn't have caught me, even on the rare occasions he *was* at home."

Something in her riposte disturbed him. "You'll have to prove your ability, the same as any crew member, Miss Sunderland. We'll take a few trial runs."

Her brows lifted again. "Certainly, sir. I have no desire to be trapped inside my locked boat with a panicking male . . . and since this is my boat, I ought to choose the crew."

And here it was — the time for truth. "The property of a woman crosses to her husband on her marriage."

"Are you saying you're going to hand the boat to my husband to pass on to Fouché or Bonaparte as he sees fit?" Her face and voice stopped halfway between incredulity and derision.

He wondered if she could see how much he

hated this, knowing how it would hurt her. "Of course not — if Delacorte was your husband. But he's not."

After all the emotional bombs he'd thrown at her since they'd met, he expected something physical from her, perhaps anger. All she did was withdraw into the shadows. Her voice came softly from the dark. "Explain that, if you please."

"Your father sent me to Scotland after you left with Delacorte." His tongue felt thick and clumsy. "There was no record of the marriage at any cathedral or kirk in the region."

"We married at the kirk in Creasy Village by Jedburgh. It's small and out of the way."

He nodded. "I was there. The rector had no memory of you. I arrived two weeks after you. It seems Delacorte had a sham ceremony performed and papers filled by his cohorts after poisoning the real rector's poached pears with syrup of ipecac the night before. He was sick for days. It means your marriage is invalid." He waited for the anger, the tears —

The last thing he expected from her was a burst of wild laughter. He stared at her as she threw her head back, thudding her fists against the wing chair's arms. "Oh, that's beyond price. He never married me — of course he didn't. Of course he didn't!" Tears rolled down her scarred and bruised face as she laughed like a Bedlamite.

Unsure of his ground, he waited for her to compose herself.

"That's why he burned my identity papers as Lisbeth Delacorte," she gasped. "Should anyone check their validity, Alain would have been arrested for forgery — oh . . ." Her eyes widened. "That's what you meant by your threats at the fort! By drugging me when I refused to go to France, he abducted a nobleman's daughter. Since he wasn't my husband, he had no right. It would have caused an international incident. He kept me watched because I was his ransom so my father wouldn't expose him, either about the forgeries or about abducting me. It's also why he took Edmond. He knew I wouldn't leave my baby."

His respect for her intelligence grew tenfold. If she'd been a man, she'd be running the bloody Alien Office before she turned thirty. "I believe you're right on all counts."

"That's why he set the town against me. With all of them watching my every move, Papa couldn't send someone to Abbeville without him knowing. That's why you took on the Gaston Borchonne identity." Her face came alive, brighter as she absorbed each new implication. "He set us up for LeClerc's murder because Alain suspected you'd been sent by my father. He needed to hide his crimes before they became public. If the

European Tribunal discovered his acts, not even Bonaparte or Fouché could protect him. They'd make him the acceptable sacrifice."

"Neither can afford to be seen as Delacorte's accomplices." He couldn't keep the wonder from his voice. She hadn't even been with him when he'd worked out that Fouché had kept Delacorte in Abbeville after the espionage rings at Le Boeuf came to light. Good God, she was brilliant.

"Alain stood to lose everything," she went on. "People have been killed for far less since the Revolution. So he made up the story of my being a whore, took Edmond, and set the entire town to watching me to protect himself. It's why he keeps chasing us. He has no choice." In the soft firelight, the wonder on her face fascinated him. "I thought he hated me because my father didn't love me enough to let my husband in the door. But it was all just a cover-up."

Alarm bells tolled in Duncan's head again. "It was to punish your father, too."

Like dawn breaking after a black night, her charming, one-dimpled smile came alive. "I'm free of him. Even Edmond — he could have told me when I was pregnant, and I'd have married him for the baby's sake. But he made his son illegitimate and didn't care."

Before he knew what she was about, she'd jumped from the chair and, balancing each step as the ship pitched, bent and kissed his cheek. "I told you the night we met that you were a godsend, and you've been just that. I don't *care* if you never tell me anything about yourself —"

"My birth name is Damien," he said harshly, hating her gratitude when he didn't deserve it, "and I haven't finished."

Instead of seeming cowed, she tilted her head, considering him. "Damien? No . . . I'm sorry if I seem rude, but it doesn't *fit.*"

How odd that she could make him smile even now. "I've been calling myself Duncan since I was fourteen."

"So that's why you could introduce yourself as Duncan, yet still tell me it wasn't your real name. I thought you were lying to me." She nodded wisely, looking like a lovable owl. "Yes, Duncan suits you perfectly. But how did you —" She bit her lip. "I'm sorry, it's not my concern."

"I was christened Damien Urquhart Charles Aylsham. I took the first letter of my names and added the 'n.' " He smiled as she nodded again, innocent and wise — and suddenly he knew he'd never intended to let her marry Fulton. "Does the name mean anything to you?"

"Should it?" she asked, frowning.

Blowing out a breath, Duncan said the words he'd refused to speak since the night he met her. "I thought your father might have told you the name of the man who offered you marriage."

Her eyes widened, her mouth fell open, and the color drained from her cheeks.

He stood and made a formal bow. "I'm the heir to the Annersley barony — the man you ran off with Delacorte to avoid meeting."

Before she could speak, he bowed once again and kissed her knuckles. "Since I dare to hope you no longer find my offer repulsive, I ask again, this time in person. Miss Sunderland, will you do me the great honor of becoming my wife?"

CHAPTER 39

"I don't like this, Pitt."

Former Prime Minister William Pitt, known as Pitt the Younger, felt his brows lift. Shivering, he pulled his chair closer to the fire. As current Lord Warden of the Cinque Ports he'd been given Walmer Castle as his home, and he loved it; but it was drafty and cold, and the Channel wind roared through the walls even in summer. In the colder months it was unbearable. "*You* don't like it, my lord." The emphasis carried volumes of incredulity.

"No, I damn well don't." From the other side of the tea table, Marquess Cornwallis drained his tea. He was too old a campaigner to care what Pitt thought of him. In America, India, and Ireland he'd performed tasks few could stomach, and as British ambassador to France until three weeks ago, he had been well rewarded for his unswerving loyalty to

British interests. "I was looking forward to my retirement after being recalled from Paris — but like it or not, I'm temporary Lord Constable of Ireland until they find a replacement for Whitworth. If there's insurrection on my watch, I ought to expose it, not sit on it like a chicken waiting for it to hatch."

Pitt hid the grin at the mental vision Cornwallis had engendered: a fat, self-satisfied chicken indeed, in his wig and the fashionable tight coat that he could only fit with a corset, the kind made for the Prince of Wales. As he shifted in the chair, the corset creaked ominously.

"Appropriate action will come at the right time. It's necessary to let this plot . . . mature, shall we say?"

"Why?" Cornwallis demanded as he took the delicate cream cake offered him.

Covering his aching knees with a second blanket, Pitt eyed the marquess with secret envy. When was the last time he could eat without care? Irritable, he drained the port in his glass. No point in repining the hand he'd been dealt.

Apart from a lifted brow, Lord Cornwallis didn't react. Everyone knew his proclivity for port had begun as early in life as fourteen. "The French and Irish are collaborating again."

"Of course they are. They're both Catholic and want this republican rule by the rabble.

All the more reason to expose an Irish plot right away."

Bulldog Cornwallis, Pitt thought, with an affection he felt for few outside his family. " 'There is a limit at which forbearance ceases to be a virtue,' " he quoted.

"Edmund Burke's words. Good man for an Irish. Why?"

Pitt knew better than to think he was asking about the famous Irish statesman. "I believe this insurrection is an old song resung."

"Which song?"

"Seventeen ninety-eight."

Cornwallis stared. "French invasion via Ireland again? I thought we'd finished with those tomfool plots in 1801 when Nelson went into Boulogne."

And had his arse soundly kicked. Pitt shrugged. "Boulogne's blockaded by land and sea. Our agents are having the devil of a time getting in, and two or three of our men have already been killed. Something's going on there, my lord, during a peace Boney engineered."

Cornwallis frowned. "Boney pulling strings behind the scenes I'll accept, but you must have compelling evidence to ask me to risk going behind Addington's back."

But he looked interested. Though Pitt had retired on ethical grounds a year ago, the day was near when Prime Minister Addington, a good man given to panic, would desert the sinking ship. Then the king, still offended with Pitt over his stance on Catholic emancipation and his friend Wilberforce's public passion over the abolition of slavery, would beg his return.

Pitt believed passionately in good government. Power by the people was asking for trouble when they didn't know what to do with it. The crazed slaughter during the French Revolution and the Terror were proof positive. Boney was a brilliant commander of troops but knew little of politics or statecraft. France needed someone bred to the task of government. "Word from the Archbishop of Narbonne and the Comte d'Artois was confirmed through reliable agents in France. There was a failed attempt to kill Bonaparte yesterday. Most of the conspirators disappeared before the day, but a massive cache of weapons was found."

Cornwallis snorted. "He has so many demmed spies and sharpshooters and guards no assassin can reach him, not even that Infernal Machine in 1800. What makes this plot different?"

"When Boney returned to Paris, he insulted Fox again at the Tuileries, accusing Britain of harboring assassins at the embassy. The weapons were found at Raoul Gaillard's house. O'Keefe was also implicated."

Cornwallis was fast to catch on. "The Gaillard brothers want the little grinder dead, I grant you — the silly gudgeons made their feelings public on the subject — but why would Boney alienate the Irish by naming O'Keefe . . . ah." Cornwallis nodded. "The Act of Union makes him British — and he has known ties to the Alien Office." He drummed his fingers on the table before taking another cake. "He's alive. So Boney's using this as a diversion. The question is why."

Relieved Cornwallis had grabbed the plot by the throat — age certainly hadn't dimmed his sharp mind — Pitt nodded. "I'm sure you know, my lord."

"Boney made the plot fail at the last moment, confiscated the weapons, and accused the British via O'Keefe, knowing Addington will panic, send every troop to Dublin, and recall Nelson from the Channel to prove he's keeping to the Amiens Treaty," Cornwallis murmured.

"Meanwhile, Boney sails his *Grande Armée* across the Channel and lands wherever he chooses on our coast instead of risking the Irish Sea again. Probably he's hoping it's *our* ships that get wrecked this time." Pitt offered the lord constable a fourth cake, which the marquess took with a self-effacing grin.

Every man had his Achilles heel.

" 'When bad men combine, the good must work together,' " Cornwallis said, quoting Burke again. "Addington makes decisions based on fear and panic. Boney can't be blind to that. Well done, Pitt. I'm on board. So what's happening in Boulogne?"

"We don't know yet. So far the European Tribunal inspectors have only been invited to the Mediterranean ports, and our spies have found just a few ships built at any port in France. Seems they've only built the agreed-upon number of warships. We have a team combing the Channel Coast, unofficially of course."

"Is it unofficial to prevent untimely war? Or because your cousin was part of the conspiracy?" Cornwallis asked softly.

Pitt held in the shudder. Nobody of good birth and breeding dared admit the head of their family was a madman, especially when one was in politics — but Thomas's acts were as well known as they were erratic, even before his latest assassination attempt and capture. For all Camelford's obsession with birth and breeding, Pitt couldn't remember the last time he'd acted the gentleman and kept his violent little peccadilloes to himself. As the saying went, he might as well have tied his garter in public.

Though he rarely felt warm these days, Pitt felt his cheeks heat. "That, also. Boney captured him just outside Boulogne. No one knows where Thomas is now. My cousin Anne . . ."

Cornwallis waved a hand. "Shall I send my

463

brother a note to ask if he'll send a patrol or two to the right region, perhaps send a few good men to go discreetly hunting for the prison that holds Camelford?"

Pitt's face broke into a rare smile. He couldn't have asked, that wouldn't be playing the game; but Cornwallis's offer of his admiral brother's influence to help find his cousin was a gift he desperately needed. "Thank you, my lord."

"So what else do you want me to do?"

Relieved to leave the subject behind — they both knew what had to be done, but one had to play the game — Pitt shrugged. "Let the Frogs think we've swallowed this."

Cornwallis's puff-cheeked countenance lit with his grin. "What am I to do?"

"Keep sending the troops to chase the usual suspects — but somehow your soldiers don't find them. Keep Dublin Castle manned and ready, but make certain it's as discreet as possible. Play the arrogant old fool making bumbling mistakes. They're bound to have their spies inside the castle."

The rheumy eyes twinkled. "I've played that part quite well before. I can see how history will paint me! What will you do?"

"The vital work now is being done by Windham's people."

Cornwallis tapped the side of his nose as he stood, signaling the end of the meeting.

"So I'm guessing this meeting never occurred."

"What meeting, my lord? Few people even know you inhabit Dublin Castle this month. I certainly didn't invite anyone to Walmer."

The marquess chuckled and grasped Pitt's hand. "You'll do, lad. I'll be back in Dublin by morning. Don't chafe too much during this lull, or watch the ocean too hard. Figureheads look pretty, but in a storm, those who steer the ships into safe waters are the ones remembered."

After Cornwallis was gone, Pitt thought about his analogy. This was but a lull before war, and Britain couldn't have a mere figurehead leader. A good man, Addington wasn't built for hard decisions. He was already bending. Soon he'd break, the government would collapse, and the king would have to give power back to Pitt . . . on the right terms.

Thomas must be out of France before that happened. When war came, it couldn't be a Pitt that started it.

With a weary smile he sat at the desk by the window of his library and wrote a note to his old friend William Wilberforce. On the surface, he asked after his wife Barbara's health; she was in confinement for the fourth time. But if a few words slipped in that resurrected Wilberforce's passion for the abolition of slavery and Catholic emancipation, it wouldn't do any harm. It would also make

Fox very happy.

Pitt needed to be ready, and he needed men of heart and courage on both sides of politics to stand with him.

English Channel, British Waters

Lisbeth looked down at the hand holding hers, his head bowed over it, lips touching her skin; but it was as if he'd spoken Swahili to her. "I don't understand."

He looked up. "It's simple, Lisbeth. I offered you marriage eighteen months ago. I offer it again now."

Her free hand wandered to her brow. "You'd go so far to secure *Papillon* for Britain?"

He let out a short laugh. "If you like, I'll sign everything you own back to you on our wedding day. I'll have the papers drawn up when we reach Jersey. I'll never own *Papillon,* in any case. Fulton's deed makes you its owner for life, no matter your marital status, and I was a signatory to the deed. Does that satisfy you that I'm not plotting against you in this?"

She shook her head. "No. None of this makes sense. Commander, I —"

"I think we've gone past Commander and madame, or even Miss Sunderland," he said, with a strange smile. "Call me Duncan, Lisbeth."

His sudden desire for intimacy between

them was one change too many in her life. She shook her head. "If you're a baron's heir, you can't be linked to a woman like me. I'd ruin your chances at politics. Society wouldn't accept me."

He stilled for a moment, then released her hand and sat back at the chair opposite her. "I couldn't care less about society or going into politics." He moved back into the chair until his face disappeared into shadow, the firelight a dancing mask across his features. "I told you I don't see you that way. You were pushed into your situation, and that was mostly my fault. I should have met you before making you an offer."

"Yes, you should." Her fingers smoothed absently at her frown. "Why now?"

He tilted his head but said nothing, watching her closely. Knowing what he wanted, she lifted her chin and waited in turn.

He acknowledged the power play with a small smile. "You learn quickly." When she still didn't speak, he nodded. "I wanted you to know you have an option other than Fulton."

A disbelieving laugh burst from her. "What am I, a chess piece in a private battle between you?" She wouldn't tell him Fulton had made his proposal days ago, even with the scandal of divorce, as disgraceful as that was in the eyes of almost any society.

As soon as Fulton discovered she was still

in truth Miss Sunderland, he'd be searching out rings and churches — and she wasn't sure how to feel about it.

She'd spent her rare quiet moments in the past few days trying to find a reason why Fulton had proposed. That he desired her was obvious; they worked well together — but his passion for invention was paramount. To gain vital funding, Fulton had to live within the rules of accepted society. It would have destroyed his career to wed a woman of a lower class, or a divorced woman. So somehow she'd revealed that she was a lady by birth, and her father a wealthy man. It was the only possible reason she could find for him to want to marry her.

The commander — Tidewatcher, Damien, Duncan — was a baron's heir. No matter what his finances were, he could have looked far higher for a wife, even before she was ruined. So why was he renewing the offer? Despite the Stewart brothers' presence in his life, he seemed an isolated man. His surname alone told her there was a history he wasn't telling her.

He always spoke of her father with deep respect, affection — and knowledge. "Are you making the offer to please my father?" It felt right — yet the hurt of it went deeper than she wanted to admit.

"If I did at first, Lisbeth, it was before I knew you. Now, when Eddie wouldn't blame me for walking away, I'm offering again because I want to."

It was an answer of sorts, true in its way; yet there was something he hadn't told her. But when hadn't that been the case? The man ate and drank secrets like ambrosia and nectar. "Why?"

"I like you," he said, and once more she hated that he said it so simply, and she believed.

"There's another reason." It wasn't a question.

"Your father knows my financial position. I can easily prove that I have no need of your inheritance, or Eddie's wealth or influence." In his eyes, she saw understanding of her turbulent confusion over Fulton's feelings for her; that she needed to know that either man offering her marriage liked her apart from the Sunderland name, influence — and wealth.

"Then what else is behind this? What do you want from me?" It was the only thing that made sense. "I brought you the boat. I'm willing to let you use it as needed. I expect to have Edmond returned to me without being coerced into agreeing to marriage, or anything else you need for British security. So there's something else you're not telling me."

"I suppose I can understand your suspicion." With a fatalistic look, he handed her a folded paper. "It's the marriage license I hoped we would use."

She looked down at it. "It's signed by Mr. Kendall, our vicar at home."

"Yes. Note the date."

He'd bought the license the day her father had announced her engagement.

"I accept that back then at least, it had nothing to do with British security." Frowning, she pushed it back at him. "It doesn't mean you're not manipulating me now."

A frozen half smile acknowledged the accuracy of her assessment. "Tell me what else I could want from you, Lisbeth, but your lovely person."

A short bark of laughter escaped from her. "Don't try charming me, Commander, it doesn't suit you."

He relaxed and grinned. "An accurate hit."

She laughed with him. It felt comfortable; too easy to imagine a life like this. Laughter by the fire. A man she could respect, desire — but she'd spend her life extracting information from him as a dentist did teeth. Would she die fifty or sixty years from now, wondering if she'd ever truly known the man she'd married?

Slowly, she said, "It occurs to me that if we return to war, I would be useful for further missions of this ilk. You could put off bringing Edmond to me while asking me to rescue this person or that, get this invention or information. As your wife, I would have no right of refusal."

The smile on his face faded. "I meant it when I said no child should be raised by that man. Your son deserves his mother, all day, every day . . . and a father whose sanity and tendency for violent behavior isn't in question."

With those abrupt words, he put her in her place. "I beg your pardon." He nodded, retreating into the darkness of the chair. Looking down at her hands, she said, "I can't answer you. I came here to fight for my place on the Boulogne mission, not this. This past week — it's all too much. I need to be alone for a while, Commander . . . um . . ."

"Duncan," he said gently.

She wouldn't look at him, or acknowledge the name. "Tell me I'm part of the mission."

He sighed. "You know you are. There's nobody else who *can* go with me."

"Thank you." What was there to thank him for? Acknowledgment of what they'd both always known? Absurd.

Looking up, she saw his face soften. His hand lifted, reaching out to her. "Lisbeth —"

She shook her head again and walked out.

English Channel, French Waters
November 2, 1802
The first fingers of daylight searched the clouds and slate-gray churning waters of the

Channel. The morning was frigid, the wind fickle, fighting Lisbeth's every step. She drew her cape tighter around her. Her heart hammered, but she was no longer afraid, only filled with a sense of purpose as she crossed the deck to the starboard side where *Papillon* hung suspended, ready to be lowered into the sea.

"Lisbeth."

His voice rumbled beneath her skin, spreading fingers of warmth in the biting cold. She turned, but knew the familiar black-cloaked figure was behind her. Water splashed up onto the deck from the insane wind, making the cloak fly around him.

"Lisbeth, we need to go. The ship can't stay here after daylight."

Without a word she headed for the gangplank stretched from the starboard rail to *Papillon*'s hatch.

Papillon shifted as the waves smashing the ship jostled her like a crowd at the theater. Weak rays of a fitful sunrise pushed through thin cloud. A touch of rose-hued light illuminated the craft. Foam from the slapping waves and dried-out tendrils of seaweed crowned her, an obdurate crown. The awkward little sister of *Nautilus,* with twice the defiance, *Papillon* filled Lisbeth with wonder and half-fearful respect every time she entered. She heard its silent taunt, lost in the morning's hard chill. *Come and take me. I dare you.*

Without meaning to, she turned to him. He held out his hand; she took it and climbed the little stepladder that led to the board that acted as a gangplank. She crossed without losing balance or panicking — one of the many tests she'd passed in the past day. The tests were to show the men she was capable, but in reality, she'd spent the time teaching the commander — *Duncan* — the inner workings of the boat she'd been given.

Bunching her cloak into her hands, wearing the ragged trousers the cabin boy had left behind when he'd jumped ship, she dropped into the two-legged piece of canvas on ropes called the bosun. Held by ropes, the crew lowered her inside *Papillon*'s cramped cabin. She'd insisted on the trousers; it made the whole mission from climbing into this bosun to exiting at the other end far easier. A simple winter dress was in a sack tucked beneath *Papillon*'s bench seat, in case it became necessary to enter the town.

When they were both inside, he pulled the hatch down. "Lower away."

He locked the hatch tight before *Papillon* touched the water. It rocked with the wind and waves. Lisbeth's stomach churned. Fulton had given her a pouch filled with his confectioner's sticks. She broke one in two and handed the bigger piece to Duncan.

What a good wife you'll be, her mind mocked

— and the words returned, typeset in her mind like a book that refused to remain closed.

My birth name is Damien . . . will you be my wife? Less than three minutes had elapsed between those two utterances. He was trying to be more transparent; he'd been opening up to her ever since. But — she pulled the peppermint from her mouth. Whenever the words came back to her mind, her gut churned, leaving her unable to eat, or think beyond the oddest proposal any woman ever heard.

She pushed it to the back of her mind again. She had to keep her focus on *Papillon;* but the jangling thoughts crept behind her, tapping her on the shoulder at the worst times. *Become an inventor's mistress, no, his wife. Get an underwater boat, now sail it to find Bonaparte's greatest secret, but you're a woman, so you can't do it. Alain didn't marry you. Abducted . . . false papers . . . stolen child. I am the baron's heir, marry me. I'll return your son.*

Had she jumped feet-first into one of Mrs. Radcliffe's novels? *The Perils of Pamela. The Adventures and Outrageous Marriages of Elizabeth.* Surely life could hold no surprises for her after this.

Then she looked at where she was, what she was about to attempt, and laughed.

"What?" Duncan asked in that too-perceptive tone, but she shook her head.

Papillon rocked as the crew released the ropes, and Lisbeth pitched forward. Duncan pulled her back, her head snuggled in the crook of his shoulder. Her heart felt constricted with the breath stopped somewhere in her chest, her concentration broken. "Thank you." She heard the stilted sound to her voice. "You seem fated to be the one to catch me."

He murmured into her hair, "We all fall at times. We should be glad if someone's there to catch us."

Pretty words. Did he mean any of it?

"We need to stabilize her," Duncan said, pulling her from her reverie.

Papillon was rocking again. She found her peppermint and sat on her side of the bench, taking everything in one final time. "The lower we go, the harder it is to go forward, and we'll run out of air faster. We should be no more than two feet under unless we need to avoid ships."

"Aye-aye, Captain," Duncan replied in a warm, laughing tone, and despite knowing he was trying to charm her, she found herself smiling. She'd given him a hundred instructions about *Papillon*'s use during the past day and a half.

Papillon settled; the world returned to its right axis. "Can you take the rudder and pump? The waves are stronger than our trial run. It will be harder for me to hold it straight."

Duncan took the rudder in hand. "Can you manage the propeller in this tide?"

"I've done it before." Making sure everything was as it should be, she threw a half smile in his direction. "*Papillon*'s mine. She'll work with me."

She was fey this morning.

From the time he'd first gone inside *Papillon,* Duncan had seen her become one with the little craft. Her eerie smile now was a vague sop to kindness, because they both knew he was the outsider. This task, this craft belonged to her.

"Of course," he replied after a minute, hearing the whoosh and slap, slap of waves against the craft. He felt like a giant inside an anthill. The craft's belly was barely five feet high, and six feet around. Almost every conceivable space was filled with cranks and hoses and pipes and levers and a handle. Even sitting, he wouldn't be able to stretch his back or neck without hitting one of the contraptions. Every time he'd stepped inside *Papillon* he'd been careful to avoid all the bits and pieces: a clumsy ox that didn't have a clue what he was doing here, except that he'd muscled out every other candidate to come with her.

From Eddie's, Leo's, and Andrew's tales,

he felt as if he'd known Lisbeth for years without ever seeing her face. Now together, they worked to prevent the cold tide of history repeating. When they were together, he felt more certain, and her unpredictable brilliance came to life.

He knew that, if he'd asked, the inventor would have gone on the mission with Lisbeth. Fulton was certainly the best candidate, but he was no hero. He hadn't even offered to come to the fort when she'd been taken; although he loved her, his priority had been saving his inventions. There was no way to trust the man with Lisbeth's life if they met with any peril.

The submersible bucked and bobbed as it moved with the heavy tide; the slap of the waves was a hard rhythm. He took the rudder and held it to the course Lisbeth showed him as she turned the propeller handle. "Can we really reach Boulogne undetected in this little thing?"

"Fulton used her as a model to build *Nautilus.* She's smaller, but I think she's easier to handle without the bomb chamber splitting her in half." She pushed a sack under the sitting bench. "We have sails packed beneath the bench with rigging attached. We can only use them in fog, at half-light or night, but there's plenty of that at this time of year on the Channel."

He knew that, but it still sounded ludicrous.

"How do you sail a sinking ship?"

"Call it a sinking *boat,* or a submersible boat — but not a sinking ship. It invokes thoughts of rats and desertion." Her cheeky grin told him she was with him again. "It's easy to sail — and we'll be grateful for it before the day ends. This voyage will be very uncomfortable. Hold the rudder hard, we're pulling too far south."

The discomfort of this voyage seemed minor besides handing control to her — but she'd earned his respect. Deciding to go with the tide, he bowed with a wink. "Aye, Commander."

When she bit her lip over that shy, eager half smile, his sacrifice seemed much smaller.

"If we arrive in darkness, we shouldn't be seen," she went on. "If we dock at the river to the south of Boulogne harbor, we can climb out and go about our business."

What she proposed sounded reasonable — probably because he *must* find what Bonaparte was desperate to hide. It was thanks to Lisbeth he had a way in. He seized her hands. "You've done it. Even if we only penetrate as far as the river mouth, and see what's going on there . . ."

He pulled her to him in his excitement, just as a wave hit them. She jerked forward, hit her head on the center pipe, fell, and landed on the sail sacking in seconds . . . all without a sound.

He helped her up and released her hands. "I beg your pardon."

She gave him a half-dazed grin. "Papa always said I needed sense knocked into me. Perhaps that's why he sent you — to prove he was right in his choice for me."

Without wanting to, Duncan laughed. "That sounds just like Eddie."

Her smile felt like sunshine in this closed darkness.

Distance was a necessary safety he'd practiced with outstanding success since he was fifteen; but inside *Papillon*'s cramped confines there was nowhere to go, and Lisbeth's complete absorption in the mission combined with cheeky charm made her the most unpredictable woman he'd ever known. Thoughts, questions, and impressions overloaded him — and the softness of her was far too close. Even with winter clothing on, he could feel her arm or thigh brushing his when they moved or breathed. He could smell her skin.

He hadn't even been alone with her an hour. How would he be in ten? Twenty?

He glanced at her. She was working the propeller crank, her hands moving with complete confidence and concentration. "How do you know when you reach the desired depth?"

"The same way you check ocean depth from a ship with the rope and its knots, except you do it from below the surface. It's attached to the torpedo screw. It's harder to measure depth through the observation dome than from the topmast of a ship, so timing the seconds also helps."

When she turned her head, a slight scent emanated from her hair, her skin, even over the sea brine. *She uses lavender water.* Ladies used it for headaches, but as a perfume, it suited Lisbeth. Less cloying than the heavy perfumes women used in overcrowded ballrooms to mask the scent of sweat, it was relaxing, comforting, yet somehow stimulating. Like Lisbeth herself.

He hadn't noticed her using it before he'd sent her to Fulton. Had he given it to her?

She's probably using the rest of the bottle Clare sent for her injuries. A comfortable conviction — but he wished he'd thought to buy her some kind of personal gift. The only things he'd given her were for the mission. *Nightwear that embarrassed her,* she'd said.

This had to be the strangest courtship in the history of mankind, if it was a courtship at all. She still hadn't accepted him, or rejected him. Or Fulton.

He struggled to concentrate on her lesson.

"The lever opens a small hatch beneath *Papillon* to let water in to fill the space beneath the floor. The weight of the water submerges us. It's a tiny keel, so we can only submerge six feet, four knots on the rope. We have to peg the air hose shut when we submerge, and then blow the seawater out of the hose when we emerge again. It's best to keep close to the surface, to keep a supply of fresh air. We need to follow the tidal eddy." In the light of the lantern, she frowned. "If Fulton had given us the breathing apparatus he'd been working on . . ."

"Yes," he agreed, trying not to be distracted by the swish and slide of her hair, the riband barely holding her braid together. Maybe he could rebraid it later, the intimacy of bumping his fingers against her skin.

He'd never seen her hair in a mess since the day she'd fainted on the path. Fulton must have dressed her until she'd healed. No wonder he'd given her *Papillon.* If he'd felt half the tenderness she'd roused in *him* when he'd dressed her — seeing the life-threatening injuries that made it impossible for her to dress herself for weeks; her delicacy, the desperate embarrassment — yes, the plan had gone perfectly. That they were sitting inside *Papillon* now was proof. Lisbeth had all the makings of a brilliant spy. If she didn't have the child —

"What did you say?" he asked too late.

"It's not important." She was peering through the tiny window. "The tide's rising. If it grows stronger, we'll be in trouble. Let's try the pump."

At least she hadn't laughed at him, but the irony *was* laughable. Just five weeks ago he'd seen the luminous desire in her eyes and pushed her away for the sake of the mission. Now, when he'd finally allowed himself to admit his feelings, to propose to her, her whole concentration was on the mission. His desire awoke only as hers died.

With a tight jaw he turned to the pump. It was like a bilge pump on a ship, but using it while sitting in a cramped position, fighting the tide, brought on a slight panic that they'd sink beneath the waves if he got it wrong. He felt them submerging, knew in his mind that this was the desired result, but he couldn't stop his mind from chanting the names.

The Mary Rose. The Flying Dutchman. The White Ship.

He didn't want to lie forever at the bottom of the ocean like those famous shipwrecks. Neither did he want to be a hero like Nelson or St. Vincent. If this mission was successful, he'd be a nameless "discovered by" in someone's files, but he'd know.

"You've turned too far south."

"I know, but it's hard to use the rudder and pump together effectively." He sounded like Hazeltine when his third lieutenant first became part of his team, and made excuses for his little failures.

He frowned. Hazeltine's clumsiness of word and deed . . . accidentally giving information away . . . turning the rowboat by seeming accident as he had the day he'd been shot —

"Then we've learned to use only one of those two at a time when possible." The words slid into his thoughts and scattered them. She spoke French, as they'd agreed to do during the mission; but the slight rasp in her English vanished, turning her voice melodious and fluid.

Damned irritating to be so distracted by her. He forced his focus onto the task at hand. "We're five feet under. The craft feels strained. Bring her back up to two feet to go forward."

When they were at two feet, she pulled the peg from the air tube and blew the water out. Even the trickle of air coming in through the hose refreshed the cabin, if only a little.

"Now we're at sea, you should take the propellers, Commander. You'll get us there faster. I'll use the rudder and pump."

"Duncan," he reminded her yet again.

She nodded, frowning. "We should stop speaking. The air grows warmer as we submerge, and we need to check the surface for ships before we can open the hatch."

He gave up. He'd created this distance, now he was stuck with it. "Let's go as far as we can before emerging again."

"That's sensible. Underwater, *Papillon*'s movements are smoother and faster."

She'd already moved on to the next task, and the little craft moved in time to the combined symphony of wave and woman.

Papillon was created for this kind of motion, and Lisbeth, with her quick intelligence, lively curiosity, and heedlessness of social norms, had been born to take her. Bringing her into his world had been the blindest stroke of luck he'd had in the game. Now he'd trust the instinct he'd had about her from the first and give her the lead. He learned to follow her hand movements and obeyed her while keeping his mouth shut and his thoughts under firm control.

English Channel, British Waters

The ship's mole watched the commander's brother deciphering the semaphore from where he lay flat on the upper deck.

It gave the code name three times, then said, *Messages still being passed to the French. Change the signalers. The sous-préfet has gendarmes everywhere in town. Do not enter.*

The mole smiled. Even if Stewart could send a message, it was hours too late to warn the commander and Delacorte's blond leftovers. They wouldn't see it.

Then he frowned. Delacorte had killed Peebles almost a month ago. So who was in Boulogne working against him? He had to be found and killed. Until then, he dared give no message even if he could. He had to wait until they were in Jersey.

CHAPTER 40

English Channel, French Waters (Inside Papillon)
November 2, 1802

Four hours later, Duncan was hunched over almost double as he tried to peer through the tiny window at the top of the dome. "We seem no closer to land than two hours ago."

"We can't fight the tide." Lisbeth was too tired for anything but truth. "That's why we started so far north, to have drifting miles. I think we're south of Wimereux. Can you see land?"

"I think you're right, but this is taking too long." He was bent so far over, his voice came warped by the dome and the smacking waves. "We won't make Boulogne harbor by sunset."

"The tide will turn. We'll go faster then." Lisbeth was miles past amusement at his grumbling. Though it made him human, she was too aware of her own fragility at this point.

At first the awareness of his closeness made

concentration a struggle. For the mission's sake she pushed away all thoughts of him as anything but her commander and limited her conversation to teaching him. His subtle irritation at her distance was perversely pleasing.

After being locked inside *Papillon* for hours, reality set in, and her body's needs became so urgent, she got over the embarrassment of using the chamber pot with him there. Though the air tube was above the waves, only a trickle of air entered — enough to breathe, but the capsule felt like an oven. They came up for air every hour, but within minutes of submerging, the heat, the smell of sweat, and their irritation swamped them.

Duncan kept watching for ships as he turned the propellers, finding it easier to go by sight than by compass. Then he snapped, "Avast and submerge!"

She worked the pump and rudder to stop, turn, and dive while he cranked the propellers, but *Papillon* rocked so hard he walloped his shoulder on the propeller lever and fell. He swore as she landed on him. "What is it?" she cried as she scrambled up, hanging onto the copper pipe for dear life.

"Cannonballs. We're close by one of Boney's new gun batteries along the coast. They probably test their cannons every day at this time. Submerge faster, for God's sake. If one hits us, we're dead."

She fought to keep them deep below the waterline as deadly hail hit the water above and around them, and *Papillon* became a crazed pendulum. *If we're hit, I can use the flotsam to hold on to . . . at least my skirts and petticoats do not hamper me now . . .*

Unfortunately for her dignity, her stomach decided to upend itself all over the floor. "Don't touch it now," he snapped when she moved to clean it. "We can do it later. Hold to the pump and rudder!"

At last they passed the gun battery, but they kept working the levers in suffocating darkness. Too little light filtered in from the observation dome, but they had to keep the lantern for when full darkness came.

"We've passed the danger. Emerge," Duncan said a few minutes later, voice harsh.

Lisbeth frowned. "Are you sure we've passed?"

"Right now I don't care if a bloody bomb hits us. I have to breathe!"

"Stubble it, Commander," she snapped, using a cant term she'd learned from Leo and Andrew. "We'll emerge to the level of sight and make certain we're safe."

The hard words brought him back to himself. He shook, like a dog throwing water off its fur, but he snapped right back, "For God's sake, call me Duncan. We're clear."

"Thank heaven for that — Duncan," Lisbeth conceded, glad they could open the hatch and breathe clean air, untainted by vomit. It was humiliating to have to clean the mess by hand, scooping it into the chamber pot and then rinsing the floor with water, but he said nothing.

An hour later, he snarled, "I'm cooking inside this thing, and it stinks. We need to rinse it again."

Embarrassed that the vile smell was her fault, she snapped as his hands lifted to the hatch, "No! We're just outside Boulogne."

"All the more reason to do it now, before we hit the patrols."

She tried to clear her mind, but it was fixed on reaching her goal, one task at a time. *Turn and crank. Check the pump. Turn and crank.* And the waves splashed and the tide rocked them, and no matter how many peppermint sticks she sucked on, she wanted to throw up again. "If we don't emerge above the line of the screws, you'll drown us both. I understand your panic —"

"I never panic." He spoke through gritted teeth. "I can't bear the smell."

"I understand." She bit back a smile. "I'd kill for fresh air myself. Let's raise *Papillon* to the surface, but check the window first."

"It's too close to sunset, which means they won't see us." He hit his head on the edge of the observation dome and swore with vicious fluency in three languages.

She sighed and rolled her eyes. "Sit down

and work the pump." But he grabbed the pump lever too hard; the craft jerked upward, and they tumbled off the bench. He swore again. "Raise handsomely," she snapped, using one of the nautical terms he'd taught her yesterday, which meant to go smooth and even. "Unless of course you *want* to drown."

He slowed his movements without a sound.

She peered through the observation window and made a stifled sound. "We're too close to shore." She took control of the rudder handle and steered *Papillon* back on a southwesterly course. "Avast *now,* or we'll founder on the rocks."

Duncan stopped, then turned the craft in the semisilence of wave and wind and cranking levers. He was dying to put her in her place, which was ridiculous, because this *was* her place. He'd sent her to Fulton to become an expert, now he resented that she'd done just that.

Using the rudder and pump, one held hard in place, one slowly lifting, she asked to distract him, "Why do you want to marry me?"

His body was right beside hers, so she felt him go still.

It was obvious he didn't want to answer. "You can't expect me to decide on something that will change my life knowing only half the story. So let's talk. We could die in this thing."

After a few moments, he said, "We will not die."

"Are you a prophet now, too?" she taunted. "It seems sharing anything of yourself with me terrifies you. If I know the truth, where will you hide from me?" With a lifting of one shoulder, she continued working the propeller with both hands. "If that's your first priority, what incentive do I have to agree to be your wife?"

"A logical argument," he muttered, sounding petulant. But he didn't say more, and she knew he wouldn't unless she goaded him into it.

"I realize how hard it is for you to trust me," she said, slow and cutting. "But this mission will only last a day or two. You're asking me to give you my life. I don't know anything about you apart from your name and title, and what school you attended. I don't know why your brothers have a different name than you, or why you wanted to marry a girl you'd never met. I don't even know how you met my father."

"He came to Harrow, to watch Leo playing cricket. I was on the team."

Intense disappointment filled her when he said no more. "So I've risked my life for you, and you refuse to trust me beyond a game of cricket? There's your answer, Commander."

"If you've risked your life for me, I've saved yours three times now. That ought to inspire trust at least." He sounded furious.

"Thank you — but you still say nothing of real value," she said coldly. "You're cranking the propellers backward, and they're fighting the pump. We're going nowhere."

Hastily he revised his actions, swearing again.

She sighed. "How about this: I bow with appropriate feminine submission whenever your masculine esteem demands it, and you'll allow me to do the job for which I have been trained. Does that work for you . . . Duncan?" she asked with mock sweetness, lowering her face until her nose almost touched her knees.

A stifled sound greeted her parody of a bow. "That has to be the least graceful show of respect I've seen in a long time."

"Why, thank you. And how many prospective fiancées or wives have you had to judge on this matter? Are you a pasha now?" she teased, hoping to see a smile in return. Disappointed yet again, she had to reach over his body to take over the pump. "Remember, this is how it's done on *Papillon*. It's the opposite of your ship, I gather." She kept pumping until she heard the swish and slide of water leaving the hull. "We're above the tide now, I think. Would you like to —"

Like lightning he opened the hatch, his head and shoulders through the aperture. "Ah, winter, I never knew how I love your cold air," he mumbled, and breathed a few more times.

"I might love it too, if I could take any in," she groused. "The sooner you sit and allow the air in here, the sooner we can be on our way. Don't forget that the rocks still exist. Keep working the propellers!"

The air must have cooled his temper, for he laughed as he took control of the propeller cranks. It was only a quick chuckle, and by the time he sat, no trace remained of it; yet the low rumbling sound lifted her mood to almost ridiculous proportions.

"Oh, that's so good," she breathed as the cool air rushed in. Then the frigid air filled the cabin, and she shivered with the fast change from overheated to cold.

"Wear this until we close the hatch." He tossed her cloak over her, and then, when she shivered still, threw his over her shoulders as well. "We need the clean air to keep going. Stand and stretch your muscles for as long as you can. But come about; we're drifting to shore."

A few minutes later, cabin as clean as they could make it, Duncan locked the hatch, and they headed south once more.

"I'm Lord Annersley's heir, but he isn't my father," he said as he took his turn at the rudder and pump. "Broderick Stewart was my real father, but he couldn't marry my mother, at least not using his real name. He was an outlaw, having fought on the wrong side at Culloden when he was fourteen. He escaped to France and Rome afterward with the Pretender and married Alec and Cal's mother there. She died in childbirth, and he sent the twins to his family in Scotland. Eventually he became disenchanted with the Pretender's drinking and self-pity and returned to Britain, where he met your father. Eddie gave him work as a King's Man under a cover name. When he met my mother — she was a chambermaid at an inn — he resigned." When she didn't speak, he went on. "They went to Norfolk a month before I was born. Annersley — he has one of the Old Saxon baronies, with a different name to the title — fought the Stewart clan at Culloden. When he saw them, he recognized the Black Stewart face — you've seen we're all rather alike. Annersley saw his chance to gain an heir he hadn't been able to get through three wives, and he betrayed my father to the magistrate. Stewart was hanged two weeks before I was born. My mother wed Annersley to give me a name and a place. When I was born, Annersley paid her to disappear without me. She left within a week of my birth. So I'll inherit the barony legally. Annersley named himself my father in the church records."

Lisbeth blinked, then opened her mouth and closed it. Like champagne shaken and uncorked, information exploded over her until she felt drenched in it, unable to find her bearings. "I see."

"Is that all you have to say?"

The odd, laughing demand made her turn to look at his face around the pole dividing them. Like him, really. Split in two, half of him keeping secrets and the other half throwing them at her in warm laughter. "Thank you for telling me."

"Oh, so polite. Thank you for telling me," he mimicked her, laughing still. She couldn't work out what he was hiding behind it. "I'll understand if your answer remains the same. Most ladies prefer their husbands to be of the legitimate variety."

She tossed off the cloaks as sweat trickled down her back. "You are legitimate. You just said so." She half stood and looked outside. "We're too close to land."

He changed tack. "Some women might want to see me as legitimate . . . those who'd like to be elevated to the peerage, for example."

"Thank you," she replied, hurt. "If that's what you think of me —"

"It isn't. Lisbeth, I'm sorry." His hand touched hers. "If you were that kind of woman, you'd have accepted me right away. I'm irritable and sore, and dying to stand upright again. Walk a few steps. Have a cool drink of ale." His face came around the pole, wearing a rueful smile. "Despite my boast of being able to bear confined places, I'm drowning in my own sweat and constantly fighting against being sick, and taking it out on you."

She smiled back, feeling oddly shy. She loved it when he looked at her like that. How weak and foolish she was. "Have another peppermint."

He took the confection but returned to hold her hand. "Forgive me?"

She could only nod.

"Thank you." He lifted her hand to his mouth.

Such a simple thing, a kiss on her knuckles, one she'd known a hundred times from a hundred gentlemen during her brief Season. Until now, none had made her heart stutter and her breath catch and her gaze cling to him as if he'd just changed the world.

He lifted the lantern before turning back to her, touching her cheek. "Poor, battered little face. You've endured so much, and still you fought to come with me. You're the strongest woman I've ever known."

When he smiled at her, she forgot her body was cooking inside the cramped confines, forgot to work the rudder. His gaze dropped to her mouth, and her breath came in rapid spurts. He dropped her hand and leaned back so his upper body was behind the pole — and she could only smile as his hand cupped the back of her neck, bringing her to him.

At last he was going to kiss her; and like a starving woman before a feast she leaned in, lifting her face. He brushed his mouth over hers —

Papillon bucked, and they both smacked their heads on the pole. Gasping, they jerked apart. "It wasn't a ship," he reported after looking through the window. "Probably just a freak wave. We're close to Boulogne now."

They returned to their stations and set the craft to rights.

As they entered Boulogne's wide harbor, she heard him mutter, "Could there be a worse time and place to kiss a woman? *Idiot.*"

Despite pain ripping through her after a day cramped and cranking levers, she glowed like steel at a forge, for the kiss felt more true to her than all his words ever had. "I won't argue, but perhaps you'll do better next time."

He grinned. "Your riband's fallen out." He handed it to her and looked out the window as she rebraided her hair. "At dusk it's a danger to use the lantern in case we're somehow seen, but we need the light to sail by the compass and circumnavigate the rocks and islands using the map." He looked out again. "There's a new gun battery by the entrance to the harbor, and another on the south side. There are twice as many gun batteries along the coast as there were before the Treaty of Amiens."

She stretched her shoulders. "Was it forbidden under the terms of the treaty?"

He sat, an arrested expression in his eyes. "I'm not certain, but added to all the excessive protection here, it's disturbing. Of course, it could be a reaction to Nelson's invasion in 1801." He dropped the lantern low on the rope so the light was hardly visible. "We'll have to bend down to read the map and compass, and we must remain in lockdown until we're inside the river."

She breathed in and out, fighting the usual traces of panic at being in this cramped place in the dark. "The tidal eddy's picked up, heading south. It shouldn't take long to reach the river."

"Even so, this trip took longer than expected, and I need time to reconnoiter the harbor and see what's inside the river. We'll leave with the morning tide."

Exhausted, she spoke without thinking. "You'll find us somewhere to stay."

His brows lifted. "You have faith in my abilities."

"I've watched you work. As you knew about Gaston Borchonne, I'm sure you study the places you go before you begin a mission and form escape methods. I know I would."

Another smothered chuckle came, an unspoken acknowledgment of her perception.

They reached the northern edge of Boulogne, and the patrols grew thicker. Wending their way across the harbor, trying to work with the shifting tide, she kept up her mantra. *Turn the cranks. Move the rudder. Check out the window —*

"Avast and submerge!" Duncan snapped as *Papillon* rocked hard yet again.

Lisbeth stopped, then worked the pump at double speed. "We can't submerge far enough. Any ship's keel will cut us in half. Bear toward land."

After a few moments *Papillon* tilted and jerked back. Duncan looked out. "The waves make it impossible to see. She's bearing down on us. Use both propellers and tack southeast."

Soon *Papillon* bucked like a terrified horse, and Lisbeth paled, fighting another urge to vomit. "Do you think they saw us?"

"I doubt it. We're underwater, and virtually in the dark."

"Of course you're right. Brace sharp." She changed course against the ship's movement.

"Damn, it must be coming to!"

They submerged as far as they could and kept bearing away, but the push-pull of the ship drew them in. As *Papillon* bucked and rocked, they hung on to hold course. Every time they fell they had to scramble up to grab the cranks and levers.

"Ease away now; she's gone at last," he muttered. "We're a full fathom beneath. We need to cut and run, or the pump will split."

It was true. *Papillon*'s pump was older than

that of the *Nautilus,* less expensively made, more fragile. Lisbeth reversed its motion.

The closer they came to the river, the more they submerged and emerged, dodging ships and rocks and tidal rips. When they could hardly breathe, they hid behind tiny islets to take in air briefly. While they were high in the water Duncan gazed out the windows, using his navigating experience to tell Lisbeth what to do next. All the while she chanted beneath her breath, *Turn the rudder. Crank the pump. Don't get sick again. Don't do it.*

After a while he said, "You're very quiet. Are you feeling ill?"

"Yes," she whispered.

"Pick up the hose and breathe." He spoke with slow clarity, as if talking was beyond him.

They took turns breathing from the hose. At last, just before nightfall, he said, "Thanks be to God, because of the streetlights here, I can see the river mouth."

She almost collapsed in joy. Never had time crawled so. *Papillon* had been well named, a butterfly fighting the tide.

"Tack leeward. We're passing Fort de Musoir," he reported in a tense whisper. "Every window's alight in the fort. There are fully armed ships everywhere." He sat again, a frown between his soaring brows. "This security is done far too brown. Bonaparte's taking a carriage to reach the shop next door."

She took her turn at the window and nodded. Yes . . . the security overkill Duncan spoke of in slang terms was obvious everywhere she looked.

"The gun batteries he's built, the ship patrols, the soldiers . . ." His expression cemented her feeling of destiny in the morning. "This is it, the proof that Bonaparte's preparing for war."

CHAPTER 41

Boulogne Harbor, France
November 2, 1802

Duncan felt the weight of certainty settle on him. "It's the only possible explanation."

Lisbeth answered in a whisper. "Bonaparte would argue: Boulogne needs the added protection since Nelson invaded last year."

"Yes, and got his arse kicked all the way home to his ménage à trois with the Hamiltons. His victory should have reassured Boney that this level of security is unnecessary."

At a statement that would have shocked any other gently reared girl, she just nodded and reached for the air hose. When she argued again, she sounded only a little better. "We're almost at the closest point to England. Why are extra security measures vital defenses when they're in Britain, but it's paranoia or preparation for war when it's in France?"

Exhausted and air deprived, she still had the unpredictable brilliance coupled with common sense Duncan had come to rely on. "Because he wants war and we don't."

"We don't?" Her satirical question was the mirror of his doubts. "Then why are there dozens, hundreds of British spies everywhere Bonaparte goes? Why are we in this boat now?"

"To prove he wants war — but I can't prove we don't," he conceded with a grin. "And we're not alone. Austria wants revenge for their losses under the Treaty of Lunéville as well as Amiens. Russia's new czar has taken an aggressive stance also. You really are your father's daughter, aren't you? Too bloody clever by half."

Her laugh was pathetic, but damn, he loved that she tried.

Papillon bucked, in the violent lee lurch that heralded an oncoming ship. Flung forward, she landed on her hands and knees on the deck and stayed down. Filled with tenderness, Duncan lifted her. "Almost there, love, and then you can rest. For now I need you."

She blinked at him. "Submerge," she whispered as she used the pump to submerge and the rudder to come about.

"It serves me right, discussing politics now," he muttered, as he worked the damn thing for dear life. "A ship's keel could slice us in half and we'd die without anyone knowing we'd ever been there. Let's get to the river."

Forced to remain underwater as they waited

for the ship to pass them, he sat in sweat and darkness so thick he felt as if he was swimming through it.

At last the creaking grind of the ship above them ended, but *Papillon* kept moving. "We're dragging on the ship's eddy." He released the pump with slow precision. *Papillon*'s observation dome broke the surface. He looked through the window and grinned. "We're headed straight for the river mouth."

Ghostlike with exhaustion, she took the compass from him to guide the rudder and tiller.

"We're entering the river mouth," he reported. "It's deep. I can't see anything we could founder on. Just hold the rudder and I'll keep watch."

She murmured something inaudible.

How much longer could she last? If he was right about what lay inside this river mouth, he couldn't allow her to rest long enough to recover. Britain's security — not to mention both their lives — depended on her knowledge of *Papillon*. "I'll take the rudder. You look done in."

"I am done in," she admitted, "but if I stop now I won't wake for hours." She pushed him off when he tried to take over. "No, just let me be. It's easier now without the waves."

She was at the end of her rope, but still did her duty. She knew he'd be lost without her.

He looked through the window. "There

ought to be a pier. If we turn leeward, we —"
Papillon turned with the river and the ship,
and he saw farther down the river mouth.
"My God, Lisbeth . . . I can barely believe it,
but . . . my *God* . . ."

She tugged on his jacket, and he leaned
back on the bench to let her up. She groaned
a little as she bent half over to look.

Moments later she sat back down and said
in a dazed voice, "Did — I just see . . . ?"

He nodded. He felt the same.

"The river's long and wide, yet there's
barely enough room for them all," she
croaked. "How has no one heard of this?"

"Their outer lines of security — the hills
around Boulogne, the military blockades, the
high factory buildings on the sea side, and
ships patrolling — are impenetrable. Who
could possibly get close enough to see anything?"

"We did." Her eyes were wide like a child's,
her crooked smile lighting her face so he
could see its vague outlines in the half dark.
"We did!" She struggled to stand, hit the side
of her head on the base of the observation
dome, and growled a word most well-bred
English ladies pretended not to know. She
didn't apologize for it or make excuses.

He grinned, loving her lack of pretense with
him.

She peered through the window. "We're
heading for the riverbank." She grabbed the

rudder, and he worked the propellers.

"How many ships are there, do you think?" she asked as they reached the center again.

"Enough to repel the British fleet in its current depleted state. Did you see the shape of the ships?"

At once she got up and looked out again. "That's odd. They're fat."

"Flat and wide," he corrected. "They're clinker ships — Viking-style longships. Look at the gunwales."

Moments later she dropped back down to the bench. "There are barely a dozen cannons. Fighting Nelson's ships with one line of cannon per ship is absurd."

"I doubt Boney's planning to fight anyone with these beauties. But without the weight of the extra rows of cannon, the ships would float higher in the Channel, and reach their destination faster." He added when she didn't react, "Caesar left from this port — William the Conqueror from this coastline, with longships much like these — and Boney loves emulating his heroes."

She sounded doubtful. "Via Ireland again, you mean? He failed before, in 1798."

"But this time, instead of being mobilized for war, our government's chasing its tail with the assassination attempt against the king and the unrest in Ireland. Marshal Ney's forces pushed farther into Switzerland. I received a semaphore yesterday that King George made formal protest to the European Tribunal over it. Boney is refusing to withdraw from Switzerland, stating that *we* haven't yet handed Malta back to the Knights of St. John. He also demands we withdraw from Egypt, and that *we* won't do until he withdraws. But even then, I doubt Britain will withdraw from Malta. It's too strategically important to have a port in the Mediterranean, should there be another war." Arrested by his train of thought, he stared at her. "That's why Boney's making a show of accusing Britain of breaking the treaty — because the king's forced his hand. If Boney doesn't launch as soon as he can, the European Tribunal's inspectors will find the fleet."

"Who gave the information about this invasion fleet to your source in England? It must be someone reasonably high up, and with an ax to grind against Bonaparte."

He felt awed. With his dozen years of experience, he *ought* to make that kind of connection, but how did a girl of nineteen, and one reared in the country, put all the plots and plans together? "Boney humiliated Fouché when he dismantled the Ministry of Police."

"So is this Fouché's revenge: to lead Britain to discover Napoleon's plot, in an attempt to bring his government down?"

He lifted his hands. "These new ships are the ultimate proof that Boney's been breaking the Amiens Treaty from the start: they'd take a year at least to build. I think Fouché set up a failed assassination attempt last week to propel us into coming here to find this. He warned the conspirators to get out, and — I think — he sent Camelford there so Boney had a convenient scapegoat, a way to accuse the English."

She drew a deep breath, yawned, and shook her head. "Why? It makes no sense to me."

"He received a massive payoff for losing the ministry, and still runs the spy networks, but he craves the ultimate power, and he knows he'll never control Boney."

"So he wants to bring Napoleon down, so he can step in as first consul?"

"It's not Fouché's way to stand in the light. He likes to inspire fear, not love," he said slowly. "He's found a suitable puppet — a Bourbon prince, I heard — but he'll be the true power behind the throne."

"How does this tie in with Alain's actions, both in Abbeville and in Ambleteuse? If anything, Alain's actions have brought Fouché's plots to light, only aiding Napoleon."

He frowned. "Delacorte's supposed to be Fouché's man. It doesn't make sense."

She murmured, "None of it does, unless Alain's playing one off against the other?"

Sitting close together in the murky darkness, Duncan said, "It's the only plausible answer. It's how he got away with so much with you. He was playing Fouché against Boney until that last night in Abbeville. Now he's gone over to Boney, unless he's Fouché's mole in Boney's camp."

"It would depend on which leader most closely suits his beliefs. He's no money hunter. He's passionate about what's best for France."

He settled the lantern between them and waited for her to say what was on her mind.

"If Alain works for both men, does that mean Napoleon knows Fouché's passed on the information to us? Could he be playing games with us, too?"

After a moment he nodded. "It's almost certain, or there wouldn't be so many patrols near the river mouth. I told you about the French informant on my ship. Alec and Flynn have taken over the signaling on ship to stop information leaking, but it may not have been in time. If Boney knows about *Papillon* — and it makes sense he does, given the interest in Fulton — he'll be racing us to get the fleet launched before we arrive."

Lisbeth stared at him with red-rimmed eyes still alive with intelligence and the curiosity that made her such a damned fine agent — the best he'd ever had. "The launch must be happening soon. Will our report reach London before then?"

"A semaphore could reach London in hours, but the problem is that the French would see it, too. Sending one via my ship could mean the double agent will also send a decoded copy to Paris. Besides which, half the British army's still in Egypt blocking Boney's forces there, and twenty thousand troops are putting down the unrest in Ireland. Boney has a hundred thousand men ready to fight on French soil, but the men in England are raw recruits, drunken lords' spare sons, or boys taken from farms or the streets. Half the navy ships have been decommissioned."

Her mouth fell slightly open. "Can the rest of the navy be recommissioned in time?"

He shook his head. "Dozens of ships are now transporting convicts, or floating prisons on the Thames. Fifty are in Ireland. The rest are in the Caribbean, fighting pirates. Unless . . ." Could he be right? He frowned, said in a slow voice, "I think Zephyr's been preparing Britain since I told him about the chance of an invasion fleet. If he's managed to get the admirals on board, and the Duke of York, who's his cousin Grenville's friend — there's a chance."

"Napoleon's ships look seaworthy."

"They are, but they're too shallow for the kinds of storms we've been getting. This has been the year without an autumn in the Channel; it's as if we went straight from summer to winter, especially at night. They'd have to launch in darkness to be hidden from British lighthouse keepers and the tide watchers

— not me; *tide watcher* is a derogatory nickname for the Customs Land Guard, excisemen watching for smugglers," he explained when she looked confused. And then he wondered how she'd heard his code name. Probably Alec or Cal. "That's why they haven't launched yet. They're waiting for calmer weather."

"Could all these ships have been built here?"

"This isn't a major shipbuilding port." He thought for a moment. "Most of them must have been built elsewhere and sailed here. He probably had a few built at each French harbor to avoid arousing suspicion and sent them here two at a time. They're all built on similar lines."

"Any British patrol would assume they were seeing the same ships sailing," she muttered, following his line of thought. "Did you notice that not all the ships have cannons set yet?"

He peered through the window, making out some of the ships in the lit estuary. "Not even half are outfitted." He snapped his fingers. "Of course — they couldn't risk sailing brand-new ships, cannon-ready, from their home port to here; it would defy the terms of the Treaty of Amiens. They'd be assembling the cannons and fitting them here. That's another reason why they haven't yet launched. Assembling a *Grande Armée* and outfitting a fleet of new ships with the lightweight types of cannons they need not to weigh these ships down has got to be damned expensive, and France was almost bankrupt when Bonaparte became first consul two years ago. This is why he invaded Switzerland and is pushing the Americans to buy Louisiana. He's desperate for the money. Even raping Piedmont and Parma of their wealth wouldn't be anywhere near enough."

"Why was Britain not prepared for this? It seems crazy to trust Napoleon to hold to the terms of a treaty he made himself."

He shrugged. "Reaction to nine years of war. The government, the people want peace — and we knew the straits France was in financially. We felt safe."

"So Napoleon took advantage," she said slowly.

"Yes — and the ultimate commander who needs to stamp his authority everywhere didn't come anywhere near Boulogne from the signing of the treaty until now: to keep the world from wondering what was going on here. If it hadn't been for a deposed archbishop wanting revenge, and my search for you . . ."

Another slow nod. "Until everything is almost ready to go . . . and it's too late to stop him."

"Yes." A brilliant double bluff, designed to keep the insecure blinders on the current British government. If it hadn't been for Fou-

511

ché's power games with Boney, the archbishop's anger, or Duncan's determination to find Lisbeth, they'd never have seen this in time.

Why had Fouché left it this late? What was his agenda?

Then suddenly it came to him. "Boney came here *because* he knew about the assassination attempt. It was the only way he could come here and scatter any British spies, while deflecting the British from noticing what was going on. I'd wager my fortune Fouché told Boney about Camelford, and about us if it would benefit him. When Boney heard of British spies on the Channel Coast he had to divert our attention. The Americans have been stalling on buying Louisiana, and the fight to get into the Swiss banks has been harder than he anticipated. The ironwrights building the cannons would refuse to do the work without pay. Boney's not stupid. Pressing them into unpaid work would mean he'd probably end up with inferior cannons, and the shipwrights wouldn't have nearly enough lightweight iron for the job without the money up front."

As if reading his mind, Lisbeth murmured, "So that's why they haven't sailed yet?"

He nodded. "Thank God the Americans stalled, and the weather's been so foul this winter. Light ships like these can almost skate over the water, but they need reasonable calm."

"So then we have a little time. To stop this," she said quietly, meeting his inquiring look.

"Yes?" he prompted her. Seeing that distracted frown again, he knew her quick mind was working on something.

She blinked a few times and yawned. "Can we use the submersible technology? Fulton told me Bushnell had ideas on how to use submersibles to sink British ships in the War of Independence."

"Go on, Lisbeth," he urged again when her eyes glazed over. "How would you use the submersible? Lisbeth?"

She shivered and whispered, "Um . . . in a way so Bonaparte won't know Britain's in violation of the treaty. No bombs."

He frowned heavily. "Have you any other ideas?"

She blinked a few times and frowned. "If only *Nautilus* was repaired . . . but we must use what we have." A hand fluttered up, indicating *Papillon,* and fell.

Another yawn, and he almost yelled at her in his impatience. "But what can we do?" he prompted after a minute's silence.

She shivered again; her head jerked up and around. "I beg your pardon, I drifted."

The jerky rocking began again. With difficulty she rose and peered through the window. "I think there's more than one ship coming. We'll be crushed if we don't move." Looking all around, she made a little, tired sound. "There's a short pier behind us and to the left, with an almost clear path to it."

They worked in silence until the craft bumped against something. "We're against the riverbank. Bring her above the waterline. We need to tie her to the posts, keeping her out of sight beneath the pier." Lisbeth's voice was fading to nothing. From pale, she'd gone to a phantom in the failing light of the lantern.

It wasn't the time to keep pushing her about her nebulous plans. But if he took over the menial tasks, her clever mind would keep thinking it through. "I'll do it." He opened the hatch as quietly as possible. His back screamed in protest as he stood straight for the first time in hours. His arm muscles bit into him as he tied the ropes to a post at each side of *Papillon* for stability.

He sat again, feeling the cold winter air flood in. Hearing a soft sigh, he turned to her. She was asleep sitting up, her head drooping onto her chest. She'd be in agony when she woke.

"Lisbeth, wake up," he whispered. "We'll find a place to sleep."

Bleary eyes looked up in the low light of the lantern. "Bed?" she whispered, as if he'd offered her a vision of heaven.

"Yes, bed, love," he murmured, thinking

briefly of their unfinished kiss, but both of them were well beyond that tonight. "But there are soldiers everywhere. You need put your dress on, quickly and quietly." But she stared at him as if he'd spoken in Chinese, and he wanted to laugh. Bloody hell, he must be beyond anything to think of undressing a pretty woman and only feel tired. "I'll help you, but you must do exactly as I tell you."

CHAPTER 42

Boulogne-sur-Mer
November 2, 1802

It had taken over half an hour to reach the back alleys up the long hill of Boulogne toward the walled part of town, where the respectable people stayed. "We're almost there," Duncan said, squeezing the arm he held to encourage her. Every few steps Lisbeth stumbled on the skirt of her winter dress. He'd helped her pull it on over Mark's old trousers, and she let him hold her arm, but absolutely refused to let him carry her, and she was right. He was in as much pain as she, and it would cause suspicion should anyone see them in the torch-lit streets.

He could only thank God she always put the mission first.

"I'll make it," she murmured, and stumbled. "I'm sorry," she whispered when he lifted her to her feet a fifth time. Her voice was so faint he had to strain to hear her.

How had she lasted so long? No other

woman he knew could have endured what she'd put herself through, and she was apologizing for her understandable exhaustion. God knows he was barely any stronger.

Holding her by the waist now to keep her up, Duncan turned into an inn near the old town walls, where the better class of people stayed. Thank God it was only evening. Most inns remained open until at least eleven. After ten it was mostly men with a whore, but he doubted anyone looking at Lisbeth's pale face, braided hair, and modest dress would believe that of her. Arriving this way was a disaster he couldn't have prevented; there was no room to carry suitcases or bandboxes on board *Papillon*.

He resigned himself to a night of little or no sleep.

Reaching a respectable inn, he shoved the doors inward with his shoulder and walked through to the taproom where he'd find the innkeeper. "My wife is unwell, m'sieur," he said to the oldest man behind the counter. "Do you have a room for us?"

The innkeeper saw Lisbeth's white face and ringless marriage finger, the fading lump on her head and the scar on her cheek. He looked for their baggage, and, finding none, a cunning expression came into his eyes. "We have but one room left, monsieur, but it is the most expensive in the house. Five francs per night."

"Don't do it, *mon coeur*. He's lying," Lisbeth whispered, and he could only be grateful again she'd remembered the endearment, proving she could keep her head in tight corners. "We can go to the next inn."

He touched her arm. "I doubt the room's usual asking price is more than three, but I'm in no mood to argue, *ma chère.*" He turned to the innkeeper. "Show us up."

The man's brows lifted. "We expect payment in advance, monsieur."

Lisbeth made a small, hissing noise.

Obviously the man knew something wasn't right. With all that was hidden here, suspicion had to be bordering on paranoia throughout town by now. Duncan said, "You'll get your money when I have made my wife comfortable. She is a poor traveler, even in the latest high-sprung carriage from London." He'd seen one on the street, and hoped to God the man wasn't clever enough to check who owned it — or that he already knew its owner.

"I'll have your bags collected for you. Do you require rooms for your servants?"

"I sent them to The Cock's Crow." It was a far cheaper inn, and naming it made the innkeeper's stance relax a little. "I'll collect our luggage after I've settled my wife. I desire nothing to find its way into the pockets of light-fingered servants."

He didn't know if his excuses were good enough, even delivered in the sneering tone of the *nouveau elite.* Before he could sleep, he'd have to steal baggage and clothing for them both, an army uniform, and weapons in case they needed to escape.

The man's face was bland. "*Certainement,* monsieur. This way."

Climbing the narrow, badly lit stairs to the third floor, Duncan felt Lisbeth's body trembling more with each step. His own muscles burned as he began lifting her up by the waist to help. "Hurry, you creaking tub of lard. I'm in no mood to wait."

At last they were on the third floor. The innkeeper opened a door. "Here you are."

With a glance, Lisbeth made a sound of disgust. Duncan snapped, "I don't know when the feathers were last changed, or the window opened. There's dust everywhere, and the beams are too low above the bed. This is a room for a child of the working classes, not for my wife and me. Now show me a room that's well aired and clean, or I'll take my gold somewhere more deserving. This is your last chance, you crawling louse."

The innkeeper cringed, bowed, and turned to the room at the other end of the hall — but he seemed satisfied. The next room was clean, airy, and the bed looked comfortable. Lisbeth nodded, her face still haughty, but even paler than it had been a minute before.

Duncan led Lisbeth into the room, sat her on the chair by the window, and turned.

"Well, come here, I don't have all night."

The chubby, balding man approached, hand outstretched. Duncan showed him the French travel papers he'd brought from bona fide spies on the ship, complete with a faux stamp as close to Admiral Latouche-Tréville as he could make it, then put two francs and five sou into his hand. "I doubt it's even worth this much, but I don't argue with underlings. Nor do I allow myself to be cheated. Accept this or we leave."

The man sighed, nodded, and took the coins.

Duncan pushed another two francs into his hand. "Leave breakfast outside the door at seven. Lunch will be served at one. My wife and I expect privacy."

Now the man smiled and bowed again. Two francs was a fortune for breakfast and lunch at an inn like this. "*Certainement,* monsieur!"

"Food worthy of a lady, with a pot of chocolate for her, and coffee for me," Duncan snapped, vertigo gripping him. "Now go before I demand my coins back."

He disappeared. Duncan turned around to tell Lisbeth his plans, but she was already on the bed, lying above the quilt, curled in a ball on her side. Good, it would at least stretch the kinks out of her back. He tugged until the quilt was over her. He really ought to undress her, but he couldn't manage it. Pulling off her boots was all he could do.

Looking with longing at the bed, he sighed and left the room, locking the door. Moving with jerking puppet steps, he left the inn.

Boulogne-sur-Mer
November 3, 1802

A knock sounded once, twice.

Lisbeth woke with a groan. Thin winter light peered in through billowing curtains; the breeze held the tang of the ocean and the crispness of snow. Horses clip-clopped over the cobblestones outside. Hawkers called for customers to sample their wares. The wafting scent of meat and pastry, apples and apricots coming from a street pie vendor made her stomach growl.

She moved, and her back seized. Frowning, she stretched her whole body, testing one muscle at a time until she'd stretched every part of her, taking a few luxurious breaths.

Deep, rumbling breaths told her she wasn't alone.

Turning her head, she saw Duncan beside her, still fully clothed if his exposed arm was any indication. Beneath his lashes there were black smudges. He breathed through his mouth, making the half snores she'd heard.

Looking down, she made a face at the sight of her crumpled dress, but it was still on. He had removed her boots and socks, leaving them to dry by a small fire.

She walked to the door barefooted, shivering with cold as the wind bit through her dress. She struggled against crying out in pain as she moved the small cupboard away from the door.

By the time she opened it the hall was empty. Though her muscles screamed protest, she picked up the tray left on the floor and brought it in, closing the door with her foot.

At the soft slam Duncan jerked up, groping beneath the pillow, presumably for a weapon, but in seconds he was at her side, taking the tray from her. *"Bonjour."*

For no reason she could discern, she blushed. *"Bonjour.* I'm glad you slept, too. It makes me feel less guilty."

He shook his head, crossed the room, and pushed the cupboard back in front of the door. "Neither of us would have made it back without sleep and good food. Can you wash and change into the dress on the chair before we eat?"

Including himself in the decision made her feel better. She saw a woolen dress hanging over an old wing chair. She nodded and asked, fumbling, "Um, can you undo my buttons?"

He nodded and undid her buttons for her, brisk and without any lingering that would make her uncomfortable.

When she was in her shift and stays, she crossed to the washbowl, shivering with the touch of crusted, semifrozen water, but it felt so good to wash the stickiness of dried sweat off her skin. She glanced at his averted face. "So we go with the night tide?"

He nodded. "If possible, yes. Eat everything you can, and drink the chocolate. Bread and water isn't good for either of us for more than a day."

She dried herself, pulled the new dress up, and rebraided her hair. "You don't have to tell me twice. Watch out for your own portion."

He chuckled and came back to help her button up her new dress. Again, though his tone was warm, his touch was impersonal, like a servant. "Go and eat," he said when he was done. "I'll wash and dress now."

She didn't ask where the new clothing came from, or the small portmanteaux on the floor. When he came to the table, she didn't ask why he was dressed as a French soldier. This was his world. To survive, she had to work with him.

"The tide changed while I was out last night. The tide should return in two hours. Eat as much as possible now, to leave no chance of being sick by the time we're back in *Papillon.*"

"Thank you," she said again, feeling stupid.

"How are you feeling? In much pain?"

Everyday questions, yet they felt so intimate, like a husband caring for his wife. "I'm much better after sleeping, thank you." Her cheeks heated with a flicked half glance at the bed.

He smiled at her, as if he knew what she was thinking. "The color of the dress suits you."

She smiled, liking the golden brown hue of it. "A uniform suits you." She took a minute to stretch out her cramped muscles before reaching for the cutlery on the tray. The curtains billowed in a rising wind. She pulled them back and held them while he arranged the food.

They ate in silence, more companionable than awkward. Yet since that moment's kiss yesterday, her awareness of him had become acute. Their long waltz in darkness had led her to a shared desire at this, the worst possible time and place. Merely looking at Duncan, she felt such a sense of rightness, of belonging . . . if only it could be.

But she knew better than to indulge in sentimentality. Not until he knew the truth.

When they were done with breakfast, Duncan moved in silence to the door, opened and closed it. He checked the windows, looking around. "A storm's on its way from the north. It looks like a hard one. But even if we don't make it out until tomorrow, we need to be ready to escape at all times. We'll have to take shifts watching the window."

Her brief foray into femininity was squashed by his practicality, yet she smiled.

They were partners in this, equals, and he didn't try to shield her.

He sat again. "If the storm comes in, we'll order a bath. The proprietor suspects us as it is. We have to behave as a honeymoon couple." He grinned at her second blush. "Do you remember saying last night you had a plan for our little boat?"

"I — what — oh, yes." She followed the careful trend of his conversation, his soft voice, in case anyone was listening. "It was to do with using the screw at the top. Do you think it could be modified so we could use it from the inside, as a drill?"

"For what purpose?" he asked, even softer now, frowning.

Unsure, she felt her way. "They're new ships, you said? What did you call them?"

"They're in the style of the Viking clinker ships, with a shallow hull for beach landings. They're light and far more portable than traditional ships."

"So they've been made quickly and might not be as strong as a warship?"

He nodded, intrigued. "Where are you heading with this? What's the plan?"

"Can we use the torpedo-attaching screw — modified by a blacksmith or shipwright — to drill holes in the bottom of the ships?" she whispered diffidently. "We'd need to make more drills in line with the first. If we made a series of small holes, to cause slow leaks . . ."

"I see . . . yes, if we made holes along one plank . . . deeper holes could be made at the lazaret — the back of the cargo hold, by the keel — it would be difficult to notice at anchor. But when the ships put to sea, it would weaken the entire rib. It would bilge, perhaps even split." Slowly he rose, closing the windows as the wind blew harder. "If only one rib bilges on a dozen ships on a new fleet, it would scare the rest. They'd need to return to port for repairs and confirm every ship's seaworthiness before launching again. It could take weeks. By then our people will hopefully have recalled the ships from Ireland and Egypt and set some land defenses in place." He sat again, as if in a daze. "It's entirely practical. More, it's brilliant."

She sucked her lips in, trying to control the blinding smile.

His voice was awed, his face alive, blazing with excitement. His gaze turned to her, filled with wonder. "You called me a godsend the night we met — but if I've saved you, it's you that keeps saving us — all of us."

Lisbeth felt the smile break out across her face, like the sun rising. Happiness blanked her mind. She could think of nothing to say that would convey her joy. *She would go home.*

I am the baron's heir. Marry me. With a single word, her ruin would vanish as if it had never been. She could have Edmond. Wife, mother, and a peaceful life in the milieu where she'd been raised. She could see her family again.

From across the table, he took her hands in his. "I called you your father's daughter — but not even he would have come up with a plan so brilliant." His thumbs caressed her palms, and all her hopes, fears, and plans vanished in the startling beauty of his touch.

She felt the blush cover her face, her smile almost painful it was so wide. "Thank you."

"It's I who should thank you. You might have saved us all." His thumbs moved over her skin. "Anything you want, just tell me and if I can give it, it's yours." He lifted her hands to his lips, his eyes sincere yet tense, shadowed.

He thought she'd say she wanted Edmond, and to go home — and part of her desperately wanted to. But the other was here and now and made her feel as if the sun was rising after a long darkness. Turning her hands so her fingers wound through his, she whispered, "I want . . ." But her courage failed her.

"Tell me, love," he murmured, leaning closer. "I swear if I can give it, it's yours."

Like a honed blade, the endearment cut her fears right off — and she remembered he'd called her that last night, too. "I want the kiss we started yesterday."

Ten seconds of silence brought the fear rushing back. "I'm sorry . . . that was inappropriate. You said we had to keep watch . . ."

She didn't know she'd pulled her hand from his until she felt her fingers on her scar.

He took her hand from her face, laughing. "That's my Lizzy. So much you could ask for, so many other things I expected, and you ask for the easiest thing I can give." His eyes grew dark, intimate. He kissed her palms one after the other.

Duncan wasn't a man for poetry or fanfares, but with two words, he changed the world. *My Lizzy.*

By using the nickname only her family and Georgy had ever used, he'd made it real; he wanted to be . . . intimate with her. Somehow it made his proposal feel *real.* "It means something to me," she managed to say.

His eyes softened and darkened. "Ah, Lizzy." With their hands entwined, he stood; she followed. He pulled her close, closer until their bodies fit against each other like puzzle pieces, two continents in their right places. "Lizzy," he murmured again, bending down to her, and she loved the nickname on his lips.

She loved everything about him. She just loved.

How could something millions of ordinary people did every day change her forever? From hiding in darkness, he led her into the light; she felt beautiful for the first time in her life. A splendid glimpse of heaven's light and her place in life came within a single kiss.

This was her man.

His hands moving over her waist and back, he whispered, "So this is all you wanted? Just a kiss?"

The happiness that came whenever he touched her had flooded her body. "*Just* a kiss? It's been like this for you so many times?"

His low chuckle rippled through her. "No, love, it hasn't. You bring the unexpected with you no matter what you do."

No romantic words or poetic syntax, just simple sincerity. "Duncan." Soft undertones in case of watchers, listeners, yet they kissed again and again. "The girls at the tavern — they said —"

"Yes?" he prompted with a soft kiss at her throat. "What did they say?"

Her head fell back. There was no fear, only joyous anticipation. "They said that with a man they desired, the act didn't hurt. They said it was like dying, but you wanted to die. I never understood before, but now I feel like I'm on the edge of a cliff and I don't care if I fall, so long as you're with me."

He smiled at her, and the shadows that haunted her from the first time she'd seen him had vanished. "We have to keep on the watch."

Blushing harder, she whispered, "I — I know. But — when we're safe . . ."

With slow kisses along her collarbone, he

whispered, "As soon as we're truly safe, but I won't risk your life now. Nor will I risk Edmond."

She froze. "What do you mean?"

In her ear, he whispered, "I told you there's a double agent among my crew. Alec and Cal are trying to find him now. Whoever he is, it's likely he reports to Delacorte."

Her blood chilled inside her. *Edmond.* The blood draining from her face, she murmured, her hands falling from his body, "Would he — the double agent — tell Alain that we'd come here together? And — and we stayed here overnight, together . . ."

"Only Alec and Cal are using the semaphore for now, and when Cal's gone, Flynn and O'Keefe take over. I trust both utterly," he said quietly. "But you're right. Once we return to the ship, we must show no sign we could be anything but commander and team member for Edmond's sake."

"Thank you for caring for my son." She went up on tiptoe and kissed him a final time before stepping away. "Most men wouldn't have put the needs of a child they'd never met before their wants. But when Edmond's safe with me in England, I'll ask you again." It wasn't in her nature to make empty denials for pride's sake.

"Lizzy . . ." From his discarded breeches pocket, he pulled out something. "I bought this when I first made the offer to your father, hoping it would be your betrothal gift. Damned if I know why I brought it to France. I thought I'd given up hope. But I brought it with me yesterday in the hope that you'd accept it — and me." He thrust it at her like a street vendor plying his wares and jerked to his feet, looking out the window.

Wordless, she stared down at the piece in her palm. It was a gold locket with a dark velvet riband threaded through as a chain. It was oval, perhaps an inch and a half high and an inch wide, intricately engraved with what looked to be climbing roses. "It's lovely."

"Open it," he said, voice gruff.

When she loosened the tiny clasp, the opened halves held two miniature drawings, of him before his scars happened — perhaps at Cambridge — and one of her, in what seemed to be a copy of a kit-cat painting of her at sixteen. Moved, she whispered, "Duncan, I . . ."

Suddenly he swore. "Gendarmes are heading this way."

CHAPTER 43

It took a few moments to comprehend his words. By then he'd stashed two pistols in the pockets of his cloak he'd thrown over the army uniform and was tying a rope to the bedpost. Lisbeth watched in fascination. Heaven knew where he'd stolen all these things. "We'll have to go out the window. Put on your cloak and follow me." He swung over the sill and scrambled down.

Following wasn't easy when she was trembling like a bowl of calf's-foot jelly in the hands of a drunken butler. Soaked through by the rain in seconds, she cursed herself for forgetting her gloves. Her hands burned as she slipped rather than climbed down.

"Let go," he whispered harshly. She closed her eyes and dropped. He caught her in his arms and put her down. "Keep to the shadows."

She nodded and moved into the shadows by the inn wall, inching her way to the opposite street corner from the gendarmes.

Knocking and yelling sounded from above, banging at the door. "It'll take a few moments to kick the door in, and move the cupboard. Head for the tavern kitchen."

Her heart hammered and she fought to control her breathing. Lightning flashed above them, the wind howled around the buildings.

"Wait," he murmured when she'd have run. "Next lightning — wait — *go.*"

A brilliant flash crossed the sky; rain sheeted down. They ran into the open doorway and closed it behind them. "Stay with me. If anyone looks at us, we stop and kiss. I'm a soldier in the *Grande Armée,* and you're my sweetheart."

Quelling an odd sense of irony, she took his hand. They walked into tavern kitchen and through, holding hands, talking and laughing about being drenched. Joking, kissing, they walked through the tavern. Coins clinked; Duncan must be tossing money at the servants for silence. In half a minute they were through the tavern and on the road.

"Keep walking to the next alley," he murmured, holding her hand tight. "If they see us, run. I'll cover you. One of us must get back with our report, and ready *Papillon* for its return mission here. It's all that matters."

She squeezed his hand. "We can't operate *Papillon* alone unless we sail it. We must stay together."

He nodded, pulled her to him, and kept walking.

Through the side alleys of Boulogne, down the hill, hiding behind crates, slipping inside open doors, and back out, a fifteen-minute walk took half an hour. "I look like a drenched cat, and I stink," she muttered, hiding behind a third crate of half-rotten vegetables.

"Be grateful for the rain, it's kept us alive." He grinned. "And it will clean us if anyone upends a chamber pot on us."

She threw him a withering look, but doubted he could see it in the murk of the heavy storm clouds turning day to dusk.

"You'll be hot soon enough inside *Papillon.*" He pointed. At least twenty gendarmes were heading up the hill at a run. "They're checking all the newer vehicles. They're after a well-to-do couple. So far they've still bought the lie. If anyone questions us from now to *Papillon,* you're a whore and I'm your customer."

She sighed mockingly. "Always the whore."

He didn't answer, and the unfinished scene at the inn came flooding back. Her smile faded. "Duncan, I left the locket behind."

Duncan swore. "Now they'll have pictures of us to distribute." He sighed harshly. "We must all get out of France now."

"Cal?" she murmured in an urgent undertone. *Edmond.*

He smiled at her, but something in his eyes was hollow. "We're taking Cal back to the closest port to Abbeville when we return to ship. I'll tell him to execute his plan to take Edmond as soon as he returns. Don't fear, Cal has a plan complete and ready to go — and Cal, Alec, and I worked out a semaphore code that the mole can't possibly know about. We'll get Edmond out, never fear."

She nodded. "Let's get to *Papillon*," she said curtly.

Rue de Miromesnil, Faubourg Saint-Honoré, Paris
November 3, 1802
Light tapping on Georgy's window startled her from calling instructions to her maid, who was seeing to her afternoon tea. A quick, frightened glance, but the face there wasn't Camelford. With a small sigh, she lifted the window sash. "There is a front door, madame. It's the accepted manner for visitors to knock."

"Calling on you once was acceptable. Any more would arouse suspicion, and your footman is suspect. Don't fear, the foul weather has kept most off the streets." The Incomparable pulled off her damp cloak and laid it over a chair by the fire to dry. In a sky-blue walking dress, she was even lovelier than in yellow — but how did the woman climb up to the first floor in it, and without loosening

535

a hair in her braided chignon? What was she, a tumbler from the circus?

Georgy shook off the useless questions and asked the pertinent one. "What do you need, madame? As you can see, we are packing to leave Paris."

"That's why I am here. You can't leave, not yet. We need you in place here."

Half expecting the command, she shook her head. "Impossible, madame. Since his return from the north Monsieur Bonaparte has been less social than usual. He spends most of his time abusing the English. Even the new ambassador, Lord Whitworth, can't soothe him. He barely speaks to me now. My mother . . ."

The Incomparable nodded. "Yes, yes, she wants to go home and begin preparing for your wedding, now that you have your duke. I saw him first. He has already agreed to stay here and keep back any announcement of your engagement until this mission is complete."

"Thank you," Georgy said, with ice in her tone. "In what manner may I serve you, now that you have rearranged my life to suit England?"

The other woman only laughed. "We all rearrange our lives to suit England, my dear. You'll become used to it. We need you to charm Bonaparte once more."

"Didn't you hear me? He's barely even talking to me now. I think he suspects —"

"Yes, he does. You must diffuse the situation. Camelford has been arrested for trying to kill Lord Bonaparte" — Georgy gasped — "and Camelford not only has information that you are an Alien Office operative, but me also, and your dearest John. He also read certain papers from Mr. Pitt's desk when visiting. He may think to use the knowledge he has to bargain his way out."

"Isn't that all the more reason for us all to leave, now?" Georgy asked, eyes wide with the fear making her heart slam against her ribs. "We could be arrested at any time!" Even protected as she was, she'd heard of the infamous French prisons, and the manner in which young women were treated, forced to use their bodies in exchange for food —

The other shook her head, looking impatient. "Your friend Miss Sunderland is in grave danger on a mission in an underwater boat," she murmured in an urgent undertone. "We must do what we can for her. We must know where Camelford is being kept before he breaks. The knowledge he has is vital to Britain's interests — you cannot imagine how vital, Lady Georgiana. You're in a position to help." When Georgy backed away, shaking her head, The Incomparable said, sighing, "Very well. These letters are from Mr. Pitt, and another from your intended. I believe they say everything you need to hear to help you make a right decision."

Before she even put out a hand, Georgy knew what she had to do for Lizzy, if for no other reason. If Lizzy could risk her life in an underwater boat, then *she* could go to some parties in a palace. With a sinking feeling, she realized that the British Alien Office had a hold of her, and they didn't intend to let her go.

Boulogne-sur-Mer

The storm abated at last, clashing chariots of light and sound over the churning sea. Huddled in their cloaks, Duncan and Lisbeth crouched beside yet another crate. They'd spent the day hiding in seedy back-alley taverns, lasting only long enough to dry off or gulp down food before heading back out into the wind and driving rain to avoid the gendarmes. Once they paid a pie vendor to hide behind his cart, but more often than not it was this, crouching behind crates of old vegetables, frantically quiet while the rats munched and scurried about.

It was nearing sunset by the time they reached the river. Hanging lanterns swung from poles, lighting the entire estuary, where armed patrols and gendarmes ran in all directions.

Here, just one street behind the river, it was dark and slippery. The night people making their way to inns and brothels would come soon. Now was the strange abeyance of twilight, the dearth of light and sound after a storm.

"The patrols will pass us soon." Duncan took her hand again. "We need to make a convincing show if anyone sees us." He drew her closer so they walked like lovers.

"Someone's coming," she whispered moments later.

He nodded. He'd seen the soft halo of fog-shrouded lanterns as well. "Be ready."

A group of green-uniformed men came out of the curling sea mist like the plague of frogs in Moses's Egypt. Throwing back his cloak, Duncan showed his similar green uniform to the soldiers. It was two inches too short and too tight, but pray God it would pass. He pulled the cockaded hat from his cloak pocket and crammed the damp and crumpled thing back on his head. "Time for the show." He turned her into his arms and kissed her, reveling in her skin's heat. How was she so warm, when the drenching rain left him half frozen?

Catcalls and whistles of encouragement came closer. Duncan leaned back to snatch his hat as it fell. "She'll be free tomorrow. This one's worth a full night's payment."

The soldiers chuckled as they passed.

The moment they were alone again she pulled away. "Let's go."

He glanced at her. Her eyes were shadowed, and she was pale. No wonder after being wet most of the day. The sooner he got her back on board the ship, the better.

Finally, after another forty-five minutes of ducking and weaving patrols, they made the pier. It was full dark, with a biting wind and the odd, dancing flake of snow. After checking all around, he lay flat on the planks and checked beneath. "Still there and safe, thank God. Watch for soldiers or gendarmes while I open up."

Instead of answering, she nodded. It seemed she didn't want to talk. Shrugging, he hung upside down at the end of the pier and opened the hatch. "Go."

He covered her while Lisbeth lay down and moved back until her feet swung onto the outer iron rungs on *Papillon*'s hull. By pushing her knees into the craft and hanging on with one hand until she could get a firm hold, she could lift her feet inside the open hatch. But she took far too long; soldiers neared just as she'd dropped inside. After spilling a little of his brandy on himself, Duncan lay flat and barely breathed, waiting for the alarm to start.

When one soldier murmured something and came closer, he snored softly. The other reached him, breathed in his scent of brandy, and spat in disgust. "Go home and sleep it off, *imbécile,* before Admiral Latouche-Tréville hears of this disgrace!"

Duncan grunted and rolled to his feet, reel-ing away. He forced out a huge belch, and the junior officers turned their backs on him, moving off.

When they were out of earshot, he ran to the pier and swung himself under as fast as he could. The second he was inside the craft she grabbed his arm. "Where did you go? What happened? I thought they'd taken you."

He peered at her. White faced and heavy eyed, she'd still managed to light the lantern and was already at the rudder and pump. After locking the hatch, he took the propellers and smiled at her. "Just drawing off interest. I'm an old hand at this, Lizzy. Don't worry for me."

She nodded and released his arm without looking at him. "There are ships going in and out constantly. The waters aren't calm, but we can navigate them. Take us down two feet, and out into the harbor as close to the bank as you can," she said, her voice strained.

He obeyed her in silence, wondering what was going on. Then he shook his head and got on with it. Probably she was just exhausted. What a devil of a day it had been.

After a while she checked through the observation dome. "Tack northwest to avoid the patrols by Fort de Musoir."

When they reached the open sea, he took the compass and used the map to guide them. As he struggled to put them on the right course amid fickle post-storm waters he said, "What is it, Lizzy? You seem worried."

"I'm fine." She sounded strange: a touch cold, like autumn's first frost.

The lingering chill in the overheated chamber confused him. Asking if he'd offended her would only put him on the back foot, so he remained silent. No doubt she'd tell him later.

The next hour was hot, with the submersible jerking and shifting as the wind changed the waves over and over, and they had to avoid the patrolling ships even more than during the voyage in. Had the rat on his ship gotten word to Delacorte? Were they looking for them in the water? Three feet below was barely a tablecloth of cover. With the hanging torches flaring along the estuary and the lantern they couldn't do without, should men with ocular devices begin to search from the forecastles of their ships, *Papillon* would become a painted target.

Duncan knew he ought to be grateful for Lisbeth's continued silence. She was the only woman he knew who was neither shy nor filled the silence with chatter on things men didn't give a damn about. But she seemed to be avoiding any form of contact with him, leaving him with half a mind on the mission, the other damned nervous. They were only hours away from the infatuated Fulton . . .

He didn't even offer to come on this mission, even for her. If he truly cared, he'd have insisted on coming. He was the perfect candidate.

If Fulton had come with her, she'd be dead or taken by now, because Fulton wouldn't have known what the hell to do last night or this morning. He'd have had no idea of how to protect her without one of his clever inventions to hand.

Fulton talks to her . . . he tells her things. So far all Duncan had told her was that he'd played cricket with Leo and his true father was a Jacobite.

What incentive do I have to accept you?

She'd put her finger on his pulsing wound and probed it without mercy. He hated saying anything about his past, especially to her — but there was little choice unless he wanted her to walk away with Fulton. "I was fourteen the last time I ran away from home."

She didn't answer; but if he stopped now, he'd never start again.

Pointing to the scars on his face, he said, "Annersley gave me these. There are many others on my body. Living with him was more dangerous for me than any duty I've performed for Britain."

Horror dawned in her eyes, but she didn't speak.

Papillon bucked. He jumped up and checked through the window. "There's no ships close enough to be causing this. We're just rocking with the outgoing tide."

He saw her shoulders relax a little. So she

543

was as nervous as he. She knew the stakes.

He checked the map and compass and adjusted the rudder, hanging on hard to keep them on course. "Yes, fourteen. I'd been locked in my room again without food or water for some misdemeanor against the great name of Aylsham, who were barons hundreds of years before the Conqueror, titled by some Saxon king. They've been inbred for centuries." He felt justified telling her a half lie — his room instead of the cupboard. She was only nineteen; the true story wasn't for her ears. "He brutalized a servant. I broke the door down and pushed him down the stairs. He's been confined to a bed since then. I'd paralyzed the only father I'd known."

She said nothing, barely moved apart from holding on to the pump. He closed his eyes for a moment and went on.

"I had no one to go to. My real father was dead, my mother left a week after my birth, and all I knew about my father's family was that they were a bunch of poor Jacobites that blamed me for my father's death. So I ran to the only other place I knew: the streets near Harrow."

After a few moments, she asked, "How did you survive?"

The sordid story of his life was something he'd hoped never to tell anyone, least of all the woman he hoped to make his wife. His stomach knotted, and sweat broke out on his skin from more than the heating chamber. "I stole a piece of bread here, a pie there, but I wasn't very good at it. A cook named May caught me and threatened me with the magistrate."

"But you were a child," Lisbeth protested.

Did she have any idea how many children were imprisoned or transported for the crime of theft? Seven years for a loaf of bread. "I didn't look like one. I've been this tall since I was thirteen. May thought I was a man — and she made a deal with me. No magistrate, if . . ."

After a bit, she said softly, "You don't have to tell me."

He forced the self-loathing down, the words out. "No magistrate, and food to spare, if I satisfied her carnal needs."

"Dear God," she whispered, sounding ill.

Though she was no virgin, it was clear she knew little about the seamier side of sex. May was the first of many women he'd pleased during his career, but her memory was the one that shamed him most. A frowsy woman three times his age who believed bathing more than once a month brought disease, her needs had been rapacious. "After a few weeks, others in town heard of it, and also approached me. Lisbeth, the propeller."

The hand covering her mouth returned to the propeller. He had to walk a fine line here

— honesty without revulsion for him, personally. He went on with care.

"I had no interest in doing it again — with anyone — but one of May's neighbors was kind to me, gave me food, and patted me on the arm. When May found out Julia and I had become friends, she threatened to inform on me to the magistrate. But Julia had some kind of hold over May. When May let me go, Julia took me in."

Lisbeth's face softened. "Oh, that was kind of her," she said, her voice husky.

His laugh was hard. "Not quite. Within an hour she seduced me."

The hand returned to her mouth. "Oh, my God."

He shrugged. "By then it seemed almost natural. I knew nothing of women before May. The cook and a few maidservants at Mellingham Hall had looked after me, but I was still very much a child when I left for Harrow, and then I only saw them during holidays. But I was well aware of Annersley's idea of women — it was to use them for cooking, cleaning, and sex, whether they were willing or not."

Lisbeth gulped. Speech seemed beyond her.

"So when Julia took me in, I thought I was lucky. Julia gave me a bed, good food, and somewhere to stay. I helped her around the house, and she taught me how to please her. This lasted about six weeks, until her husband returned from the north." Again he prompted, "The propeller, Lisbeth."

It seemed she'd run out of ladylike expletives. She worked the propeller, her slanted gaze fixed on him, asking him to go on.

"Mr. Wapping was almost sixty to Julia's twenty-nine. It seemed he'd been threatening to turn her out on the streets for her barrenness. The day he left, she took me in. When she heard he was returning, she told me she was pregnant, and thanked me for proof that she wasn't barren, but she had to turn me out of the house. She gave me two shillings." He looked at Lisbeth, but only saw only Julia's pretty, scheming face. "I'd turned fifteen the day before."

The trembling hand touching his brought him back from the darkness.

"The propeller," he said for the third time, but smiled. Thank God, he hadn't repulsed her; his brave, sympathetic Lisbeth was back. "Unfortunately for Julia, Mr. Wapping suspected the child wasn't his. He made inquiries, and within a few days, he met May. Unable to bear being cuckolded in front of his town and laughed at by his people, he bludgeoned Julia to death and disappeared."

"Oh, Duncan," she whispered, eyes brimming with tears.

He shrugged. "I ran to the streets of London and stole to survive. I avoided all women and learned to avoid men who wanted the same thing as May and Julia. A few months later, a man caught me picking his pocket. He knew who I was at a glance, had known my real father, and despised Annersley. He'd been looking for me for months. He made me return to school. In the holidays, he sent me to an older man who treated me well. He trained me in the game right alongside his sons and treated me as one of them. That man made me what I am."

A smile like the dawn breaking crept across her face, lighting her dimples. "Papa." He smiled at her, thinking she was still too pale, her eyes black ringed. When they got to Jersey, she'd do nothing but rest for a week.

He nodded. "Eddie saved my life. I know he wasn't at home for you often, but I'd either be dead or owned by some street-gang king but for him. I owe him everything. It's time for more air." He unlocked the hatch. "You go first."

She stood, breathed and stretched for a moment, her body jerking. He was about to ask her why, when she dropped down fast. "A ship's light's close, coming fast," she croaked.

"This has been going on too long. Somehow our double agent must have got a message to Delacorte. I think they're looking for us. Drop down a full fathom for as long as possible."

The ominous rocking began seconds after he'd battened down the hatch. The next few minutes were taken up with the necessities of staying alive.

It took almost half an hour until the ship was out of sight. Gasping with relief, they emerged again and reopened the hatch; but after she'd stood and drawn in fresh air, she looked even paler, and somehow hollow. She shivered. "Your turn now."

He took in air and gave her more time to breathe, but she stayed up only moments before her body jerked again. He watched her, concern growing; but she said, "Please turn your face."

They performed the necessities of life, cleaned the chamber pot, and ate the last of the food he'd bought at a tavern before bringing the hatch down. After, she sucked on one of the remaining eight peppermint sticks.

Disturbed by her white complexion and heavy-lidded eyes, he said, "Only two hours to go, if all goes well. We're clear of any small islets, and the patrols have stopped for the day. I think we can use the sails."

Lisbeth nodded, but she looked strained.

He affixed the sails, working *Papillon* by the compass and map. He didn't have to be outside, except to check for ships every few minutes.

After a bit, she asked the question he'd been expecting ever since he'd told her his identity. "Did you offer to marry me to please Papa?"

He wanted to smile in blinding relief. She wouldn't be asking if she didn't care. "I would have — I'd always wanted to. Becoming part of your family was my dream for so long," he admitted. "But though Eddie spoke of you and your mother often, taught me to be a King's Man, trained me in the ways of a gentleman, and called me his son, he never brought me home to meet you. I was scared sick he knew about May or Julia and didn't want to infect his wife and daughter with the likes of me. He only invited me home once, when you were staying with your grandmother near Bath. He wanted me to meet your mother." He had no idea how she'd react to his next words. "Then when you were nearly eighteen, he told me you'd had a Season but didn't find a single gentleman who interested you. He said he wouldn't be surprised if you turned out to be as hard to please as your mother."

She smiled, but it was a weak, pale thing, like first light at the winter equinox. "That was because I thought I was in love — with Alain or the dancing master, I couldn't be sure."

He chuckled, but said, "I didn't know what Eddie wanted me to say. I'd wanted to go to London and meet you during the Season, but he sent me on a mission. I thought it his way of telling me I wasn't good enough. Then he gave me this" — he brought out the miniature of her that he'd carried from the day Eddie had given it to him — "and said, *Here is your way into our family, if you like her.*"

After a few moments, she started laughing, punctuated with strange snuffling sounds. "Oh, that's so — so like my Machiavellian papa. He . . . he meets a ragamuffin vagabond who happens to be a baron's heir, and — and thinks, 'This boy's p-perfect for my rebel daughter. I'll keep them apart so they don't think of each other as brother and sister, and — and then propose on her behalf.' " She kept making odd sounds as she spoke: not quite a laugh, closer to choking.

"Good God, I never thought of that." He grinned. "That sounds exactly like Eddie." He checked for ships before he went on, taking the time to think out his words. "I wanted to be a Sunderland so badly I'd have married you no matter what, but I took one look at your miniature and blurted out a proposal. I fell in love with a face — but when I met you, and took the time to know you, I came to love the brave, surprising woman you are." He hesitated, but decided to press on. "The moment we're safe I will marry you, Lisbeth."

In a flash her warm vivacity was gone behind a wall of stone and mortar. "I can't marry you, Duncan."

Though she'd said it with quaint dignity and tired honesty, in a voice strangely hoarse, that old sword tip ripped his belly; all he heard was the rejection. "So I'm good enough for sex when nobody's around to see, but not to marry?" he asked, voice cold.

She made a small sound. He couldn't decipher it because she moved the propeller at the same time.

"I suppose you'll marry Fulton," he went on, not knowing whom he punished more with this. "Go to America, so you won't have to face your past. He'll be happy to have a pretty young wife and a bottomless pit of funding. You'll have a nice life. Just don't ask him to save you, because he won't even notice that you're gone, or he'll hide behind his principles when it means risking his own neck to help others."

Another sound, just like the last: distress or exhaustion, he didn't know. But this time he refused to fill the silence.

Eventually she said, "Please. We need to concentrate on the mission."

Good sense told him to keep his mouth closed. But like an idiot he pressed on. "By all means, let's return to the ship, saying nothing."

"It's what you're good at," she mumbled. When he turned on her, she sucked her lips in, shook her head, and whispered something, apology or defiance. Her body jerked again, making him irritable. Why didn't she just tell him what was going on?

"Whatever it is you're thinking, say it out

loud," he said, but without heat. Only a fool would let this descend to a full argument, given where they were now.

The look she turned on him was touched with betrayal. "I thought you knew I wasn't a whore. Yet you just treated me as one. How could you think I'd ask you to kiss me, to — to — and think I could go back to marry Fulton?" Her voice sounded gravelly. "You know nothing of me, to think I could do that."

He shifted on the bench, fiddling with the sails to hide the flush covering his cheeks. "I beg your pardon," he mumbled.

She shrugged and spread the map across her lap, peering at the compass. The stiffness of her position screamed some kind of warning to him, but he had no idea what it was, or what to say. He'd never been in such an intimate place before with any of the women he'd bedded. With Julia, he'd been the supplicant; with every other woman, he'd made certain he was in control, always keeping a vital part of himself back, keeping his emotions in check.

He'd been doing that with Lisbeth from the start, yet here they were, sitting in a darkness that was as emotional as it was physical, and she wasn't trying to fix it. She was the only woman he'd met who didn't demand, ask, cry, or beg, and it left him floundering in unfamiliar waters.

"I think we've drifted east with the tidal

changes," she said in a rasping voice after standing for a moment. "We seem too close to land."

"What's wrong?" he asked in quick concern. She shook her head, but by the light of the lantern, she seemed more delicate and pale than she'd been yesterday, or even an hour ago. "Are you well?"

At last he saw what she'd been hiding: she was shivering. He touched her, and while her clothes were still damp from the last drenching hours ago, her skin was hot. Her body jerked again with that strange choking; then a cough erupted from her, hard and barking. She coughed half a dozen times before she could stop. "I'm sorry," she whispered.

"Why didn't you tell me?" he growled, pulling his cloak off and over her. But he knew. He'd told her he expected her to be as tough as a man on this voyage. He'd forced her to prove herself, to endure travails that would have broken most men he knew, and all without complaint. "I ought to beg your pardon." Loathing filled him for what he'd done to her. She'd been the only one small enough with the necessary qualifications for the mission, yet he'd punished her for being right. "I relied on you too heavily."

A slow blink, and then she frowned at him. "It's what I came for, what I was trained to do. I'm proud to have served with you on this mission. Don't take that away from me."

And then she broke into another coughing fit.

He frowned in turn. "It's too cold for you with the air coming in. I'll close the hatch."

Quivering fingers, too hot, touched his arm as he began to stand. "You have to leave the sail up. I don't think I can help you now."

He lifted the lantern to look more closely. Good God, her skin was hot and dry, her eyes red and burning. "You should have told me."

"We couldn't stay in Boulogne," she whispered. The damned little heroine that she was, she'd done it to save him, kept going until she could no longer move.

Even around the pole splitting *Papillon* in half, he leaned back and drew her close until the next coughing fit subsided. He checked the compass every few moments with his free hand, using the tiller by instinct. All he could think of was getting her to the ship's surgeon, as fast as he could. "No one else could have done as well as you. The past two days have overwhelmed me, and I'm used to the rigors of a mission. Spending the day getting wet and dry again, hours in the rain — I should have thought to bring a blanket —"

"Not much use if it ended up as wet as we were," she whispered with a weak chuckle.

"Naughty chit," he murmured. Even now she could make him smile — at least until another hacking cough erupted from her. He patted her back and turned so she could lean her head on him. "Rest now. I'll get us safely back."

"Mmmm." Her head touched his shoulder, rested there as she sighed. "Nice . . ."

Something inside him shifted as he felt her snuggle into him. A lifetime of fears as uneven as the welts across his skin softened, as if a balm covered them. Checking the compass, he adjusted the rudder and tiller as he said, "You like me, Lizzy. You wouldn't have wanted to kiss me if you didn't."

"Not now," she complained, but she'd tensed. She was still awake, still thinking. Wishing she wasn't.

He brushed his hand over her cheek — too hot — and down the back of her neck. Feverish and aching to the touch, by the way she winced. "You like me." It was no longer a question.

She sighed again, lifting her face. Her eyes held fever and illness and a world of fear and hurt, and he cursed himself for pushing her so hard. "I do. I love you, Duncan. I want to be your wife."

The words he'd dreamed of hearing from the only girl he'd ever wanted to make his wife, but the fact that she'd spoken in a voice shaking with illness and terror took the brunt of the joy from him. "Then why won't you marry me?" he asked, because he couldn't stop himself. Because she wanted to tell him.

She put a hand to her forehead and shivered

again. Another racking cough burst from her.

Cold fear gripped him. He'd seen the symptoms before — this was either influenza or, worse, inflammation of the lungs. Either could kill her. She needed the hatch closed — but he couldn't work *Papillon*'s machinery alone, and she didn't have the strength to work the levers. By the look of her, unless he got her back quickly, he could lose her.

He pulled her head back onto his shoulder, his arm around her to warm her. Everything was set; he could sail via the compass almost right to the ship, so long as no French patrols passed nearby. "Rest, love," he said gruffly. "We can work everything else out when you're better." He only felt a smidgeon better when she snuggled in again.

"Did you really think I'd encourage Fulton?" she rasped after a while.

He drew in a breath and made an admission he'd never have thought to speak before she'd said she loved him. "My experiences with women haven't led me to believe the best. I was angry and jealous, and punishing you for rejecting me. Trying to prove I could take better care of you than Fulton would. Look how true that turned out to be," he muttered in self-disgust. "I should have noticed you were sick."

"I do like Fulton, very much," she whispered. "He's gentle and kind, interesting, brilliant and . . . safe. If — if I hadn't met you, I might have . . ."

"But you did meet me." He kissed the top of her head, happy and wretched and flat-out terrified. *Please, God, just let her get through this,* he prayed again, realizing how often he'd prayed since meeting her. She had that effect on him. Making him see his illusions of control were exactly that. Right now he'd never felt so helpless.

Despite the fact that she was fevered and shivering, the silence felt companionable as he held her, kissing her forehead.

After a while she spoke again, but her voice was cracking, her breaths quick and uneven. "Duncan, I wasn't rejecting you." She lifted a shaking hand when he would have stopped her, urged her to rest. "Edmond's birth . . . took too long. I'd worked all day, all week. I was so tired . . . lost blood . . . kept falling asleep. Alain went for a midwife, and then the doctor. Edmond came out blue. By the time they had him breathing . . ." He felt her tremble and tense against him, her skin heating even more as she mumbled, barely audible, "If — if you want . . ." She shook her head and pushed out a few words, racked with coughing. "There won't be any more children."

English Channel, British Waters
Since word came out that there was a suspected French agent aboard ship, the ship's

558

mole had accepted he'd be found and killed here. What he couldn't tolerate was failing his assignment, letting down his master, or his country. He'd let Mark run off with Camelford, thinking it spelled disaster for Britain; knowing the Mad Baron, the boy would end up dead for certain. Now the cunning little bastard was hiding in Boulogne-sur-Mer, finding secrets his lord couldn't afford the English to know.

He had to warn his lord of the infiltration — but with the commander's brothers manning the semaphore paddles in the forecastle, he couldn't do it. Neither could he escape, with Flynn watching the rowboats like a hawk.

Wanting to kill Camelford for the disasters he created wherever he went was useless. He had to get a message to France.

He began making new plans.

CHAPTER 44

St. Aubin's Harbor, Jersey, Channel Islands (British)
November 6, 1802
"Lad, I think we've narrowed the search to two, maybe three."

Having carried a semiconscious Lisbeth into a warm coach waiting at the land end of the gangplank, covering her with blankets, Duncan started at the soft voice near his ear. He whirled around. Alec was right behind him. "What? Who?" He hoped to God it was neither Carlsberg nor Flynn.

Alec put a finger to his mouth. "Come back on ship."

Without meaning to, Duncan turned to where he'd just left her. Fulton had climbed in the coach and had her lying across his lap to keep her warm. As he leaned out to shut the door he gave Duncan an odd look. It wasn't competitive, or triumphant, but — reassuring. Fulton had told him last night that he'd once nursed his mother through influenza. "I know the herbs to give, the teas to make her drink. West and I will see her well, Commander," he'd murmured, laying a warm cloth over Lisbeth's forehead. "Warm is better than cold, ice baths will make her shiver, and get hotter inside," he said when Duncan tried to protest.

Damned if he knew what Fulton was talking about — but to leave her now, after their unfinished exchange inside *Papillon,* felt like he was courting a rejection. Damn it, why couldn't he remember what he'd said in answer to her revealing her secret?

There won't be any more children.

He thought he'd said something, but whenever he thought of it, he drew a blank. Lisbeth had become so sick after her last words he'd had to concentrate on getting them to the ship as fast as possible. Would she even remember what he'd said? If he'd said anything of what he'd been thinking, he hoped to God she never remembered.

"Carlsberg's the best engineer I've worked with. Flynn's not only a man I'd trust with my life; he's also a shipwright's son. I need them for the work on *Papillon*'s modifications." Especially since he doubted Fulton would leave Lisbeth until she was well.

Uncharacteristically serious, Alec nodded. "I think Carlsberg's cleared of suspicion, but Flynn has to stay on board, lad. He's a highly competent messenger, and he's the only one

I'm anywhere near certain of right now, apart from West, and the lass needs him."

He gave Alec a sharp look. "You *think* Carlsberg's clear?"

"We have to be sure." He put a hand on Duncan's shoulder. "Thank God O'Keefe found us. I can use him, and I'm going to hunt up a few good agents left kicking their heels here since the peace. I heard they've been forced to highway robbery to survive. They'll be glad of honest work, and the promise of work later. Best of all, the rat won't know them. You have enough on your plate. Leave flushing out your rat to me."

Duncan wished to God Cal could have stayed as well. Leaving only two on board was a hell of a risk, even half a mile out to sea. "Excellent plan. Buy or hire every possible rowboat the rat could take out to a ship, including this one," he said quietly, handing Alec a full pouch. "Recruit every man you can to the cause."

Uncharacteristically serious, Stewart nodded. "I've been here a few times on assignment. The Jerseymen trust me. I'll organize for food and beer to be sent to the ship daily. West can bring it when your lass is asleep."

The coach took off at a steady pace, West walking grimly beside it. It was Duncan's only comfort. West wouldn't allow Fulton to do anything stupid.

He turned back to the ship. Flynn was

562

already organizing the transporting of *Papillon* to the smithy. He'd left the ship at first light to negotiate a price for commandeering the smithy for the three to four weeks Fulton said they'd need for Lisbeth's suggested modifications to the craft, and to make enough drills. Now Flynn was back, his invaluable lieutenant. Duncan hoped to heaven he wasn't the rat, because if Alec was wrong, God help them all. Flynn knew the ship and the mission inside and out.

Once *Papillon* was on its way to the smithy he'd dismiss the men for well-earned leave. Then he had to stay on board, watching the damned semaphore like a hawk. "First, you need to speak to the councilmen of Jersey and arrange to have the Martello towers fully manned."

Alec nodded. "I'll do it while you're on semaphore duty. I'll message the agents while I'm there. I'll take one of my main suspects with me. The other I heard making arrangements for drinking and dicing with the men, so he can wait until the agents arrive."

"It's a good plan, but I want both followed, all the time." Duncan wished to God it wasn't necessary with Lisbeth so ill, but he couldn't break squares on this. "Ask O'Keefe to follow the other suspect until tomorrow. If your friends come on board with the mission, you and O'Keefe retire and handle matters from the inn." He almost asked the suspects' names, but until it was confirmed, it was best he didn't know.

"Aye, an excellent plan." Alec's eyes softened. "I'll check in every few hours with your lass and send word."

Duncan's smile was touched with the gratitude he felt. "I'll want you to pass a daily note to her, asking after her health." He put out a hand: a sign of trust.

The bridge was crossed. He could trust his brother to be at his back, armed and ready to defend him and those he cared for. After years of denial, he'd chosen to become a Stewart.

He wished it could be so simple with Lisbeth.

As if reading his mind, Alec said gruffly, "Don't lose her now, or you'll always regret it. Black Stewarts rarely love more than once, lad," he went on quietly. "I'll give her any message you like." His half brother turned away, his eyes black with ancient grief.

He looked like a statue Duncan had seen of Romeo on waking and seeing Juliet dead . . . but whoever Alec's Juliet had been, she was long gone.

Why did he only see the reality of people when they were in pain? Fumbling, he touched Alec's shoulder. "My thanks again." He strode off to oversee the transport of *Papillon,* and to get the would-be assassins off ship.

"Monsieur *le Capitaine,* welcome to France, to Paris, and to my home." With one of the little flourishes he was said to love, Boney bowed.

The tall, dark, and handsome blue-eyed sailor known to friend and enemy alike as "Guinea-Run" Johnstone smiled and bowed in return, imitating the flourish to a tee. *Neatly done,* he flattered himself. "Very glad I am to be here, m'lord. A signal honor and all that."

Once they were seated and Boney had poured him some of the finest French brandy that ever passed his tongue, the first consul said softly, "You must be wondering why I requested your presence, *Capitaine.*"

Dragged from the bathtub was more like it, me lord, by four soldiers, à la Bathsheba to King David, he thought, more intrigued than sour. He nodded but said nothing. In a long and varied career, he'd learned how to wait with a smile.

"I hear it is — shall we say, dangerous for you to return to your homeland currently," Boney said, smooth as water on glass, mellow as the brandy he was drinking.

Johnstone laughed outright. "Because I escaped from the Fleet Prison, you mean, m'lord? Aye, returning might have its drawbacks until I can pay me debts, but it'll work out right in the end." He swirled the brandy in its glass before taking another swallow. *One left. Make it last.*

"I can make your debts disappear, make certain you are not only pardoned for all outstanding charges in Britain, but also given a place of honor, with a title and wealth beyond any you could ever make by smuggling."

Johnstone laughed again, turning it to an unconvincing cough when Boney frowned. "An' how would ye be doin' that, m'lord, seeing as how you're leader of France?"

Boney's slow smile filled with promise. "Of course it would be impossible — unless I became the leader, as you quaintly call it, of Britain also."

Every sense went on screaming alert: a silent blasting of the ship's horn. *Enemy approaching!* Johnstone leaned forward, trying to appear eager. Part of him *feeling* eager. Why shouldn't he listen? It wasn't as if anyone in England cared if he lived or died. "An' what would ye be wantin' from the likes of me?"

Boney, too, leaned forward. Smiling. Gentle. A friend or foe depending on Johnstone's answer. "As a smuggler of both contraband goods and information, you know the ways in and out of Britain that are not, shall we say, heavily watched by those — what do you call them?"

"Damned nosy tide watchers, that's what we call 'em," Johnstone muttered. "Excisemen, if you're of the official kind."

"The tide watchers, *oui,* that is it. Excisemen," Boney said slowly, drawing out the syllables. Johnstone tilted his head, watching more closely. Checking the room without seeming to do so. "You know where to land a ship — one, or even several — without being seen, *oui?*"

Damn, damn, damn. Aye, whatever the first consul wanted now, Johnstone knew it was something perilous, not to say traitorous, and he was in the heart of the beast, in the bloody lion's den. And he felt more than ever like Bathsheba, dragged to a palace to face a king with the power of life and death over her soldier husband. "That I might," he said, feeling his way.

"It is clear that the day of serfdom and lords nears its end. The power of the ordinary man, the man extraordinary in every way but birth, has dawned. It is so in America, in France — and it must be so for all the oppressed in Britain and all her enforced territories. Those in servitude to the class who will not even work to earn what they have should be set free!"

What did he say to that? Hear, hear? Vive la France? "Um, right, just so," he blurted, when it seemed Boney had noted his lack of enthusiasm. "I'm a little confused as to where I come in, m'lord."

"Citizen Bonaparte will do," Boney said gently. "We are all brothers here."

And I'd be believin' that more readily if you weren't livin' it up in a palace while yer "brothers" are beggars on the streets not too far off, and your soldiers bivouackin' in tents. But Johnstone smiled and murmured, "Citizen . . . where do I come in?"

"You come in as the second in command, the pilot to the man who will lead the *flottille nationale,* a pilot of capability and brilliance, helping us to free the common man and woman from their bondage."

Johnstone coughed. "Um, not meaning to upset the applecart here, m'lo— . . . um, Citizen Bonaparte . . . but we British were freed from serfdom centuries ago."

"Oh? And can a man born into the lower classes become a lord through his brilliance, or must he be fated to clean the excrement of a drunken lout with a title he did nothing to earn, but simply inherited?" As if seeing the little dagger cut he'd made in Johnstone's confidence, Bonaparte went on, softly, "Are you destined to remain nothing but a despised half spy with the degrading nickname of *Guinea-Run Johnstone,* from whom your so-called superiors will take information and help, but will never reward you in the manner your intelligence and ability deserve, simply because you are the son of a fisherman and smuggler?"

The questions burned into Johnstone's brain like hot wax poured into his ear. He felt his cheeks grow hot. He couldn't answer. Now he knew how he felt to be his poor friend Brownlow, who'd believed in his adored wife's fidelity only to see her legs spread for his brother.

Was that how outsiders saw him? A lifetime of adventure on the seas since he was nine years old, charming women and gathering information, became small and stupid, defined and defiled by the birth he could never escape, no matter what he did. At least in England . . .

"In France, a man is rewarded according to his deeds, not his birth," Napoleon said softly, walking into the room of his thoughts and snuggling in for a long rest. "Why should a man who already has too much be given a position of honor when he has no talent and will not fulfill the role to anyone's satisfaction? Why should a man of ability and strength be forever held back simply because of a heritage that exists in no one's mind but that of his oppressors? Why can he go no further in life while the glory and riches go to a man who did nothing to earn it?"

Damme, he'd hear the questions in his head until Gabriel blew his trumpet, so he would.

Johnstone drew himself up. "I might be just a smuggler, sir, and never go any higher; but I am a true lover of my country. The one thing they will never call me is a traitor."

Expecting a violent outburst, Napoleon took Johnstone aback with his smile and nod. "Somehow I had expected such an answer. You're a good man, Johnstone. Such a shame all they will ever do is exploit your loyalty for their gain."

"Still," Johnstone said, a dog hanging on to its bone, "if I betrayed my country, what would stop me betraying you later? It would always be in your mind, and in mine. That way lies corruption of a man's soul, and we both know it."

A tiny sigh. "I am sorry, *Capitaine.* You don't know how sorry."

He snapped his fingers, and those four soldiers returned, bearing cuffs and leg irons.

St. Helier, Jersey
December 7, 1802
From a hill to the town's north the ship's mole could see everything right out to Elizabeth Castle, sitting splendid and armed against invasion in the harbor. It was the first time in weeks he'd been able to get away alone, even for a short time. Alec Stewart knew, or suspected the truth; O'Keefe had suddenly become his barnacle, keeping nearly constantly in his company. In desperation,

the mole had set up his scapegoat in a suspicious situation, and Stewart needed temporary help chasing that down. He'd easily lost the inn's boot boy. He was too young to understand that buying a whore didn't always mean spending the hour with her.

Twenty minutes left.

He squinted through the bilocular lenses. As part of the Royal Navy, he'd passed through here many times before the war began in '93 — but now he barely knew the place. Since his last visit, the entire town of St. Helier seemed to have moved a few hundred feet back. At the rocky promontory at the tail end of town, there were new fortifications. Trenches surrounded the round tower forts built after the Battle of Jersey. Every road into town had been cleared of vegetation. There were smaller trenches beside the roads, like rainwater ditches.

His frown deepened as he traversed the hill, looking in every direction. On every road in and out of town, and along the walls and ramparts at both Elizabeth Castle and at the round tower, armed men and even women patrolled in uniform. No doubt the same was occurring at Mont Orgeuil Castle to the northeast, at Corbiére Point farther west, and every promontory on the island. They'd made it impossible for any sizable force to sneak onto the island — even a single stranger without credentials wouldn't make it.

Thank God he was a bona fide member of an English ship.

The island was militarized, and Delacorte, Fouché, and especially Bonaparte needed to know about it *now.* If the other Channel Islands had similar fortifications and were set up with semaphore, it could be deadly for their leader's plans.

Squinting, he saw the semaphore poles on the roof of Elizabeth Castle. Any suspicious ship coming in from anywhere would be known across the island in an hour.

Since Delacorte's arrival in Ambleteuse just before the assassination attempt, nothing had gone right. Since the commander's brother had taken control of the ship, watching them all closely, it was ten times more dangerous.

He needed to create suspicion. Luckily, he had a scapegoat close to hand.

CHAPTER 45

Blacksmith's Forge, St. Aubin's Township, Jersey
February 9, 1803

"I can't believe you thought of this plan, my dear." His face glowing with the forge's heat, Fulton beamed at Lisbeth. "The master is overtaken by the pupil."

Standing by the bucket of water, ready to cool the finished drill, Lisbeth felt her cheeks warm. "I can't believe you're here, helping us. With your scruples against Britain . . ."

Fulton sobered. "My republican principles don't cover the enforced invasion of other nations, Lisbeth — even if it means Britain becomes a republic. Bonaparte is the best and most conscientious leader France could have asked for, but in this, his passion for conquest overcomes his good sense. No man should have to die to fulfill another's ambition."

She nodded. "That's just how I feel."

With tongs in the fire, molding the tensile

steel and twisting it into a drill shape with delicate care, Fulton said, "Another thing we have in common, my dear."

Lisbeth fought against stiffening. Her nine long weeks of influenza that had turned into an inflammation of the lungs had made him even more loving and tender with her. During those weeks Fulton had nursed her like a babe, fed her, and tended the fire himself. He'd worked double time at the forge while she bathed or slept, day and night. He'd only returned to full-time work when the doctor decreed she could leave her room in mid-January. And not once did he remind her of his proposal during her recovery. The pearl drop pendant he'd given her at Christmas, and that he was working for Britain to remain close to her, only doubled her painful confusion. She'd never expected a man to love her this much.

She'd put him off as long as she could. Now it was February, and he'd still demanded nothing from her — but she felt it coming. "Thank God the winter storms have grown in ferocity. It's slowed down any chance of the French fleet's launch."

"Yes. It makes our task slower, but I'm glad of it. You've had time to recover." Another warm smile made Lisbeth want to squirm in guilt.

She'd run out of time; the proposal was coming again, and her stomach twisted in knots. "I — think I should go in for lunch . . ."

"Wait a moment, my dear. Stay with me. Please."

His tone held pain and hope. She bit her lip and nodded, fighting against pleading her recent illness as an excuse to leave. She owed him far more than this hearing.

Her silence seemed to daunt him. He finished working on the drill part. "I'm not certain this steel is strong enough. You'll have to do a test run."

"A test run?" she faltered, confused.

"There are old ships and boats in the shipyard, I dare say, or perhaps the shipwright's son could build a mock-up of the first consul's ships you saw. We must be certain that these drills won't break off when you attempt the holes."

Awed, she smiled at him. "How stupid of me not to have thought of that."

After passing her the new drill part to dip in the water with the tongs she held, he pinched her chin. "You can't think of everything, my dear. We men have delicate sensibilities that need constant stroking by conceiving at least some of the brilliant ideas."

Nerves growing, she laughed, and moved just enough so his hand dropped. She turned and saw West watching her like a hen over its chick. Reluctantly she nodded, and West left to find his lunch.

Before she'd even turned back to him, Fulton said, "Lisbeth, you do like me, don't you?"

Her stomach dropped. "Of course I do . . . Robert. Very much." He'd insisted she call him Robert, but it brought back unpleasant memories of the first time she'd been forced to be on so intimate a footing with him.

"I know you, ah, like the commander. No," he said, lifting a hand when she would have interrupted. "Please give me the dignity of honesty, my dear. You care for the commander."

Strangely ashamed of her feelings, she nodded.

Fulton selected another piece of steel from the high-quality German metal he'd brought with him from Ambleteuse. "He's sent notes daily that you haven't answered, or even read. Since your recovery you've made every excuse to avoid him though he's come to visit many times." He looked up. "It seems to me that he's hurt you."

She bit her lip. "He hurt me no more than any other gentleman would." She almost choked on the admission. How many more times must she endure this? "My son is the only child I'll ever have."

The silence was profound. In the quiet he selected a piece of steel and leaned over the forge. His apron glowed golden in the light; his spectacles gleamed like twin mirrors, warming his kind face. "I see. And this made a difference to the commander?"

She shrugged, putting her wall back up. Duncan had said but a single word in response to her confession, but its foulness had spoken volumes. "It would to most gentlemen, I believe."

"I dare say." He kept twisting the steel. A minute passed, two, and her throat filled. She was about to leave the forge when he spoke again. "Perhaps in time you might consider an offer from someone who considers your worth to be far above the mere bearing of children?"

She stared at him so long he turned back to her. His eyes were serious, kind, affectionate. In the light of the forge, his gentle face was at its best. He put the piece of steel down on the iron plate lying on the table behind him, then came over and took her hands in his. "We didn't start on the best footing, but during our time in Ambleteuse I came to admire your quick mind, your lively intelligence, your courage and kindness, as well as your lovely face." He smiled and shrugged. "I don't have the flowery words women want to hear, but if you knew what's in my heart . . ."

"You — you don't care about having children?" she whispered, amazed.

His smile turned rueful. "Probably as much as most men. But though I could find many other women to provide children for me or feed me when I forget to eat, there is only one Lisbeth. You can stand beside me in my work and bring it richness and unexpected brilliance, make me laugh and think, brighten my day with your smile, and put me in my place when I treat you as anything less than the lady you are. If you'll accept me as your husband, I'll raise your son with all the love a father can provide."

Tears slipped down her cheeks. "Thank you, Robert," she gulped, gripping his hands. "You have no idea how much I needed to hear that."

He gazed at her with such tenderness, she knew he meant every word he'd said: his first consideration was his love for her. He wanted her even without Papa's funding. "Will you please do me the honor of thinking about becoming my wife? I'll wait as long as it takes, so long as you'll say you're considering it."

Her head drooped. "You deserve more than a woman who loves another man."

He fumbled with his answer. "You are too close to him now. Perhaps after this mission, when you have your son . . . would you come with me to America? I swear I'd treat you with all honor. I wouldn't press any, ah, attentions on you. In time, away from him, your heart might change. If it doesn't, you're free to pursue your own life. I would make certain you and your son are both provided for."

Moved, she looked in those kind eyes, and saw their masculine beauty in strength, kindness, and tenderness for her. She was ashamed that a small, vain part of her still felt resentful for the past neither of them could change.

America.

In England she'd have no hope of meeting a man who'd see beyond her past. Perhaps he was right — once she was away from Duncan . . . if she and Robert traveled to America without his asking for anything from her father . . . again she felt ashamed for suspecting that he'd write to his new father-in-law, hoping for Papa's funding in exchange for rescuing his daughter.

She lifted a hand to her mouth, feeling off her balance, her thoughts heavy as a glop of mud in a pond. "From my heart, I thank you for all you've said. I have doubts, but, I — Robert, I'll consider your offer, will consider going to America with you once I have Edmond." Moved, shaken, she leaned forward to kiss his cheek. "You have been —"

Fulton turned his face and kissed her mouth.

St. Aubin's Bay, Jersey

During the murky end of a sunset filled with scattered cloud, Duncan heard splashing oars approaching across the small, calm bay by St. Aubin's township. His was the only ship not docked close to land. Unable to see the boat's occupants in the dark, he swarmed back down the forecastle mast. Once on deck he made sure his pistols were primed and ready.

He didn't need to call Flynn; his first lieutenant was already in the shadows by the bow. They'd taken shifts in the commander's cabin for the past few weeks, never achieving more than uneasy dozing. He didn't have to ask if Flynn was armed. They'd been waiting for this for the past three months, knowing the Martello towers were too well manned, and how easily they could be outnumbered here aboard ship. He nodded. Flynn came over to him; standing as one, both were armed and ready.

"Who goes there?" he yelled.

"Ho, Commander," West's strong Welsh brogue called. Duncan didn't have to ask who he'd brought with him, or even why. West refused to leave her for any reason.

He looked at Flynn, cocking his head upward. Instead of melting back into the darkness of the commander's cabin, Flynn climbed up the forecastle three hours before his turn would begin, at twelve bells.

Still, Duncan called down in a hushed tone, "Who's with you?"

"It's me, lad, and Miss Sunderland," Alec called back, sounding subdued.

It was warning enough.

Duncan lowered the rope ladder over the port side, knowing West would dog Lisbeth's every step until she was safe on deck, and inside by the fire. Alec would tie the boat and guard the ship with Flynn until Lisbeth said what she'd come to say.

Moments later he saw Lisbeth's face for the first time since his last day off two weeks ago. Though she still seemed delicate, he was happy to see that waiflike translucence had given way to a glow of health. Fulton had taken good care of her, along with the nurse Duncan had paid to stay and perform all intimate tasks for Lisbeth during her illness.

He grasped her by the waist and lifted her onto the deck. Her face was serious, a little sad, but mostly turbulent as she looked at him. West saluted his commander and waited outside the door when Duncan led her inside to her favored wing chair in front of the fire. "Please, be at comfort." He stoked the fire. "I'm sorry I can't offer you tea, but I have some ratafia —"

"No, thank you, Commander. Please sit down."

Knowing what was coming, he sat, wiping his face of all expression.

It wasn't long in coming; she had too much emotion churning in her to hold it in. Watching her fiddling hands in her lap as though they contained the mysteries of life, she said, "Commander Aylsham, I thank you for the great honor —"

His laugh was hard with no humor in it. "Shall we put the word without any bark on it, Miss Sunderland?"

She stiffened and looked up. "Certainly, sir." Her tone was gentle and cool. "You know what I've come to say. I only wish you'd saved me the trouble by withdrawing your suit."

He felt a brow lifting. "Why would I have done that?"

She turned her head to the side. "I thought it obvious. I suppose, given the love you bear my father, it was awkward for you to retract."

"That obligation ended the day I found you." It took some self-control not to snap the words, but he refused to hand her the power of knowing she could hurt him.

"I am here to —" She shook her head in apparent frustration. "Thank you for your offer, but I think you will be grateful for my rejection of your suit."

"You've accepted Fulton, then." He spoke calmly.

Both her brows lifted. "That would be unpardonable in me without answering you, even though he proposed first," she said gravely, but her eyes still held storm clouds. "He proposed days before you did — days before he knew my father's name."

"Why not say what's on your mind?" he demanded, reining in the temper he'd claimed only weeks ago he never lost. She was still not fully recovered, as evidenced by the thick winter dress and the cloak she'd put off, the shawl tied about her shoulders.

"It's obvious you have something to say to me."

She sighed, staring at her hands, twisting together on her lap. "You don't wish to marry me now. You want children."

In the quiet, a wave lapped the side of the ship, and the pendulum swung on the ormolu clock on the mantel. "Yes, I do," he said quietly, before realizing the ambiguity of his answer. Unsure if he wanted to clarify her first statement, he said, "I've never had a family of my own."

"It's understandable, sir. But I find myself offended. I want another man to come on the mission with me. I think perhaps Robert would do it now — for me."

It took a minute to make the connection. "Fulton knows, and still wants to marry you."

When at last she looked up, her eyes burned with betrayal. "He said he would raise Edmond with all the love a father can provide. That any woman can give him children, but there is only one Lisbeth. I want a husband who feels that way for me."

Looking at her, he knew how much it had taken for her to break Fulton's confidence. How much it meant to her to have Fulton feel that way. He chose his words with care. "I'm certain you do. As certain as I am that Fulton would wish his wife to feel that way for him," he said bluntly. "But you love me. If you didn't, you wouldn't have come straight from him to me."

In the warm firelight, she paled. "Damn you."

He waited for the rest.

"Damn you," she said again. "He's willing to wait. Once we're in America —"

Sudden fury took hold of him. "No, damn you. Damn you for running off instead of waiting to meet me. Damn you for a wasted year of my life searching for you, worried for your safety." He jerked to his feet and paced the room, refusing to look at her. "You're the best bloody team member I've had the privilege of working with. Despite being injured or ill, your brilliance and your insight have taught me to depend on you, and to miss your clarity when you're not with me. Now you're leaving me when I've carried your bloody portrait around like a lovelorn youth for a year. You think it's just you who hurts?" he said softly, even now remembering her illness, her need for gentle treatment. "All my life I've been alone. Is it so wrong to want my own family?"

"No, it isn't," she said quietly, her gaze back on her lap. "Nor is it wrong for me to want a husband who won't resent me later for the children I couldn't give him." She lifted a hand when he would have spoken. "You want a family of your own. I respect that. I want a quiet life with my son far from Alain's reach. Robert can provide that. So I'm here to say thank you — thank you for everything — and farewell."

Vicious words escaped his mouth, but he snapped it shut when he saw her flinch. "I seem to beg your pardon on a regular basis," he said, dropping to his haunches in front of her. "I'm sorry, Lisbeth. It seems neither of us is wrong to cling to our wishes, and though we love each other, it's not going to work."

She didn't look up. "I need to go."

When she stood, he rose with her, looking at her averted face. He could smell the lavender on her skin, the rosemary in her hair; he saw the pain he'd caused her. "Damn you," he whispered fiercely, but his fingers on her cheek were tender. "Even now, all I can think is that if I lose you to Fulton I'll never meet another woman like you."

"You will," she said softly. "I'm not so unique."

Something snapped in him. "Marry me, Lizzy." He took her hands in his.

She looked up then, her eyes filled with that same turbulent confusion. "Why?"

The sadness in Lisbeth's voice caught him off guard. He watched her, puzzled.

"Why are you asking me again now, when you've barely been near me in weeks? Is it to destroy the only prospect I'll ever have to be respectable, to have a good life with a man who values me beyond the bearing of children? Haven't I done everything you've asked of me? I — I don't understand."

He frowned. "You knew I couldn't come. I told you why. With the double agent on board, Carlsberg working with Fulton, my trusted sailors manning the outside of the Martello towers, and only Alec and Flynn to trust, I had to man the semaphore. Didn't Alec tell you his visits were to reassure me of your health? Did you not read the notes I wrote to you every day? You didn't answer once."

She frowned, staring at her twiddling fingers; she always did that when she was hiding something. "It hurt too much," she said eventually. "I found the illness left me weak and tearful."

"Did you read them?" he asked, gentle with her again. "I came to you, Lizzy. You refused to see me."

She didn't answer that. "You want children, a woman who can give you a family. So why are you doing this? Can't you just be glad to have me off your conscience?"

What did he say to that?

A man who values me beyond the bearing of children.

Fulton's clear vision humbled him. Any woman could bear children, but there was only one Lisbeth. Dreams could change, but his feelings wouldn't. "Edmond will be my heir," he said curtly. Within seconds he cursed himself, waiting for the fury to come.

"I could never subject my son to *being an heir,* Duncan." She took him aback again with her sadness, so much stronger than anger, and harder to fight. "You of all men know how it feels to be that boy."

"You're right." He sighed and made a rueful face. "I'm putting this badly, but Fulton was right. Your worth is far beyond the bearing of children. You know I love you. If you'll be my wife, I swear I'll love Edmond as if he was my own."

"I won't give my son into the control of a man who'll resent him one day for not being his own son." Her words weren't a challenge. She meant it.

"If there's anyone who understands that, it's me." Her brows rose in silent challenge, and he sought the right words to convince her. "I wish my mother had loved me the way you love Edmond. No" — he shook his head as her eyes flashed — "this isn't some stupid plea for sympathy. I'm telling you I've never had a family. I'm making one mistake after the other. I love you, but I don't know what it means, or what to do."

She stilled.

"I never had a mother, or sisters." The words tumbled out. "The only kindness I had as a child was from servants. The only father I've known is yours. The women I've known only wanted me in bed. But from the start you've challenged me, shown me new ways

587

to do things, and taught me how to treat a lady. I've failed you over and over, but you're still here now. I want" — his lips pressed together, but seeing her chin lift, he knew he had to say it — "I see Alec and Fulton saying things to you that make you laugh or smile. I never learned how to flatter and charm." He shook his head in frustration. "Show me how to be the man you want."

Her expression softened, then turned questioning. "You've said nice things to me before."

"I practiced. I listened to other men to work out what women like to hear. What *you* would like to hear — but it rarely worked." He knew his frustration showed in his tone. Lord, how he hated admitting to any weakness. Too much like a soldier going into battle without weapons.

A pensive look crossed her expressive face, and then a little chuckle came. "That's why they never felt real to me."

Her adorable expression invited shared laughter, but the moment was too serious. "Does this feel real?"

She blinked, bit her lip, and nodded. "And you've made me laugh many times, Duncan, just being yourself. I — I do like you."

Relief flooded him. "I'm sailing in uncharted waters here — but you make me more than I am, better than I was. I want that for the rest of my life."

"That doesn't mean you won't regret your decision later."

"You don't trust me." She only shrugged in response, just as he did when protecting himself at her expense, and he wanted to smile. "I don't deserve your trust. Despite working together all these months, you barely know me."

"No — because you don't trust me, either. I don't think you trust anyone."

"I trusted you with my past. I've never told anyone about that, not even Eddie."

He saw her mouth tilt up in a half smile she soon smothered, but something in her expression was a lantern leading him on a path he hadn't known was there. She'd had an idyllic childhood compared to his — yet her experiences with Delacorte, and in France, had given her no reason to trust any man.

Still, she'd come to him. Because of his advent in her life she'd nearly died — twice — yet she was still here, giving him the chance to prove himself.

He returned to his chair, but leaned forward, taking her hands in his. "I'm not saying all this because I want to win some game with Fulton, Lisbeth. You're the only woman I've ever wanted to marry, and I don't think that's going to change. If you'll accept me, I'll never give you or Edmond cause to regret it."

Her gaze was so full of doubt. Pretty words weren't the way. He wished to God he did know the way. If Eddie was here —

Eddie. "You've said things about your father I can't understand. I think he's made mistakes with you — and with me — but I can't see them. Help me, so I don't repeat them."

After a few moments, she said, "You said Papa wanted to whip me, that Annersley whipped you."

It was only now he saw how bad it was to have made that joke. "He wouldn't have done it, Lizzy. He said all you ever had to do was smile at him and he'd forget why he was angry."

Her smile was still pale, wintry. "But you were raised on whippings."

He got the point. "If you'll make me Edmond's father, I swear I'll never whip him." The promise might be harder to keep at times than she knew, but he'd do it. "I have more reason than most to know how it damages a child. I wouldn't want my son to grow up terrified of me."

She tilted her chin up, her eyes glittering. Even before she spoke he felt the stakes rising, a desperate woman putting her whole fortune down on one throw. "You will *not* raise my son to be a King's Man. Edmond will choose his own path."

Then what the hell can I teach him? About to say it, he saw his youth, his years with Eddie, Leo, and Andrew. Like a plant, Eddie had fed and watered the three boys a steady diet of loyalty to king and country until they'd bent in that direction as to the sun, leaving Caroline with no husband or sons, Lisbeth with no father or brothers.

"Edmond will be his own man," he vowed, hating the words as he said them.

There was a visible hesitation before she spoke, and again he saw the image of the crazed gambler, throwing down all he had. "You won't leave us when we need you. You won't disappear for months on end and re-appear, expecting a welcome home."

He frowned, opened his mouth, and closed it. There went another of his cherished dreams — but now he knew why. She'd spent her entire childhood *without* her father.

"Swear to me," she said fiercely.

"I will be a husband and father first."

Her shoulders relaxed a fraction, yet her defiance grew. "You once said, *needs must when duty drives.* I won't tolerate that, Duncan. I am not my mother."

His eyes widened. "Your father was never unfaithful to your mother to my knowledge, and neither will I be to you."

She nodded, but closed her eyes, and he knew this was it, the final challenge. "Tell me why you flinched when I mentioned Mama."

Cold sweat broke out fast as a lightning strike. If he told the whole truth — that he'd written to Eddie dozens of times during the past six months asking after Caroline's health, and received nothing — no, he couldn't do it to her. "Eddie asked me to bring you home once the mission's done. He said your mother's pining for you. It's all I know for certain."

She frowned. "But you suspect more."

"I heard she was ill from a man who'd never met her. That's all I know. I don't even know if it's serious illness or not."

"Mama is ill, and Papa didn't send for me." Her gaze dropped to her hands, twisting.

The words came out, King's Man to the end. "As my wife . . . as the person who helped save Britain, he'll be so —" He couldn't go on. "Eddie will welcome you home now, no matter what, Lisbeth." She deserved to know that.

She shook her head. "No." It was all she said, but as fierce and heartfelt as anything else she'd said today. So strongly she believed Eddie would never forgive her, that he simply didn't love her.

What kind of father had he been? What had he done to her?

Send her home now, before it's too late. But again, the equation was simple: Lisbeth or his country. Hundreds of thousands of lives against one young woman's happiness — the woman he loved. "He loves you, Lizzy. He just doesn't know how to talk to women."

Her eyes still closed, she shook her head. "I want to see my mother as soon as this mission ends." Closing the door on her personal house of ghosts, all with her father's face.

"We'll leave for Norfolk the hour it ends."

The doubt in her eyes flashed up to him like a semaphore flag, bright red with warning. "Don't say it if you don't mean it. If I ever discover you've put nation above family, I'll be gone by the next day — and that's my vow to you."

She knew him so well. The shame and the resentment mixed in a toxic potion. He loved his life as a King's Man — and he loved her. How many compromises did she expect?

Unwilling to make a vow he didn't know even now if he'd break, he lifted her hands to his lips. "These weeks since we left Boulogne have been — hard. This is the most important mission I'll ever take part in. I can't leave the ship until the double agent is found, but I've resented that the whole time. Next time you're ill or in need, I want to be the man with the right to care for you."

Her head drooped again. "I'm afraid to love you, Duncan. I'm afraid Edmond will love you, will need his father, and you'll leave us over and over when duty calls. Robert will be there for Edmond, I have no doubt of that."

"You're right." He felt her trying to tug her hands free. "Lizzy, I can't guarantee I'll never go if something dire comes up. But until now,

I've never had a reason to say no, never had anything or anyone that needed me more. Give me that reason, Lizzy. Give me a family."

"Like Mama did with Papa?"

That was a facer. "Eddie always had the luxury of taking family for granted. I'm not Eddie."

Her chin lifted and her mouth curled down. "If you're not my father, I'm not my mother, waving her husband off with a smile and crying for weeks, watching the window for hours every day for his return."

Her words took a half lifetime of blinkered vision from his eyes. Eddie's portrait of a happy wife and charming rebel daughter, so proud of his duty and awaiting his return, had been painted in all the wrong colors. "Is that why you took all those mad risks as a child, behaving like a boy? To get Caroline to bring Eddie and the boys home?"

She shrugged and turned her gaze to the fire. "She was happier when they were home."

"When you were twelve," he said slowly, remembering a story Eddie had told him, "you rode your horse in a hard frost, fell and broke your wrist and ankle, and had a concussion."

She shrugged and grinned. "A little too extreme, you think? But Mama wrote to Papa, asking him to come home."

He felt no urge to laugh. "But he didn't."

He knew, because the Sunderland men had all been with him in Paris until summer.

Another shrug. "They wrote to me, telling me to stop being such a hoyden."

"And your mother — ?"

"Cried for weeks while I was laid up in bed."

Another wave lapped the ship; a log crackled in the fire as the cabin grew into darkness, hand into glove. "Did you have friends in your childhood?"

She smiled. "Grand-mère, who taught me all the French accents."

Again, he couldn't smile with her. "No girls your age?"

"During my Season, I became quite friendly with Lady Georgiana Gordon, until her almost-fiancé died, and the duchess took them home. Then a month later I ran off with Alain, and that was that."

"No friends at all, until you were seventeen?" he asked, stifling the incredulity. "No wonder you thought you loved Delacorte."

"And the dancing master. Never forget poor Ludwig," she giggled, and for the first time since they met, she looked and sounded like the girl she still was. "I probably would have loved the local blacksmith's son if he hadn't been married. I spent some of the happiest hours of my childhood at the smithy's forge."

Moved by the sadness she didn't see in her life, Duncan took her hands in his. "I am not your father," he said again, and for the first time, he meant it. "If circumstances ever force me to go on a mission, just write if either you or Edmond needs me. I'll be home within days."

The smile faded from her face. She turned to the fire, her hands limp in his. In the silence, the disbelief and a hundred fears screamed all the louder.

"Do you want me to stop trying to convince you?" he asked softly. "If that's what you want — if Fulton will make you more secure . . ."

The fire crackled; a log popped, sparks danced like fireflies, lighting her sadness and confusion. "He kissed me. Robert kissed me."

"Is that why you came to me?" he asked, when she said no more. Her head shook and her shoulders shrugged before she frowned and nodded at last, the distress plain to read in her eyes. An eloquent silence indeed, and he read a three-volume novel into them.

She'd come to him.

In the warm firelight, whispered echoes of the night they met returned, and he knew why she was here. "I was shot because I refused to leave you to Delacorte and the Jacobins. I broke the first rule of a team leader: leave injured members to die if it endangers the mission. I should have let you die then. I should have left you alone with Fulton. Instead I slept in a tent in the bushes, close enough to hear you scream if you needed me." After a few moments, he went on. "If my duty came first, I would have let you have your say today and leave. I've been fighting it for months, but since you were hurt I factor what you would think, what you'd want me to do, in every decision I make. I'm asking you to marry me because I like the man I am when you're in my life. You make me more than I was, better than I ever thought I could be."

He thought he saw a faint glimmer of her lopsided smile, but it faded. "No more missions for me. I will never *charm* another man, no matter what Britain's need may be."

He closed his eyes. Behind his lids he saw the man he'd been taught to be through her eyes. "After you ran off with Delacorte, I was convinced you'd never want me. When I found you, I believed I couldn't fulfill my desires at the risk of others. I thought I was making the sacrifice. I told myself Fulton would propose when he knew your father's name, and you'd be safe and happy in America. I refused to look at what damage could be done to you because I'd have to see what I'd become."

"The man my father taught you to be." Soft, bitter words.

"He protested against this mission, Lizzy," he said, hoping to soften the pain.

"But he never came for me. He never wrote to tell me Mama was ill — and don't tell me he didn't know my location. You told him, didn't you? He's known for months where I've been, and I've heard nothing from him."

He sighed. Eddie was a King's Man to the end. In his devotion to king, country, and, yes, his own glory he'd betrayed them all, none more than Caroline and Lisbeth. In refusing to influence the mission, Eddie had abandoned Lisbeth and left his only grand-child with Delacorte despite knowing what kind of man he was.

And he'd left Duncan to judge whether he could risk an entire nation on an untrained girl's brilliance.

The more Duncan had come to care for Lisbeth, the more he'd despised the choices he'd made. But with a government in denial and a bare dozen ships patrolling the entire Channel, even since her illness, Lisbeth was still their only hope of stopping the invasion. He couldn't send her to her mother in case she refused to return to France. Even if Caro-line was dying, he couldn't risk it. There was no time to train anyone else.

"I came for you." Floundering words of re-assurance, inadequate because he hadn't rehearsed any others.

"You did. You always have." Her lopsided smile, so damned trusting, almost hurt him. "I'll teach you to be the kind of husband and father I want."

Thank you, God. "You saw the special

license. It means we don't have to post banns for three weeks, and the double agent need not know anything. We'll marry here in Jersey, tomorrow if possible, with Alec and West as witnesses, and keep it discreet. We can fill in Edmond's birth details at both our parish churches when we return to England, naming me as the father. All anyone need know is we toured the Continent on our honeymoon, and Edmond was born abroad."

When she lifted her head, her eyes glowed. "You're saving my reputation, and making Edmond legitimate. I can go home. Duncan, you don't know what that means . . ."

When he moved to kiss her, she pulled her hands from his, with an apologetic smile. "Not until I've spoken to R— Mr. Fulton. It's only right."

A painful kind of wonder filled him. How a woman like her, a lady to the fingertips, wanted a man like him he'd never understand. "You make me a better man." He meant every word. Her promise was made, and she'd keep it. He released her hands, tucked her arm through his, and escorted her to the ladder.

The Smithy, St. Aubin's Township, Jersey
A half hour was all the mole had needed for months, but he'd had no chance. Now, his fear at desperation point, he'd take any time he could get to get a message to a ship.

Miss Sunderland's belligerent demand to see the commander had made Stewart careless enough to hand him that time. Why so many men rushed to do the woman's bidding he'd never know. Right now the commander was probably hearing she was leaving the mission to wed the American.

He had to move fast. The message must be received.

Standing outside one of the two Martello towers near St. Aubin's township, he flicked his knife. A swift gurgling sound, and poor old ship's master Jones was on the ground, the sharp point at the base of his throat leaving the blood pumping from his neck. "I'm sorry, Jonesy," he whispered, taking the knife back. He hated that he was forced to betray people he liked and respected. When Jones was dead, he slipped past the body, inside and up to the parapet. He killed the Jerseyman on the watch before fixing the semaphore paddles to the poles, winding the torches around and fixing them well before lighting them. Dozens of French ships patrolled this area from sunset. One was bound to intercept his message and pass it on.

He moved the semaphore's arms with practiced ease, careful to be exact. Using the torches was a big risk, especially with the township on the alert and Flynn or the commander able to see everything he signed, but he had no choice.

English spy in Boulogne. Jersey militarized. Compromised here. Do not approach.

Two minutes later, a winking light in the distance told him *Message received.*

The mole looked across the land. Someone had arrived, was watching; he could feel it. People were moving from the west. They'd seen the message.

He slipped down the stairs and out. Back to the whore he'd paid to keep making noises until he returned.

CHAPTER 46

St. Aubin's Bay, Jersey (English Channel)
February 10, 1803

"I performed my part. I made your drills and the modified brace," Fulton said stiffly. "I want the promised passage with all my things to Amsterdam."

Standing in the commander's cabin, Fulton looked only at the windows behind, his color high but eyes flat. Duncan didn't need an explanation.

"My ship cannot be spared right now. I'll arrange passage for you on a smaller ship passing by Jersey as soon as *Papillon* is complete. If you prefer, I'll hire a room at a different inn for you until that time, and hire another smith to help you repair *Nautilus*. But first I need you to strengthen the pump and lengthen the air hose."

"I'd appreciate somewhere new to stay." Spoken like a substandard actor reading unfamiliar lines. Duncan would have done the same if he'd known Fulton was to spend this night in Lisbeth's bed. "Order the pump and hose to be brought here. I'll do it at the forge here aboard ship with nobody watching me. It should take no more than a week."

"Thank you for all you've done," Duncan said, low. "Please remember, none of this discussion can be spoken outside this ship."

If anything, Fulton became more somber. "I have no wish to die, Commander. Nor do I wish anyone else to die. Now may I leave?"

Duncan nodded. "I'll organize a ship — and your payment — as soon as may be."

All he got in reply was a bitter look from over Fulton's shoulder as he left the cabin.

Duncan had won — won it all, at the expense of a good man's innocence.

The long-familiar price of saving Britain. Under his tutelage Lisbeth had spied on Fulton, captivated him, taken his boat and his skills, allowed him to nurse her to health, let him believe she'd accept his hand, only to reject him in favor of the man he hated. All that was left was the bitter aftertaste of betrayal in the name of duty and loyalty.

Rule Britannia, the life of a King's Man . . . or woman. No wonder Lisbeth wanted no more of it. Watching Fulton go on this, his wedding day, Duncan wasn't certain he did either.

The plump, middle-aged rector, brought in haste from St. Helier, looked resentful as he pronounced them man and wife. Without time to heat with the day, the church was half frozen; its high stone walls and ceiling seemed to bounce the cold from outside onto them. The minister kept his cloak on over his vestments, and his traveling hat, but still he shivered. Torches in their sconces lit the ancient walls, but they gave no warmth. On a heavily clouded day, the saints in the stained-glass window behind stared down at them in sorrow.

The wedding party shivered along with the minister. West and Alec were their witnesses, while Flynn manned the semaphore on ship, and two midshipmen cleared of suspicion followed the suspects. Three months, and still no results. Whoever the mole was, he was damned good.

As weddings went, it was a quick, joyless affair. Lisbeth wore a dark winter dress, pelisse, cloak, and bonnet, her hair in a chignon. She felt positively plain beside Duncan, who wore his best commander's uniform. There was none of her family or friends, no party planned for later. Lisbeth saw in this day the warped mirror of her first wedding, and infidelity to all her younger self's dreams. Somehow, after all her defiance, she'd married the baron's heir.

She stifled a giggle.

"What?" he murmured so only she could hear.

Her eyes twinkling, she whispered, "If Papa could see us now, how he'd crow over me."

Duncan chuckled and squeezed her hands. "He'll have his opportunity, soon enough." Then they turned to accept the hurried congratulations of the rector, and the heartier handshakes of Alec and West. Hardly had they spoken when the rector guided them to the register, rushing them through the necessities before pushing them out the church door and climbing onto his pony and trap, disappearing into the cold misery of the day.

It amazed her still that they could wed so soon. That Duncan had never burned the special license, that it was still in force and he'd had the proof of it with him — he was saving her, saving Edmond, and giving her a life in England. It hardly mattered that they had to return to work, and her only wedding trip would be inside the cramped confines of *Papillon.* No hidden kisses, no pretty ball gowns, no flicked looks across a room — no family apart from an almost unknown half brother and a bluff old Welsh sailor; even squashing inside the carriage with West and Alec as they rode back to the task at hand didn't disturb her tranquility.

"I am a strange woman," she whispered

aloud, shaking her head.

"If you were not, you wouldn't be my wife," Duncan murmured into her ear.

She smiled at him.

Catching her whisper across the carriage, Alec grinned. "You're a Stewart woman, Lisbeth, a strong woman of the clan. You may not fit in with the English simpering misses, but in Scotland you'll meet many such women as yourself."

She felt Duncan's reserve, saw it in his frown, but Alec seemed unmoved. It seemed Alec also knew Duncan needed time to adjust to new relationships.

Before the horses had even stopped at the inn, the door was yanked open. "Commander, Commander, sir, ship's master and the Jersey guard at the Martello tower are missing. There's blood at the door, and on the parapet. The semaphore paddles are gone."

Alec and West left the carriage and ran, taking the young midshipman with them. Left alone, Duncan took her hands in his. "It's a rotten wedding day for you. I'm sorry, my dear."

"Go," she urged him when he hesitated. "You must."

"Thank you, my dear." He handed her from the carriage. "Tell no one about the marriage until we know Edmond's safe."

She didn't know whether she felt disturbed

or reassured by that.

He saw her inside the inn, bowed, and ran out. And Lisbeth broke the first promise she'd ever made herself, to never be her mother's daughter, for she was watching through the window as her husband left her.

CHAPTER 47

St. Aubin's Township, Jersey
February 10, 1803 (Late Afternoon)

Unable to send or receive messages for weeks on end the ship's mole had had no choice but to follow his training. Now, with everyone shocked by Jonesy's disappearance, they'd left Carlsberg alone at the forge, working. Fulton had stormed out last night and hadn't returned.

He liked Carlsberg, and he truly regretted Jonesy's death. Perhaps that was why he tied a scraggly kitten to the handle of the smithy's front door to distract him, or maybe because a death here would draw attention to the smithy. It didn't matter. Carlsberg was always sneaking tidbits to the ship's cat, even if it meant she wouldn't be chasing rats that night.

Soon the kitten's mewing got the big man's attention. He untied the kitten, cradling it to his chest, petting it and speaking nonsense. The kitten's crying grew more urgent. "Oh, ho, laddie, what do you do here?" The kitten meowed again. "I think someone's hungry." After a glance around the smithy, he took the kitten to the inn's kitchen for food scraps.

It took no more than a minute and a half for the mole to do what he had to. He slipped out the back way and down to the small, rough bay that was difficult to reach, where he'd set up camp the day Stewart left him to run after the Sunderland whore.

Mission accomplished.

English Channel, Near Jersey
February 10, 1803 (Evening)
The night was thick with mist and drizzling rain. They used the two-legged canvas bosun swing to lower in. She shuddered during her turn, the ropes tossing with the tide, banging her legs, hips, and shoulders against the brass coopering around the observation dome. The moment she was in, she felt squashed beside Duncan.

"Good God, but it's awkward," he muttered as he pulled the ropes to help her out of the canvas confines. When she was finally free of it, Duncan yelled up for the men to lift the device. "No wonder you prefer breeches for this. I can only imagine the difficulty if you wore skirts."

With a droll expression, she looked down at herself. "Perhaps these were breeches once. They can't be called such now."

"That's base ingratitude on your part. I'm

sure wherever he is now, my cabin boy Mark misses them, not to mention the all-weather coat you wear is mine." In the murky light of a half-lit lantern, she saw the anxiety behind the smile. The doctor had come this afternoon at Duncan's insistence, dosing her with vile concoctions until she complained she'd turn as green as his herbs.

"I doubt your cabin boy misses anything about this outfit." She pointed at the crisscross of sewing and patches. "His mother probably blesses me for not having to sew them up again."

"At least they've been washed." He called up, "Lower the rowboat, and anchor it."

The sound of the hatch thudding closed made the jokes wither on her tongue. *No air, no air,* her mind whispered though there was enough to breathe for an hour. When Duncan twisted the wheel to lock it down tight, she longed for that rocking cold wind only inches away.

"Don't think about it." He touched her hand. "It's only an hour or two this time. We need to test the drills before we undertake the voyage." He grinned. "I have a range of new medicines to pour down your throat for the next few days before you can be deemed well enough to go."

She laughed and pulled a face. "Submerge as soon as we're free of the ropes."

The submersible heaved as the divers

released *Papillon* from its ropes. In the bosun now, Flynn thudded on the side wall: their sign that the launch above them was anchored in place.

Lisbeth worked the pump, feeling them submerge. "Don't use the top propeller. We could damage it against the wood of the boat."

The next half hour was taken up with maneuvering *Papillon* into place. "Damn it," he growled. "If we have to do this every time, we won't get more than a few ships done."

Guiding him via the observation dome, she said, "We'll be in the river, which is far easier to manage than the open sea. Ease up; yes, that's it." She turned to the new contraption above her head and turned the handle, watching all three drills turn at once, lifting upward.

"Remember the noise factor. We can't afford to attract attention when we're there."

She nodded and slowed, keeping it steady. *What an oddly appropriate wedding night for us.*

Five minutes later she beamed. "It worked!" With the removal of the drills, she could see little bubbles of water spiraling up into the launch.

Duncan smiled back, but said, "Let's practice changing the drill, and try again."

She shrugged and nodded. "Do you know why Alec insisted on this test tonight?"

"No, but Alec never asks me to do anything

without a reason." He added, "If you start to cough, we'll stop."

An hour and five drills later, a drill broke off at its base within a few minutes, blocking the hole they'd made.

They had Alec's reason.

"I had two main suspects after you were shot in that rowboat. From what you told me, the boat moved so you were in Delacorte's line of sight," Alec said quietly. "Then Cal sent a note. Delacorte was on the trail within a day of your sailing out of Valery. It made it certain: it had to be either Burton or Hazeltine. I had my friends Prigent and St. Hilaire — the former highwaymen I told you about — following Burton. Hazeltine's clumsiness was suspect, so O'Keefe and I stayed with him. When we couldn't be there, the boot boy was well paid to follow Hazeltine wherever he went."

Sitting at his desk in the commander's quarters, Duncan heard the doubt and pain in his voice. "Hazeltine's clumsiness has seemed suspect to me, too. Are you sure . . . ?"

Alec shook his head. "So certain I sent O'Keefe to London himself with the message rather than trusting a semaphore. We both saw him, Duncan."

Duncan felt his shoulders slump.

"Prigent was with Hazeltine for weeks. He

played cards and dice and got drunk with him, but Hazeltine never did anything else. Burton seemed innocent too, apart from a proclivity for whores. But the attack on the Martello tower couldn't possibly have been Hazeltine; he was drunk and snoring at a card-table. I'd also put the inn's boot boy onto Burton two days ago, when I brought Lisbeth to you. The boy's only thirteen. He was terrified at seeing Jones's death and ran to his grandmother's for the night. When he came back early this morning, he told Hill everything about the Martello tower attack. Hill came to us. I put one of my highwayman friends on Burton, who followed him all day. The proof is positive."

Duncan felt his shoulders drop even more. "Well then."

A scratch at the door, and Hazeltine and Flynn frog-marched a trussed Burton between them. His second lieutenant was pale, dark hair mussed, but his eyes flashed with defiance.

"He entered the smithy today while we were investigating Jones's disappearance. St. Hilaire saw him enter and leave and followed him to a bay to the west of town," Alec said grimly. "I checked everything when he reported to me. *Papillon* seemed sound. That's why I asked you to check the drills. Swapping the drills for some of inferior make seemed the easiest type of sabotage. St. Hilaire sent his men to every smith on the island. Burton had them made by the smith at St. Clement's Bay, to the east. The smith identified Burton beyond doubt."

Duncan looked at the man whom, apart from Flynn, he'd thought of as his right hand for five years. He'd entrusted Lisbeth to his care when he went to England, had trusted the man with his own life more than once. He turned to Alec, eyes pleading. Gentle with regret, Alec nodded.

"That's why Miss Sunderland wasn't attacked when in your care, only mine," he said, just now realizing a truth he ought to have seen months ago. "Delacorte wanted no attention drawn to you. You were too important."

"I don't know anything about that, sir, but the man following me saw nothing, sir," John Burton said. "I was merely curious and looked at the drills —"

"It wasn't St. Hilaire who followed you to Petit Port in St. Owen's Bay, but O'Keefe, a highly placed King's Man. You replaced three dozen of the drills with some made from poor-quality steel. You got to damage a dozen of them until the alarm sounded from the ship, recalling the crew. O'Keefe saw you toss the rest in the harbor late this afternoon. I found the semaphore paddles there as well. Ingenious, adding the torches for night use. Unfortunately for you, both O'Keefe and another King's Man, Le Brigand, saw and reported you there. From then, we knew where we were. Hazeltine was deep in a card game with half the crew." With a contemptuous half smile, Alec held open an oilskin packet filled with steel drills. "Unfortunately for you, I was a navy diver."

Seeing Burton's shoulders drop a fraction, Duncan grieved anew. "Why didn't you expose him this afternoon? Why put us through all this rigmarole?"

Alec's face was neutral. "Would you have believed me if you hadn't seen the inferior drills breaking off in the hull? Would you have accepted my word over Burton's?"

Duncan surprised even himself by saying, "Yes, I would. You're my brother."

Alec smiled in a way he hadn't seen before. "If you ask me, we'll get nothing from him."

Two hours later, Duncan had to agree. "This is useless. Burton's father bought him the commission as midshipman when he was fourteen. He's been on my ship five years. This will break the Burtons' hearts. They lost him once before — he disappeared at five years old and was returned to them when he was nine."

Watching Burton, Alec said, "Perhaps he's one of those stories I've heard about — a street urchin trained in the game from childhood, a French child replacing a missing English child. They have a blind devotion to

France, being taken off the streets and given everything."

Burton remained silent, but the air fairly crackled with hate.

"Where's Jonesy's body?" Duncan asked, his voice cold. "At least give us his body to bury. He loved you like a son. You owe him that much."

Burton didn't even turn. "I demand to be returned to the Admiralty for trial."

Why that convinced Duncan he didn't know, but looking at Burton, he saw a true French loyalist. He'd give nothing away. "String him up," he ordered Hazeltine and Flynn.

Hazeltine gasped. "Sir, he asked to be handed over to the Admiralty —"

"Extraordinary circumstances, Hazeltine. He claims to be a British national, so he's guilty of treason on the evidence of two high-ranking King's Men," Duncan snapped. "I'll take the responsibility. String him up."

Flynn said quietly, "I ask to be recused, sir. Burton and I joined your crew together."

"Permission denied," he snapped, thinking of Burton carrying him to the midwife's, or when he covered Duncan with his body during a sea battle. He wondered at the duality of the man he'd have trusted with his life. Had it all been a lie?

Faces ravaged, his first and third lieutenants marched Burton out, their friend, drinking mate, and confidant until this hour.

Swinging from the yardarm, Burton said only three words before his neck snapped. *Vive la France.*

Duncan turned away from the jerking body with the tongue sticking out, the bluish-purple face and staring eyes. "Take him down, and throw him over," he said to his sailors.

"He was my best signaler," he muttered to Alec. "At least we know how so many secrets found their way to Paris."

Alec put a hand on his shoulder. "Delacorte's probably got ships waiting to hear where to drop anchor to stop *Papillon.* Burton must have truly felt desperate to kill Jones. The man was like a father to him."

Duncan glanced at Flynn, who watched the sailors taking down Burton's body, his face expressionless. Duncan knew Burton's last words would ring in Flynn's ears, too, until Gabriel blew his trumpet. "What type of signal did he use?"

"Only Nelson's style of messaging in my sight," Flynn replied, voice guttural.

"Did he ever send a message you didn't understand?"

With a frown, Flynn shook his head. "I'm sorry, sir. I didn't think to look until we all came under suspicion, and he hasn't been on the semaphore since then."

"Ask every man if they saw anything, no

matter how ridiculous it seems to them. Go," he snapped when Flynn kept staring at the corpse of his friend.

Flynn saluted and strode away.

Alec said when Flynn was gone, "Sometimes these spies work in pairs. We don't know if Burton was the senior or junior partner made a scapegoat."

Duncan gave him a helpless look and swore. "It's February as it is. The winter storms will end soon. Boney is pushing hard for the sale of Louisiana. It won't take long now. Even if the Americans are finding it hard to raise the money, the slave rebellions in Louisiana are growing in violence, and the government needs the right to end the unrest the Spanish are fomenting through Florida. We can't go until we know which drills work and which don't, and finding another mole could take months we don't have. We've wasted enough time."

Alec put an arm around his shoulder. "Give me two weeks. I'll sleep on the forecastle — I did it as a midshipman — and watch for messages from Boulogne. I'll send all messages myself. Flynn can work with Carlsberg in the smithy, since Fulton's done a runner. Since West has been absolutely proven innocent by being with Lisbeth throughout her sickness, he can do semaphore with me. Hazeltine and the midshipmen can take the night watches from below. We'll flush this mole out if he exists, never fear."

Duncan nodded. "It's a good idea. I can take shifts with you on the semaphore —"

"You have a wife now," Alec said gently, smiling. "It's after two in the morning. She must think you've forgotten her. Go, lad, and trust me. I'll captain the ship in your absence."

Duncan stared at this brother he'd tried so hard to push away from the day they'd met, Cal too — but they were still here. Now, during the final hours of this imperative mission, he thanked God he had a wife and family he could trust to the death. He, who'd always been alone, now had a family — and he hadn't done a damn thing to earn their loyalty.

Feeling strange and awkward, he held out his hand. "I'll inform the crew."

Alec grinned and pushed him. "Go to your lass. She's waiting for you. If there's another mole, he has to come on board with us. Half a dozen Jerseymen guard every Martello tower. If a second mole exists, he can't get a message to Delacorte about your marriage, or where you sleep at night. So go. Maybe you think you don't deserve a honeymoon, but Lisbeth does. A week or two of recovery time, and a bit of happiness, will only improve her outlook for the mission."

Duncan grinned, feeling foolish and uncertain. "Strip all suspects of weapons or anything that can make fire and keep them out of the galley." He wished to God the rest of this day hadn't happened. Wishing he could still count on Burton's loyalty, or that any part of his relationship with Lisbeth could have followed a normal course.

"Go. She'll forgive you." Alec clasped his hand and held out the other crossed over the first. Duncan took the double clasp and, grinning, gripped in return: a cementing of brotherhood.

Acceptance.

CHAPTER 48

The Ship Inn, St. Aubin's Township, Jersey
Lisbeth woke with a start and shiver. The
room was cool; she didn't remember going to
bed, but she lay on top of the blankets. The
candles burned low, but the fire was bright.
Turning, she saw a figure crouched in front
of the hearth, stoking the fire.

It took a moment to understand why he
was here. "Duncan?"

He turned and smiled at her, as uncertain
as her tone. The winter in his eyes made her
shiver again; the memory of the evening
returned. He'd sent her back to the inn with
West and Carlsberg after the testing of the
drills was done. "Who was it?" she asked
softly.

He faced the fire again. After almost a
minute, he said, "Burton."

She pressed her lips together. Only the
name of Flynn could have hurt Duncan
more. Slipping off the bed, she came up
behind him, forgetting all the embarrassment

she'd expected to feel tonight. She knelt and put her arms around him. "I'm so sorry."

The stiffness in his body slowly gave way, and he leaned back against her. "He's dead."

The warmth of the fire seeped into them. There was nothing to say. Her legs had begun to grow numb by the time he turned and put his forehead to hers.

The log he'd put on the fire crackled, sending a tiny shower of sparks up. His eyes opened. "Lizzy," he said hoarsely.

Her fears seemed petty in the light of his grief. She kissed him, but he drowned the tenderness in his desperate need to forget. "Come to bed, Duncan." She stood, took his hand, and led him across the room.

Whitehall, London
February 20, 1803

Windham slapped his desk with an open hand. "Hawkesbury, this is a farce! You've seen the confirmation we needed that Boney's been breaking the Treaty of Amiens from day one! Addington's seen this. How can he possibly deny —"

Seated opposite Windham, Foreign Secretary Lord Hawkesbury merely lifted a tired shoulder. "Do you think me privy to the workings of Addington's mind? The Treasury's in a mess; the bulk of the trained army's in Egypt, and recalling the troops from Ireland would invite insurrection there.

Though we can recall half-pay officers and sailors in a day, there aren't ships enough for them all, and no time to build. We've recalled two dozen ships from the Caribbean, but they won't arrive for six to eight weeks, depending on the weather. The king's, ah, indisposed again" — ah, the delicate political term for another bout of madness — "and the Prince of Wales doesn't want to send his dear friends to fight the French. Take your choice, Windham. Addington won't declare war or even push back at Boney unless he's forced into it. But since *he* isn't in Paris . . ."

There was a slight emphasis on the final words. Windham searched the other's face, but saw no expression. "Whitworth's new to the embassy. He appears to be doing well."

The slightly hawkish nose twitched. Windham caught the trace of pleasure in Hawkesbury's eyes in an otherwise morose face. He must be picking up the right crumbs. "He's the essence of a gentleman, Windham. Tact personified."

"I've heard he has quite the temper when pushed," Windham pressed, delicately for him since Hawkesbury tended to ride his high horse if he became offended. "Wasn't he, ah" — he scrambled to think of a subtle enough word — "provoked by the Irish once or twice?"

Hawkesbury merely lifted his brows. Windham sensed he was waiting, but Windham had no idea for what, so waited in turn. Eventually Hawkesbury spoke. "Certainly he can, as can all gentlemen when pressed. And his lady wife can be quite haughty."

Windham held in the grin. Yes, Lady Whitworth could be unpleasant, but much was forgiven in the former Duchess of Dorset, who had a stipend of thirteen thousand pounds a year.

"It's true," Hawkesbury murmured. "However, Addington says that in post-Terror France, it's easy to see war where there is only violence and savagery. However, a push in the right direction to an easily agitated leader, by a man he is known to fear . . . ?" Again, that little, tired shrug; but Hawkesbury's fine, dark eyes seemed to be conveying a hint.

Windham hadn't gained office by connections alone. "I've heard Captain Wright has a yearning to visit Paris again. If he were to ask you for a recommendation . . . ?"

The gentle set to the peer's shoulders relaxed. Boney had hated Wright since his escape from the infamous Temple prison with Sir Sidney Smith in '98. "I'd be delighted, dear fellow."

Eaucourt, France
February 22, 1803
"Did you hear? Alain Delacorte is dead!"

In the tavern on the Eaucourt road leading

to Abbeville, one of the men assigned to watch Delacorte's home and family looked around sharply, slopping his ale on his jacket. With a low curse, he shook it off. Asking for a towel meant losing precious seconds of the news.

From a shadowed corner, hat shading his face, Cal Stewart listened as the drama he'd created unfolded.

"No!" one of the wenches gasped, and then she pouted. "He was one of my best customers."

"*Oui,* he always paid for his whores on time, if nothing else," the tavern keep muttered with a sour look.

"You wouldn't have customers without us," the wench retorted with a sneer. "It's not like your ragout or goulash is world famous, and you water the ale and wine."

General sniffs and sniggers followed.

"Well, he's dead — killed in the attack on Fort Vauban in Ambleteuse back in October — the same night someone tried to kill the first consul," the carter yelled over the laughter. "I heard the tale when I was picking up my load in Abbeville this afternoon. The Jacobins were celebrating good and loud, after what he did to them."

Everyone stopped and turned to him again. "What was he doing at Fort Vauban? He's no soldier!"

"I heard tell he was chasing that wife of his

who disappeared. I heard she was playing house with some American or Briton, and when Delacorte tried to take her, her lover killed him."

"Well, which is it? Did he die in Fort Vauban or did his wife's lover kill him?" one man asked in exasperation.

"I don't know, but look here. I got the list on the reward notice for any trace of the killer. The Jacobins were handing them around. Delacorte's on the list of the dead."

News like this was bound to cause a sensation in a small place like Eaucourt. Everyone crowded around the carter, looking for the name, seeing how much was being offered.

The faces on the reward sheet were nothing like those of the Stewart brothers, naturally. Cal had paid the pamphleteer well.

After seeing Delacorte's name on the list of mostly military victims, Delacorte's man left the tavern. "So much for being paid double when he returns," he muttered. They'd run out of money weeks ago. "Delacorte can go straight to hell! I'm for work that has payment up front!"

Cal watched Delacorte's man run to his friends. Within a week of receiving Duncan's letter, the mission was almost complete, and all for the price of two carts of logs, three hundred pamphlets, and the promise of public revenge on Delacorte. The conspiracy with the Jacobins had a lovely irony he was sure Delacorte wouldn't appreciate.

Cal drained the last of his watered ale. Now he'd take Lisbeth's baby and the child's grandmother, get the midwife, and leave France. No more perfect revenge could he have on the bastard.

Late that night, the carriage was heading north, Madame Delacorte holding the sleeping child and weeping for the choice of love she'd been forced to make. Cal had left a note on Delacorte's dresser. It had but two words: *For Clare.*

St. Helier, Jersey
March 6, 1803
Called to the nearest Martello tower to receive an urgent message from Alec, Duncan returned to the inn to find Lisbeth. In the near month since their marriage, she always understood when he had to go, but he refused to break his word.

He found her at the forge, where Carlsberg and Flynn had taken over Fulton's task. Flynn was twisting the metal in the super-heated fire. Once each drill piece was cooled and in its place inside Fulton's clever drill bar, Carlsberg soldered them in. The bar had a cunning device to make the drills move together. If one drill broke, the entire bar would need replacing. They'd have to take *Papillon* to a safe place above the waterline to do it, but there was no other way.

"All's going to plan, Commander. We'll be done with this lot in a few more days," Carlsberg pronounced cheerfully. "You'll have five dozen triple drills, as planned. I'm just sorry I'm doing the job so much slower than Fulton."

Duncan clapped Carlsberg on the shoulder. "Thank you for taking over the job."

The older man winked at Lisbeth. "I'm happy to oblige, so long as you promise me this little girl will get a real wedding trip when the mission's done."

Duncan grinned. "Now there's a promise I'm delighted to give."

Flicking a glance at his wife, he finally understood the term *blushing bride*. She slipped out of the forge with murmured excuses.

Duncan smiled. As soon as Flynn and Carlsberg discovered their commander had wed, they conspired to ensure she and Duncan had time alone — and both men gave wedding gifts. Carlsberg had given them a bottle of his old mother's homemade mead to ensure fruitfulness — and Flynn had given Duncan a wedding ring for his bride. "I'm sorry it's only silver," he'd said gruffly, the tips of his ears red, "but I noticed Mrs. Aylsham has no ring. My grandfather was a silversmith. I know it's not fancy. I crafted it in haste . . ."

Duncan slipped the simple ring on Lisbeth's wedding finger with quiet thanks.

Tears in her eyes, Lisbeth had shaken hands with his men. "I'll treasure this ring, Lieutenant Flynn. I'll never forget everything you've done for Commander Aylsham and me."

They'd used the mead that night for a toast, wishing the couple health and happiness together.

A few minutes after Lisbeth left the forge, Duncan found her in the cobblestone lane behind the smithy. It climbed up to the hill above in a world of soft-falling morning rain and lush gardens. They'd taken the spot as their own for the past week. Lisbeth loved the budding flowers and early spring rains, so soft after the hard winter. Spring usually came early to Jersey.

"What was the message from Alec?" she murmured in his ear.

Duncan grinned and held her close. "Cal has Edmond, love."

With a cry of joy, she slumped against him. "Thank God, oh, thank God!"

"Thank the Stewarts also," he said, low. "There are too many French patrols for Alec to drop anchor close enough. They're traveling to Calais as a family, with the wet nurse acting as Cal's wife. Edmond's grandmother is with them. They have papers to take the packet to Dover."

"Marceline's coming?" she asked, with open doubt in her eyes.

Duncan nodded. "Probably she can't bear to leave the child."

"What if she regrets it later — or if . . ."

He sighed and took her hands in his. "Don't play that game. I doubt she knows where he is; he's been gone for months. Could you leave the poor lady alone after taking her grandchild?" Slowly she shook her head. "Can you accept her as part of our family, Lizzy?"

She thought of the gift Marceline had given her months ago, seeing and holding Edmond when she had no reason to trust her, and nodded. "But I'll want her correspondence vetted."

"Of course. Now smile, Lizzy. Our son's coming home."

She hiccuped, blinked back tears, and smiled up at him. "You don't know how many nights I've stayed awake worrying for him, missing him."

Disturbed that she must have done that while he slept beside her at night, he said, "Our son's coming home to us."

Another hiccup, then she nodded. "I so want to show him to Mama." Her smile was radiant with joy, and Duncan's stomach jerked. *Tell her.* He couldn't.

"If Alec can't anchor near enough for Cal, what does that say for our mission?"

"French patrols are everywhere. It seems Boney's recalled ships from the Caribbean," he whispered back, glad of the distraction. "We'll have to sail behind Guernsey and Alderney islands into English waters facing Boulogne, and go from there. It will be longer than the first time, and —"

She put a finger to his mouth. "Don't say it. You won't make it without me now."

He laid his forehead against hers. "You've been through so much. I worry for you, Lizzy."

"As I'll worry for you on every mission you go on when I'm at home."

"You really know how to take the wind from my sails," he mock-complained.

She grinned. "No, it's just the reality of family life that my mother never taught my father."

He sighed and kissed her, but after a while he murmured, "Your dress is damp. You should get out of this weather and change into something warmer. Sit by the fire."

"I think we should both change." Impish smile, invitation in her sparkling eyes, and the happiness that was marriage to Lisbeth flooded him anew. With her past abuse, he'd hardly expected to know this kind of joy with her; but his need for her after Burton's hanging seemed to have broken any barriers she could erect in fear. He'd taken care to be tender with her, both then and since, but even now, he could hardly believe it was enough.

He grinned, unable to resist teasing her. "I only have a few drops on me. I could dry by the fire downstairs."

"No, you can't," she retorted, her chin jutted. "Come upstairs with me."

He tweaked her braid. "You're a wicked woman, Elizabeth Aylsham."

She smiled, slow with promise, and tugged at his hand. "Come to bed, Duncan."

It occurred to him that he'd never felt this happy. "I believe they're fast becoming my favorite words." He allowed her to lead him inside through the back door of the inn.

CHAPTER 49

The Tuileries, Paris
March 8, 1803

Standing beneath the bright chandelier, Georgy chatted to friends and acquaintances alike in the stifling room. The servants had already stoked the fires high, because the first consul would walk through in exactly fourteen minutes, and he liked to be warm.

By now she knew Napoleon's likes and dislikes. She wore a demure, round-necked dress of faint primrose, no longer of the sheer or damped variety, but the highest-quality silk. About her neck and ears was the simple diamond set Mama had passed on from Grandmamma, suitable for a well-dowered virgin of high birth, accepted in all royal and diplomatic circles. Her hair was in a simple, braided chignon with pearls woven in. Serious, sweet, she was a young lady of high estate with a hint of the Mona Lisa about her. Napoleon was ensnared, but he'd still said nothing of Camelford's whereabouts.

She wished she knew how her presence here was helping Lizzy; but she had a feeling she wouldn't know until she saw her friend again. That she was determined to do — and John agreed with her. "We're in a position to help her, Georgy, and from what I've discovered, she deserves far more than simple acceptance in society."

She loved it when they made plans for after their marriage.

With a faint frown, she became aware of a strange ripple of sound behind her, murmurs of mingled shock and speculation. She turned to see what was going forward.

The new British ambassador to France, Lord Whitworth, stood in the center of the noise. Nothing unusual in that; he came to the levees every week. A charming man with waving silver hair and a wonderful smile, he stood a full head above almost every man in the room. It was no wonder the lovely Duchess of Dorset had married him so soon after she became a widow.

His wife was still on his arm. Odd — they normally parted, speaking to all in the room before Napoleon's entry, leaving everyone smiling. Now they moved from group to group within two minutes, leaving ripples of confusion and fear behind them.

Georgy's head tilted, watching. With a smile she crossed the glittering, overcrowded salon to where the Whitworths stood, presenting a united front — against what, she had to know.

"What mean you by that, my lord?" Fox was demanding, his cheeks and bulbous nose the shade of a ripe plum.

As one, Whitworth and his lady turned a frozen glance upon the leader of the Whigs. "I do not waste my explanations on Devon pig farmers masquerading as intelligent men. If you have a brain, use it to think."

As the group gasped, Lady Whitworth nodded. "Come, my dear, these *persons* are not worth our staying for." They walked off without appropriate farewells or looking back.

Georgy realized she was gaping and closed her mouth. The group they'd left consisted of British nationals — the very people the Whitworths represented in Paris. Lady Whitworth's choice of word felt deliberate. *Person* was used by butlers to tell their employers a visitor was not worth their consideration.

They approached Georgy. She swept a curtsy, but they passed by her without a word or glance. Overlooking a duke's daughter who was not engaged in conversation was a grave offense. She stared after them, then took a slow, circling walk around the salon. With every conversation she joined, she heard how the charming, well-bred Whitworths were insulting the French and frightening their own people, which they'd never do —

Unless . . .

Her gaze covered the room, but The Incomparable wasn't here. She glanced at John, standing in a corner and watching her with brokenhearted moodiness. The question asked. A half shrug in response.

The trumpets sounded, the doors flew open, and everyone hastened to take their places. The first consul strode up the stairs with his usual morose half smile — but as he glanced about the sumptuous salon, it vanished like the sun behind summer storm clouds. "What does he do here?" he demanded, his ringing tones filling the salon as he pointed ahead of him. "Well?" Bonaparte demanded again, turning to Lord Whitworth.

Georgy turned, saw a man slipping through the back doors, tall, broad shouldered and curly haired, with a definite kind of bearing about him, soldier or sailor. She hadn't noticed him until now. Odd — she normally noticed everyone.

"Of whom would you wish to ask, *Citoyen Premier Consul*?" Whitworth asked, in a tone reserved for tradesmen or encroaching persons. "I see no man who would bring forth this level of . . . agitation."

Georgy heard the collective gasps. No one spoke to Napoleon this way, especially not before a crowd of people. This had all the earmarks of a well-rehearsed play.

As if he'd recognized it, too, Napoleon collected himself. "Captain Wright is a fugitive from French justice. He would not dare show his face here if you had not sanctioned it, Whitworth. He is staying at the embassy. Do you want an incident? Are you pushing for one? Is this little dispute over Switzerland worth war to you?"

Whitworth looked bored. "I assure you, *Citoyen* Bonaparte, Britain values peace as much as you do — as I am certain do the people of Piedmont, Parma, Venice, and Switzerland."

Everyone in the room gasped at the deliberate provocation. Bonaparte's face turned ominously dark. "You say this to me, when you refuse to hand Malta to the Knights of St. John? Woe to those who do not honor treaties! What right do you have to dictate to me over those few little places, when your nation has invaded more countries than any other, not even giving the peoples the dignity of choice or keeping their religion or culture?"

Whitworth froze in place, his smile hard, cold. Eyes glittering. Tall and handsome and disdainful. "As you say, Monsieur Bonaparte."

Bonaparte lifted his chin, fire meeting ice. "Shall I call you Mr. Whitworth, then, and not the title you have earned? Shall I name your king Mr. Saxe-Coburg, since he did nothing to earn his titles but be born into the right family?"

The whole room was silent. Waiting. Barely breathing. Long moments later, Whitworth bowed. "My lord Citizen First Consul," he murmured, acknowledging the point.

Even lower did Bonaparte speak, almost a lion's growl. "I demand an answer, and not this stupid prevarication over bagatelles. *Was Captain Wright sent to the Tuileries as a deliberate provocation?* What does Britain want from me now? Have I not given enough?"

Whitworth sighed. "I saw no man resembling Captain Wright here tonight, my lord."

"Ah, bah! I know what I saw!" Napoleon threw down his treasured tricorn hat and stamped on it. "You are lying. Do you think I do not know your nation is rearming, forming another army, or that I have not heard that you've recalled your ships from the Caribbean, bringing your best troops back from Egypt? I have more spies in Britain than you have free citizens! You say you're fulfilling the Treaty of Amiens, yet your government is recalling ships, gathering an army. Obvious preparations for war!"

Lady Whitworth stared down her nose at Napoleon, saying something to her husband about lowbred histrionics in a cultured but carrying tone.

Everyone gasped again.

Bonaparte stood very still. "What mean you, Lady Whitworth? Do you have the ill breeding to insult me in my own home?"

Lady Whitworth curtsied in return. "This home belonged to others before you, sir." She spoke in English, putting Bonaparte at a disadvantage, since he'd need a translator.

Lord Whitworth stood to his full height, towering over the first consul. "I believe Lady Whitworth and I may be *de trop, Citoyen* Bonaparte. You are probably wishing us long gone. We bid you a good evening and will take our leave."

After a brief bow bordering on insolence, the Whitworths left the room.

As they passed Georgy, Lord Whitworth murmured to the stunned girl, "Leave France with Bedford tomorrow. Your role here is done."

As Lady Bessborough, sister to the great Duchess of Devonshire, joined her, Georgy's mind was in too much of a whirl to discuss the deliberate drama that had unfolded before them all tonight; but one thing had been made crystal clear. Her mission had ended, very publicly.

She didn't care if Camelford saw daylight again or not; but she hoped she'd done enough to help Lizzy. And she fully intended to invite Lizzy to her wedding.

Boulogne-sur-Mer
March 9, 1803
During his time with Camelford, Mark had spent the few spare hours he'd had making signs, painting the most basic of ciphers on palings of a broken orange crate. Crude

semaphore, and he'd meant to make proper paddles and flags, but now it would have to do. He'd run out of time.

Camelford thought he'd killed him. Bleedin' idiot was too thick witted to realize any mojer with a brain in his cock-loft could see the pleasure he took in killing people or animals. So by the time Camelford came at him with a knife, Mark was ready with a leather jerkin under his shirt. Bloody inbred, believin' he were superior. Even thought he 'ad blue blood. *All men shite the same color, lad,* his da had always said. And that gave a smart bleeder the edge. Let 'em play off their toff airs and you could run rings round 'em.

Not Commander Aylsham. Though he'd been cheeky as all get-out, he never got the best of the commander. Mark was right proud to serve with him. He just hoped Aylsham had found the note he'd left in his desk on board ship . . . and had caught the last semaphore he'd sent.

It was ruddy cold sittin' on the roof of the rough inn he'd come to after his recovery. Masclet's doctor had saved his life and his shot was paid at the inn, long as he wanted it, but it still felt like a piss-poor kind of thanks for savin' their leader's life. No doubt Masclet had taken all the credit, and got all the rewards, too. But if the commander got this message today, he'd ensure the lowborn

Cockney cabin boy would benefit from his loyalty.

Thanks to him, that freak Camelford had been caught in the act. Keepin' him in prison in Boulogne was clever of Boney. These days it was like a bleedin' fortress with all its security.

Lucky for Mark he was above suspicion. He was the current messenger lad at the offices of the *sous-préfet,* catchin' tossed coins and scraps of conversation as well.

'Twas a good thing the roof of this old inn was above its immediate neighbors.

It was time for his final semaphore. He'd stored his signs in the attic. Nobody went there. He just hoped it made sense to some British-paid coder in the farms outside town, the ones right by the sea with real portable semaphore sets on their roofs, to send messages direct to the ship. He might've learned by watching Flynn and Burton, but he'd never have a future as a signaler.

It was up to him now.

The Bull Inn, St. Aubin's Township, Jersey
   (English Channel)
March 9, 1803
Alec came into the inn's dining parlor as Lisbeth and Duncan were finishing afternoon tea. "Lad, a strange semaphore came very early this morning. It said Marcus René Balfour three times, and then said, *Limey in the*

right place. Hell to pay for a sailor in the morning."

"Damn it, that's the signal. I was hoping for another week." Duncan scraped his chair back hard and fast. "My dear, are you ready?"

Lisbeth opened a sack she'd kept by her chair, put bread, cheese, ham, and boiled eggs in it, and picked up two containers of small beer. "What about the extra drills?"

"We have five dozen now. It has to be enough."

Lisbeth headed for their room to put the cabin boy's outfit on once again.

Duncan watched her, thanking God for her good sense — and that Mark had managed to send the messages. The little smart arse had been right on all counts. Boney had known about Camelford and wanted the unstable lord under his eye, so he'd let him get *in* to Boulogne. But nobody bothered to look at the skinny urchin with him.

I ain't nobody, sir, so's I can get about with nobody noticing. Don't tell nobody about me, Commander, sir, specially not the nobs, the note had said. *Somebody ain't right on board ship. We can't trust nobody.*

Mark had a real future in espionage, if he could get himself out of Boulogne as easily as he'd made it in and return to England on his own. Somehow Duncan had no doubt he would.

He turned to Alec. "Return to ship. We set sail within the hour, going around Guernsey and into English waters south of the Lydd promontory, but no time for us to take the long sail. Take us into French waters facing Boulogne, and then get the hell out. You have command, Alec. Flynn alone is to use the semaphore. West and Carlsberg will stay continuously by the forecastle, protecting Flynn from the deck. Hill and Marks will watch either end of the galley. We take cold food only, no cooking allowed until I return. All men are to hand in their weapons, plus any tinder and flint before boarding; no smoking allowed. Everyone is to be thoroughly searched for spare weapons, incendiary devices, or flint and tinder. You'll stay in English waters at all times: no need to use cannons. The sailors you've cleared of suspicion will take turns guarding the galley, the gunpowder store, and the weapons room at all times. They can only open them for you directly. Your suspects sail the ship only, while under constant guard. Anyone who argues goes overboard."

Alec nodded, snatching some bread and butter from the table, shoving ham on it. "Consider it done, lad — and God go with you both."

CHAPTER 50

English Channel, French Waters
March 9, 1803

"We need to test against any kind of unseen sabotage before we leave the ship," Duncan said when the lines holding *Papillon* were released. "Work the propellers as hard as you can. I'll lower us. We need to be sure everything works underwater."

Lisbeth tested every piece of equipment possible. "The floor's damp." Frowning, she touched everything. "The air intake hose has a leak."

They watched the water slipping in. It was barely noticeable, something they'd never have discovered until they were well out to sea, and probably out of air.

"Why didn't we notice this on the last test?"

"It didn't happen. Either this happened by accident when Fulton was making the new air pipe and the leak's only sprung now, or Alec was right about a second mole. But how he got to the smithy and into *Papillon* I don't know." Duncan swore. "We'll use the sail as long as we can while I check the damage."

"What about when we submerge?"

Another shrug, but she could tell he was worried. "We'll use the peg, tie it tightly beneath to hold the pipe together while we're drilling. If I can repair the horn, less water will get inside."

"But if we must outrun a ship? Our hands are all taken up with the equipment."

"We'll use every tie in the craft to tie it hard. The rudder stays in place once it's wound up, and we can use the chamber pot to catch drips."

As they lifted to the surface, Lisbeth shuddered. Cold air flooded in as Duncan opened the hatch, and breathing it in felt as if she'd returned to life from the tomb. She reveled in the sweetness of it, but still shivered, even after Duncan wrapped his cloak around her.

"Give me the dark sail, Lizzy."

She pulled the sail from the sack and used the steel hooks and eyes Fulton had created to fasten the sail to *Papillon*'s walls. After checking the tide and what coastline was visible in the misty evening, Duncan unfurled the sail. He remained standing, continuously dipping down against sail movements, watching through the ship's second bilocular device for tide changes and enemy activity. Meanwhile, he kept checking the air horn. "It's merely out of place, Lizzy. It could just be a mistake on Fulton's part — he was fairly upset before he left. If I use the tiller to hammer it down, it might hold."

She didn't want to think about Fulton, how he'd left Jersey without a farewell. "And if it doesn't?"

He frowned. "Then we do it as many times as we must."

Shame washed through her. "Of course, Duncan, I apologize."

He nodded and pulled the iron tiller from its canvas hold.

"The fog's closing in," he reported after an hour of sailing and making repairs to the air hose. "The moon's well above the horizon, but I don't know how much longer we can keep sailing. With the rolling tide, a ship could cut us in two before we even know it's there."

Dread touched her. "How close are we to shore?"

"By the compass direction and time we've sailed at about four knots, we're perhaps three miles, and the tide's running in to harbor. Sailing has cut our travel time by hours. It should only take another hour to reach the river mouth. The hose is as good as I could make it, and it's best for you to be warm."

She couldn't afford to be a liability to him, tonight of all nights. "Hold until we can see the lights of the harbor and the patrolling ships."

After a moment, he nodded. "There's an islet a mile out of harbor with treacherous rocks. We're far safer sailing around it."

When they'd passed the island and saw patrol ships in the distance, he looked at her. She nodded and, taking in her last breath of fresh air, took the tinderbox to relight the lantern.

He handed her the sail, and she packed it. She lifted her hand for the hooks and eyes, but he said, "It's best if we leave them in place. We'll need them ready for fast escape."

Taken aback that he seemed to have more hope of living after today than she did, Lisbeth opened her mouth, closed it again, and nodded. After all he'd done to secure her future in England, and bringing Edmond home to her at last, she had to fight for her life. She smiled when the hatch closed and the closed-in panic she'd dreaded didn't eventuate.

"Take the rudder and hold it to shore," she said, as she worked the pump. "We should submerge three feet before working the propellers."

"We need to take care. It's a shallow tide, heading fast to the shore."

She held the pump fair until the pump gauge tipped onto three. She had to slide against Duncan's body to turn without tipping the tiny craft. She said, "Last time we did this I could hardly stand the closeness, touching so much, wishing for more."

He smiled before returning to the compass. "I thought you didn't notice —" *Papillon* rocked hard, and he glanced through the window. "Two ships approaching from north and southwest. Submerge and head east."

When the danger passed, they raised the craft until the air horn was above the waterline, visibly slowing the steady drip of water dropping into the chamber pot from the ties.

In a fast tide, even while playing catch-as-catch-can with passing ships, and holding the air hose, they made the river mouth in under an hour. Another ten minutes and they'd turned under the pier. At last Duncan opened the hatch.

The thuds of booted feet on the pier warned Lisbeth to keep silent. They breathed, ate, drank small ale, and Duncan made quiet repairs to the air hose. When he'd done all he could, he looked at her; she nodded, and he pulled down the hatch and locked it.

Anything but breathing was a waste of air and precious time. She pointed to the rudder and he took the handle. She used the propellers until they were away from the riverbank.

Soon they were beneath the first ship's stern. The cargo hold was the safest part to drill, but the river was too murky to see if they were at the right spot. He took one end of the crank that turned the drill. She took the other. With a slow, methodical pattern, they drilled.

But soon the drill snapped off in the wood. So did the second. She looked at him in dread. "Do we still have inferior drills?"

He shook his head. "This is the lead ship, older and double hulled, made with aged oak. Let's hope the others are easier."

Returning to the pier, they changed the drill. "I'd hoped to have five ships done by now," Duncan growled as they moved on to the second ship.

As she'd predicted, the river was calmer than the churning Channel, but each passing ship rocked their equilibrium and churned the silt through the water. Every maneuver took precious time. They kept checking for a glitter on the water with the advent of sunrise, though it was still hours off.

At last they were in place. With exquisite care, they pushed the drills into the wood. The resistance she'd half expected wasn't there. Within a few minutes, they felt the release of tension that meant they'd made the breach.

As one, they halted. "Thank God, it's a single-layer hull," he murmured. "We were lucky. With this clinker style of hull, the planks overlap for strength, and the planks may be caulked for flexibility of sailing instead of having iron rivets that will break our drills. The rush to have them made in time has worked in our favor."

Unfortunately, they discovered some of the ships had the iron rivets and caulking, and the drills snapped more often than they could afford.

"Our success depends on if they do a preparatory check of the ship before setting sail." He lifted the lantern, lit the third wick, and stared into the murky river water. "I can barely see the hull. I can't be certain if we've drilled the rib cleanly, but I think so."

She chewed on her lip. "If we drill across two planks three times along each ship, we'd have reasonable certainty that we'll hit at least one rib in a line and weaken it enough."

"It's worth trying. We won't be able to drill as many ships as we planned. We'll be lucky to drill forty before they launch — that is, if the drills last." Then he nodded. "If only ten ships founder, it would convince them to return to port."

The triple drills working sideways cost them far more time than they'd calculated, and they had to keep surfacing for air. "We'll become more proficient with each ship," he predicted, as they moved toward the tenth ship.

Lisbeth said nothing. Since her illness her body grew tired much more easily from the heat and lack of air. She was sweating from her toes to her scalp, her body filled with a dull ache. Luckily the disgusting medicines the doctor had given her killed the cough for hours at a time.

Soon talking was beyond them both. They only came up for air when she felt faint. Hiding between ships, they opened the hatch, ate and drank, breathed and did what they must.

"Twenty-two," Duncan muttered four hours later, when they finished the ship they'd been working on, triple-drilled sideways over three ribs. "We should drill at least one or two at the tail of the fleet before returning to the final ten here."

She looked at him in helpless pleading. "I'm going to be sick."

He took the propellers and worked them until they were between two ships. He opened the hatch, emptied the chamber pot, rinsed it quickly, and handed it to her. "Close it again if you're going to make a noise," he whispered.

But the fresh air lessened her body's urgent need. She sipped at the small beer and sucked on a peppermint stick. She looked up, saw the gray-rose lighting the murky sky. "It's dawn. We should go to the back —" But then she heard the sound of marching boots, wave after wave. "Can you hear that?" Suddenly a coughing fit came, and she couldn't control it.

Men began shouting orders, and booms sounded as gangplanks fell into place.

Duncan brought down the hatch, quick and silent. "They're boarding. We need to leave now."

"We didn't do enough ships. You said fifty was the minimum we'd need. We only did half of that. I failed you."

He touched her face. "Nobody could have done better than you." He reached into the food sack. "Now take your medicine, and eat bread and a boiled egg, love. You'll feel better, not to mention you'll need the energy until we can make use of the sails."

Oddly, he was right. Her cough stopped soon after taking the vile green stuff, and she revived a little when she'd eaten. She took her place at the pump and rudder when he began using the downward and forward propellers. Staying submerged meant it took almost an hour to reach the outer harbor, nearly two to reach a mile out to sea.

The ominous rocking began.

Duncan peered through the window and swore. "That was fast. The lead ship's almost on us." When she blinked at him, he snapped, "Submerge and avast."

The sea around them was white with mist and sails by the time they reached the rocky islet to the northwest of Boulogne, hours later. Duncan shook his head when her hand hovered over the pump. "We can't risk it until we see where they're heading. There's a little cove to the south. Let's hide there and eat."

When they reached the cove, Lisbeth peered through the window. "They're heading north-northwest. Surely they're not risking the Irish Sea after the terrible weather we've had?"

"It's been worse there this year than 1798 by all accounts." Duncan shook his head. "Despite the mist rolling in, it's still daylight. Either Boney's run mad, or he knows Addington ordered the fifty ships to Dublin. That means the Irish rebellion *was* a French distraction for this purpose. They're not heading to Ireland at all, but western England."

She frowned. "The French have set sail without their cannons complete. Look, quite a few are unfinished. What did the British do to provoke Bonaparte into this foolhardy act?"

He grinned, shaking his head. "If they allowed women into politics, you'd have my vote. My guess is that's exactly what Whitehall has done. Made him angry and scared enough to set sail in a way that almost guarantees failure . . . and the admirals will have sent as many ships as they can to cover the expected entries into Britain."

Her forehead crinkled. "But they wouldn't go without a landing port in mind. Ireland is out; everyone expects invasion via the Thames. So where are they heading?"

"St. George's Channel is a protected harbor. Wales has nothing but a few excisemen watching the tides for smugglers." He added grimly, "Two hundred United Irishmen crossed the Irish Sea a few weeks ago, going where only God knows. Addington merely ordered extra protection around London."

Her eyes grew wide. "There were thousands of soldiers on that fleet. They could take England via Wales in days."

He nodded. "The Irish foment unrest at home and set up the assassination attempt on the king. Boney uses his assassination attempt to divert us with accusations over the treaty and invades Switzerland. While we're distracted with all the balls he's juggling, he sails in where nobody's watching." He thumped his fist on the thigh that hadn't been shot. "*Damn* Whitehall! Boney stays awake every night until he's read all his dispatches, while the vital *communiqués* we send pile up in corners. If the lords would *read* them instead of attending bloody parties . . ." He risked another glance through the open hatch. "They worry more about gossip and royal scandals than whether the conqueror of Europe will invade."

She didn't know how to answer. "How long before we see if our sabotage worked?"

"You ask because I would know, having drilled so many ships before?" Before she could take offense at his tired sarcasm, he shrugged. "The sun still sets by four this time of year. We should leave. If they begin to sink, they could use this islet as the closest shallow water."

She frowned. "The white sail will be less noticeable in this mist."

"Yes, but we can't use it until we're out of sight of the harbor."

They prepared to shove off from the rocky cove *Papillon* was wedged in. Opening the last sack, she saw a little barrel and frowned. "What's this?"

"You know what it is, and how to use it." Duncan made a face and half shrugged as she stared at him in furious repugnance. "It may come to us or them, Lizzy. I swore I'd get you home to your mother, and I'm bloody well going to do it."

A smothered little chuckle took him by surprise. She mock-saluted him, grinning. "Aye-aye, Commander."

She knew him so well. Only weeks ago he'd hated that — now he loved it, relied on it.

Don't let them fool you, son. It's when they seem to be meekest and gentlest that a woman wields the highest power over a man. You can't do a damned thing about it, so you might as well enjoy it. Eddie was so right. Even now Duncan was fighting the urge to smile at that cheekiness that was intrinsic in her.

"Duncan."

The sharp word shook him. She was standing, staring south, holding the bilocular device to her eye. "The ships are turning back, signaling from ship to ship with lanterns. I can see flags moving on the lead ship." She coughed again.

"Sit down, Lizzy, and wrap the cloaks around you. Take more medicine." He stood, checking the lay of the rocks. "Use the rudder the moment you feel it come free."

"In which direction?"

"Wait." The highest rocks were barely submerged — damn, the tide was too low to help. They bumped against a rock. "Hold the rudder in hard against the craft! If it breaks off on the rocks we'll really be in the basket."

They bounced off rocks, going nowhere. He had to feel around each rock to push off it gently, without hitting another too hard. "How the hell did we get inside this inlet at all?"

"I think the tide was still then. It's going out now."

He saw with dismay she was right. He, the experienced sailor, had made the most basic and stupid of mistakes, forgetting to watch for tidal changes. Rocks he hadn't noticed when he'd entered the inlet were visible now, sharp enough to split *Papillon* in two. "The fleet can't dock here, but the tide won't be back for hours. We have to be gone before the patrols see us."

Helpless, he watched for the next hour as the ships slowly came ever nearer — but then, even in the thickening sea mist, he could see the lead ships were deeper in the water than they had been. "The fleet's sinking."

"What did you say?"

He dropped down. "That's why they've come about. They're sinking!" Her face lit, but he held a finger to her lips. "The ships are heading this way. If they anchor near the island . . ."

Lisbeth's shining happiness faded. "Maybe if we spin slowly, we'd have momentum but not enough to damage her against another rock?"

"It's a good idea." Grabbing at two of the highest rocks, he twisted his body, and spun as he released them. He tried again and again, and they barely moved.

The fleet changed tack, heading for the mainland, exactly as he'd do in their position.

The sun had sunk in the sky when shouts came on the wind, the splashes of rowboats put to the water; a long, creaking groan that wouldn't stop. With a ripping sound of rushing water and a jagged symphony of human screams, he saw the lights slowly dropping.

"Was that what I think it was?" Lisbeth sounded horrified.

"Four of the ships are going down. They couldn't get back in time," he murmured in revolted fascination. "There are hundreds of men in each ship, and hardly any real sailors.

It's every man for himself."

"Stop," she cried.

He looked down. She'd covered her ears with her hands and sat curled over herself in the lantern's uncertain light. "They're only a few miles out to sea. Most will make it back, or the town will send rowboats. And remember, we only sabotaged twenty-two ships. That means there are dozens of others seaworthy to save those in the ships that founder."

There was a jerking motion as the outgoing tide pulled *Papillon* around a rock and into the sea. They were free at last — but Duncan couldn't stop the forward momentum. He pitched forward and curled over double as the brass rivets bit deep into his stomach. He scrambled to grab hold of the hatch and drop through it — but another thump came, and he whacked his back on the brass of the observation dome. Stomach and back seized in the grip of sudden pain, he grunted and let go of the hatch. It landed square on his head and he knew no more.

CHAPTER 51

English Channel, Near Boulogne-sur-Mer
Lisbeth took her hands from her ears. *Papillon* was bobbing with the tide, bouncing against rocks. Then there was nothing but the splashing of water. Were they free? Duncan was neither bringing the hatch down nor setting up the sail.

"Duncan?" she called, uncertain. "Duncan, what's happening?"

No answer came.

Don't panic. Gritting her teeth, she shook his legs. No response. She shoved his hip. Nothing. Grabbing him by the waist she tried to pull him in, but he got stuck at the shoulders.

She went cold with panic. What if he'd been shot? If she moved him, she could kill him. Her mind froze; she dithered for long minutes. If he were shot, he'd die either way; she had no choice. She pushed him, then twisted and pulled and shoved at him until she was swearing like a sailor, covered in sweat, and her arms were shaking with exhaustion. At last she heard a cracking noise and his body fell inside. His face was pale, but he was breathing. A thin line of blood trickled down his neck. She'd probably broken something getting him inside.

Pulling him around so he was curled in a ball on the wet floor of the submersible, she checked him all over, but the only blood was on the back of his head, oozing from a lump, the only holes in his jacket were tears from when she'd dragged him in. Sick with relief, she grabbed the sail from under the other side of the bench where Duncan had left it, and set it up.

The sounds of the sinking ships and screaming men made her fingers shake and fumble. The sudden descent into night, and the whistling cold wind, made it harder. But before she'd even set it, wind filled the little sail. She pulled the tiller hard right. One side of the sail pushed against her cheek as *Papillon* sprang forward, heading north.

Though the fleet hadn't moved and *Papillon* kept moving, the screams of the drowning men took a long time to fade.

Holding the tiller in place with an elbow, she tied the brass compass to her rope belt, so it hung by her waist. She turned the rudder to the right angle to maintain course.

Duncan hadn't moved. She put her hand

to his nose. Thank God, he was still breathing.

The wind turned fickle. Checking the compass, she saw she was heading northeast, and adjusted the tiller. The craft moved around, and she drew a sigh of relief. Then she coughed; she could feel the pain begin. She took a massive slug of the medicine and wrapped herself up well.

Time passed without meaning. There was only the whistling of the wind on the skin of her frozen ears. The tip of her nose was numb. Her face ached, her arms hurt from shoulders to fingertips, and every breath was more painful than the last, but though it grew colder as night turned deeper, the coughing subsided. She hung on by grim will, moving only to correct course.

The wind screamed like the sounds of the men crying for help, the yells of others trying to save them.

What was the difference between her life and those of the French soldiers? They lived, loved, wed, and had children. They wanted to save their country, had to obey their leader. The only disparity lay in where they'd been born.

She sailed on, praying for the French soldiers' lives, praying she was heading in the right direction. Praying for forgiveness with half-frozen windy tears dribbling down her face. Making a deal with God: *I'll never hurt another living thing if I can have Edmond, and see Mama again.*

No wonder Duncan seemed so haunted when they first met. No wonder Papa came home from every mission and slept for a day and drank too much brandy for weeks.

Fool! Just get Duncan to British waters! Her world narrowed to tides and wind, cloud and moon and scudding mist, a compass needle, intense cold, and Duncan's slumped body.

"Don't you die on me," she muttered fiercely, sailing as fast as the wind could take her.

Then out of the mist, a ship bore down on her. A flag flapped above the lit forecastle, and another from the flying jib: French flags.

She jerked the tiller right, the sail moved, and *Papillon* bore away. The little craft swung ferociously, up and down with the waves as the ship passed. Fighting a wave of nausea, she kept going. *Papillon* was tiny. With luck they hadn't seen her. But the ship moved in an arc; the port side faced her. A double row of cannon faced her, twenty-two oiled barrels blocking her path to England. The sound of pistols cocking simultaneously froze her blood. She turned the sails right again, heading east —

"Don't do it, *ma chère*. One cannonball will send your boat to the bottom of the sea."

Lisbeth's hand froze on the tiller. With half her body above the hatch, there was nowhere to hide. She looked past the planks of the ship to the starboard. He was leaning far over the edge, smiling. In the light of the lantern he held she saw that beautiful face, now scarred like hers. Eyes glittering with the vengeance that no amount of killing had satisfied since he was fifteen.

Leaning even farther over the starboard rail, Alain called in a voice tight with fury, "Elizabeth Sunderland, I place you under arrest in the name of the first consul for an unprovoked act of war: the murder of hundreds of French soldiers."

She closed her eyes; her hands shook with more than cold. For once it wasn't clever torture or manipulation. Alain was a loyal Frenchman to the bone. "Where were the first consul's ships heading, M'sieur Delacorte? Can I not protect my country as you do?"

"I will bring you to account," he snarled. "You're still in French waters, and you killed a true French loyalist on your lover's ship. Our fleet would have brought freedom to an oppressed people and ended the reign of a sad madman oppressing other nations to keep his useless soul in luxury, and self-satisfied lords taking the rights of the people."

She'd never heard such passion from Alain. He truly believed all he said.

"Don't think the men that saved you before are so clean," Alain went on in that furious tone. "I've been investigating them. A man of their description was responsible for killing seven children on the rue Saint-Nicaise, and another took part in the assassination of Czar Paul of Russia." He lifted his lantern higher, smiling down at her. "Yes, I thought that would shock you. They must be turned in to the European Tribunal for trial. What are their names, Lisbeth?"

Overwhelmed, she shook her head. *It's not Duncan. It can't be Duncan.*

"Give me their names, and I'll let you see Edmond," Alain called down, voice sweet. "Isn't that what you want, *ma chére?*"

Lisbeth closed her eyes. A few months ago, she'd have —

He's baiting me. He has no intention of fulfilling the promise. As soon as he has Papillon, *he'll kill us both.*

It might come down to them or us, Duncan had said.

Her mind raced. The ship could outrace and outgun *Papillon,* but it couldn't change direction so fast. In the dark, beside the hull, they'd be forced to shoot blind — it might work.

Dropping as far down inside *Papillon*'s hull as possible, Lisbeth released the tiller and added the propellers to the sails, heading hell-for-leather straight toward the ship, a tiny, onion-shaped boat blending into a deeper shadow of night.

In answer red fire came from the ship's gunwales. Being this small had its advantages. Cannonballs hit the water around her, but missed by enough not to sink her. Yanked back and forth, Lisbeth held on with all she had — but the cannonballs just kept missing.

Then she realized. Alain didn't want to sink *Papillon.* He wanted to deliver it as a gift to Napoleon — and that gave her the courage she'd almost lost.

The ship's bow faced full west as it turned around, men hanging over the rails to find her.

She had only seconds. A fresh gust of wind came from the south. She jerked the tiller to follow it. *Papillon* sprang forward, straight into the wide curve of the ship. They wouldn't shoot the cannons straight down or the ship would sink.

"Come, let's show them what we're made of!" She patted *Papillon*'s brass coopering and yanked the tiller until she was almost beneath the ship. If the ship turned back north . . .

Even in the lee of the ship the wind was strong. *Papillon* leaped forward, heading east, but she'd only bought a little time. When the sun rose, they'd use pistols and rifles, and those would not miss. Alain might want *Papillon,* and Duncan delivered alive — but it was imperative she did not survive.

The ship's stern turned north, coming at her.

One minute. One chance.

After yanking the tiller to turn away from the ship for a few moments, Lisbeth used both hands to pull the barrel bomb, tinder, and flint out of the sack. With shaking hands she pulled the cork, lit the short wick. Without time to heat wax to make a seal, she pushed it back down hard.

Shots fired and cannonballs fell around her as she waited for the right moment to toss it.

She turned the tiller south as fast as the wind would take her. The ship came at her, and she threw it as hard as she could. In seconds the ship sailed right over the barrel. If the cork and wick got wet —

Papillon almost overturned in the rocking waves as four cannonballs landed around her with hard booms. A bullet embedded in one of the propellers, and she cried out, eyes blinded by the flash as the wet wood exploded. *Papillon* jerked hard forward. She counterbalanced by jumping across Duncan's body, almost falling on him. The next shot would kill her. All she could do was keep moving. Small and dark, *Papillon* was hard to see and harder to hit.

If the bomb were going to explode, it would be any moment. She had to chance it. She jerked the tiller again, heading north. Shots and cannonballs followed, churning the waves and slowing the craft. Yes, Alain wanted to bring the craft, safe and whole, to his leader.

A *boom,* and startled, pain-filled screams filled her ears. She turned her face: a brilliant golden-red flash flew up from the port side of Alain's ship, a false sunrise. A silhouette of a corner of the stern flared up in sudden clarity, men, sail, and mast. The ship rocked back.

Though she was on the other side of the blast, *Papillon* bucked like a horse being broken in. Less than twenty feet from the ship, Lisbeth held on for dear life, keeping *Papillon* on a grim nor'westerly course, wishing she could take her hands from the tiller and sail to block the creaking of breaking wood and the panicked screams of the sailors that filled her ears.

As if compelled, she turned to the carnage she'd wreaked.

The ship was listing badly to port side. Fire covered the corner of the stern. The ship would be at the bottom of the Channel in less than ten minutes.

Again she turned *Papillon* back toward true north, tacking around the hapless ship.

"What the hell's going on up there?"

The voice wasn't steady, but it was loud enough to hear over the wind. Her knees sagged, and she fell forward over the tiller in relief and joy. "I just bombed Alain's ship. It's sinking."

"You did *what?*"

"We're close to British waters." She felt him scrambling to move. "Hold still. It's hard enough maintaining balance with a sinking ship nearby and my feet stuck either side of you."

He stilled. "I can't move my left arm. What happened?"

The irritable demand would have made her smile in any other circumstances. "I broke your arm or shoulder to get you back inside. I had to get you to British waters."

After a few moments, he said, "I can't manage the sail. Can you get us there?"

"We're close," she replied in grim determination, though in truth she felt frozen stiff and as shaky as an autumn leaf; she was coughing again. "Can you manage the lower rudder?" she yelled, coughing again. She took the last swig of medicine.

She felt him move up to the bench. "Take these."

It was her leather gloves; he'd fallen on them. She fumbled into them, warm from his body. For the first time in hours she felt her fingers.

She'd tacked around the fiery carnage that had been Alain's ship. A few rowboats were in the water, all heading southeast to the closest part of the French shore.

Setting her face, she turned north. "Turn the rudder west, toward the closest point in Britain. I think we might be near Dungeness."

"My ship should have joined Nelson's

blockade by now, at a point southeast of Lydd — the big promontory. Can you see any lights?"

She looked around. "Yes! There are lights about a mile due west!" Her voice cracked on the final word, and the coughing fit wouldn't stop.

"We're in British waters," he yelled over it. "Go!"

Tears streaming down her face from coughing, she turned to England.

She couldn't believe she was home, not even when they reached a ship of the line. Dozens of cannons turned on them, and a cold voice demanded to know who the hell they were. Duncan yelled at her to sit, for God's sake, and she dropped down. Duncan struggled through the opening, gave the required code and showed the captain a curious little shape painted onto the dark sail to prove they were British spies.

It all felt like a strange dream.

Clapping, cheering sailors surrounded them as they were lifted by the bosun and helped to embark, then given brandy and blankets. The ship's doctor examined Duncan's head and strapped up his arm. The one-armed ship's captain introduced himself in beautifully clipped English and bowed to Lisbeth, but the unfamiliar face blurred before her eyes. Uncertain, she put out her hand, and coughed again. Duncan murmured a few words. The doctor hurried to her, and snapped orders to fetch the herbal medicine.

The captain said something about meeting the admirals in Portsmouth.

"My lord, we must transfer to my ship. My wife needs to get to Norfolk. Her mother's ill," she heard Duncan saying, but as if through water; a rushing sound overtook it. Duncan put his good arm around her.

She looked at Duncan. "I want my mother," she whispered, and coughed again.

"A damned little heroine" were the last words she heard as she fell asleep standing up.

Lord Nelson is . . . patrolling English waters. Was that the national hero Admiral Lord Nelson she'd met? Was she really home at last?

CHAPTER 52

Norfolk, England
March 12, 1803

In the hired chaise Lisbeth and Duncan sat tense and still, watching the gently rolling hillside roads into the village of Sunderland, north of the greater town of Sandringham.

She didn't remember boarding Duncan's ship, only waking in a hammock in his quarters, by a fire. She remembered being woken to take the new medicine Nelson's doctor gave her two or three times. The next thing she knew Duncan entered the quarters, his right arm in the same kind of double sling she'd worn a few months ago, and gave her more medicine.

They'd docked near King's Lynn. A sailor carried a bath in. Others brought in jugs of hot water, soap, and lavender water, and for twenty minutes she luxuriated in being clean.

Afterward, Duncan brought in a bandbox with a new cinnamon-colored walking dress, a pretty bonnet, satin slippers, and a lovely redingote — even the required three petticoats. He ushered in a woman whom he introduced as Mrs. Margot Bailey, a local dressmaker, honored to help the future Baroness Annersley into her new outfit and dress her hair.

When she was fit to be seen, he'd led Lisbeth out to a near-new post-chaise, well sprung and perfectly comfortable. "We'll be there in an hour and a half. I'll write to my valet and tell him to bring a maid for you when he comes."

Home. Unable to speak, she'd nodded, tried to smile. *Mama . . .*

Ninety minutes later the chaise turned the final corner, past the gates and around the great sweeping curve. For the first time in almost two years, the beloved, eclectic jumble of buildings came into view. The original house was a Plantagenet-era abbey ruined during Henry VIII's dissolution. Every successive owner had made improvements or additions, so the manor was a sprawling jumble of Tudor, Jacobean, Charles, and Queen Anne. When the last scion of the family died, it was sold to Lisbeth's great-great-grandfather. The messy pile of stone and wood, bricks and mortar amid half-wild rambling gardens.

Never had she seen anything more beautiful. Barton Lynch. *Home.*

She drank in every sight and scent as the

carriage drove down the drive, with old-growth pines, juniper, and the hedgerows at each side. They stopped outside the front entrance. Footmen emerged from the house and let the stairs down on the chaise. Duncan exited, helping her out with his good hand.

"Miss Lizzy!"

Lisbeth wheeled around. The family butler, Conway, stood in the open doorway, his dear old face ablaze with emotion he couldn't hide. Then, covering his trembling hands, he bowed deeply to her. "Miss Lizzy, I mean Mrs. Aylsham, if I might be so bold to congratulate you on your recent marriage, it's good to see you home." He turned to Duncan and bowed again. "Commander Aylsham, thank you for bringing Miss Lizzy home to us, sir."

Duncan bowed his head. "I take it my letter arrived, announcing our marriage."

"Yes, sir, as did all your other letters. If I might be so bold as to wish you happiness?"

Duncan smiled and clapped a hand on the old retainer's shoulder.

Turning aside, Conway gave orders to a footman before leading the way up the stairs.

"Thank you, Conway. Is my mother well?"

Conway jerked to a stop halfway up a step. Then he turned to her, his eyes holding deep sorrow. "Miss Lizzy . . . Lady Sunderland . . ."

Too late, she noticed the black riband

around his arm. Slowly she looked around, saw the black curtains on the windows. She looked at Duncan, the sadness and knowledge in his eyes.

Her father came down the stairs, attired all in black, his face ravaged. "Lizzy . . ."

She swayed. "No. *No.*" Duncan moved to her, but she put an unsteady hand on the stair rail, in a blind need for distance.

Sir Edward sighed. "Your mother held on as long as she could, waiting for you, Lizzy. If she'd known you were coming . . ."

Whirling around, she stared wild-eyed at Duncan. "What did you do with my letters?"

He whitened, reached for her again, but she held herself so stiff he let go. "I sent them, Lizzy, I swear to God I did. If you mentioned anything you shouldn't, the Alien Office —"

"They *opened* my letters? Did you?" she demanded. He was wise enough to remain silent. "You did know she was ill when you recruited me, didn't you? *Didn't* you?"

His face filled with grief and regret. "I'd hoped it wasn't as serious as I feared —" He closed his eyes as she made a mewing sound. "Ah, Lizzy . . ." he muttered, his voice thick.

A rush of sourness filled her throat; with another sound of distress she pushed past Duncan and ran back out through the door.

"She still hasn't spoken?"

Duncan shook his head. "Not a word."

With whitened hair and eyes dark ringed with sadness and fatigue, for the first time Eddie looked the sixty-one years he was. "Caroline wouldn't forgive me for not writing to Lizzy. She didn't understand the importance of the mission . . ."

Duncan shrugged. Eddie never listened to things he didn't want to hear. But then, had he? She'd warned him . . .

"Try again," his father-in-law snapped, but the suffering in his eyes took away any sting in the words. "Make her see sense."

"What sense?" Duncan heard the weariness in his voice. "That the mission was more important than if she saw her mother again?"

Eddie's jaw tightened. "Don't support her in this ridiculous vengeance —"

"She's *grieving.* Who else does she have to blame but us? *You* blamed her when we arrived, said she ought to have come earlier. You knew what we were doing!"

Eddie looked startled, and Duncan realized he'd never treated his mentor with such contempt. The older man said, "You could have brought her home."

"You could have come for her a year ago. And don't say fear of Delacorte prevented you. He couldn't stop us for long once we knew the marriage was illegal. All you had to do was approach Boney through legal means. You didn't. You never once wrote to her when you knew where she was. You didn't ask her to come home. It would have meant the world to her."

He heard Eddie's teeth grinding.

"I've tried to comfort her," Duncan said quietly. Every day he had to bring her home from her mother's grave, shivering, coughing. Night after night he found her curled in the large wing chair in Caroline's sitting room, her salt-streaked face telling him she'd cried herself to sleep. Though she took the medicines he pushed on her, and let him lead her to bed, her look of fury warned him to find another room to sleep in. "Why don't you try?"

"What do I say? We've all made sacrifices in the game —"

Without warning, Duncan lost control. "Lisbeth was never *in* the game. She was illegally wed, her baby stolen from her, dumped in a town of strangers who despised her. She didn't agree to the mission; she desperately clutched at her only way to get home, only to get here too late." He stood over Eddie, for the first time realizing how much taller he was. "She's *nineteen,* for God's sake, and she's your daughter. All she knows is her mother died, and we betrayed her trust."

Eddie sagged. "I've tried to talk to her. Leo and Andrew took turns speaking to her. But she won't even look at us. Something must be done."

Goaded by the way he spoke, Duncan snapped, "She's not a mission, Eddie. She's hurting, and she needs time to forgive us." But he didn't know if she could, or would. "Apart from having Edmond, all she talked about in quiet moments together was seeing Caroline again."

"Well, I'm here, aren't I?" Eddie snapped, "Talk to her, Duncan! She can't keep ignoring us this way."

"Why is that? Is it only acceptable when you do it?"

Before they'd even turned to the door of the library, Lisbeth was inside. Dressed in a gown of deepest mourning, her hair pulled up in a severe chignon by her mother's maid, she stared her father down, not with fury, but with haunting sorrow. "I'm sorry, Sir Edward. I don't know how to comfort you. I don't know who you are."

"What did you call me?" After taking a few moments to gather his wits, Eddie said with obvious wariness, "I'm your father."

"I'm sorry." She shook her head. "I don't know you. I never knew you."

Eddie flinched and threw Duncan a helpless look.

"You wanted her to speak." Coolly, Duncan moved beside his wife, showing her where his loyalties lay — but she stiffened beside him. He'd give anything to turn back the clock a week, a month, and tell her everything.

"You shouldn't speak like that to me," Eddie faltered at last.

Lisbeth lifted her fingers in a tiny, sad shrug. "Is that all you can say? Shouldn't and don't, and you ought to have taken to me with a birch switch? Would it have made me more the daughter you wanted?"

Eddie drew himself up and focused on the one deflection he could make. "Are you saying I should blame myself for your mistakes? If you'd obeyed me, your father —"

"I remember when I was about eight, I asked Mama who you were. *Papa* was just a word. Every time you left I used to wish you'd never come back. It always hurt her so."

Eddie's gaze lowered. "Talk to your brothers if you need to blame me. They need you."

"What should I say to them?" Said without rancor: the power of her words enough to flay, gentle cat-o'-nine-tails. "When I went to Jeremiah the blacksmith's wife's funeral, I knew what to say to him, because he was my friend. I barely know your sons, sir."

"Well, get to know them. Duncan knows them well."

She closed her eyes. "Of course he does." A

river of disillusion in that pitiful little laugh.

After the longest minute of his life, Duncan saw Eddie soften, but it was like the wax of a candle, bent out of shape by callous fingers. "You felt neglected. I see that now, but you don't understand. The terror that the Revolution would come to Britain — that everyone I loved would die horribly — I had to make sacrifices, risk my life. Then Bonaparte —"

"*I* don't understand sacrifice." She pointed to her scarred cheek, and something in her look chilled Duncan right through. "I have three of these, sir. I nearly died twice." She turned to him, and Duncan waited in silence for the attack. "Is what I did so trivial that you haven't even reported it to your superior officers?"

A slow-moving tide of sadness, loss — bewildered disillusionment — it was all in her eyes. What the hell was he supposed to say? "I didn't want to leave you —"

Her lifted hand stopped him, the pain in her face. "Please, no more lies. Stop pretending you care. You have everything you wanted — you've won. You're a Sunderland. At least give me the respect of honesty in return." She pressed her lips together to stop the tears, but they had their way, along with pathetic, noisy little gulps. The men waited in wretched silence. "When Cal and Alec bring my son, I'm going with them to Scotland. Their family sounds nice." After a moment she added, "I thought I was too ruined to have Edmond — but I can't leave him here. Not without Mama."

Long moments passed, marked by the ticking of the grandfather clock and the birds tweeting outside. It was obvious Lisbeth had said her piece. "You're certain the Stewarts will bring your child?" Eddie asked, without a bite of mockery.

Lisbeth's smile was a ghost of her normal sweetness and life. The blind distance was back, familiar enemy. "I've only known them a few months, but Cal has been risking his life for months to save Edmond. Alec did everything to help Duncan, while he made Alec jump through hoops to prove himself worthy." She glanced at Duncan. "You never need doubt his loyalty to you, Sir Edward. Duncan even said he loved me so I'd fulfill the objective. I congratulate you on your creation. He's just like you."

Duncan felt sick. All this time he'd bargained on her forgiving him, loving him against all odds. He'd never been more wrong. Long-instilled training in silence when others spoke was a habit now, but he forced words out. "I do love you. I always have."

She closed her eyes again. "Then God save me from your anger or vengeance." She spoke to her father. "Cal and Alec will bring Edmond to me. They're the brothers I never had."

"Lizzy," Leo whispered, taking a faltering step forward.

The grief in Leo's voice made her swing around. She paled at the sight of her brothers' devastated faces. "I'm sorry." That same shaking little shrug. "I don't know what you want from me. I only came home for Mama, and she's gone." Her glance turned to Duncan, hopeless, lost. "Enjoy being a Sunderland." She lifted her black skirts, moved past her brothers with quiet dignity, and walked outside.

Eddie looked at Duncan, with the same unspoken plea as a year and a half ago. "How many times do I have to bring your daughter home?" Duncan asked, low. "When will you show her you care for her, or tell her you were wrong?"

Eddie fell into a chair behind him and covered his face with his hands.

Barely able to stand seeing the feet of clay Lisbeth had always known were there, Duncan said, "Then you really have lost her." Sickened, he looked at her brothers, who shrugged helplessly.

He spent the rest of the day at Caroline's grave standing fifty feet from his wife, her unwanted sentinel.

CHAPTER 53

Her father was gone by the time Lisbeth woke up the next morning.

Leo and Andrew at least had waited to say farewell, but they'd been so stiff and cold she wished they'd sneaked off as well. Their coaches had barely disappeared beyond the gates before she turned on Duncan. "When are you leaving?"

He regarded her with eyes gentle with compassion. "I'm staying."

"Please don't." Her knees were shaking. Half afraid she'd fall down, she turned away, walked in the house, and up the stairs.

Duncan followed her to her mother's sitting room, her mother's chair. Saying nothing, not even always looking at her. Just there.

"When are you leaving?" she repeated.

With difficulty he knelt at her feet, balancing awkwardly with the broken shoulder. "I gave you my word. I'm not going anywhere, no matter how you push me away."

"What if I want you to go?" she demanded,

low and quivering.

The growl that shivered into her soul from the first time he'd spoken to her was still quiet and gentle. "I understand now. We stand on the same side of the mirror. If I don't know women, men are strangers to you. You believe all the men in your life will leave you — your father, your brothers, Alain, me. Even Edmond left you."

His damaged warrior's face rocked back with the force of her slap. "My baby is innocent!" Her hand stung and burned.

He remained at her feet, his cheek red with the imprint of her blow. "That's it, love. Hit me, hate me, I deserve you to."

In his words, she saw herself through a new, horrified set of eyes. She dragged in a breath and looked at her hand as if it had betrayed her. "No. I won't hit you, not ever again. I won't be like them."

But he wouldn't give up. "Edmond couldn't help leaving you — but it's what you're afraid of, aren't you? That he'll become like your father, like me, and leave you to save the world, the nation, or someone else. That's why you made me swear not to train him."

She fought the childish urge to cover her ears. "Stop it."

From his kneeling position he looked up at her. Just as in her romantic novels, a knight vowing fidelity to his lady. The irony of it was almost ridiculous. She'd have believed it only a week ago. "Every man you've ever loved has left you. So you're pushing me until I go."

"No, I'm not." She looked in his eyes and saw his fear, a reflection of her suffering. He did understand. "You can't make this right. You didn't tell me about Mama, and it makes all your vows worth nothing. The only man who ever loved me, who never let me down, was Robert." She stared out the window, unblinking in the weak sunlight, silvery scudding cloud. "I chose the wrong man."

He kept his gaze on hers, the shutters into his turbulent soul fully open. Too late. A week, a lifetime of choices too late. "I'm sorry."

"I loved you," she whispered. "I thought I'd finally found a man to believe in."

After a few moments, he said unsteadily, "I'm still not leaving. You promised to teach me to be a family man. You're teaching me now not to walk away when life gets hard. I don't care if it takes a lifetime, I'm never leaving you."

His declaration only brought stinging tears. Lies, all lies.

He remained on his knees before her. When she finally stopped crying, he said, "All my life I've been taught to obey, to put duty above everything — as a child, a King's Man, in my short stint in the navy. With your father. Duty was the highest calling of man.

It was only when we came here that I realized the real cost, the true sacrifice."

It sounded like something her brother Andrew had once said to her, and most likely he'd taken it from their father. "My father told you to say that. Say something to make me pity you, and I'll forgive you. I'm not my mother."

This time he remained still. The silence was almost hopeless. "So that was wrong, too?"

A helpless shrug. "I don't know if anything could be right."

After a minute of unspoken acceptance of her accusations, he said quietly, "You'll remember me telling you that the only thing I knew nothing about was women? If you'll —"

With remembered nausea at his story, she could only look at him with bleary eyes. "You won't leave me in peace until you've had your say. I've lost the only person who ever loved me, and you still push for what you want."

The tired pain in his expression, and she knew what he was going to say. "Lizzy, please believe that —"

"I don't." She kept her voice down. Back in England, keeping up appearances for the servants. Accepting what wouldn't change. "The girl you married died last week. As my father created you, this is what you made me. Now live with it. God knows I have to."

He whitened, got to his feet, and backed

away. "Alec wrote to me today. He said Cal's had trouble leaving the continent with Boney's soldiers everywhere. He's made it as far as Amsterdam. Alec is sailing to Holland to get them. They'll be here in two weeks. If you want my house in Frampton Lacey for you and Edmond —"

She shook her head. "Grand-mère left me her house in the Cotswolds. I'll go there if the Stewarts won't have me."

He opened his mouth, closed it, and nodded. How could he answer that? His own family was as unfamiliar to him as they were to her. "You'll have my best carriage, a generous quarterly allowance, and a full contingent of staff. If there's ever anything else you need, write to me."

Her hand crossed her brow, covering her eyes. "For God's sake, Duncan, give me a little peace — *please.*"

Ten seconds of silence. "If you need me, I'll be in the study." He bowed over her hand and quit the room without another word.

Barton Lynch, Norfolk
April 10, 1803
The uncertainty of cold, windy spring finally gave way to warmer days, but Lisbeth was like the half-frozen nights that followed. Sitting by a fire didn't melt the ice in her. It walled around her, and nothing she did

686

warmed her up or broke her out of this prison.

She walked the gardens in the watery sunshine. It grew a bit warmer each day, but the breeze was cool and playful, loosening the careful chignon. Her skin itched and sweated beneath her heavy black dress, but at least she felt something other than this awful numbness.

Duncan, still at his post half a garden length from her. Watching.

Irritation swelled up in her; but at least she felt something other than the bitterness of his betrayal. He did nothing but give to her, but it was weeks, months too late. He was putting her first at last, but it was all aimed at gaining forgiveness. Perversely, she couldn't blame him for that. He was so alone, and she was so tired of fighting, of pushing him off. If . . . if she gave into her shameful craving and allowed him back into her bed —

Then I'd be the thing I despised. Hasn't Duncan been used enough by selfish women?

Nobody had ever told her grief was such a stupid thing, turning her into a total lackwit.

A cloud scudded across the washed-out blue of the sky. A bird cawed. Rumbling slowly came to her ears, the wheels of a coach. Lisbeth held her breath as she did every day, waiting until the sound passed, leaving her in the same disappointment she'd felt for the past three days.

The sound slowed, the carriage trundling over stones as it turned into the gates. The gatekeeper let it in, and it began the long drive up. Lisbeth had to stop herself from running. If it was another condolence call by curious neighbors, she'd —

A face appeared at the window of the big, brand-new carriage with the Annersley crest on it. A face with hard features, black eyes and hair, and a smile as wide as the sea. Alec met her agonized gaze and nodded.

She almost fell to her knees. Now beside her, Duncan put his good arm around her waist and led her to the coach.

The driver let down the stairs. Alec alighted, his smile blazing, holding a blanket-clad bundle in his arms. "I think you've met this little lad before." And he handed the baby to her.

Edmond was asleep. The warmth of the blanket, the sight of satin skin, the dreaming crooked smile . . . for the first time in months, her son was in her arms. So much bigger; so much she'd missed. He made a soft baby noise, opening his mouth. He had teeth.

Vaguely she saw another form coming down the coach stairs. Absorbed in her son, she knew it was Cal by the endless silent grief emanating from him. *Thank you,* she mouthed, and saw the strange, hurting half smile that was uniquely Cal. He was limping.

A young woman emerged, holding another child. Edmond's wet nurse, she assumed.

Then another face appeared. Thin, hollow eyed, with frizzled gray hair. Marceline's gaze met hers, asking the question.

How could she do less for Marceline than she'd had done for her in Eaucourt, and at far more risk? Lisbeth nodded. Her son's grandmother left the coach on Cal's hand. Trembling fingers touched Edmond's hair. *"Merci,"* was all she said — but Lisbeth knew her gratitude would turn to hatred if Marceline discovered it was she who'd killed her son.

CHAPTER 54

Barton Lynch, Norfolk
April 14, 1803

"What a beautiful boy." Sitting on the floor in her old nursery, Lisbeth cooed in her son's face, making the baby giggle and bounce in her lap. She'd discovered he liked it when she said "boo-ful," and said it at every opportunity.

For days she'd spent every waking moment with Edmond, playing with him, changing him, feeding him, and holding him. The wet-nurse, who'd brought her own child with her, a toddling girl, only took Edmond to give him milk. Lisbeth hung over his cradle in ecstasy when he slept, spoke to him in English, in French, and held and kissed him constantly. Edmond was fascinated by her in seconds, loved her within a day, and Marceline did everything she could to strengthen the bond between mother and son.

"My son was damaged by the Revolution," was all she'd said of Alain's abuse.

Lisbeth had bit her lip and said, voice breaking, "Edmond needs a grandmother."

"We'll do better outside of France," Marceline whispered, patting her arm.

"He is beautiful," Duncan agreed now, but he felt slashed by the sword of her uncertain half smile. She was trying to be nice but clearly wished him at Jericho. She was still leaving him, and guilt held him back from forcing her to stay.

Marceline stood from the chair beside where mother and son played and left the room.

Lisbeth's gaze dropped. "We're leaving in the morning."

He couldn't help it. "I'll come with you. Or stay with me here. This is your home."

"This will never be home again." Her lips sucked in, drawing slow breaths. "Your love is an anchor pulling me underwater, drowning me. I can't forgive you."

Closing his eyes, he nodded. "What do you want done with *Papillon*?" he asked at length, gruff with the pain he couldn't hide.

"Give it to the Admiralty," she murmured, caressing Edmond's hair as he bashed wooden blocks together. "I never want to see it again."

"They'll kick up a fuss, but I'll make sure they won't demand your presence." He tried to smile, but he was shaking. "Poor Fulton, they'll probably kidnap him for his expertise."

"Alec has written to prepare the family for our arrival." She hadn't mentioned Fulton since the day she said she'd chosen the wrong man. She didn't deny her part in destroying Fulton's love and his faith. She never excused her actions as others did.

Loyal, faithful Lizzy, she'd be fond of Fulton until she died, wishing she'd married the American instead. Duncan's throat ached. The only woman who'd ever just loved him, and she was leaving. He'd scraped empty the barrel of her forgiveness. "They'll love you."

Though she hadn't hit him or even spoken harshly to him since their shattering scene, the echoes of her anguish were all the louder for their remaining unspoken. *My mother died believing I didn't care enough to come home, that everyone in her family put duty above her.*

She spoke again. "When I was in France and Jersey, I thought I could forgive my father — and you — anything. But I can't."

Platitudes, useless and stupid, filled his mind again. What if time *didn't* heal all wounds? How the hell would he know, when he had never healed from his own wounds in more than sixteen years? "If you wanted the world, I'd try to give it to you. You're everything to me."

She looked in his eyes. "I don't care." She unwound her legs and stood, carefully holding Edmond. "I'm broken, and you just keep hitting me."

He didn't answer. Keeping a lid on all the love he felt inside, because every time he spoke it aloud, her numbness flayed him.

At the door she turned, holding her sleeping child, mother and son so beautiful they made him ache. "You should talk to your brothers. Something happened to Cal. I think he needs you."

Moments later, the door closed, and his wife and the only son he'd ever have left his life.

He found his brothers in the garden. Cal stood staring into the washed spring sunlight, where the poppy buds emerged from green sheaths, and lavender stalks had a hint of the luscious purple to come. Alec stood behind his twin, a hand on his shoulder. Neither spoke.

Duncan felt like the worst of blundering intruders. The last thing he wanted was to be here. But the promise he'd made Lisbeth only minutes ago — *If you wanted the world, I'd give it to you* — would be worthless in her eyes if he didn't do the first thing she asked of him.

"Lisbeth thinks something happened to you, Cal, and you need to talk," he said, cursing his bluntness. Cal and Alec had each other. What possible use could he be?

Cal turned his head, and Duncan forgot his stupidity. His brother's eyes were dry and red, filled with the well of blackness Duncan knew well. "She was already half dead when I got there. I had to finish it. I was ordered not to kill the bastard, and I had to save his son, his mother. I can't look at them, not even the baby."

Clare. Duncan didn't know what to say or do.

"All I want is to kill him, slowly and painfully. The bastard, the . . ." A sound came from the door behind Duncan, and after a quick glance, Cal ground out savagely, "the filthy boggin-faced clag-tail, what he did to her . . . to them both."

He guessed either Lisbeth or Marceline stood nearby, and he'd modified his language only in changing it to Gaelic, calling Delacorte an unwiped arse. It was far less than he deserved.

"How could you have made his death worse?" he asked in Gaelic, in case Marceline was behind him. "He died at the hands of the woman he'd abused and ridiculed as weak. He'd tried over and over to kill her, and she destroyed him instead. To a man like him . . ."

He ran out of words; but Alec smiled at Duncan and nodded. "He's right. How could his death be worse at your hands?"

Cal stared narrow-eyed at his brothers. "Are you certain he's dead? They never found his body." He stalked away.

Duncan glanced at the door, seeing Marceline disappear. "I only made things worse."

"No, lad." Alec shook his head, smiling. "He hasn't said this much about himself since Rose and little Frances died. I gather he was fond of this woman?"

I think Cal's suffering, Lisbeth had said. "He had a wife and daughter . . . and they died," Duncan muttered in horror. "And now Clare's dead."

The subtle glow vanished from Alec's face. "Our father cursed the people of Tyburn as they watched him hang. He said they'd suffer until the German kings stopped ruling Scotland."

Confused, Duncan asked, "But wasn't he a King's Man? Eddie told me . . ."

"It's true. But at heart, despite the Bonnie Prince's faults, our father was a Jacobite. When Annersley turned him in, he said at an open hearing he wanted a return to the Stuart throne — and Scottish freedom — with all his heart and soul. The government couldn't save him after that. He was bitter that at the end his life amounted to nothing. He cursed the people watching him die for entertainment." He curled his hands into fists. "I believe the curse rebounded on us, his sons. We've each had a wife and child and lost them."

Alec's voice was cynical, touched with self-loathing, taking Duncan aback. Before he could think of anything to say, Alec said, "Cal lost Rose and Frances through no fault of his own. My wife and son aren't dead, but I lost them fifteen years ago. Don't make the mistakes I made. Do what you can to repair the damage you created with Lisbeth while you still can."

Finally the laughing mask had been snatched from Alec's face. After all he'd lost, Alec kept reaching out, trying to bring Duncan into the family. Humbled, he touched his half brother's shoulder. "I think it's too late."

Alec's eyes stopped looking inward at blackness and turned to him. "Lad, don't mistake suffering with finality. Let her grieve; let her blame you. Give her room to breathe, to think, to forgive — but don't give up. Somewhere inside she knows you had to make the choices you did."

He shrugged helplessly. "I've been trying to reach her for weeks, Alec. I don't know what else to say or do." It was the closest to a cry for help he could make.

Alec's hand landed on his shoulder. "It's only been a few weeks, Duncan. Think about it, lad. Why is she coming to Scotland with us? Look at that, and you'll know what to do."

For once Alec was the one to walk away from him, leaving Duncan feeling as if he'd been handed a gift he didn't know how to unwrap.

CHAPTER 55

Jermyn Street, London
May 19, 1803

He'd been alone for more than a month now.

The streets of London were filled with boys selling newssheets, screaming that they were again at war with France. The screaming and the war suited Duncan's mood. Even the vile smell of the city, the piss and the vomit mixed with cooking smells and befouled rivers six feet beneath his feet, felt appropriate.

Then the rain drizzled over his head. Perfect. London mirrored his life, a dirty shambles.

Then it's time to change it.

The problem was, until Caroline's death, he'd liked his life. Marrying Lisbeth had been the realization of everything he'd ever wanted. He was a successful King's Man, with a home and family, a wife and son —

The first time you put duty above family I'll be gone — and that's my vow to you.

Well, she'd kept her vow. Three months

married, and it had been over for more than a month. It hadn't even lasted a month. What was so wrong with him that he couldn't keep her love even for a few months?

Why is she coming to Scotland with us? Look at that . . .

What did Alec know that he didn't? Why had she gone to Scotland? To Duncan, it was the one place he planned never to go: the embodiment of a life of rejection and ridicule.

No, there was something off in that.

He turned into his building, and he ran up the stairs to his rooms. Letting himself in quietly so his valet, Dobson, wouldn't fuss over him, he picked up his letters and headed for the chair by the fire in the small sitting room. He'd planned to open up Annersley House in town for them. Now he couldn't be bothered leaving his bachelor's digs.

Scotland. Why had she gone to Scotland? It was something he ought to know. Alec thought so, and Duncan had learned to trust his brother's advice. If he'd listened months ago —

He sighed and sorted through his letters.

One had a Norfolk direction. Though he knew she'd gone, he tore the thing open before reading the sender's address.

Swallowing his disappointment, he read the letter from the Aylsham man of affairs.

698

Dear Lord Annersley,

I regret to inform you that your father passed two months ago. As you were not in England for the reading of the will, I take leave to inform you that everything passed to you, including the title of Baron Annersley. Mellingham Hall is in urgent need of repair, as are the villages and lands surrounding. The tenants desperately need repairs to their homes. Your father dismissed the steward some years ago, among other servants. If you could find the time to make an inspection, and release some funds, I would be most grateful.

> Yours, etc,
> Jerome Fairmont

"So I'm Lord Annersley," he murmured, feeling only emptiness. He'd expected to be grateful the abusive old bastard was dead at last, but what he felt was cheated. God knows it would have been useless, but he'd wanted to see the old man one last time, take Lisbeth and Edmond, show him even a traitor's unwanted bastard could find happiness.

He frowned, thinking about why the thought disturbed him.

Our grandparents pray every day to see you before they die.

Why is she going to Scotland?

I don't know who you are.

His life had been built on more lies than he'd realized. No wonder he'd chosen to be a King's Man. A life of deception was all he'd known. Annersley gained his heir by killing Broderick Stewart by legal means. Then he'd fed Duncan a steady diet of half-truths and crazy stories that prevented him from wanting to meet his real family or discover the truth. By the time he'd run from Norfolk at fourteen he'd become so comfortable with the sham that was his life, he hadn't considered truth to be an option.

Then Eddie saved him, cared for him, and filled him with ideals of duty to king and country. If Annersley had spun ugly stories to keep an heir, and Julia had made love a lie, it was Eddie who'd made deception noble in Duncan's eyes. Thrusting him into the shadows and telling him it was acceptable, right, even honorable to keep secrets, to maim, kill, or die in the name of king and country. And lying, always lying. It was normal for him to push truth away, apart from factual reports to his superiors. But everyone else was fair game. Being like Eddie had been his holy grail for half his life; emulating Leo and Andrew was his aspiration, gentlemen spies.

Did they even know who they were, if their own daughter and sister didn't know them?

Did *he* know who he was?

No wonder he refused to accept Alec in his life. His brother had thrust an unwanted light on his life from the day they'd met, handing him unpalatable truths, leaving him uncomfortable with who and what he was. And then he'd met Lisbeth, who didn't know how to lie; and Cal, with his bluntness and his pain. Three people who'd risked everything for him, who would do anything for him without agenda or cost.

The three people he could trust with his life, because they'd never deceived him. The people who'd shown up his life for the glass castle it was, a fragile house built on shifting sands.

Why is she going to Scotland? Think about that, lad, and you'll know what to do.

A slow smile spread across his face.

Admiralty House, Whitehall, London
May 20, 1803

"Where is this underwater craft? We must test it and make replicas."

Duncan stood facing the long line of desks. "My ship's docked at Brunswick. It takes time to bring such a contraption here, my lords. It will be in the stables by Spring Garden Mews this afternoon." He waved a hand behind the assembled admirals and rear admirals to the park behind Admiralty House, viewed through wide windows.

"Will Fulton come?" The Admiral Earl St. Vincent demanded, voice eager.

"No, my lord," Duncan replied without

inflection. "Though he donated *Papillon* to our cause when he heard of the invasion fleet, he is of firm republican principles."

"Then why did he donate *Papillon* to British interests?" Admiral Baron Elphinstone asked in his Scottish accent, heavy white brow knitted. "It seems rank foolishness to me."

Duncan chose his words with care. "By then Fulton knew of the invasion. One of our team had been taken for questioning right from the house where he was staying, and it terrified him. He left France that night."

Sir Edward Pellew had sat in silence until this point. He was merely a rear admiral, but a man of famed acumen and heroism. "What's her name, Aylsham?"

Duncan met the sharp gaze. "That's a delicate matter, Sir Edward."

Pellew's brows lifted. "I will be answered, Commander! Who's the woman you sent to Fulton, what does she know about submersible boats, and why isn't she here?"

Duncan met fire with cool obedience. "You're right, Sir Edward. A woman was sent to Fulton as an assistant and learned enough from him to conceive the manner in which we disabled the French fleet. She came with me on the final mission. Though she'd just recovered from weeks of illness, she saved my life that night, and her courage and brilliance saved Britain from invasion." As Pellew was about to speak, Duncan lifted a hand. "But whatever her name was, Sir Edward, it is now Aylsham. The lady did me the great honor of becoming my wife, my baroness. She is currently in Scotland with my family."

Mutterings greeted this announcement. It was a facer, indeed. British law dictated that no man could force another man's wife into any form of work. Even the king himself couldn't force a peer's wife into the kind of labor needed to create copies of *Papillon*.

Admiral Lord Nelson spoke. "I have met Lady Annersley, my lords. She's a lady of the highest duty and principle — but when I saw her, she was in a state of collapse."

Throwing Nelson a grateful glance, Duncan said, "My wife is indeed a lady with a high sense of duty, but she is currently in sore need of rest."

Once again Pellew harrumphed, but his eyes were touched with regretful determination. "You're aware, of course, that neither of your names can be recorded as the authors of this heroic endeavor, especially that of Lady Annersley. It must remain forever secret."

Duncan fought the urge to growl when all the other men nodded in emphatic agreement. In their eyes, a lady couldn't conceive anything but children, a drawing-room decoration, or a new hat style. Anything else was indelicate and unfeminine in the extreme. He doubted any man here but Nelson or possibly Pellew would like Lisbeth, or admire her strength. Her insight would probably terrify them.

He replied coolly enough, "My wife and I did none of this for public honors."

Pellew nodded and smiled, as if he'd agreed. "Quite right. She is your baroness, will meet the king, and receive our thanks in private."

And that's reward enough for risking her life over and over, because she's a woman? Duncan saw Pellew, a man who lived to shower heroic men with praise and rewards, through new eyes. He truly believed Lisbeth's part in saving England must be kept secret merely because she was a woman. Her footnote in history would only be as the thirty-sixth Lady Annersley.

"I have another appointment. Good day to you, my lords." He bowed and left the room. As soon as the admirals had *Papillon* in their meaty paws, he'd —

Halfway down the hall, a voice came. "Aylsham, a word if you please."

Unsurprised, Duncan turned to face the haughty, thin face of his spymaster. "It's Annersley, if you please," he said coolly. "Did you withhold my wife's letters to her mother?"

Zephyr's brows lifted. For the first time, it left Duncan unmoved. He waited.

Eventually Zephyr snapped, "You don't need to create a fuss about it, Annersley. It was a necessary precaution. She'd talked about being in Ambleteuse and Jersey. It's about time you returned from Norfolk. I have a mission —" He stopped when Duncan shoved a sealed envelope into his hand. "What's this?"

"My resignation from the Alien Office, effective immediately."

Zephyr looked at him coldly. Again, Duncan felt nothing, but waited. "So you would desert us on the commencement of war?"

Words that had always moved him before now left him cold. "There will always be a war, a cause, an assassination, or a sacrifice. I've made mine willingly. My wife, however, did not, and neither did her mother. My resignation is effective immediately, sir."

"Do I not have the right to an explanation?" Zephyr demanded as Duncan turned away.

"You do not."

"Damn it, Annersley, I will have an explanation!"

Knowing the veiled threat meant something against Lisbeth, he turned back. "The former Lord Annersley left the land and villages in bad heart. My first duty is now there. Take that as my reason, if you like. I assure you, you wouldn't like the other. By the way, if young Mark Henshaw returns from Boulogne —"

"He hasn't as yet, and if he does, it is no longer your concern," Zephyr said coldly.

"True." Duncan nodded. "I recommend thorough training for him. He has a stellar future in the Alien Office, if you can look past his birth. I sent in a complete report this morning."

"I demand your word you'll be available for future missions, should they be vital!"

"Then you'll be disappointed, sir. You can't force a peer into service." Unmoved by the disapproving growl of his commanding officer, Duncan sketched a final bow, turned, and walked out, feeling lighter.

He knew what he had to do. An arrow landing on a hayrick, maybe; perhaps she'd kick him out. Either way he was heading to Scotland, to meet his true family, to become a Stewart. To become the man Lisbeth wanted him to be.

The British Alien Office, Whitehall, London
May 20, 1803

"I'm afraid you won't see Campbell for some time, sir. Seems he's disappeared."

In his Spartan office in the Whitehall buildings, William Windham stared at the sturdy, pleasant face of Captain Wright. He'd newly arrived in London with vital papers — and information. "Campbell was taken? Lord John Campbell?"

"We can't confirm it, sir, but more than

fourteen hundred British nationals have been captured and taken to detainment camps across France. He could very well be one of them."

What a damn day it had been. Bloody women ruined everything. The best team of alibis he could have, done with; Calum Stewart was useless without his brothers. Furious, Windham put his hands to his hair, only to growl in pain when he encountered his wig. "Damn it, he's son and heir to the Duke of Argyll! He ought to have been released!"

Poker-faced, Wright replied, "Perhaps we counted on that a little too much when we entrusted him with this mission, sir."

How the hell was he to explain the disappearance of his son and heir to the fiery Duke of Argyll? Or to the king, when English-Scottish politics were in a delicate state with the Irish insurrection coming closer by the hour? He caught sight of his hair in the beveled mirror, standing on end like a Bedlamite, and began smoothing it. "Well? You told me you had other matters to report."

"Yes, sir, I do." A short hesitation that wasn't in Wright's style. "There was — an incident — on Boulogne Beach a few days ago, sir."

"Well? Don't make me wait!"

"As you know, Talbot and Mandeville were left to bring certain items of value with them when the embassy in Paris closed." A quick, delicate glance at the trunk at his feet, then around the room. A trained agent never said more than he needed to, even here, because if the British had hundreds of agents in France, Boney had thousands here, many of them English born and bred. "Unfortunately they were refused permission to board the packet at Calais. Diverted to Boulogne, they endured questioning by the *sous-préfet* who told them that Boney was ready to detain them and confiscate the items. So they decided to burn the ones that have their counterparts in this office."

Windham swore hard, realizing what Wright meant: the essential list of British espionage agents in France. The names and covers of over three hundred of their best. "What happened?"

"Most were burned, sir, never fear — but two bundles escaped. We can't know who's implicated as yet, but we had to hide for two hours before we could escape. As we left the town with this gift for you" — indicating the trunk — "a boy jumped on the runner board. I gather he's Tidewatcher's cabin boy."

"Annersley," Windham corrected in cold precision. "He's no longer one of us."

Wright didn't waste time on semantics or indignation. "The lad has vital information for us, sir. I brought him along with us. He's outside the door now."

"Bring him in."

Wright called, and a lad strutted into the room as if he owned it. A shock of spiky red hair, a cheeky grin, and eyes alive with intelligence, the skinny youth couldn't be more than fifteen. Windham had a vague recollection of him. The boy made a jerking bow, his eyes filled with a mixture of hero worship and wariness. "Mr. Zephyr, sir, you're gunna wanna hear what I got to say, cos some o' your best ones are in mortal danger."

ACKNOWLEDGMENTS

As this book took years to get right — from first draft to final production — I have so many people to thank that should I forget any, you have my deepest apologies.

First, to my wonderful, supportive agent, Eleanor Jackson: There are no words. Four years ago I had to make a choice, and I've never regretted it. You're the agent I want to keep until I can no longer move my fingers to write. Your commitment to *The Tide Watchers* through the years, your certainty I'd create the version that would sell to the right publisher and editor and give me a career that would, in your words, keep me happy as a writer, kept my faith alive. You never gave up on me or on the book, which meant I couldn't either. Thank you for everything. I hope we work together until I fall off my perch!

To Emily Krump, my brilliant editor at William Morrow: You brought this book to greater life with your comments and questions and constant willingness to call me and talk things through. Your commitment to making this book the best it could be kept me focused. Thanks for loving this book as much as I do. I hope we work on many, many more projects together.

To Fiona McIntosh, wonderful author and excellent course-giver: Thank you for offering the Popular Fiction Masterclass. It inspired me to the rewrite that led to the sale to my dream publisher. Thank you over and over again for your no-nonsense, no-excuses course on how to be a professional mainstream writer. The sheer amount of published authors that have come from your course is proof of what a fabulous teacher you are.

I have so many writer friends who have helped me through the years with this book: to my creative partner of fifteen years, writing coach extraordinaire and heart sister, Mia Zachary — I honestly don't know what I'd do without you. Rachel Bailey, Hayson Manning, Barbara de Leo, your critiques on the earlier versions of the book, our group chats, and emails helped me focus on Duncan's character and strengthen him. Big thanks to All of Us, email group extraordinaire, dear friends of many years who are always there for me. And massive thanks to the Beau Monde, a historical writers' group that constantly inspires me with its deep knowledge and willingness to share, never rude or competitive.

To my local critique group, the Valleygirls, and Kerri Lane in particular: you've been a big sister, a mentor, and a loving bully at times, but your incredible work ethic is ever inspiring, your generosity and kindness limitless.

Absolute massive thanks to Heather Cleary. You didn't know what would happen when you gave me those hard-to-find books on espionage in Britain and France in Napoleonic times; you just understood that I thirst for historical knowledge as you do. Without your generous gift, the core plot of *The Tide Watchers* wouldn't be what it is, its knowledge halved.

Diane Gaston, you always read parts of this book when I needed it, put me up in Washington when I cross the ditch, and always happily argue plot points with me (bulldog). Margaret Riseley, thank you for reading parts of this book over and over, and always giving encouraging advice. Your advice about seeing every scene as part of a movie has remained with me through the years.

Barbara and Peter Clendon, the lessons you gave me on raw beauty, and writing what is essential without self-indulgence, have never left me. Fiona Brand, your advice way back in 1999 on "the overreaching arc," or describing my book in three lines or less, helped me focus this book to the best of my imperfect ability.

Special thanks to Dallas Gavan, friend and military expert: your knowledge will hold me in stead throughout the book series. Thanks to Gail Mellor, dear friend for many years, for the reintroduction, and just being a friend still.

To Helen Selvey: I'm so glad we met at the Popular Fiction Masterclass. We don't just work together on historical detail, we're friends and inspire each other. History nerds unite — and there's always The Admiral!☺

Big thanks must go to the excellent staff at the State Library of New South Wales in Sydney, especially Jaisong and Cathy for finding a map of the exact region I needed in the era I needed, and for helping me with the order. You went above and beyond. Thank you both so much.

To my former critique partner, Maryanne Cappelluti: I wish you knew, my darling friend. To my soul sister, Helen Yde, who wanted me to write historical mainstream along the lines of *The Scarlet Letter,* a book she loved — I wish you could see this book. I still love and miss you both.

To my dear friends Dan and Liz Eliza: You read the book, gave good advice, put us up, fed us excellent food, encouraged and listened, and let me have hours to write when inspired, and took us on great walks too. You even came to Scotland on my research trip. I'll never forget your friendship (or the hours watching Eureka when I needed to unwind!). Thank you for being who you are.

To my fantastic "ideas person" and brilliant friend, Olga Mitsialos: I don't need to say it; you know. You always understand. How many times did you read this book for me and give me great ideas? You even read a book on Napoleonic espionage for me — a great sacrifice! Beach walk soon? Or a research trip? ☺

And finally, to my wonderful and very grounding family: to my husband, Jim, who read this twice and gave me excellent insight into the male mind, bluntly letting me know when I'd overwritten or made something "too girly." To my mother, Mary Price: thanks for reading over and over, for listening to new ideas, and being a general cheerleader. To my daughter Katie for all her technical help, advice on social media, and being a good ear; to daughter Jaime and son Justin for being proud of my achievements, loving history, and being willing to bring me down to earth when I need it. I have no doubt I'll need it again in the future! And Chris, my darling son-in-law, I just love you.

To all my extended family and dear friends I haven't mentioned, I love you and just thanks for being there.

P.S.
INSIGHTS,
INTERVIEWS & MORE . . .

ABOUT THE BOOK

THE STORY BEHIND
THE TIDE WATCHERS

Though I'd always wanted to write historical fiction, I was writing contemporary romance when a friend from the United States visited Sydney with her family. In April 2006 I showed them around Sydney, including Darling Harbor and the maritime museum. Touring the museum fired my imagination for historical writing. I wandered around, dreaming up stories. Then at the museum store, I picked up a book called *The Terror Before Trafalgar* by Tom Pocock. I looked at the first few pages and knew I had to buy it.

As I read Pocock's book, a brief reference caught my attention. Unnamed English spies found a fleet of ships in the Liane, the river behind Boulogne-sur-Mer harbor, in late 1802 or early 1803. The ships launched in March 1803, after a horrendous winter of storms. Some ships sank eight miles out to sea and the rest returned to France. Two months later, war resumed. I knew I'd found a story I *had* to tell — the story of the unnamed spies who'd found and sabotaged Napoleon's secret fleet. I read the book cover to cover, making notes throughout, making special note of who was in France at the time and what they did, especially what trouble they got into. I bought more books and researched online. Reading about fascinating people like Captain Wright, spy extraordinaire; Robert Fulton, brilliant American inventor; the Mad Baron, Lord Camelford; and what we'd nowadays call a colorful identity, Captain "Guinea-Run" Johnstone — not to mention learning such weird and wonderful facts as the Archbishop of Narbonne's false teeth — I knew I had to include them.

With each new fact I discovered about the era, I realized the sabotaging of this fleet had been almost totally shrouded in history. I even had people tell me it didn't happen. *You mean 1798, when the fleet sank in the Irish Sea,* or *No, there was only the 1805 invasion attempt from Boulogne.*

These were knowledgeable people, and I began to doubt. But then I discovered some crucial facts. In late 1802 British spies discovered Bonaparte's *Grand Armée* of 100,000 men, half of them bivouacked in the Channel region. Just after the war resumed in July 1803, over 1,400 ships and boats were anchored in the Channel region. Under the terms of the Treaty of Amiens, neither side was to accumulate more ships than it already had. Bonaparte had five hundred more than he had in 1801. Though since 1798 he'd invaded Piedmont, Parma, Venice, and finally Switzerland, and had taken their wealth away; he was pushing the Americans hard to buy Louisiana for fifteen million dollars — a massive amount back then. He'd already brought France back into economic balance. Why did he need all this money? By the time he stopped hiding his invasion fleet in late 1803, boats and ships filled the region from Boulogne-sur-Mer to Audresselles, over ten miles away. Why, if he was committed to the peace he'd created? He was too *prepared* for this open invasion to have only begun building ships and buying armaments less than a year before.

I kept searching for more of this hidden history, the invasion that "never happened," and Bonaparte never talked about. Why hadn't he? Of course, from pharaohs of old to Charlemagne, leaders never spoke of their failures or allowed historians to write about it. But why would *Britain* keep this stunning success secret? There had to be a solid reason why, when so many victories were publicly celebrated and spies had their achievements credited to them in history and this one did not.

The more I read of the time, the more I

saw that while *men* were credited, the women working for the British Alien Office (the forerunner of MI6, started by Prime Minister William Pitt in 1793) were rarely even named. Researching the etiquette of the times and how women were expected to behave, I began to feel excited. Was the secrecy because a *woman* had been, not just a saboteur, but the instigator of an idea? That was when the book really began to take off.

In 2007 my family moved to Switzerland, and I left the idea as I explored my new world, learned German, and kept writing romance novels. But I kept researching, until I had twenty-four books, three DVDs, and endless web pages on the era and the subject. I wrote earlier versions under another title, which didn't sell. It was a case of "write what you know" — in my case, romance — meeting far too much research for a genre focusing on the relationship, not the history.

In 2009 my beloved sister-in-law died. Before she passed away, she made me promise to write a story with substance about a woman who mattered. When I returned to Switzerland burned out, I took a year off writing but couldn't leave the promise to Vicky unfulfilled. I began rewriting the book. In 2010 I signed with my agent Eleanor Jackson, who tactfully began steering *The Tide Watchers* into the genre she believed it belonged in from the start. In 2011 I visited the Channel Coast region of France and bought a DVD that again mentioned the amount of ships in the region *before* war resumed in May 1803, the river ports built not just in Boulogne-sur-Mer, but in surrounding villages; it was mentioned only in passing references, but it was there. I watched it over and over, convinced I was right: a secret invasion attempt had occurred, but it remained all but secret 208 years later.

We moved back to Australia in late 2011. I was still feeling unenthused about writing romance. I fulfilled my last contract, and quit in 2012 to concentrate on getting the book right, but it was missing something.

Then my friend Heather Cleary, a librarian and historical author, lent me a book: *Secret Service: British Agents in France, 1792–1815* by Elizabeth Sparrow. This fabulous book had the inspiration and information on politicians, spymasters, missions, spies, and code names I'd been missing. I raved about the book to Heather, who generously told me it was mine. I rewrote my book again and it came close to selling, but again, something wasn't right. Finding veiled references to spymaster Joseph Fouché wasn't enough. I bought *Joseph Fouché: Portrait of a Politician* by Stefan Zweig, and it rounded out the book still more.

Then I realized my romance voice was still too apparent in my mainstream writing. I began attending mainstream courses. I heard about a master class course run by fantasy and historical bestselling author, Fiona McIntosh. After a week with that blunt-spoken and inspiring woman, I knew what to do. I went home, rewrote the book from the first line to the last, and submitted to my agent. Eleanor said, "This is it!" Three weeks after sending it out, I found my home with William Morrow. Since then I've been continuing my apprenticeship on writing historical mainstream, with my editor's help.

READ ON

FOR INSPIRATION OR PLEASURE

For you history buffs out there, anyone considering a writing career, or just lovers of excellent books, here is a list of books that inspired me in each arena. The first two are for research purposes; the third and fourth books are writers' resources, no matter what genre you like; and the final books are pure reading pleasure to me.

1. *The Terror Before Trafalgar* by Tom Pocock
2. *Secret Service: British Agents in France, 1792–1815* by Elizabeth Sparrow

These two books set me on my current writing career. They made me realize the depth of untold history in the world. They taught me that complete disclosure isn't in the history books that are written by the victors, or by the vanquished — it's somewhere in between. Digging deeper can teach you so much; and, as in my case, change your life.

☺There are many others, but I'm afraid listing them will put you to sleep!

3. *Writing the Blockbuster Novel* by Albert Zuckerman
4. *Screenwriting Tricks for Authors* by Alexandra Sokoloff

These two books taught me about writing stories with a wider scope, and to create each scene as if it's a mini movie: alive and vibrant. These books have both novels and movies as references to help you understand where the author's coming from. Both are brilliant resources to help aspiring authors bring their books to huge, screaming, 3-D life!

5. *Lord of the Rings* by J. R. R. Tolkien
6. *The Book Thief* by Markus Zusak

These are magnificently written and vividly imagined novels with beautiful, lyrical language that haunts me long after I close the book again. They taught me to find beauty in every moment you can; find joy amid danger and never give up. No surprise that both were inspired by, or written about, the world wars that changed our society so much — no matter what side you stood on.

ABOUT THE AUTHOR

Lisa Chaplin has published twenty contemporary romances under a pseudonym, but the publication of *The Tide Watchers* marks her mainstream debut. Lisa, her husband, and their three children currently reside in her home country of Australia.

The employees of Thorndike Press hope you have enjoyed this Large Print book. All our Thorndike, Wheeler, and Kennebec Large Print titles are designed for easy reading, and all our books are made to last. Other Thorndike Press Large Print books are available at your library, through selected bookstores, or directly from us.

For information about titles, please call:
  (800) 223-1244

or visit our Web site at:
  http://gale.cengage.com/thorndike

To share your comments, please write:
  Publisher
  Thorndike Press
  10 Water St., Suite 310
  Waterville, ME 04901